ACCLAIM FOR CATE HOLAHAN

HER THREE LIVES

"Starts with a bang and never lets up. If you think you've got this one figured out—think again."

—Liv Constantine, international bestselling author of
The Last Mrs. Parrish

"Slick and twisty. A high-tech spin on the domestic thriller that's packed with secrets, lies, and suspicion."

—Riley Sager, *New York Times* bestselling author of
Home Before Dark

"A deliciously twisted thriller. Holahan is three steps ahead the whole time, expertly stripping away each character's secrets until the shocking conclusion."

—Kimberly Belle, international bestselling author of
Stranger in the Lake

"The plot twists keep coming with every chapter until the shocking reveal. An outstanding read!"

—Wendy Walker, international bestselling author of
Don't Look for Me

ONE LITTLE SECRET

"A psychological thriller that will keep you up all night...Get ready."   —*Good Morning America*

"A domestic thriller that's actually filled with lots of secrets."
                                                                    —*Kirkus*

"Well-drawn characters...[an] absorbing page-turner."
                                                                    —*Booklist*

"A great beach read for those with a penchant for scandalous secrets and gossipy suspenseful mysteries."
                                                            —*Library Journal*

"Solidly plotted...Holahan does a fine job portraying fraying marriages and artificial friendships."
                                                            —*Publishers Weekly*

LIES SHE TOLD

"A suffocating double nightmare."
                                                —*Kirkus* (starred review)

"Recommended for anyone who enjoys Paula Hawkins or Gillian Flynn, primarily because it's better."
                                                            —*Library Journal*

"Engrossing...Holahan keeps the suspense high...until the surprising denouement." —*Publishers Weekly*

"A swift and intriguing psychological thriller heavy with surprises." —*Foreword Reviews* (starred review)

"Pure, binge-worthy entertainment...readers looking for an addictive, layered suspense novel will feel right at home in Holahan's world." —*Crime by the Book*

THE WIDOWER'S WIFE

"One of those rare thrillers that really will keep you reading all night, especially if you pack it to take on your next Caribbean cruise." —*Kirkus* (starred review)

"In this chilling cat-and-mouse tale...Holahan keeps the action going." —*Publishers Weekly*

"Investigator Ryan Monahan is so intriguing that readers will be anxious to read about his further adventures." —RTBookReviews.com

"Ingenious and engrossing. *The Widower's Wife* is a twisting, *Gone Girl*–esque thriller full of lies and secrets that kept me delightfully off balance right to the end. Cate Holahan is a star on the rise." —Brad Parks, award-winning author of *The Fraud*

"Impressive, exceptional, original, *The Widower's Wife* is a compelling page-turner of a novel from beginning to end—and clearly established author Cate Holahan is an especially skilled novelist of the first order."

—*Midwest Book Review*

DARK TURNS

"Holahan nails the preppy ambience, the cliques, the conspicuous consumption, and the coltish beauties."

—*Publishers Weekly*

"In this twisting danse macabre of jealousy, obsession, vanity, and revenge, Cate Holahan gives more than a superb debut performance. *Dark Turns* provides a master class in murder."

—Jan Coffey, *USA Today* bestselling author of *Trust Me Once*

"[*Dark Turns*] has a dark, sinister atmosphere that will suck you in completely, and you won't be sure who you can trust as the story races through twists and turns."

—*BookRiot*

"Holahan's debut will appeal to fans of precocious teen conspiracies like Sara Shepard's Pretty Little Liars series, as well as to fans of grown-up, plucky-heroine-must-fight-for-herself thrillers."

—*Booklist*

HER THREE LIVES

CATE HOLAHAN

GRAND CENTRAL
PUBLISHING

NEW YORK   BOSTON

Grand Central Publishing
Hachette Book Group
1290 Avenue of the Americas, New York, NY 10104
grandcentralpublishing.com
twitter.com/grandcentralpub

First Edition: April 2021

Grand Central Publishing is a division of Hachette Book Group, Inc. The Grand Central Publishing name and logo is a trademark of Hachette Book Group, Inc.

The publisher is not responsible for websites (or their content) that are not owned by the publisher.

The Hachette Speakers Bureau provides a wide range of authors for speaking events. To find out more, go to www.hachettespeakersbureau.com or call (866) 376-6591.

Library of Congress Cataloging-in-Publication Data
Names: Holahan, Cate, author.
Title: Her three lives / Cate Holahan.
Description: First edition. | New York ; Boston Grand Central Publishing, 2021. | Summary: "Greg Hamlin's kids think he's having a mid-life crisis. With his youngest off to college, the wealthy architect has divorced his wife and begun designing a new life with Jade, a struggling lifestyle blogger whose Bronx-upbringing and Caribbean roots seem an odd match for a suburban-Connecticut dad. But before Greg's second act can truly start, a savage home invasion leaves him housebound with a traumatic brain injury and glued to the live feeds from his omnipresent security cameras. The more Greg watches, the less safe he feels. Soon, he and his kids suspect his fiance of hiding something. Greg begins monitoring Jade's every move, watching her on the cameras, tracking her phone, and digging into her past. Jade is keeping secrets. But do they relate to her involvement in the break-in? Or, is Greg's battered brain playing tricks, pushing him to terrorize the only person who truly loves him? Is his life in danger? Or are Greg and his family the ultimate threat?"-- Provided by publisher.
Identifiers: LCCN 2020053584 | ISBN 9781538736340 (trade pbk) | ISBN 9781538736357 (ebook)
Classification: LCC PS3608.O482864 H47 2021 | DDC 813/.6--dc23
LC record available at https://lccn.loc.gov/2020053584

ISBNs: 978-1-5387-3634-0 (trade pbk.), 978-1-5387-3635-7 (ebook)

Printed in the United States of America

LSC-C

Printing 1, 2021

For Danielle Breakfield
This book could not have existed without your
dedication to your students and my daughter.

For My Daughters
Childhood is brief and beautiful.
The pandemic has cut both of yours short.
I am sorry, and I am ever so grateful for your
independence and love.

All human beings have three lives: public, private, and secret.

—Gabriel García Márquez,
Gabriel García Márquez: A Life

HER
THREE
LIVES

CHAPTER 1

She would make them late. Greg paced between moving boxes, fighting the urge to call Jade a second time and remind her of Friday traffic into the city. He didn't want to nag his new fiancée about the importance of their presence at a cocktail hour, in which she couldn't partake, for an event that neither of them wished to attend. They both knew what awaited them at the building's unveiling, the critical assessments they'd face from his colleagues and, worse, their spouses. Over the years, several of the wives had become friends with his ex. And even those with whom Leah had never ingratiated herself were unlikely to welcome a two-decades-younger replacement.

Late midlife crisis. That's what they'd all hiss after seeing his beautiful thirty-two-year-old betrothed with her lineless brown skin and cascade of thick black curls. Greg didn't want to consider what they might whisper about Jade herself.

The time on Greg's cell added another minute. His Pac-Man imitation in the narrow living room wasn't making her arrive any faster. He perched on the couch's arm and peered over a stack of boxes partially blocking the front windows. Jade's SUV wasn't parking outside.

She had to be on her way though. He'd explained that social events were obligations at his level. If he didn't show, Marcel would make it seem like a deliberate snub, evidence that Greg was still bitter about losing the Hudson Yards project to an up-and-comer, despite the firm tapping Greg for the Brooklyn building, for which Marcel had also campaigned. Greg needed to ooh and aah with the rest of the architects, if only to pretend no hard feelings.

Sitting wasn't calming his anxiety. Greg walked to the staircase, leaned on the banister, and tried to distract himself by picking at the rental's poor design. The builder had failed to install a front door with windows or place any in the above hallway. As a result, no natural light fell on the landing. The second floor appeared as a black hole, swallowing everything beyond the last step.

Greg had corrected such mistakes in his current project. The renovated house would be a new beginning for him, just as he'd hoped when he'd purchased the fixer-upper a few towns over from the shingle-style he'd called home for eighteen years. Leah had gotten that creation. After twenty-five years of marriage and raising two children inside it, he figured she'd earned it.

His future home would have fifteen windows in the front alone. He'd considered more but had, ultimately, restrained himself. Destroying the original Tudor exterior wouldn't have made him many friends in a neighborhood defined by old-world facades.

The sound of a car barreling up the driveway snapped

Greg's attention to the front door. He opened it, a gentlemanly gesture that would also emphasize to Jade that he'd been waiting. She seemed to catch the hint, changing her stroll up the walk into a sprint.

"Fastest shower ever. Promise."

Before she entered the house, he might have said something snippy like *I should hope so.* But the sight of her brown eyes, red-tinged like an iron-rich soil, smothered his annoyance. Suddenly, all he wanted was to gaze into those dark irises and slip his hands around the slight swell of her belly.

He grabbed Jade's left palm, restraining her from racing up the stairs. The five-carat diamond fit between his interlaced knuckles, advertising his claim. He was glad that she wore it around town and not simply for special occasions.

"How are you feeling?"

Jade's full lips pinched into a not-impressed smirk. "Belchy. Bloated. But the books say it should be getting better." She smiled. "Honeymoon trimester."

Greg planted a kiss on the corner of her uncertain mouth. If she actually felt sick, she didn't show it. He suspected that Jade complained about the pregnancy as a way of reminding him that a baby hid beneath her near-flat stomach. Either that or she was giving him an excuse to skip the event altogether. He supposed he could blame the baby for their absence. *Jade wasn't feeling well. She's barely entered the second trimester.* People would believe him. Though his colleagues would also mutter about the ridiculousness of a fifty-two-year-old man having a newborn. A thirty-something struggling to raise young kids while keeping up with the office's relentless pace was entitled to sympathy and leeway. He was supposed to be past such concessions.

Blaming anything on an unborn baby was bad luck anyway. He released her hand. "We should get out of here soon."

Jade started upstairs. "I need to make myself pretty."

"You're the prettiest woman in any room."

She turned and draped an arm over her head, striking a pose on the staircase before sniffing toward her exposed armpit. Her nose scrunched, transforming her striking appearance into something cute and cartoonish. "Well, I don't want a reputation as the ripest."

She hurried to the second floor, swearing to break speed records with her beauty routine. Greg settled on a step, knowing that she wouldn't simply wash and throw on a dress as she had pledged. Jade was her own biggest critic. She believed her bronze skin was tarnished above her cheekbones, even though he couldn't see any so-called dark circles, and she had a habit, particularly around his peers, of smoothing down invisible flyaway strands. It was all so silly. Jade didn't need to be self-conscious.

He checked the time on his phone: 5:20. Marcel had planned the cocktail hour for six to ensure that the whole firm could appreciate the brightening of Jersey City's gap-toothed skyline from the new building's omnipresent windows. If they were more than forty-five minutes late, they'd miss the show.

"Jade," he shouted up the stairs. "Twenty minutes tops. Okay, babe? It could take an hour to get into the city."

He listened for a response. Water ran through the wall pipes. Greg also heard footsteps. Heavy, yet fast. They approached the house, stomping up to the front door.

He rose from the stairs, continuing to listen. Jade had begun shopping for the baby online. Several times a week, packages landed on the stoop. What dubious necessity had the mommy blogs demanded she buy this time, he wondered. A bottle warmer? (A cup of hot water worked fine.) Teething rings painted with edible, organic vegetable dyes that, somehow, didn't break down from saliva? He waited for the familiar thud of a box landing on the outside doormat.

"You sure this is the address?" The muffled voice was gruff. Male. A new deliveryman in training. Greg braced himself for the squawk of some radio dispatcher, reaffirming coordinates.

"Yeah...what...said," answered a second voice, higher and more jittery than the first, the speech broken and even less intelligible. Two new guys, Greg decided, with a package either for him or for a neighbor that he'd end up delivering himself if they dropped it at his door.

Carting something heavy enough to require two deliverymen did not appeal to him. Greg flicked back the top lock and turned the knob. "You can leave it if—"

Wood struck his left cheekbone. Instinct drove him from the source of the blow, forcing him toward the wall when he should have thrown his entire body weight behind the opening door. Two men stormed into the foyer. Ski masks hid all but slivers of pale skin around their eyes. Their hands were covered in black leather gloves.

Greg assessed their sizes. One was skinny. He could tell by the folds in the man's bulky black sweatshirt. A drug addict, perhaps, seeking cash for his next fix. The other man was larger, nearly Greg's height and significantly broader.

Greg rushed the bigger guy, not allowing himself time to consider the stranger's hulking physique. He thought only of

Jade upstairs. Her subtle smile. Her delicate frame. The baby nestled inside her belly.

He rammed the man into the wall, recoiled his right arm, and brought it as hard as he could into the guy's stomach. The intruder absorbed the hit like a body of water, barely shuddering as Greg's fist connected with the soft flesh beneath his shirt. The ski mask muted an epithet. Greg bent his elbow, aiming again at the man's torso.

Footsteps on the stairs distracted him. The thin man was headed toward Jade.

Greg turned to give chase. Before his foot hit the second step, the larger intruder rammed a fist into Greg's kidney. Lights exploded in his head. He struggled to catch his breath.

"What do you want?" he panted. "Money? I can get money."

The larger man reached into his back pocket. *Gun*, Greg thought. *I'm going to die.* A silver cylinder flashed in the air. The masked man held the weapon above his head. Greg thought the stance wrong for a gun. For a fraction of a second, he wondered whether real people held firearms one-handed. He'd never shot one.

As the weapon swung down, he realized his mistake. Not a gun, a crowbar. The thought resounded as the tool connected with the top of his head. He heard the amplified crack of a breaking eggshell. *Jade.* Her name reared in Greg's mind, a sound wave cresting and crashing in his brain. *Jade. Jade. Jade.* It deafened him before he plunged into darkness.

CHAPTER 2

"Pride goeth before destruction." The proverb was one of Abigay Thompson's favorites. Growing up, Jade had heard her mother mutter it many a time after hearing that misfortune had befallen a seemingly upstanding individual. To her mom's credit, Abigay never uttered it with the smug satisfaction of some of the other churchwomen, as though she'd personally warned the poor soul that his luck would change if he didn't show God more gratitude.

She tended to say it in the same tenor as an apology. Abigay regretted that heaven's standards were so impossible, but it wasn't for men to judge the laws of the Lord. The Savior didn't punish without reason. If tragedy struck a decent family, then, in Abigay's mind, Jesus must have determined them insufficiently thankful for their blessings.

Jade had little use for Proverbs 16:18, or any other biblical victim-blaming. As far as she was concerned, the universe meted out vengeance with the precision of an atomic bomb. Storms leveled cities. Men and women were murdered. Raped.

Babies died in utero. There were myriad reasons, and chief among them was being in the wrong place at the wrong time. But prayer, or the lack thereof, wasn't one. She'd learned that lesson at age seven when she'd still been a true believer, and she was certain that what had happened a week earlier had nothing to do with the divine or justice.

There'd be no convincing Abigay of that though. Jade could feel her mother's disapproving gaze boring into her back as she draped a bright orange cloth over the kitchen table. In her peripheral vision, she could see Abigay's pursed lips above the newspaper held roughly in her hands. Part of Jade wanted to tell her mother that she had no right to judge at the moment. Abigay was not the one with a fiancé in the hospital. Abigay had not been attacked. But Jade had long learned that fighting with a woman who believed in preordination was pointless.

Jade slipped into the neighboring kitchen. She grabbed a white plate from the cupboard and brought it beside the still-sizzling cast-iron skillet. The air was saturated with the smells of frying oil and fish, reminding her of Lenten Fridays as a child. She grabbed a spatula from a basket beside the stove, slipped it under the small snapper, and transferred the fish to her plate.

Scales shone pink around the snapper's gelatinous eye and glowering mouth. Jade's stomach twisted with sudden revulsion. She pulled back the fridge door and dipped her head inside, sucking in the cold air to settle her stomach. Ever since the attack, the weirdest things set off waves of nausea.

Jade pressed the heel of her hand into her flat stomach until the feeling subsided. She then yanked the pickling jar from the fridge's top shelf and shut the door. Twisting off the metal lid released the trapped fumes of fermenting Scotch bonnet peppers. Jade's eyes watered as she grabbed a spoon from a drawer beside the stove and scooped out several slices of carrots, bell peppers, and gingerroot, spreading them like jam across the top of the fish.

Even with her blurred vision, she could tell the plate would look pretty on the orange backdrop. She carried her culinary painting to the table and placed it in the center of the fabric, taking a moment to admire how the cloth's color highlighted the carrots atop the fish. She returned to the kitchen for a fork and a knife, a deep purple napkin, and the flowers that she intended to take to the hospital later: a lavish arrangement with two bird-of-paradise blooms emerging from a nest of violet orchids.

As she staged the area around the plate, Jade could feel her mother's anger intensifying, heating the air between them like a blast from an opened oven. She tried to ignore it, focusing only on the still life framed in her iPhone screen and the sumptuousness of the food at the photo's center. The pictures looked appetizing, although a tad too brassy thanks to the afternoon light streaming through her mother's west-facing window. The right filter would tone down the color.

Jade grabbed the fork and carefully peeled a morsel off the fish's side. She stabbed it along with a bright yellow pepper and then brought the lot up to her coral-painted mouth, smiling as if unaware of the cell phone camera clicking in her extended left hand.

Her mother jostled the newspaper. "Sweetheart, for shame."

Jade placed the bite back on the plate. "It's been nearly a week. If I don't put up a post soon, I'll lose followers."

"Lose them then." The paper smacked against the table. "Your husband-to-be is in a coma."

Abigay leaned forward in her seat, thick biceps bulging over her folded hands, an arm wrestler waiting for a challenger. Her hair was pulled off her face in a low ponytail. The style, coupled with the fact that Abigay lacked a single wrinkle on her walnut skin, made her appear to be Jade's older peer rather than her parent.

Jade placed her phone on the table. "You don't think I know where he is?"

Abigay stiffened. Jade reminded herself of the respect due the woman who had birthed and raised her alone—regardless of how absurdly judgmental she might be acting. She lowered her voice. "I've been there plenty since it happened. Greg doesn't know that though. He's not responsive, and he may never become so. You want me to hold a round-the-clock vigil until the doctors say it's time to make a decision?"

Jade's eyes watered more, a drizzle threatening a true shower. She pushed the pepper-covered fish farther from her face. "I can't lose my livelihood too."

Her speech did little to soften her mother's expression. Abigay gestured toward the plate. "So, you're gonna what? Share a picture of you smiling beside an escovitch fish?"

Her mother's accent, muted from four decades in Brooklyn, became more prominent when she was annoyed. Abigay would have slipped into a Jamaican Patois, Jade bet, had the recent home invasion not demanded some extra show of sympathy for her child.

Abigay Thompson would never see the blog as anything other than her daughter's indulgence. As a nurse, her mom believed that the value one provided others should be physically measurable, obvious in the reduced fever of the infected patient or the stitched arm of the fall victim. Jade provided enjoyment calculated by an amorphous formula involving clicks and time spent on pages.

Clicks could add up to real money though. The blog brought in six thousand dollars a month in advertising, enough to support her as she continued to work out how a BFA in design could yield steady contract work. In her mother's defense, Jade supposed that she'd downplayed the site's importance in the beginning, dismissing it as a "hobby." In truth, Jade had always hoped to build an audience. When she'd installed the advertising widget on her site, she'd silently planned to gain enough of a following to pay off her student loans—a sum that had remained undented by bartending and sporadic modeling gigs.

Jade suspected that her mother secretly thought the whole enterprise sinful, albeit in a venial fashion. In her mother's eyes, *LifeinColor* profited off of bragging and frivolity. It probably encouraged idolatry by diverting attention from God to home decor and other vain pursuits.

"You honestly think telling the world about your lunch is a good use of your time when your fiancé's eating from a tube?"

The words stung. Fresh tears welled in Jade's eyes along with a recent image of Greg. His head bandaged and his neck braced, a plastic tube ran into his open mouth beneath thick white tape, hiding his thin lips. His skin, always pale, had the powdery appearance of albinism.

Jade glanced at the graying fish on the plate. Whatever

morsel of hunger she'd felt disintegrated. "Why don't you have it? I can't eat."

She started toward the front door. Abigay was wrong to criticize her. Even the Bible didn't contain a playbook for how she was supposed to respond to her situation. Her fiancé wasn't dead; he was comatose. Donning a black dress and wailing would be putting the hearse before the horse. And why should she do that? Because her mother came from a tradition that urged public displays of grief rather than stiff upper lips?

"Jade, wait."

She wanted to head through the door and slam it behind her, let the building shake with her fury. But she'd been raised to come when her mother called or face the consequences. She froze in the hallway beyond the kitchen, preserving a little dignity by refusing to retreat.

"Your phone is ringing. It may be the hospital."

Jade could just hear the staccato chords of a reggae song, her ringtone for anyone she didn't know. Her stomach lurched into her throat. It seemed she'd been riding a carnival swing that twirled people in the air and the centripetal motion had suddenly stopped. Her urge to fall was almost as strong as her desire to vomit. She did neither, however. Instead, she walked, shaking, toward the table where she'd abandoned her cell.

Her legs vibrated as she accepted the call, shutting off the shrill music. Would they tell her Greg had died? Did hospitals deliver that kind of information over the phone?

"Hello?"

"Ms. Hamlin?"

Her response caught in her throat. Ms. Hamlin was,

technically, Greg's ex. "Jade Thompson. I'm his fiancée." Nerves lifted her voice at the end, turning her title into a question.

"Mr. Hamlin is awake."

Emotions, too powerful to be identified, crashed over her. She clutched the phone like a lifeline and held her breath before finally speaking. "He is?"

"He's asking for you." The words barely registered beneath the rush of her own heartbeat.

"What are they saying?" Abigay had stood from the dining chair. She held her arms out, prepared for some burden to drop into them.

"Thank you. Please, tell him I'll be right there." Jade didn't know how she'd managed to form the response. Some subconscious part of her was taking over, leading her to deliver the proper polite statements that she'd been conditioned to make since childhood.

She hung up and slipped the phone into her back pocket. Abigay stood in front of her wearing an unrecognizable expression—worry, perhaps, but mixed with another feeling that flared her nostrils.

"Greg is conscious."

Abigay clapped her hands together like she was calling for lightning. "Oh praise Jesus. Oh dear God, thank you. Thank you." The clapping took on the rhythm of a church hymn. "Oh dear God in heaven, thank you. Jesus, thank you. We thank you."

The gratitude chorus followed Jade around the apartment as she grabbed her purse and car keys. It grew louder, covering for the congregant failing to join in. Jade's own voice shriveled in her throat. She'd read stories about people who woke from comas. Some couldn't walk or had to relearn to talk. Some came back fundamentally different, the spark of their intelligence permanently snuffed by the blow that had failed to kill them, their thought patterns and personality irrevocably altered. Would Greg be the same man? Would he be injured but capable of getting better? Or would he be reduced to some childlike state, needing her help to tie his shoes and wash himself?

When she'd said yes to Greg's proposal, Jade had imagined herself swearing before a priest and God to love and honor him for the rest of his life, come what may. But she'd also fervently believed in probability. Six days earlier, her betrothed had been a handsome, fit man barely in his fifties who ran triathlons and had enough income to afford top-of-the-line health care. The smart money had been on Greg's *not* becoming an invalid anytime soon. It was why he'd been able to obtain such a large life insurance policy.

Jade mumbled something to her mother about calling later and hurried out the door. Her fiancé was alive. But she didn't know whose prayers had been answered.

CHAPTER 3

Part of his head was missing. Greg gathered that much from the suited man at his bedside who gestured to a model skull with million-dollar words. Dr. Hsu was tall, at least from Greg's reclined vantage point, with a perfect noggin. Seen head-on, the neurosurgeon's forehead rose to a Moorish arch, framed by architectural haunches of buzzed black and gray hair. Greg had never paid much attention to the design of the human head before. As Hsu rotated the plaster cranium in his left hand, however, Greg found himself fixated on the shape.

"The crowbar hit here." Hsu indicated a spot about four inches back from the top of the skull's forehead, on the left side. "It broke through the bone, injuring a portion of the parietal lobe and requiring the removal of a two-inch section to relieve the swelling."

As he spoke, Hsu's pointer finger traced circles and triangles atop the replica. Greg could almost see the imaginary lines, as though the camera working his eye had been set at a slower shutter speed to trap taillight trails on a dark highway. He hoped the effect was a consequence of the pain medication and not a permanent issue.

"The good news is that removing the section of skull was successful in reducing the pressure on the brain and preventing additional damage. Very little tissue was impacted by the actual blow. Your scans have looked good, and the reflex, vision, and motor tests I performed when you woke didn't show any significant impairments." Hsu's hooded eyes pressed into tight crescents from the force of his smile. "You're very fortunate, Mr. Hamlin."

Greg felt the opposite of fortunate. His last memory before waking was of two masked men rushing into his home. After that, everything was gone. Not a blur, but completely missing, as though a yard of negatives had been excised from the film of his life, and his inner projectionist had fused together the remaining reel. The crushing blow to his skull and the subsequent days he'd spent comatose weren't experiences that he'd consciously endured. As a result, he couldn't feel real gratitude for the life he'd nearly lost. Instead, he felt frustrated with his current circumstances: trapped beneath blankets in a hospital bed, head weighed down with bandages, in the dark about how he'd ended up in the hospital or the location of his soon-to-be wife.

"Excuse me, Dr. Hsu, but Jade— The other doctor said that she was on her way?"

The man's lips folded in, as though there was some fact he didn't want to escape. "Um. She's been called. I believe so, yes."

"And you said she's okay."

Hsu's eyes darted to the side before resuming focus on Greg's face.

"You said she wasn't hurt," Greg repeated. "What happened?"

"I know that she was seen and discharged," Hsu said. "The same day of your attack."

The answer was more nuanced than the blanket "she's fine" that he'd been given earlier. Asking for Jade had been his first act upon waking. In his coma, he'd dreamed about her—or, at least, his effort to find her. He recalled something about walking through a desert canyon, the sun blaring down on his chest, a fiery comet on a slow trajectory to the rock bed that Greg had combed for his fiancée. He remembered calling Jade's name over and over, searing his parched throat with the sound of its single syllable. The sensation had felt so real. In some way, Greg realized, it had been. The feeding tube had inflamed his larynx.

"I believe she was here yesterday," Hsu added. "We can ch—"

"And the baby? Is the baby okay?"

Doctor Hsu took a breath. Greg pressed his hands into the sides of the mattress and pushed himself more upright against the frame, bracing for a blow. "Your wife will be here soon, Mr. Hamlin. In the meantime, I need to make sure you understand what happened to you and what we must watch out for."

The surgeon's buck-up grin was gone. Greg guessed brain surgeons weren't accustomed to being interrupted. Either that or he'd saved the worst news for last.

Hsu tapped the area of the model skull that he'd traced moments before. "The parietal lobe is a key processor in the brain's mainframe. It sorts sensory information required for balance, impulse control, and other things we don't even know about yet. Any injury to the area risks complications with those functions, and I'm afraid only time will tell if there are lingering issues to work through. As I'm sure you would imagine, we'll need to follow up pretty regularly as you continue to heal over the coming months and year."

The surgeon held the replica head a little higher. *Hamlet lamenting Yorick*, Greg thought. He had a flash of watching the play with Leah and Violet in Central Park years earlier. Leah had believed seeing Shakespeare would help Violet understand her tenth-grade AP English curriculum. His daughter had, of course, rolled her eyes through the whole performance. Surfacing the decade-old memory made Greg feel better about his brain function, even though forgetting Violet's teenage years might have had mental health benefits. Perhaps, he thought, he'd remembered the play only because Violet's raging adolescence had been so trying.

"You'll need additional surgery in about six weeks," Hsu continued, "a cranioplasty to restore the shape of your skull and your brain's protective covering. Fortunately, the piece of bone that we removed was sufficiently small that you won't need any extenders to grow more tissue. Believe me, that's a good thing."

Hsu's tight smile returned. Greg guessed that, like all people, his surgeon enjoyed focusing on problems that he could fix. "We'll slip a porous plate composed of 3-D-printed titanium mesh and polyaryletherketone, a kind of biocompatible thermoplastic that . . ."

The big words blended together as Greg again tested his memory of the attack and what had happened after. He'd opened the door. Two men—one skinny, one much larger— had charged him. He'd wanted to keep them from the second floor. Jade had been up there getting ready for Marcel's event.

She'd been showering.

That last detail was a new one for Greg. His heart raced at the realization that his pregnant girlfriend had been in the bathroom, likely naked, when the men had knocked him out. They'd nearly killed him. What had they done to her?

Hsu stopped talking to frown at the monitors. "Perhaps this is too much to take in at the moment."

Before Greg could respond, a woman knocked on the open door. The white coat partially concealing her green scrubs indicated that she, too, was a doctor. Her hair had been braided into dozens of blondish-brown ropes and tied into a knot at the top of her head—her perfectly shaped round head. Nearly everyone had one, Greg realized, except, apparently, him.

"Excuse me, Dr. Hsu. Mr. Hamlin's wife is here to see him."

Hsu's face relaxed. "Right. Good. He's been anxiously awaiting her." The surgeon forced his umpteenth terse smile. Greg wondered if the expression was a form of treatment, a visible sign of the positive outlook that Greg should adopt in order to heal and the gratitude he should feel at having a second chance courtesy of modern medicine.

"We'll talk again soon." Hsu headed toward the door, taking his model head with him. His stride seemed extra long, as though he'd remembered being late for a meeting.

It wasn't until the surgeon disappeared into the hallway that Greg realized he should have asked him to wait before ushering in Jade. He hadn't seen his reflection in nearly a week. At best, he looked haggard. At worst, monstrous. His skull, apparently, had a large dent in the left side. He had no idea whether his nose was broken or if his eyes were black. He didn't want Jade's first thought upon seeing him to be *I'm not, really, going to spend my life taking care of that beaten, old man.*

Heels clapped toward the door. By the sound of it, more than one pair. Whispers hissed in the entryway. Greg braced himself for his soon-to-be new wife, likely with her mother in tow. No doubt he'd look older and more infirm than Abigay. She was just three years his senior.

"Oh, Greg!"

His name rang out, part anguished wail, part epithet. Only two people had ever called out to him that way. One of them, his mother, had died three years earlier. The other strode into the room, golden tendrils coiling at her breasts. "Look at you."

A pitying smile tightened the bow of Leah's mouth. Greg hated how she conveyed kindness by infantilizing him. Toward the end of their marriage, he'd often had the sense that she was indulging his whims like an exhausted parent with a tantrum-prone child. *Let's go to Colombia*, he'd said once, marveling at a magazine spread celebrating the juxtaposition of postmodern architecture with wild jungle and sparkling beaches. *We should do that*, she'd answered, flipping back a page from whatever book she'd been reading. *We'll have to check the calendar.* Her lack of eye contact had made clear that she'd had no intention of looking into it.

She looked down at him now from the other side of the bed's metal guardrails, her wide-set eyes narrowed with a pain greater than sympathy.

"That bad, huh?"

A flush pinked Leah's cheeks. "No. Not *that* bad." She forced a smile. "It wouldn't make the Christmas card."

In spite of himself, Greg's mouth curled. When they'd been married, Leah had created elaborate Christmas cards with a variety of photos culled from various trips and events throughout the year. Though he'd always griped about posing for the pictures, the cards had made beautiful keepsakes, and he'd been proud to mail them out to friends, family members, and colleagues. He'd felt a twinge of regret the prior December when he'd received the card without him in any of the photos.

"Here, I'll show you." Leah yanked a leather tote around her shoulder to the front of her torso and began digging through it. After a couple of seconds, she pulled a rose-gold box from her purse. It snapped open, revealing a mirror, which she passed toward him. "See? It's really only the bandages."

Greg held the mirror at arm's length, trying to capture his whole reflection in the small square. From the center of his forehead down, he didn't appear to belong in a hospital, let alone an ICU. His aquiline nose was straight and free of tubes. His face had been shaved. The bruises he'd expected to see were not apparent. He looked pasty, perhaps, though not sickly. Most importantly, his eyes appeared alert and intense, as though the same soul sparked behind them.

The reason for the coma wasn't evident until Greg's hairline. Bandages wrapped from the peak of his right ear around the top of his forehead until they covered his cranium. So much gauze encircled his head that he couldn't see the depression in his skull that Hsu had warned about.

Greg passed the mirror back to his ex. He didn't want to look too closely. He'd have to confront his injury soon enough.

"All things considered, you look quite handsome, really. More like a soap opera actor playing a man awakened from a coma than the real deal." Leah reached for his hand. Right before she grasped it, she seemed to reconsider and let her fingertips rest atop his knuckles. "I was worried. I'm . . . " She paused and glanced at the ceiling. "We're all happy to have you back."

Guilt squeezed Greg's insides. Leah had always loved him—he had to give her that (even if he didn't wish to give her the many other things she was asking for in their divorce). And she *had* been a good wife by any fair accounting: dedicated; loyal; extremely focused on the kids, but then they had been her primary responsibility. Seeing her at his bedside with tears in her ocean-blue eyes, Greg had to admit that she'd never lost her looks either. Age had sharpened the angles of her face and added faint outlines around her mouth and eyes, but that hardly mattered. Leah had a classic beauty, the kind possessed by starlets of black-and-white films. Men and women of all ages had always found her alluring and intimidating. Even Leah's photos made Jade nervous.

Jade. Again Greg's thoughts returned to the woman he wanted to spend the rest of his life with. Where was she? Why was it taking her so long to arrive? What were the doctors not telling him?

He had a sudden thought that perhaps Jade was sitting outside, patiently waiting for his ex to finish her business. It wasn't inconceivable that Leah had demanded to see him first. *I need to know what to tell our children, Jade. They are worried about their father. You can see him all you want afterward.*

"Is Jade out there?"

Leah's hand retreated from his knuckles to her side. "No. But the kids are." She sniffed. "I'll get them."

Before he could answer, she was waving his son and daughter through the doorway. Greg felt a sudden dampness on his cheeks. He didn't know whether the tears were due to his ex's tenderness, his gratitude at seeing his kids, or the fact that Jade was nowhere to be found.

Violet and Paul approached his bed, each looking very young and yet somehow older than he remembered. Violet had turned twenty-three in December. Tall and blond, she was her mother's mini-me but with a ferocity to her style that Leah never would have adopted. Unlike his ex, who wore minimal makeup and her hair in loose waves, Violet's mane was chopped in an unfortunate, jagged bob. Her bangs grazed her brows, emphasizing the large blue eyes that Leah had gifted. Violet had lined them in black for the occasion and coated on mascara, making them even more overwhelming on her delicate face. Clearly, she didn't plan on crying.

In contrast to his daughter, Greg's son was his spitting image. Paul had straw-blond hair, as Greg had possessed before he'd gone gray, and clear blue eyes like his pop. His boy had also inherited his tapered jaw, a feature that would forever doom his face toward pretty and boyish rather than ruggedly handsome. The similarities weren't only skin-deep either. Paul—also unlike Violet—had inherited his own relentless drive. It was the trait Greg had most wanted to pass on.

"Dad. Thank goodness." Tears clouded Paul's eyes as he squeezed Greg's hand. His grip was stronger than seemed possible for a man so slender. Paul's cheeks had the sunken look of someone who had not been eating well. Nearly losing his father had apparently sapped Paul's appetite.

"It was touch and go there for a bit." Violet blinked at the ceiling. "We were afraid you'd lose your head. Literally."

Paul glared at his sister. "Really? Dad comes out of a coma and you're going straight to the bad jokes?"

Violet bit her lip. "I figured you'd be sappy enough for both of us."

Paul returned his attention to Greg with an irritated groan. "Are you in any pain?"

"Can we get you anything?" Leah asked. "Are you hungry?"

Greg tried to shake his head. The slight movement blackened the edges of his vision. "No. I'm okay. I'm happy that you're all here." He clapped his hand on top of his son's. "You came down from Boston."

"Of course, Dad. You were in a coma. Where else would I be?"

Violet looked to her right and then to her left, as though searching for an answer to that question. "Where's Jade?"

Greg's throat tightened. Jade's absence worried him, but Violet's noticing almost bothered him more. His daughter was nine and a half years younger than his fiancée—old enough, as Violet had pointed out on numerous occasions, to be Jade's little sister. When he'd announced plans to marry his pregnant girlfriend, Violet had called him up to rail about the impossibility of a thirty-something woman actually being in love with him. *Unless she's all sorts of messed up from some serious daddy issues, a woman that age should have no interest in you. Sorry, not sorry, Dad. Someone has to tell you the truth. That woman's either crazy or has ulterior motives.*

"Jade's on her way," Greg said.

"Oh? From where? She wasn't here this morning." Violet kept her voice light and nonthreatening, as though she were merely commenting on a peculiar choice of color for a window shade. "Now we're back from lunch, you're awake, and she still hasn't arrived."

This was how shouting matches always started with Violet. In conversation, she practiced a form of kyusho-jitsu, finding her opponent's weak points and pressing, while at the same time easily parrying whatever angry comments slipped between her verbal assaults. Greg didn't know where she'd learned it. Leah was not like that.

Greg recalled a particularly contentious conversation with his daughter over college, specifically Violet wanting to defer her acceptance to the middling safety school where she'd been accepted. He'd predicted that any "gap year" would turn into Violet's forgoing college completely and failing to launch. She'd refused to address his fears, though, zeroing in on his own frustrated desire to travel and her consequential determination not to end up "stuck" in the prime of her life. Ultimately, as was always the case with Violet, she'd won—despite his being right. While her brother had gone on to Greg's alma mater, Harvard, Violet's gap year had morphed into four years of finding herself. Whether she had, Greg didn't know, but his savings account could attest to her effort. For a year, Violet had checked for her missing piece on seemingly every beach and tropical city on the planet. She currently lived with her mother.

Greg cleared his throat. "She probably needed sleep."

Violet's lips pressed together as though she was trying to refrain from saying something. "I guess. Funny, though, Mom and I have been in and out, and I haven't seen Jade once."

The bedside monitor's beep pierced the silence. Greg could feel his son's and his ex-wife's energy heighten, like people in a blast zone anxiously watching to see if the bomb squad would defuse the explosive. He had little energy to argue with his daughter. The thought alone made his temple throb. But Leah and Paul certainly weren't going to say anything in Jade's defense.

"I'm sure there's a good reason." He knew the weak response wouldn't be enough to stave off the argument, but it was the best he could manage.

Violet shrugged and walked to the other side of his bed, ruffling the navy curtain cordoning off his section of the ICU. "So, are we all going to keep ignoring the elephant in the room? Or, not in the room, as the case may be."

Leah's eyes darkened. "Your father just woke from a coma."

Violet held her open palm out toward Greg's bandaged skull. "I can see that, Mom. I'm here. Like any loved one would be."

Leah raised her hand like a stop sign.

"No." Violet shook her head, tossing her choppy mane. "Someone tried to kill my father and I will *not* simply ignore the facts. Jade not being here is a fact. So is Dad knowing her less than six months before changing his life insurance policy to give her a generous amount, not to mention altering his will to divide his remaining estate among all of us and any of their future children. He did all that, what, a month ago?"

The question was rhetorical. Violet had left a furious message on his voice mail protesting any changes to his finances or reallocating funds their family had come to consider communal.

"I was getting things in order for the baby." Greg rubbed the center of his forehead, trying to stave off the coming headache. "I added Jade and any of your future siblings to the life insurance policy, and I took out a policy on Jade too. That's just sensible financial planning."

"Another fact," Violet continued, the rise in her tone indicating she was through with the warm-up, "the only thing taken was Jade's ring, which is, of course, insured. No doubt in her name."

The robbers stealing Jade's ring meant the men had confronted her, Greg realized. She must have been attacked. "Just because she wasn't hospitalized doesn't mean she wasn't hurt!"

Raising his voice unleashed a string of explosions behind Greg's eyes. He shut his lids tight. He wouldn't cry in front of his kids, especially not after what Violet had said. She'd view it as evidence that he doubted Jade's intentions when, really, he was furious at his family's suspicions. He wanted to throw something. Hit something. Scream.

"Two men tried to kill you." Violet's voice broke. "We have to ask ourselves hard questions. Why would that happen? What has changed? I can't let you go back to Jade when she might have—"

"Stop, Violet." Paul shouted his sister's name, shocking her into silence. He gave Greg a small smile that both apologized for yelling and declared his allegiance with his dad. "Have the doctors said anything about your recovery? There won't be any long-term damage, right? No problems with—"

The squeak of rubber soles interrupted the question. Greg expected to see a nurse in the doorway, ready to check his blood pressure. Instead, there was Jade.

CHAPTER 4

Greg's first family gathered around him like ivory chess pieces guarding their king. Jade recognized them from photos posted to her husband's Facebook account. Leah stood in the queen's position closest to Greg, stately in her creamy cashmere sweater, her blond waves framing an alabaster complexion. Beside her was Greg's youngest, Paul, a skinny, solemn bishop, protecting his mother. Violet lorded over her father's legs on the opposite side of the bed, the clear knight with her Joan of Arc hair and defiant expression.

The abrupt silence as Jade moved through the room announced how the original Hamlins perceived her role. She wasn't the family rook, nor even a pawn. In their minds, she was the opponent. The black queen perpetually trying to take their marquis piece. Jade could see their combined assessment in Violet's narrowed eyes: Usurper. Enemy. Thief.

She hadn't stolen Greg's affection from Leah though. When she'd met him at a design conference the prior October, they'd been separated. Moreover, Greg had initiated everything, asking for her business card, inviting her to dinner. He'd even decided to forgo protection—*because it never happens the first time*—despite her admission that she wasn't on the pill.

I didn't tell ya true? Jade imagined her mother's admonishing Patois. She envisioned Abigay hovering over Greg's hospital bed, self-righteousness inflating her heavy chest. *Your place is by your intended's bedside, Jade. But your ears hard, and now there's no place for you.*

"Greg, thank God." Tears welled in Jade's eyes, but for the wrong reasons. Instead of being fueled by gratitude at her fiancé's return to the living, they were filled with disappointment. The shame of her lateness, coupled with the frustrating need to explain it to his hostile family, made her want to cry. "I am so sorry. I've been staying with my mom because the rental was a crime scene, and I hit some traffic. I should have been here sooner."

"It's okay. You're here now." Greg lay on the hospital bed, thin lips pulled into a smile. His clear blue irises sparkled as he looked at her. The plain excitement bestowed a boyishness on his narrow face, belying the etching around his eyes. Bandages covered the creases across his forehead, making him appear younger and more vulnerable than he might have otherwise.

Jade had the disturbing sense that she should leave Greg to heal with his "real" family. It seemed she'd lost her claim to the man on the bed. She was little more than a girlfriend now, lacking a blood tie or even the overwrought symbol that had once weighed down her left hand. She didn't belong here among Greg's wife (an ex in name only given that his divorce had yet to be finalized) and the two children that Leah had borne him and raised into healthy adulthood.

Greg's eyes fell to her torso. His smile disappeared. "Jade, honey? The baby . . . ?"

The question caught her off guard. She reacted to it like she'd been sucker punched, instinctively holding her belly. Hot, acidic drops tumbled down her cheeks. She hadn't expected Greg to suspect anything simply by looking at her.

Jade could feel the tenor of the attention on her change from threatened to concerned—or at least genuinely interested. The last thing she wanted was any pretend pity from Greg's first family. Deep down, she knew they'd be relieved to hear she'd miscarried. Without the baby, Greg might not feel compelled to go through with the wedding.

She glanced at Violet and then stared at her fiancé, attempting to communicate that this wasn't the right time for that discussion. He took her cue, facing his ex and asking for "some time."

Leah's posture stiffened. To her credit, though, she didn't protest. Instead, she said, "Oh, of course," with the kind of overdone graciousness that the haves so often bestow upon the have-nots. Violet and Paul followed her out, though at a slower pace, like they thought their father might call them back in as reinforcements.

The kids left the door ajar as they exited. Jade knew they weren't supposed to close it. Medical personnel were constantly running in and out of ICU rooms. Fiddling with door handles could cost valuable seconds. Still, she found it difficult not to assume some malice on their part. No doubt they preferred the door open so they could eavesdrop.

Jade strode over to the door and shut it quietly so a nurse wouldn't hear the click and shout for her to leave it open. Greg seemed to hold his breath as she came back. A flush crept up his neck and to his ears. It might have been her imagination, but Jade could have sworn the monitor beeps came faster.

"I lost . . ." She choked on the pronoun. Whether "it" had been a he or a she, Jade couldn't know. "I'm not pregnant. I'm sorry."

Jade expected Greg to tear up. Instead, his face took on a deeper shade of pink. "Those men. What did they do?"

"One punched me in the stomach." The words sputtered out between sobs like steam bleeding from a broken radiator. "He wanted the ring. I would have given it to him, but he came in and . . ." She pressed her lips together, unable to say more.

Greg's upper lip peeled back, as though some spring screwing it closed had been overtightened and broken. A tear slipped down his cheek. For a moment, Jade thought he was having a stroke. She feared that she'd broken the news indelicately, causing a blood vessel to burst in his battered brain.

"Greg?" she whispered. "Greg, are you okay?"

"They're going to pay." The single tear dribbled from his cheek and around the edge of his nose, coming to rest on his upper lip. He swatted at it like a fly. "They're going to fucking pay."

Jade didn't want them to pay. Or, rather, she had no desire to be *involved* in making them pay. What she wanted was for the clock to rewind to a week earlier. Barring that, she wanted to forget the whole thing had happened.

Veins bulged in Greg's neck. "They're going to suffer. We're going to find them, honey. We're—"

Sharp breaths punctuated a litany of horrible things that Greg intended to do to the men who had killed their baby.

His desire to punish the people who had hurt them, despite his split skull, made Jade feel equal parts enamored and angry. Obviously, he couldn't make the robbers atone for their crimes. But even so, his fury was admirable. He'd wanted to protect her six days ago, and he still did. She leaned over the handrail and wrapped her arms around his shoulders, bending to put her head on his chest.

A knock interrupted the moment before Jade could register the feeling of it. She pulled upright, expecting to see Violet's revulsion or Leah's haughty discomfort. A familiar woman in a dark blue pantsuit stood in the open doorway. Behind her loomed a man with a military buzz cut. Detectives Stella Ricci and Michael McCrory. Jade had met them briefly after she'd been discharged from the hospital. They'd asked her what the men looked like and she'd provided a sparse description: one slender and one large. Both in ski masks.

Detective Ricci stepped into the center of the partitioned room. She was older than Jade but not by much. Late thirties, if Jade hazarded a guess. The detective had the build of a field hockey player, lean torso attached to thighs that could snap a neck. Her brown hair was blond at the tips, the result of a balayage dye job that hadn't been refreshed in some time.

Her partner hovered by the door. Detective McCrory had the frame of an offensive lineman, slimmed down for the off-season. The man's head nearly hit the top of the doorjamb. Greg seemed to shrink beside her as he took in his size.

"We're sorry to interrupt," Ricci said, pausing to introduce herself and her partner for Greg's benefit before continuing. "We'd like to ask you a few questions."

Greg regarded Ricci with an openmouthed grimace. "I just—"

"We know you're healing, Mr. Hamlin, but anything you can tell us could be important to catching your assailants."

The detective spoke slowly, articulating every word. Jade wondered whether Ricci had been told Greg might have trouble processing speech or, possibly, that he'd be in shock. "What do you remember about that day?"

Greg circled his index finger and thumb over his closed eyelids, as though trying to drag pictures from his peripheral vision into full view. "Two men broke into the house. I fought with the larger guy." His voice became more gravelly, like a car pushed onto the unpaved shoulder. His face contorted. "Nothing after that."

Jade had read on the internet that such memory losses were common for survivors of traumatic brain injuries. Greg had seemed so alert, however, that she'd let herself believe he'd escaped unscathed. If Greg didn't remember the attack, what else might he have forgotten? What other symptoms might he have?

"There were no signs of forced entry."

The male detective trailed off after making the point, inviting Greg, or perhaps Jade, to clarify. Jade had already told him that she didn't know why there wouldn't have been signs of a break-in.

"I opened the door." Greg's face reddened. "I thought they were deliverymen. We'd had a lot of packages coming for—"

He looked up at her, seeking permission to tell the news. Jade didn't want him to say it. No one outside of family knew about the baby.

"We needed things for the new house," Jade grumbled. "Like I'd mentioned."

Detective Ricci cleared her throat, possibly a subtle admonishment for Jade's speaking out of turn. "Mr. Hamlin, can you think of anyone who might want to hurt either of you?"

Days earlier, the cops had asked her the same question. She'd answered with an emphatic no, which the detectives had refused to accept. They'd pressed her about her blog and whether she had any online trolls or obsessive fans. Again and again, she'd said no. Blogging about Caribbean American culture and style didn't upset too many people (save for her mother). Her audience comprised mostly stay-at-home parents and DIY designers. She'd never had a problem with any commenters.

However, as Jade watched Greg rack his brain, she realized that she hadn't considered the question seriously enough. Obviously, Leah and company didn't like her. Perhaps she should have mentioned the tension there.

There was another name also that Jade had not shared with the cops. Odds were, it didn't matter. The man whom she thought of wouldn't have had any way of knowing what state she lived in, let alone where she'd been renting. And he hadn't reached out to her in a long time.

Jade glanced at Greg's tearstained face and held her tongue. Little good ever came from stirring up long-settled matters, especially those that would serve only to freak out her fiancé. Besides, the most logical explanation was that the two attackers had been after jewels. The cops had even suggested to her that they'd been professional thieves who had seen her ring and followed her home.

As if reading her mind, Greg asked about the stolen diamond: "Wasn't this about Jade's engagement ring?"

The explicit mention of it pulled her gaze to the depression still visible on her left hand. The ring had been obnoxious: a five-carat stone flanked by two baguettes in a pavé setting. When Greg had proposed, she'd understood that his jewelry choice had been less about what would look good on her finger than advertising his success and importance to his friends and colleagues. Since they'd become engaged, Greg had enjoyed showing her off at events, perhaps a little too much.

"It certainly could have been the motivation." A steady nod emphasized Detective Ricci's sincerity. "A ring like that would fetch a hefty price, even on the black market." She turned to Jade. "And you do have an active social media presence. The ring is on there." Detective Ricci lowered her voice on the last sentence, as though she were embarrassed for Jade's stupidity—flaunting a fifty-thousand-dollar diamond in front of three hundred thousand unknown Instagram followers.

"I didn't post about the engagement," Jade protested. She felt Greg tense beside her. No doubt he'd hoped that she would have shouted about their coming nuptials to all of her followers, pushing away any who might have been checking out her posts because they wanted to see her selfies rather than her recipes and interior designs.

"We've been through your blog," Detective McCrory said. "There's a post with you in a hard hat in front of the house you're building. You're holding a sledgehammer. The ring is in that picture."

Jade recalled the photo. She'd staged it after they'd popped by to see progress on the house, en route to a fancy dinner. The opportunity to tease the fact that she'd soon have a whole home to decorate had been too good to pass up. Plus, she'd been in full makeup for their night out, making for a nice picture. Jade didn't remember getting the diamonds in the shot, but she'd been wearing them.

"How would anyone know where I live?" Jade muttered the question, even though she could already guess. It was the internet. Anyone could find anybody. Her "About Me" page on the blog certainly spelled out a lot: her full name, her college and major, the state where she resided.

"Some of your Instagram posts have location tags, indicating the place," Ricci said.

"Location? I don't tag the—"

"Maybe it defaulted to it. If the robbers knew the town, they might have come here and somehow tracked you down. They could have asked around, perhaps followed you. The ski masks indicate that at least one of the men was expecting you to be at home."

The female detective gave her a thin smile, as if to say *it's not your fault*, despite her having outlined so clearly how everything had been her fault. She'd inadvertently flaunted her ring to thousands of strangers. Also, she'd been running late, forcing Greg to still be at home with her when the robbers came.

"The other possibility that we have to consider is that the ring was a bonus, and you and your wife were the targets." Detective Ricci let the horrible thought sink in. "Is there anyone who might have had a grudge?"

Greg averted his eyes to the curtain. He regarded it as

though examining a photo array of enemies. "I have a colleague, Marcel Bellamy."

For a moment, Jade wasn't sure she'd heard right. They'd been heading to Marcel's party before the attack. Surely, Greg wouldn't have encouraged them to attend an event hosted by a man he believed might try to kill them.

"He's made it painfully obvious that he wants my commissions," Greg continued, "supposedly when I retire, though I think he's a bit too ambitious to wait."

Jade glanced at Detective McCrory. Greg was clearly being paranoid. The police couldn't actually suspect a rival architect would put out a hit on her fiancé?

Greg must have sensed her disbelief because he started to elaborate. "The building I'm working on will cost at least half a billion to construct. Design fees typically run twenty percent of the total. The lead architect gets ten percent of that."

Jade hoped her eyes didn't betray her surprise. She knew her fiancé was wealthy, but she hadn't realized he could make ten million dollars with a large project. Even good people were capable of very bad acts when a life-altering amount of money was at stake. She knew that all too well.

"Anyone else?" McCrory asked.

Greg chewed a piece of dry skin on his bottom lip. Jade watched, wondering if another name might slip past. When a couple married, they shared each other's enemies as well as friends. Who else should she know that might have it in for them?

"Not at the moment. I'll keep thinking," Greg answered as he scratched at the top of the bandage covering his forehead.

"Good. Okay. So that's it for now, Mr. Hamlin. Thank you.

We'll let you rest and keep you both apprised of anything we find out." Detective Ricci deftly withdrew her wallet and pulled a card from the front flap. She'd given Jade the same one. "You remember anything else or have any concerns, call me."

She pressed the card firmly into Greg's hand. "We'll find the people who did this."

McCrory turned his hulking form toward Jade. "In the meantime, perhaps lay off the social media."

CHAPTER 5

His future mother-in-law said God had opened a window. Greg could almost believe her as he watched Jade leading Abigay around the light-filled house, exclaiming over details like the teak planks embedded in the living room's tray ceiling or the white-painted brick of the sunroom's sole opaque wall. A month earlier, a door had slammed—into his cheek, followed by a crowbar breaking his skull. But here, finally in the house, basking in the sunlight streaming through the addition's floor-to-ceiling windows, surrounded by the smells of fresh paint and new leather, Greg could almost forget the attack and focus on the next chapter of his life.

The sunroom windows overlooked the Long Island Sound. He settled onto a gleaming white couch to watch the catamarans passing tiny islands, each too small to fit a dock let alone a house. The view beat his former residence in Greenwich, despite the property costing much less (a result of the less tony zip code). Greg suspected that his new house's original ancient state had also depressed its value. Not many buyers wanted to purchase a million-plus gut renovation and risk doubling the price on architectural services, builders, permits, and construction. He'd been willing only because he'd known that he would do the design himself and work with his own trusted contractors.

"Don't you love this wall?" Jade's voice emanated from the spacious bathroom he'd tacked on to the addition.

"It's an interesting stone." Abigay's compliment was more of an observation. She didn't express like or dislike. Probably, Greg thought, she felt just as ambivalent about the whole house. He'd pegged her as a bit of an ascetic. Neither grand architecture nor grand gestures would impress her.

"It's granite. I forget the name." Jade's excitement made her sound girlish. "It reminds me of a wave."

Greg smiled at his fiancée's gushing. He wondered if she'd noticed the skylight yet. Showering there during a storm would feel like standing in a warm rain. Greg almost wished the bright blue sky outside would devolve into a thunderstorm so they could try it out.

The thought stirred a familiar twitching in his groin. Greg held his breath, as though he'd happened upon some beautiful, wild creature. Since the attack, he'd had difficulty getting—not to mention maintaining—an erection. Though he'd been in his new home for four days, and out of his coma for nearly three weeks, he hadn't yet been able to christen a single room.

Greg had quietly called his neurosurgeon earlier, after Jade had left to pick up her mother. Dr. Hsu had assured him that any inability to sustain arousal was natural after a traumatic brain injury. The doctor said his dysfunction was most likely a symptom of stress rather than any permanent, physical disconnect between his brain and his boner. Hsu had recommended a psychiatrist.

Greg didn't want another doctor. He wanted his general not to shirk the call of duty. And, if he'd learned anything as a boy, the best way to avoid a complex was to immediately rejoin the battle. Don't overthink it. Jump back in that saddle. He couldn't exactly ask Jade for a joyride while her mother was in the house, of course. But perhaps he could create enough pent-up energy to ensure that he would have little problem when Jade undressed for bed later.

Greg pressed his hand into the arm of the couch and slowly stood, a yogi performing a new exercise: upward ape. He'd learned the hard way that rising too quickly rattled his unprotected brain, sending painful tremors through his back and blurring his vision. With his spine finally straight, he took a deep breath and then grabbed the cane leaning against the edge of the couch. His balance, he'd also learned the hard way, could disappear at a moment's notice. Dr. Hsu had assured him that his equilibrium and pain would improve as his head healed, though he hadn't been able to supply him with a timetable.

After two weeks of round-the-clock rehab, Greg had been discharged from the hospital with a drab gray cane and black wrestling-style headgear, the combination of which had made him appear severely disabled. As soon as he got home, he swapped the helmet for a Harvard cap, loosened to the largest setting so as not to squeeze his vulnerable, misshapen skull. The hat sat atop his head nearly 24-7. Greg took it off only to sleep.

The cane had been upgraded too. Standard issue had been a stick propped atop a square base with four squat legs, the kind old people stuck tennis balls onto. He'd immediately traded up online for one with a silver handle and sleek black base that he thought read more stylish accessory than piece of medical equipment. When it arrived, Jade had joked that he'd gotten a delivery from Pimps-R-Us.

He leaned on his "gentleman's walking stick" as he moved away from the sofa. His leg wobbled on the first step but then stabilized. After a few paces, he felt sufficiently sure-footed to put less weight on the cane, allowing him to enter the bathroom standing tall and straight—for the most part.

Jade turned as the pole tapped the tile threshold, a grin stretched across her face. She had her color back, he thought, the golden glow that shone like weathered bronze. "Honey," she said, gesturing to the marble tile behind her, "I was showing my mother the shower backsplash."

"It's Azul Bahia granite from Brazil," Greg said. He enjoyed being able to share such details: material names, architectural jargon for shapes and decorative elements, tips that he'd learned from thirty years spent designing buildings, surrounded by artists and sculptors. Jade soaked it all up in a way that Leah had never bothered.

"The stone's base is white, actually," he continued. "The blue color comes from all the sodalite mineral deposits."

Abigay stood in front of the vanity, her face reflected in the large mirror above the marble sink. Her black eyes slid toward his flipped image. A sideways smile pulled at the corner of her full mouth. "The mind's working fast as ever, I see."

Greg smiled back, unsure whether he was being

complimented or patronized. He could never quite tell with Abigay. He thought she liked him. She often asked him how he was doing, and she smiled at him often—though, admittedly, not with teeth. Jade had said she'd been pleased when he'd proposed, though he understood that Abigay, as a religious woman, would have expected nothing less from the man who had gotten her daughter in *a family way*. He'd expected to hear some grumbling about the age difference, especially when Jade had explained that her mother had only a few years on him. But Abigay hadn't said a word.

Spiral curls shook on either side of Abigay's head as she turned to face him. He could see Jade in her, though only slightly. His fiancée had the same full mouth and short face. The eyes and nose were different, though, apparently from her father. He'd never met the man. When he'd asked Jade about him, she'd said he wasn't a part of her life in a tone that had told him not to press for more information. Greg assumed that he'd gotten her mother pregnant and then skipped town, which perhaps explained why Abigay hadn't balked at his age. Abigay certainly carried herself like she'd always been a single mother, a woman with the weight of the world on her shoulders who would never be crushed by the load.

"Let me see the upstairs," Abigay requested.

Greg turned back into the sunroom, happy to take part in the continuation of the tour. As he entered the brighter space, vertigo took over. Greg pressed a palm to his temple, trying to steady his swirling head. His right leg buckled as hot needles stabbed into it. He shifted his weight to the cane.

"Honey?"

Greg shut his eyes. Even the darkness behind his lids seemed to spiral. Jade's soft hand grasped his bare forearm. He could feel his skin sweating beneath her fingers.

"Babe, are you all right?"

He panted. "Yeah, sure. Turned a little fast I guess." He leaned on the doorframe, hating himself for seeming so feeble in front of his young fiancée and her force of a mother. "Why don't you go on ahead? I'll be right up."

Greg pried his eyes open long enough to see Jade's furrowed forehead and Abigay's admonishing stare. "Go get him a glass of water," Abigay instructed, her inner nurse clocking in on her day off.

Greg forced a smile. "I'm fine. I'll be up in a second."

Abigay's brows retreated to her hairline.

"Okay." Jade's voice sounded feeble. She patted his arm. "I'll be right upstairs if you need me."

He waited for them to leave before hobbling over to the sink, removing his Harvard cap, and splashing water on his face. The coolness calmed him. He reached for a towel and patted the droplets dangling from his chin. As he did, he caught a full view of his face, complete with the sharp slope of the left side of his skull and the defiant scar protruding through his buzzed silver hair.

He winced, though he knew—aesthetically—it could have been far worse. The segment of removed skull had been sufficiently far back to leave his forehead fully intact, enabling him to retain his face shape, not to mention most of his functionality. Before he'd been discharged, the hospital had also removed the staples, which had given him the appearance of a hastily stitched burlap voodoo doll. Still, it was painful to see the deformity so close to the organ that, for all intents and purposes, defined his very soul.

He pulled his spine into a standing position, articulating each individual vertebra as he rose. A hazy darkness crept into his peripheral vision, blurring the edges of the room visible in the mirror through the open bathroom door. A shadow moved behind him.

"Hello? Jade?" He squinted at the glass, trying to better make out the room's reflection. Had the door to the patio been opened? He hadn't heard it, but the room suddenly felt different, cooler, as though fresh air flowed inside. Again, something fluttered in his peripheral vision, this time in the area of the glass door leading outside. Someone was standing there. Hiding.

He whirled to face the intruder. Pain shot through his head and reverberated down his spine. His vision began to blacken. *Not again.* The thought screamed over his audible heartbeat and the sound of blood rushing to his head. *Not again.*

He grabbed the cane and hobbled across the room, resting for a moment to squint at the closed French doors and the shadow outside. Someone was there, watching. He could almost see him. The man would try to break the glass, he thought. Practically the whole house was glass.

He gripped his cane and entered the sunroom, legs trembling with every step. The men wouldn't get in this time. He wouldn't let them. If it was the last thing he did, he'd ram the round end of his cane into their eyes.

Greg's vision continued darkening as he traversed the bright room. He forced himself forward, gripping the stick, prepared to swing it like a baseball bat into someone's face.

Fear shortened his breaths. His heart threatened to break through his chest.

Greg reached the door and grabbed the handle. It didn't move under the weight of his hand. It was locked. Where was the shadow? An icy knife stabbed into his rib cage. He leaned his cheek against the cool glass and peered out into the yard and the beach beyond. The sun seemed to explode atop the water, blinding him in a white haze. Darkness spread from the corners of his vision. The shadows! Their shadows were everywhere.

The thought was his last before slumping to the floor.

CHAPTER 6

"Focus on my finger."

Jade watched her mother's index finger move slowly from one side of Greg's face to the other. How the act might help the heart attack that Greg swore he was having, Jade didn't know. But she also knew better than to question Abigay Thompson about anything health-related. The woman had been a registered nurse in Calvary Hospital's emergency room for seventeen years. Surgeons didn't question her mother's methods. She wasn't about to start.

"Good. Okay."

Abigay lowered her hand onto the sofa where they'd moved Greg moments after finding him. He'd been sitting on the floor with his back against the door, breathing like he'd run at full speed. Sweat had beaded on his forehead. A vein at his temple had protruded like a parasite, attempting to break through the skin. Jade had thought he'd needed an ambulance. But her mother hadn't suggested they call one. Instead, she'd asked Greg to tell her what hurt.

"My chest. It's like I'm being stabbed," Greg had croaked.

Abigay had knelt beside him, put her ear against his heart, and barked for Jade to put her phone on its timer function so that she could see the seconds. Jade had stood there, impotently, for over a full minute as Abigay listened to Greg's ticker and monitored the clock. When she'd finished, her mother instructed her to steady Greg's other side so they could help him to the couch.

"Now, breathe slow," Abigay ordered like a drill instructor. "In, two, three. Good. Out, two, three. Again. In, two, three. Right. Out, two..."

Greg followed her mother's instructions, though he clearly didn't see the point in them. Jade could tell by the way he looked over her mother's shoulder to sustain eye contact with her as she hovered by the coffee table. No doubt Greg wanted an ambulance and an EKG. Electric paddles to shock his heart back into a normal rhythm. The lines deepening above the prominent bridge of his nose conveyed as much. What Greg didn't realize, though, was that he already looked better. The pastel colors of his undertone had returned, and his eyes no longer had the glassy quality that she'd seen moments before.

Her mother must have also registered Greg's frustration because she abruptly stood and declared that his heart was fine. "You had a panic attack." She brushed invisible dust off her black pants. "Your heart rate was elevated but normal. No arrhythmias. You had a stabbing pain in a localized area that subsided. With heart attacks, the pain spreads, and it keeps getting worse—plus, I'd have heard an irregularity in the rhythm."

Greg's cheeks pinked. He looked to Jade like he needed her to come to his defense.

Abigay gave Greg the closemouthed smile that she always reserved for strangers and people she didn't like. Jade had gotten it herself when she'd announced her pregnancy and plans to marry a man twenty years her senior.

"There's no shame in it, Gregory," Abigay admonished. "They're often mistaken for heart attacks." She glanced over her shoulder through the French doors. "Tell me, did something unnerve you right before? You thought you saw something outside?"

Greg didn't answer. However, the way his shoulders rounded told Jade that her mother had diagnosed him correctly. Given the violence he'd suffered, the doctors had warned that Greg might experience symptoms of post-traumatic stress disorder. Flashbacks, frightening thoughts, increased irritation, and anxiety were the main symptoms. What was a panic attack if not the union of all those?

"Your brain is healing. It's probably sending all kinds of strange signals and aftershocks through your system." Jade deliberately shifted the focus from Greg's mental state to his physical injury. He'd be more comfortable blaming his actions on the latter than admitting he was *seeing things*. "Perhaps you should rest. Your body is trying to rebuild your skull. That's no easy feat."

He nodded at her, visibly grateful for the second opinion, even if it hadn't contradicted her mother's assessment. Jade passed him his fancy walking stick, an eighteenth-century accessory transported to an era of business casual. She then extended her arm to help him up.

He leaned heavily on the cane rather than grasping her capable hand. She walked beside him out of the sunroom anyway. "Perhaps the downstairs bedroom? We won't have to worry about the stairs."

The expression on Greg's face nearly stopped Jade from completing the sentence. "I'm not an invalid. I can handle stairs fine."

Jade bristled at his clipped tone. In the six months that they'd dated, Greg hadn't uttered anything remotely caustic to her. She'd never seen his temper, and he'd never witnessed her own. Jade could taste the acidity of the retort on her tongue. *It's not my fault you're having panic attacks. Don't take it out on me.* At the same time, she could hear an internal voice assuring her of the opposite: *Yes, it is. It's all my fault. I'm the bad seed. I brought this on you.*

They ascended like toddlers, pausing at each step. It took several minutes to reach the second floor and another minute to traverse the hallway. They both stopped outside the closed master bedroom. A massive twelve-foot double door, more fitting for the exterior of a house, blocked the entrance. Besides the obvious aesthetics, Greg had chosen the piece because its thickness made it virtually soundproof. "Can't have the kid hearing what goes on inside Mommy and Daddy's room," he'd said.

Greg moved toward the enormous door. The doctors had been very clear that he shouldn't exert himself at all while his brain lacked an intact outer shell and was still knitting together any damaged gray matter. He could stroke.

Was he stubborn enough to attempt opening it anyway? Jade watched, dumbstruck, as he grabbed the knob. Before he turned it, however, he seemed to remember his condition. He winced and stepped back, allowing Jade to move in.

Greg grumbled a thank-you as Jade wrenched open the door and held it back with her hip. His surliness wasn't really directed at her, she told herself. He felt humiliated by his temporary limitations. She passed him to pull back the pristine white duvet. "A nap might be a good idea."

His death glare made Jade regret her word choice. She hadn't meant her suggestion of sleep to come out as a snide comment on his irritability, but she could understand why he would take it that way. Telling an older spouse to "take a nap" smacked of condescension.

"Let me grab you a tea."

Greg grunted as he lowered himself onto the mattress. Jade chose to interpret the sound as an affirmative response. She headed toward the door, happy for an excuse to escape the tense atmosphere. "Be right back."

"And my computer."

Jade looked over her shoulder to see if Greg was serious or simply testing her. The doctors had been very clear about him not working for a month at least, maybe more. Straining his eyes and brain at this critical time could cause lasting damage, they'd said. He didn't need to frustrate himself with creating CAD drawings that would take him two or three times as long due to his inability to stare at the screen for more than a few minutes at a stretch. Greg's firm was massive. They could get someone else to take over the project he had started, before the assault, of refreshing an office space and the preliminary designs for the tech start-up's Brooklyn headquarters. Healing was supposed to be his chief priority—that and improving his mood.

Greg's stern expression made clear that he wasn't kidding about the computer. Jade closed her eyes, taking time to choose her words. "The doctors," she started, subtly assigning the blame for her objection to someone else, "recommended avoiding work for the—"

"Not work. I need to order some things from Amazon. This place isn't secure. Half the walls are made of glass."

Hearing Greg call their house "this place" rather than "our home" bothered her. It was as if he were already thinking of selling it. Starting over. And after she'd just fallen in love with it. "I'm sure it's a safe neighborhood."

Greg either didn't hear or didn't consider the statement worth additional comment. Apparently, the ceiling was of considerable interest. He lay down like a mannequin: back straight, his neck and head precisely positioned on the pillow. Their conversation was over.

Downstairs, Abigay was waiting. She sat at a banquette that shared its back with a kitchen counter. Her elbows were propped on the white table. She held a mug of steaming liquid. Another cup was positioned across from her. As Jade entered, her mom gestured toward the unclaimed drink. "Come sit with your ol' mother, nuh?"

Jade sensed a trap. Her mother often referred to herself as "old" in semi-jest, but her expression didn't seem to joke. Abigay was highlighting her age. And if she was old, so was Greg.

"I promised to bring him a cup of tea and his computer." Jade strode past the table to the area where Greg's MacBook sat, plugged into a charging station designed to look like an old-fashioned bread box. She'd found the piece cute in a kitschy way, though she suspected Greg didn't like it. His aesthetic was clean lines, hard surfaces, and bare white walls. No clutter. Sometimes, she felt like she was still in the hospital.

When things settled down, she'd decorate. Add some color. The before-and-after shots could go on the blog, which she'd been neglecting since Greg's discharge. If she didn't come up with something traffic-grabbing soon to make up for it, her advertisers would be furious.

"Pride'll be the death of that one, ya know." Abigay's voice switched from the singsong British accent with its omnipresent *schwa* sounds to the more relaxed diction that she used among relatives. "Proverbs chapter eight, verse thirteen: 'I hate pride and arrogance, evil—'"

"Enough with the proverbs, Momma." Jade grabbed Greg's computer. "The man's irritable because he has a literal hole in his head. Cut him some slack."

Her mother looked at her sideways. "He wasn't prideful or arrogant before?"

Jade couldn't pretend that Greg had been humble. Her mother had seen the ring, after all. But pointing out her fiancé's failings minutes after he'd suffered a panic attack seemed especially harsh—even for Abigay. "Like you said, Momma, my place should be by my sick husband."

Abigay opened her mouth as though she wanted to say something else. She picked up her tea and took a pointed sip.

Jade walked back to the table and snatched the waiting mug that her mother had prepared so that they could sit in the kitchen, gossiping about her fiancé. Before she could march away with it, her mother called her name. "You know that the Lord works in mysterious ways." Though her mother hadn't moved from her seated position, her eyes were active. Like two black holes, they pulled Jade back, keeping her from advancing to the staircase. "Now you know I would never, ever, have wanted anything bad to happen to your baby, and I would have supported your marriage. But did you ever think, Jade, that there might have been a reason for what occurred?"

Jade hugged Greg's computer to her chest. She was so tired of her mother searching for blame in every bad thing that came to pass.

"Think, sweetheart. Maybe God, in his wisdom, was giving you a way out." Abigay pointed to the stairwell. "Maybe the person up there is not the man with whom you're supposed to start a family."

Jade glanced behind her, praying that she wouldn't see Greg hovering on the steps. If he realized that her mother opposed him so vehemently, he might decide that Jade and her family were too much trouble. She didn't have the promise of a baby to keep him around anymore.

"I love him."

Abigay looked at the ceiling, either praying for God to give Jade some sense or, perhaps, rolling her eyes. "You're attracted to him. He's good-looking for his age, and he has money. Success. He's smart, I'll give him that. But do you really love him? For real, Jade? You sure you didn't find out you were pregnant and think you had to get married, or you got excited about finally having a father figure in your life?"

The words picked at old wounds. Abigay knew how much

what had happened with Jade's father had hurt her. And Jade knew that, deep down, her strained relationship with her dad had probably contributed to her attraction to older men. But there was more to her and Greg than that. Moreover, Abigay was forgetting that Jade wasn't some young thang anymore with her pick of suitors. She was past thirty, past her prime according to many guys her own age. And she had other problems, too, which Abigay knew all too well.

Jade turned toward the steps. "Sorry, Momma. I have to give my husband his tea. Then I'll take you to the train."

CHAPTER 7

Greg waited for the delivery van to pull all the way down the street before opening the front door. A cardboard stack stood beneath the portico, each block slapped with Amazon's blue-and-black Prime sticker. He brought the boxes inside individually, aware that carrying the lot could invite a stroke.

The large boxes contained smaller packages. He opened each in his study, a back room with two glass walls segmented by shutters to keep the sun's glare off his television-sized computer monitor. As he unpacked in the hazy glow, he took inventory, checking items off the sizable order he'd placed the prior night. He'd purchased twenty cameras in all: five outdoor devices, three interactive doorbells, and twelve indoor units—one camera for every exterior wall of the house and nearly every room without a toilet, as well as one destined for above the garage. The entire lot had come from the same manufacturer, ensuring that they'd all link up with the same home security application on his cell and computer.

It pleased him to see how nondescript the devices in fact

were. Each camera was hardly bigger than a hundred-watt
lightbulb and encased in a forgettable white that would blend
into the home's siding. The units would turn his house into a
fortress, without making it resemble Fort Knox.

In addition to the cameras, Greg had bought several alarm
stations. These devices hooked up to a variety of tubular
motion sensors intended for the top of ground-level windows
and the inside of exterior doors. Thanks to the sensors, when
a window or door was opened, a tone would sound throughout the house. If the system was armed, the alarms would
go off once a door or window was opened. To shut off the
alarms, all he or Jade had to do was brush one of two key
fobs against any of the alarm base stations.

All in all, he'd spent six thousand dollars on the setup.
Hiring a security firm to monitor the place might have been
cheaper, at least in the short run, and he'd initially intended
to do so before the break-in. But this way, he retained control.
He would see who was entering his space and when. He'd be
able to call the cops or not. He'd be ready.

He was finishing an online instructional video on wiring
the doorbell cameras when Jade knocked. She came in right
after, carrying a plate of something that resembled scrambled
eggs but didn't smell like it. Jade was a great cook. Sometimes, though, Greg wished she would prepare more foods
that he recognized. With his head hurting, he didn't feel like
embarking on any culinary adventures that could upset his
stomach. He wanted the American food pairings to which he
was accustomed: bacon and eggs, ham and Swiss, burgers
and fries.

"It's ackee and saltfish." Jade's eyes widened as she took

in the sight of all the cardboard and plastic littering the bare wood floor. No doubt it seemed like somebody had enjoyed a very lucrative Christmas. In his excitement at opening all his new purchases, Greg hadn't noticed the mess that he'd made.

She navigated around the paper land mines, holding the plate like a waitress. Watching her tiptoe made Greg feel a little bad about the explosion of packing materials. He cleared a small space beside his keyboard for her to set the plate down, mumbling about bringing in a garbage can.

"Honey?" If Jade intended to hide the concern in her voice, she wasn't doing a good job. "What's all this?"

"I bought a home security system." Greg settled back into his deep leather desk chair, an Eames lounger that had actually been his Christmas present to himself many years earlier. The chair was the epitome of form meets function. He could think of no better place to recover than between its cushy arms. "What's ackee and saltfish?"

Jade's eyes flitted from open box to open box. She appeared to be counting them. "It's a Jamaican breakfast. You'll like it. Ackee is a fruit. It's packed with protein but doesn't have the cholesterol of eggs."

Greg examined the yellow curds on his plate. Cut tomatoes—he recognized those—were mixed in with it, along with something that smelled like fish. "What does it taste like?"

"To me, it tastes like ackee." She pointed to one of the cameras. "What company did you go with? Is someone coming to set all this up?"

The question was more of an admonishment than a real query. Jade had to know that if he'd hired an installer, the technician would have brought the devices. She meant to suggest that he was incapable of setting up the system himself.

"Don't worry. I'm doing it. Most of them are plug-and-play."

Jade's frown confirmed Greg's assessment. He swiveled his desk chair away from his breakfast. If she wasn't going to be supportive about him securing their home, he didn't need to feign enthusiasm for eating a strange fruit with fish first thing in the morning.

"We don't want some stranger monitoring our comings and goings all the time," Greg said. "Imagine some guy, glued to screens all day, watching you heading off to the gym in your tight yoga pants, bending down to pick up your packages, all the while figuring out the best time to pay a visit."

"There are systems without active monitors." Jade spoke quietly, as though trying to calm a crazy person. "My friend Belén has one in her house. They automatically alert the company when an alarm goes off. Then they call. If you don't answer, they notify the police to send a car. If you do, they ask for a code word. There's one word for 'I'm okay,' and another for 'intruders in the house,' or something like that."

Greg leaned back in the chair, as if he were considering the alternative despite having already settled on an option. Jade wanted the police to protect them. He guessed that he couldn't blame her. He hadn't done a good job of it, after all.

"Those systems have a boy-who-cried-wolf problem." Greg softened his tone. "Dispatchers get so many false alarms from folks not punching in the right code, or not doing it quickly enough, that the cops assume the calls are mistakes, leading to slow response times. With this system, we will be alerted and able to dial 911 ourselves, conveying the urgency."

Jade picked up one of the empty device boxes. She flipped it over and began reading the marketing material on the back. "The video goes out over the web. Doesn't that make it hackable?"

"To access it you'd need the user name and password on the account, just like online banking." Greg extended his hand for the box. "Trust me. We'll both feel much safer when this is done."

Jade gave him a small, surrendering smile. She handed him the box and then rested her hands on his shoulders. "What do you need me to do?"

Greg patted her arm. "Nothing. Don't worry. I've got this."

Installing the cameras took the better part of the day. Setting up the indoor units had been as easy as advertised. Greg had simply needed to locate a suitable spot atop a dresser, windowsill, or counter near an electrical outlet and then angle the camera to best capture the room. The outside units, however, had proved more challenging. Greg had propped a ladder against the house and donned his unwieldy medical helmet, intending to demonstrate to Jade that he was up to the task, only to be assailed by vertigo as soon as he'd climbed a couple of steps. Ultimately, he'd asked Jade for help. She'd installed the remainder while muttering about Greg nearly killing himself.

Sitting at his desktop computer in his office—the command center of his secured castle—Greg felt certain that the crick in his neck, throbbing temples, and peeved fiancée were worth it. A grid of color images dominated the wide-screen monitor in front of him. The majority appeared static, due to the lack of motion in the frame. Only the front cameras betrayed that Greg watched live video feeds. In those two, Jade headed down the walkway dividing the green lawn in front of the house. At the end of the path was a charcoal post with an attached mailbox.

Greg monitored her journey to the curb. The day's silver sky had sprung leaks and she was stepping fast, almost jogging toward the street. Several times she held a hand to the top of her forehead to keep the rain out of her eyes. When she reached the mailbox, she struggled with the lid, apparently not realizing that she needed to pull the top down rather than slide it up.

After a moment, she figured it out, yanked it open, and reached inside. Her hand emerged with a paper bundle—a stack of legal-sized envelopes and a catalog, if Greg had to judge from his computer monitor. Mail in hand, she slammed the lid shut and then hustled back toward the door, her image growing ever larger on the screen until she disappeared beneath the portico.

She was still visible on the front doorbell camera. Greg clicked the live feed of that unit, an act that expanded its video to full-screen, started the audio, and opened a visual list of recent clips, recorded when that particular camera had sensed motion. The videos were time-stamped and then stored in a secure online account for thirty days, which only those with the log-in information could access.

Had such a system been in place at the rental, the police would have been able to watch the whole attack, freeze-framing the robbers' masked faces for a photo array. They might even have been able to catch the men coming up the walkway, perhaps before they'd slipped on their balaclavas. Of course, the presence of security cameras probably would have prevented the attack to begin with. The criminals would have seen all the recording devices and run.

Greg continued to watch Jade on the doorbell cam. If he was going to test the alarm, now was as good a time as any. He clicked a button on-screen to arm the system and then returned his attention to the live video.

Jade muttered under her breath as she entered the door code on the electronic lock and jiggled the knob. It didn't open. She tried a second time and was rewarded with a pleasant ding. Greg heard the tone from the speaker in the door's motion sensor, located several rooms over, and simultaneously from the audio outputs on his computer and phone.

He braced himself as the tone outside his door turned into a steady beep. Jade had to swipe her key fob over the base station on the entry table or she'd set off the alarm. He shrank the doorbell video back to thumbnail size on the security grid and then clicked the image with Jade's puzzled expression. The real-time feed of the foyer took over the screen. As it did, the accompanying audio played. Steady beeps continued to emanate from his computer monitors.

A microphone icon sat centered at the bottom of Greg's screen. It pulsed when he clicked on it. "Babe."

Jade's head shot up at the sound of his voice. Her straight eyebrows pulled closer. She looked over her shoulder. "Greg?"

Again he clicked on the microphone icon, holding his cursor over it to keep the intercom open. "You need to swipe the fob over the base station within thirty seconds or the alarm will go off."

Jade turned her head right and left, looking for the sound of his voice rather than the key fob. The beeps picked up speed. She stepped farther into the foyer.

The alarm started blaring its threatening loop: INTRUDER ALERT. INTRUDER ALERT. LEAVE THE PREMISES. THE POLICE HAVE BEEN CALLED. INTRUDER ALERT.

The computer speakers amplified the warning already blasting through Greg's office door. He slapped his palms over his ears and watched Jade pace on-screen, a confused rat in a complex maze. A white piece of plastic peeked from a back pocket of her jeans.

Greg removed a hand from his ear to press the microphone button. "It's in your pocket."

Jade spun toward the sound of his voice, pressing the mail to her breastbone. She zeroed in on the entry table and the black camera.

Greg tried again, shouting through the computer speakers. "It's in your pocket."

She patted all around her waistband before finding the device. Palming the fob, she headed over to the base station on the entry table, running as though the police actually had been called. The alarm shut off with an indignant beep.

Jade's open mouth closed into an annoyed expression. "Well, that was unpleasant."

"We'll get used to deactivating the alarm."

Jade looked into the camera. "It's not just the alarm. It's odd talking to you through a speaker."

Greg pressed his cursor into the microphone icon. "Just think, no need to shout across the house."

He released the button, cutting off his verbal connection

with the room. Jade's sigh hissed in the monitor. She began walking away from the camera, tilting her head to consider the envelopes in her hand.

Greg watched her exit the frame and then clicked on the edge of the image, causing it to shrink back to normal size and reveal the rest of the grid. Jade entered the living room. She added the catalog to a stack of home design magazines atop the coffee table and then continued on, carting the envelopes into the addition.

Greg watched her disappear from one camera only to appear in another before, ultimately, settling in the sunroom. He pulled the corresponding video up to full-screen. There was something so alluring about Jade's face when she didn't realize anyone was watching. Her features, often animated around him or company, relaxed into introspection. He could appreciate the fullness of her mouth. The quiet of her doe eyes.

She sat in the corner of the white couch and then leaned over to the coffee table. Two of the legal envelopes landed on the surface. From the sight of the cellophane windows with his address, Greg guessed that at least one bill had arrived, either for the house or his lengthy hospital stay. He winced at what he imagined might be the deductible on brain surgery.

Jade held a white card-style envelope in her left hand. She slipped her right index finger under the fold in the corner and slid it beneath the triangle of the envelope, freeing the lined piece of paper inside. Jade held it at her waist as she read it. Greg considered tapping on the image to zoom in but thought better of it. His fiancée was reading her mail. As much as he was enjoying his new toys, he shouldn't use them to spy over her shoulder. Either way, the angle at which she held it wouldn't let him see anything.

Jade's brow lifted suddenly. She jumped from the couch, folded the paper, and jammed it back into the open envelope. Her hand seemed to shake. She paced for a moment and then called out his name.

Greg almost hit the microphone button. Seeing Jade's apparent nervousness made him reconsider. He rose from his leather chair, rounded the desk, and opened the door. "Babe?" he shouted through the open floor plan. The sunroom was on the other side of the house. "Is everything okay?"

"Um, I have to run an errand." Jade's voice was louder in the computer speaker behind him. "I'll be right back."

"Sure, what—"

Before he could finish, Greg heard the tone caused by an opening door. He hurried back to his screen and returned to the grid view. Jade was visible in the camera facing the backyard. She'd exited and was heading around the side yard, toward the garage.

Greg watched her approach the detached structure. He brought the north camera up to full view, enabling him to see her key in the unlock code and hear the rumble of the opening garage door. Jade hurried inside, as though she were late for an appointment. Perhaps she'd gotten an overdue payment notice and was heading to mail a check directly from the post office before it closed. Greg wondered if those came in card envelopes.

He switched to the garage camera. Beside Jade's BMW sat his Tesla, unused these past weeks as he'd healed. Jade beelined to her own vehicle. She flung open the driver's-side door, jumped into the seat, and slammed it behind her in one continuous motion. The engine roared to life.

The car reversed down the asphalt drive. Through the windshield, he could see Jade's face. She looked at the dashboard, no doubt at the reverse camera. She was biting her lip.

Something had rattled her. Greg grabbed his cell and hit the button for recent calls. Jade's number was second on a list that included his ex-wife's cell and the hospital. As it rang, he tried to come up with a delicate way to say he'd seen her looking worried. *Was anything in the mail? You left on your errand so quickly.* No. That was too accusatory. He would start out simply asking where she was heading under the guise of wanting her to pick up more aspirin for him at the pharmacy. From there he could segue to the mail.

Jade's voice mail answered. He hung up and dialed again. The second time, voice mail picked up after one ring, indicating she'd hit the ignore button.

Greg clicked over to the sunroom camera and expanded the empty room to fill the screen. He scrolled through the video history on the side for the clip with Jade sitting on the couch. The recording took over his monitor. He pressed play on the feed.

Jade put the bills on the table. She brought the card to her lap, obscuring whatever was inside as she opened it. Her expression morphed from mildly annoyed to extremely agitated. She bolted from the couch.

As he watched, Greg's temples beat to the rhythm of his heartbeat. Dr. Hsu had warned that too much screen time could strain his eyes, adding undue stress to his healing parietal lobe. He felt the headache coming on. Even still, he couldn't pull his gaze away from the computer monitor. Something had scared his wife. And whatever it was had sent her running.

CHAPTER 8

A "welcome" note. Jade's first thought upon taking the small envelope from the mailbox was that a local vendor had sent a card congratulating her and Greg on their new home. Such mailings were staples of landscapers and gutter cleaners. The fact that the letter had been addressed to her hadn't set off alarm bells. She'd figured the woman of the house would receive more advertising pitches than the man.

As she sat in the police station, waiting for Detectives Ricci and McCrory to speak with her, Jade realized that her full name and address on the center of the envelope should have been a dead giveaway that something was wrong. Greg had purchased the property well before he'd proposed. The records wouldn't have had "Jade Thompson" on them.

She jiggled her knee and drummed her fingers against the plastic water cup given to her by the desk officer. Fifteen minutes had already passed in the small interview room, a homely space that was, thankfully, a far cry from the interrogation sets on television. Instead of reminding her of a jail cell or a sparse office, it recalled an ancient living room. There was a small bookcase stocked with dolls and kids' board games. A floral couch straight from an estate sale was the main seating area. Jade guessed the room was reserved for victims. She couldn't imagine cops putting the screws to anyone inside Grandma's parlor.

The one similarity that the space shared with TV interrogation rooms was the camera. Jade spied it, mounted high in a corner, a clunky, oblong device that reminded her of the eighties Panasonic with which her mom had taken home videos. It pointed at the couch. Jade had an urge to wave to it, as though the detectives might be behind a monitor in some neighboring room assessing her behavior.

Instead of drawing attention to herself, she set the water on the coffee table and grabbed her phone from her purse. She'd ignored a couple of calls from Greg. He was probably worried. But telling him where she was would only upset him more.

She opted to scroll through her photos, soothing herself with the images she'd taken hours earlier for an upcoming blog post. She'd baked a Jamaican hard-dough bread the prior night, putting her own spin on it by adding cardamom to the thick flour. The bread had come out light brown on top and fluffy white in the center, exactly as planned, which wasn't something she often experienced with her baking. She credited the oven. New appliances were more exact about temperature.

In the photograph, the bread was centered on a platter with its end carved off and lying white side up beside it.

A sunny slice of yellow cheese and a dollop of bright red strawberry jam shone atop the cut piece. Juxtaposed with the shot was an image of the electronics charger disguised as a bread box. Later, she'd write out the recipe along with a post about preventing the kitchen from turning into a cord-cluttered, pseudo office space. It was the kind of advice that her audience would appreciate.

Concentrating on her upcoming work dulled the image of the letter. Each glance at the lined paper had threatened to open wounds she'd been trying to ignore, pushing her to remember the sight of the men and the police rushing in with their weapons drawn. The blood that hadn't been her own.

Heavy footsteps sounded, followed by a gentle knock. "Ms. Thompson?"

Jade straightened as the detectives entered. The female officer, Ricci, wore a gray suit this time. She held a clear plastic folder in her right hand. Her jacket was buttoned, concealing the gun that Jade could see outlined beneath the fabric. Her partner had opted for a black suit. In the re-creation of Nana's sitting room, he reminded her of one of the hit men in *Pulp Fiction*, sans the skinny tie.

"We apologize for the delay," Ricci said. "Detective McCrory and I are with the county Major Case Unit, headquartered in Hawthorne. We came as soon as we heard."

Hawthorne was on the opposite end of the county, border-ing the Hudson River rather than the Long Island Sound. It took Jade twenty minutes to get across. The detectives, she realized, must have used their siren. They thought the note even more of a threat than she did.

She mumbled her thanks as Ricci sat on the cushion beside

her, the folder propped atop the detective's thighs. McCrory stood near the exit as usual.

"So, tell us how you got this letter." Ricci passed her the plastic sheath containing the note. Jade glimpsed the heavy blue ink, the lines thicker in spots where the sender had nearly pierced the paper. She felt a phantom pinch in her gut and averted her eyes. It didn't help. She'd already memorized the handwritten, all-caps message.

NOW YOU KNOW HOW IT FEELS. THE PAST CAN'T BE FORGOTTEN.

"I found it when I got the mail, tucked in with a magazine and some bills. It was stamped. The carrier must have dropped it off this morning."

The detectives eyed her as though she'd said something wrong. "It's pretty concerning," Ricci said.

Jade had thought so in the beginning. As she'd had more time to digest the contents, though, she'd stopped worrying as much. He wanted her to be scared, and she was tired of giving him the satisfaction. She handed the folder back to Ricci. "Sure. It's upsetting."

McCrory tilted his head like a confused puppy. "You don't seem that upset."

"It's definitely alarming. I'd hate for Greg to see it. That's why I brought it to you."

Ricci stared at her. "Do you know who sent it?"

Jade couldn't continue to look at the officers. She watched herself curl her hands into fists and press them into the brushed fabric of her jeans. The room, which had felt comfortable moments ago, suddenly seemed chilly. "Why would I know?"

Ricci leaned toward her, invading her space in an effort to reestablish eye contact. "If you suspect someone wants to hurt you, Ms. Thompson, you have to tell us. For your safety and the safety of your fiancé."

"Can't you just track down who sent it?"

"This is an attempted murder investigation." McCrory was speaking now. His voice was raised. "Whatever you know, you have to tell us. Otherwise, you're protecting the robbers. What are you hiding?"

The officers were looking at her like Dobermans waiting for a dinner bowl. If she didn't give them what they wanted, they'd rip her to shreds. But once she did, Greg might want nothing to do with her. Already, his family regarded her like a stray that had snuck into their house, someone without their breeding or pedigree. Her story would only confirm all their prejudices and inflame Greg's worst fears.

Hot tears built behind Jade's eyes. "I believe it was sent by a man named Carlos Bernal." She lowered her voice on the name, as though saying it too loud might somehow make him materialize in all his fury. "He's tormented my mother and me for years."

McCrory crossed his arms over his chest. "You didn't tell us someone had been harassing you."

"Well, he hadn't sent a letter in almost a decade before this. It didn't seem relevant." Jade pressed her knuckles harder into her jeans, kneading her frustration into her thighs. "It still might not have anything to do with the attack. I think he's just gloating. I came because I thought you might be able to get him to stop before Greg sees this. It would only upset him, and he doesn't know anything about Carlos."

Jade heard the desperation in her own voice. "Will you have to tell him?"

Ricci offered a cautious smile. "Why don't you explain it to us from the beginning?"

A fiery, frustrated tear slipped from Jade's lower lid. Over the years she'd told people the story, hoping for understanding and, maybe, compassion. For a time, she'd get it. College friends would say how sorry they were for her. Teachers would express admiration for the way she was "making something of herself." Boyfriends would be extra loving and protective. But they'd all look at her differently. Eventually, their sympathy would morph into disdain. Who was she to remind her roommate to tidy up given where she'd come from? She might have an artist's eye, but she obviously couldn't afford an MFA, so what was the point of spending much time on her? How dare she complain about her lover's behavior? Her father hadn't been a prince.

She could imagine how the detectives would treat her admission. They'd spend fewer resources on finding the men who'd nearly killed her fiancé and ended her baby's life. No need for the detectives to battle karmic justice.

Telling them everything was not an option, Jade decided. Still, she had to give them something. "When I was about seven, there was a shoot-out in my neighborhood between rival gangs. A young boy, one of my classmates, was caught in the cross fire. His name was Mateo Bernal."

Jade paused a respectful moment. She always said the child's full name. Remembering it was her duty. "He died."

Her throat tightened. She cleared it, forcing out the difficult part. "My father had some involvement with one of the gangs. Mateo's father, Carlos, blamed my family for what happened. He thought if anyone's child deserved to die, it should have been my father's kid. It should have been me."

The last sentence barely emerged from her constricted larynx. Jade picked up the nearly finished cup of water and drained the last of it. The detectives watched without offering a refill.

McCrory looked at her like he wished they were in the real interrogation room. "But why would he harass you?"

Jade shrugged. "You would have to ask him. All I know is that every April 25, on Mateo's birthday, Bernal would send a card reminding us that his son was still dead and of all the milestones that I had no right to achieve given that fact." Jade gestured to the note in Ricci's hand. "The cards had stopped years ago. I thought he'd lost track of us. Maybe he had. I suppose he's found me now though. As you know, April 25 is in a few days. He must have wanted to make sure I got Mateo's birthday card in time."

Ricci scanned the words through the plastic. "He doesn't mention his son."

Jade closed her eyes. On the back of her lids, she could see the sharp capital letters cutting into the paper. "That stuff about not forgetting the past has to be him."

Ricci shook her head. "But he says now you know how it feels..."

In her mind, Jade filled in the possible endings: To lose a child. To suffer random violence. To have your hopes and dreams and peace shattered by a stranger. To go through a day so distracted with grief that you're not sure of anything you're doing or feeling or thinking.

"How would he know what happened to you?" McCrory asked.

The question's past tense seemed wrong. As Jade struggled to find an explanation, the attack seemed to occur simultaneously. She could see the skinny man in the black ski mask, the fabric darker around the top of his head and his neck where he'd been sweating. She could feel the aftershocks of the leather-clad fist that had connected with her torso. Once. Twice. Before those hits, Jade had never fully understood the expression "having the wind knocked out of you." She'd realized that it was apt. All the air in her diaphragm and lungs had fled her body, leaving her gasping, choking, unable to suck a breath into her injured stomach. Organs that she would never have been able to pinpoint had pulsed with pain. She'd become acutely aware of the placement of her kidneys, her liver. Her uterus.

Jade pressed the heels of her hands into her closed eyelids and exhaled long enough to transform her staccato breaths into a solid one. "I'm guessing he still has friends in my mom's neighborhood. My mother has her whole church prayer group working on Greg's recovery. They pray for people by full name and with all the details. Someone in the congregation probably still knows Bernal and relayed the news. With Greg's name, he could look up our property record."

McCrory nodded as though he'd placed another piece into the puzzle.

Jade turned away from his satisfied expression. "The friend probably thought it evidence of Exodus."

Ricci glanced at her partner. Jade caught the quick shake of his head. "Punishing the children for the sins of the father," she said.

Ricci considered the letter again. The lines deepened around her mouth. "Could a mutual church friend have also told Mr. Bernal where you'd been renting?"

"I don't think so..."

Jade's chest suddenly felt as though someone sat on it. Bernal had never been violent with her, and she'd gone to the police station assuming he was only trying to pour salt on her wound. But she didn't know that for sure. It had been a decade since he'd sent the last hate letter. Perhaps, instead of moving on with his life, he'd been plotting ways to get back at her all this time. "God, if Bernal did this, then it's all my fault."

Ricci patted her arm. "No, it's not."

The gesture didn't reduce the pressure on Jade's lungs. "Greg's family will blame me. They already think I'm a gold digger. If they think I brought this on him... If he starts to believe it..." Voicing the fear broke the dam that had held back her tears. Jade sobbed into her palm. "Who would want that kind of baggage?"

McCrory's aggressive stance softened. He sat in a chair opposite the couch, apparently no longer trying to intimidate her with his size. "Maybe we don't have to tell Mr. Hamlin until we know more. We'll talk to this Carlos Bernal first."

The knot in Jade's chest loosened a little. "Thank you. Last I heard, he still lives in Bushwick, but in a nicer part. He has a plumbing business."

Jade's bag shook. Her phone was vibrating. Probably Greg

again. She'd already been in the police station a half hour, and she'd need another ten minutes in the car to compose herself. "I should get back. Greg must be wondering where I am." She stood from the couch along with the detectives. No one offered to shake her hand.

"If it helps, you can tell Bernal that I think of his son every day." Jade's voice broke. "I know it could have been me."

CHAPTER 9

Greg lay on the chaise appended to the living room sectional with his bare head pressed into the back cushion. His eyes shut. A steady pulse beat between his ears, its rhythm reminding him of a nagging spouse. *This is what happens. You hate to listen. Doctors know better. Now look what you've done.*

A buzzing hummed beneath the drumbeat. He opened one eye to the blaring orange light. The sun had broken through the clouds and barreled into the open living room through the sunroom's floor-to-ceiling glass windows. Rays exploded on the west wall. In front of him, fake logs burned in a stone fireplace, an original outdoor feature that Greg had converted to gas when he'd built the L-shaped addition. The fire in the hearth, coupled with the view of the water through the windows in the adjacent room, should have created a Zen balance. Instead, Greg felt disoriented. Where was Jade?

The buzzing continued, like a bee or fly had been trapped beneath a cup. Greg reached forward to the glass-and-wood coffee table and collected his cell. A warning blared on the screen: *Motion Detected! Garage Exterior!* Greg clicked on the text, opening a video captured moments before of Jade's BMW advancing toward the detached garage. Through the cell speakers, he could hear birds twittering. He hadn't heard her car pass on the road or turn into the long asphalt drive. The fact bothered him. He was inside an interior room, but the house had an open layout. He should have been able to hear some street noise. Had he lost hearing in the attack? Or had the pain medications dulled his senses?

Greg squinted at the video, searching for Jade's face on the small screen. The sun, somewhere outside the shot, shaded the driver's-side window in a painfully bright halo, obscuring any view inside the vehicle. Greg had a flash of Jade in the front, a gunman behind her, dictating her movements from the backseat. *Drive into the garage. Call for your husband. Don't say a word.* He was aware that the image came from a mob movie. The hammering on his eardrums picked up nonetheless, as though his daughter's idol, Meg White, had handed over the sticks to Dave Grohl.

He opened the full home security app on his phone and scrolled to the garage's interior camera. Jade had already exited the vehicle. She opened the SUV's passenger door, reached inside, and reemerged with a plastic CVS bag. The garage bay door began lowering behind her.

Greg dropped his cell onto the couch and grabbed the crimson baseball cap beside him. He placed the loose hat on his head, pulling the back low on his neck so that the one side didn't obviously pucker over the impression in his skull. It was an odd way to wear a ball cap. But it was better than exposing the scar, which ran down the side of his dented head like a curved spine beneath a thin, hairy back.

Cap on, Greg refocused on his cell, switching to the security application's grid view so he could determine whether Jade had gone to the front or back of the house. She walked past the camera mounted on the home's north side and then into view of the east-facing cameras, the units that monitored the whole backyard and the water. He watched as she passed between the deck's barbecue area and the sandy bank beyond the house, her chin angled down to avoid the wind whipping off the water.

On the doorbell camera, Jade leaned toward an unseen keypad mounted above the back door's electronic lock. Her elbow jostled in the frame as she tapped in numbers. His son's birthday: 12801. The digits, he realized, would mean nothing to Jade. That was why she'd had trouble with the front door earlier.

He resolved to change the code as he watched her elbow move backward and forward several times in front of the camera, trying different combinations. Finally, a tone sounded. Greg heard the sucking sound of a seal being broken, followed by the soft but steady beep of the alarm countdown. He pulled his attention from the video to the very real woman standing in the adjoining room.

"The base station is on the credenza."

Jade rounded the couch to the floating cabinet. Greg heard the plastic bag jostle on her forearm as she fished into her purse for the key fob. She swiped it, silencing the steady beeps.

"Hey, you hungry?" Her voice had the hoarse quality of someone tired of talking. She entered the living area and dropped onto the foot of his chaise. "I have chicken brining in the fridge." She pulled off a sneaker, releasing it to the floor with a jarring clunk. "Otherwise, I can leave it overnight and cook up something simple like burgers." The other shoe dropped. "What are you in the mood for?"

Jade looked over her shoulder at him, brown eyes deep as pools, sad as mud puddles. What had she read in that letter?

Greg sat straighter on the chaise. "How are you doing?"

"All right." She shrugged and offered a hint of a smile. Even troubled, she was beautiful. Rather than feel pride in his fiancée's looks as he usually did, though, the observation made him nervous. Why would she want an old man with a dented skull?

"Where did you go?" He tried to sound nonchalant while simultaneously closing out of the security app on his phone. Though he'd been watching to protect them both, revealing that he'd seen Jade enter the house—and open her mail before that—could make him seem stalkerish.

Jade grabbed the plastic bag from the floor and placed it on the coffee table. "I bought more aspirin. How is your head?"

Greg returned Jade's shrug. "Intact."

"Thank God for that." She rose from the couch. "So, start the chicken then?"

His fiancée had just returned and already she was rushing away from him. Was she uncomfortable being in the same room, or trying to avoid discussing where she'd really disappeared to and why? "You were gone awhile for aspirin."

Jade's chin pulled toward her neck. "Um, well, I went there second. I visited the library first, actually."

She hadn't brought in any library books. Greg braced

himself on the sofa arm and reached for the cane resting against the side. "I didn't know you had a library card."

Jade grabbed her purse from the couch cushion, as though it was in his way or she worried he'd look into it. "No time like the present. Everyone should have a local library card." She started toward the kitchen off to the left, easily rounding the white table in the breakfast nook. "You know what, I'll save the chicken for tomorrow so it will be juicier. Do burgers tonight, right?"

Greg's vision swam as he rose from the couch. He leaned on his cane, closed his eyes, and counted breaths until the floorboards felt firm beneath his feet. It took six inhalations before he could follow Jade into the kitchen.

"What book did you get?" He leaned against the bright white counter. If he stumbled, a bolted surface would be better at supporting his weight than the cane.

"I didn't." The sound of water nearly overwhelmed her words. Jade stared out a picture window facing the street as she worked the liquid soap beneath her nails. "They didn't have anything I wanted."

Greg waited for the water to shut off and Jade to turn around. He was good at reading faces. When his kids had been little, he'd been able to discern when they were hiding something simply by looking them in the eye. Of course, anyone could have figured out when Paul was fibbing. The kid became verbose, trying to hide his untruths under tons of verbiage. But Greg had also known with Violet, and she'd been an expert prevaricator in her teenage years. Often she'd told untruths staring directly at him, daring him to call her bluff.

Jade's tell hadn't revealed itself yet. Greg assumed that was because she'd never lied to him before. Once she did, Greg felt certain that he'd recognize some out-of-the-ordinary affect.

She silenced the faucet and then pivoted toward the pantry. He couldn't see her behind the half-open white door. "How many burgers can you eat?"

"Two, maybe." Greg shifted his position, ensuring Jade would be visible once she emerged from the closet. "You just went to the library? Not the post office or bank?"

"Well, the convenience store too," Jade said in a louder voice. "Sorry I was gone so long. It took me some time to realize that the library didn't have what I was looking for."

So much for his theory of a late-payment notice sending his upset fiancée flying to fix the issue. "What were you looking for at the library?"

Jade shut the pantry door with her elbow. She balanced a cutting board on one hand and held a box of salt in the other. The items landed on the counter by the range. "A Caribbean cookbook." The answer came over her shoulder as she opened the paneled fridge door.

"A specific one?"

"Not really. Just something else, you know. Something to expand my repertoire beyond the stewed chickens and fried fishes that I know best. Maybe recipes with more spices or different spices."

Jade's words were half swallowed by the Sub-Zero. She opened a fridge drawer, pulled out a butcher-paper package, and then unwrapped it on the cutting board, exposing the wavy red block of beef. She then crouched beside one of the spice cabinets, pulled it open, and began picking through the glass bottles on the tiered rack.

"Don't you think my audience would like a post about spices? Maybe something on creating a great rub for the grill coupled with backyard entertaining tips?" Jade tossed out the questions like scraps for a bloodhound. Greg was determined not to be thrown off the scent. Something had arrived in the mail that had upset her. And for some reason, she wanted him to believe that everything was fine, and she'd only gone to the library for a cookbook.

"It's surprising that the library didn't have *anything* on Caribbean cuisine. You'd think there would be at least one book in the cooking section."

Jade shook one of the spice bottles over the ground meat. She began folding the green and brown flakes into the beef with her knuckles. "Well, they didn't have . . . jerk."

Name-calling, Greg thought. That was Jade's tell. She'd been lying about the library.

"I'm a jerk?" His voice lowered to a hissing whisper. Twenty-three years of parenthood had taught him that yelling was pointless. Making someone listen required speaking at a volume that forced them to shut up. "Why? Because—"

"Jerk spices. You know, jerk chicken? Jerk pork? I realized that's what I really wanted, and they didn't have it." She looked at him, lips parted to bare her bottom teeth. Her eyes examined his face and then rolled up to the cap hiding his injury. "Are you feeling okay?"

Greg felt sheepish. He'd intended to back her into a corner and force a confession, one that wouldn't require that he first admit to spying. Instead, he'd snapped over something stupid. "I didn't know jerk was a spice."

"You seem a bit on edge." She lifted both hands from the

meat in a surrender gesture. Little pieces of graying red flesh stuck to her palms. "You can talk to me, you know. Feeling agitated, nervous—overwhelmed—it's all natural. We should be open about it."

Greg didn't appreciate the hard turn that the conversation had taken. He'd been questioning her about her supposed library trip, and she'd turned it back into a discussion of his mental health. If he mentioned her reaction to the mail now, she could dismiss whatever he'd seen as PTSD-related paranoia.

Jade returned her attention to the lump on the plate. She pulled off a chunk, sprinkled it with spices, and then rolled it into a large meatball on top of the cutting board. The heel of her hand slammed into the sphere, squashing it into a patty. She ripped off another chunk of bloody ground meat and held it out to him. "Want to try smashing one? It's therapeutic."

The anxiety he'd felt since Jade had rushed out abated. Perhaps he was unnecessarily on edge. He could have misread his fiancée's expression or ascribed it to the mail when, really, she'd had an unpleasant thought about lacking blog material. She certainly didn't seem worried at the moment. If she said she went to the library, then that had to be what she'd done.

Greg approached her, hugging the counter in case he needed it for balance. Jade placed the hunk of ground beef in his open palm. It was room temperature from sitting in her hand. The wavy red mass reminded him of the wrinkles in the human brain.

His heart began racing. His stomach lurched into his chest. It felt like he held loosed bits of his own mind, ready to pulverize them into dinner. He dropped the wad on the cutting board. The ackee and saltfish that Jade had prepared for him earlier bubbled to the base of his throat in an oily acid. Needles stabbed his stomach. "I need the bathroom."

He barely made it to the closest toilet before half-digested food flooded his mouth. As Greg heaved, he swore he could smell what Jade was doing to that meat. She hadn't even started cooking the burgers outside on the attached gas grill so he shouldn't have been able to. But the scent of searing, sizzling flesh seemed to penetrate the walls, stinking up the bathroom air, making him retch.

By the time he reentered the sunroom, Greg felt like a used sponge left out in the sun. Shriveled. Smelly. Sapped of usefulness. From the kitchen, Jade saw him walking toward the sunroom and immediately ran over to help.

"Let me bring the plates to the coffee table. We can eat here." She gestured to the wall of windows and the lines of white surf in the darkening water beyond. "Enjoy the view."

Greg lay back against the couch as Jade began clearing the table, moving a decorative vase to the console table behind the sectional and picking up the mail. For the dozenth time that day, he pictured Jade's face as she'd gone through the letters. Had he really misread her expression that much?

He gestured to the envelopes in her hand. "What came for us today?"

Jade placed the lot beside the vase. "A catalog, a pack of coupons from town businesses, and your credit card bill, I think. It's from Chase."

Greg slid to the edge of the couch to better see her. "That's it?"

"Mm-hmm." Jade turned back to the kitchen. He definitely could smell the burgers cooking now. The scent no longer churned his stomach. Still, he couldn't eat something as heavy as beef after being sick.

"I think I need a little time before dinner," Greg called out over his shoulder. "I'll probably just have a sandwich later after my stomach settles."

Jade stopped in the living room. "All that work with the cameras and then watching them for hours. It can't have been good for you."

"The cameras will keep us safe, Jade."

She blanched at his tone. Greg realized he'd been too gruff. He'd never responded well to being told what was good for him. "I should install the app on your cell so you can also check them."

Jade grimaced. She'd just scolded him about his screen time, and now he was suggesting that he spend time on *her* phone. "You can shut off the alarm remotely with it." Greg knew the fact sweetened the deal. Finding the key fob quickly was clearly not Jade's forte.

"Okay. But I need my cell to blog later."

"I'll download it and be done. Ten minutes tops."

Greg watched Jade return to the kitchen. She retrieved her phone from the bread-box charging station, an item that he found clever, if a bit folksy. Before sharing the unlock passcode and handing it over, she warned a second time about needing it after dinner. Again he promised to be done in ten minutes and then shooed her back to the kitchen to tend to the burgers and eat hers while it was still warm.

Installing the security application was simple. Because Jade was on his carrier's family plan and he'd already set up the app on his device, all he had to do was find the software in the online store, download it, and create a log-in for her. The program had already been paid for on his phone and synced with the cameras on the network. He actually finished in less than ten minutes, before Jade had even polished off her meal.

Greg rose from the couch to deliver the phone, perhaps along with a playful *I told you so* or a joke about how millennials weren't the only tech-savvy generation. Things had become so heavy between them since his injury. They'd fallen in love because of the fun they'd had talking with and teasing each other. He wanted that joy back, to kid around with his love, to flirt, and, yes, to also have sex—though he doubted he had the energy post puke session, or the balance.

As it was, his switch from sitting to standing had forced him to grab the sofa table and repeat his closed-eye countdown until his vision stopped swirling. When he opened his eyes, he saw the stack of mail. There was a catalog and a Chase bill, just as Jade had said. But no card envelope.

He glanced back at his girlfriend, scraping off her plate in the kitchen. She'd told him that all the mail was beside the vase. But he'd definitely seen the card envelope on-camera.

Greg reopened the phone's home screen and returned to the app store. He had five more minutes with her cell, and there was one more program he needed to download.

CHAPTER 10

Fashioning a replacement skull and fusing it over a human brain was not a routine matter, but it was still a feat any ol' trauma hospital could execute. Jade supposed that was a good thing, though it didn't feel like it as she waited in Westchester's main medical center, struggling to bat away a barrage of bad memories. The entrance reminded her of when she and Greg had both been rushed inside, in different ambulances. Her arrival subdued. His frantic. The trauma ward recalled the sour-faced hospital staff who hadn't permitted her inside to see her dying fiancé since she was not yet "family." Even the imaging suite, which she'd entered earlier for the first time, brought back the nights she'd dozed in the chair to the steady beeps of Greg's bedside monitor, nights interrupted by nightmares in which nameless doctors explained that Greg would be stuck in a childlike state.

She waved from behind the radiation-proof glass, unsure whether Greg could see her from his reclined position in the adjacent room. The female technician leaned into an intercom. "Are you ready, Mr. Hamlin?"

"Let's see what's on my mind."

Greg's answer echoed in the viewing area. The joke was for her benefit, Jade thought. There was nothing funny about being strapped to a table and fed through a giant microwave, modified to invade every part of the body with ultraviolet radiation. Greg had to be nervous. He just didn't want her to know.

Lights blinked on the donut-shaped CT scanner. Jade heard the rushing of a dozen air conditioners cranked to full blast. If the noise was this loud in the neighboring room, she thought, then Greg had to be deafened by it. A low buzz, like a foghorn being blown during a storm, interrupted the sound of hurricane winds. Pictures flashed on the television-sized monitors in front of the technicians. Jade could see the cracked walnut of Greg's skull.

She turned away from the screens. Blood and guts had always made her squeamish. Seeing Greg's interior in black and white was worse. There were some sides to a loved one that no one should have to stomach. She hoped that Greg never had to see her like that.

The machine's buzzes grew sustained, like an annoying note held on a piano. No, worse, an alarm. Jade became aware of a similar buzzing beside her. She opened the purse hanging from her shoulder and fished out her phone. A Westchester area code was on her screen. Only one person in Westchester, other than Greg, knew her cell number.

The female technician shot her an annoyed look. Before the woman could scold her about not turning off her phone, Jade mumbled an apology and hurried out the door. Missing this call wasn't an option.

The scream of the CT scanner was blessedly inaudible in the empty hallway. Still, the space echoed with the sounds of medical monitors. Jade cupped the phone to her ear as she answered: "Hello."

"Ms. Thompson?"

The voice was exactly whom Jade had expected—and feared. As Detective Ricci confirmed her identity, Jade's mind raced through the possible reasons for her call. They'd found the attackers. They'd located CCTV footage of a strange car speeding from their prior rental. They needed Jade to confirm whether the jewelry in an eBay auction was her engagement ring.

"We spoke with Mr. Bernal," Ricci said. "He swears he didn't send that threatening letter, and I'm inclined to believe him."

The excitement filling Jade's chest turned leaden. She felt it thud somewhere in her bowels. Bernal had won Ricci's sympathies. Of course he had! No cop would want to arrest the father of a murdered child over a mean letter. Ricci probably thought Jade should suck it up and deal with the hate mail.

"I see." Jade's own actions compounded her disappointment. She'd not only gambled that the police would intimidate Bernal enough to stop the letters before Greg got one, but she'd doubled down on that bet by hiding the whole thing from him. If she confessed now, Greg would think her a bald-faced liar.

"He and his wife still live in Bushwick so it's possible he heard through the grapevine about your attack and the move. But my take is that he's too wrapped up in his new life to track you down. The Bernals have twin boys—nine years old—born, I gather, around the time he stopped sending you and your mom letters."

Jade did a quick calculation in her head. They'd received the last letter when she'd been in college, perhaps her senior year. His wife would have been pregnant.

"Before having the boys, Mr. Bernal said he'd been depressed and drinking too much. Eventually, his wife got him into Alcoholics Anonymous. He got sober. They decided to try for more kids. Things are going well for them."

Was Ricci trying to convince her that Bernal was a good person? Jade didn't need to hear from the man's PR team. She'd never said he was a bad person. She'd said he'd sent her letters wishing horrible things on her family, specifically her, for more than a decade.

"I'm happy for him." Her tone didn't sell the statement. "But I don't understand how his having more children makes you certain that he didn't write the letter. He's sent threatening notes before, and now I've gotten another one. There's no one else who would have said that about my past."

Ricci let Jade's statement hang, like a blatant lie. "I agree that a solid family life isn't proof that he didn't send the letter," Ricci said finally. "But he also has an alibi."

"For when? The attack?"

"Both your attack and the day you received the note."

"It was mailed. He could have sent it days earlier, whenever was convenient."

"Not exactly." Ricci took a long breath, a tennis player shutting down a volley. "As it turns out, the stamp on the envelope was never voided. It's likely that the letter never made it through the postal system."

The moisture evaporated from Jade's throat. "You think someone dropped it in the mailbox?"

"We're strongly considering that." Ricci coughed. "The day it arrived, Mr. Bernal was at work and then at his boys' baseball game. We checked. Even if he knew where you had moved—and there's nothing to suggest that he did—he wouldn't have had time to drop off the threat."

Ricci's logic was sound, Jade supposed. But the rage-filled man she remembered from her youth had seemed capable of anything. She tried to imagine the man Ricci described, a subdued fifty-something with twin elementary schoolers. It didn't seem likely that such a person would drive over an hour to her house, missing his sons' ball game, just so he could toss a Molotov cocktail into her mailbox. But she also couldn't picture Bernal as a friendly family guy. He had to have delivered it somehow.

"There's a possibility that this letter is related to the break-in, Ms. Thompson." Ricci's tone took on a stern tenor. "You need to discuss things with your husband, ask if he knows anyone who might have sent it."

Jade thought of Greg in the neighboring room with x-rays whirling around his head. She pictured him as he'd been the past week, glued to the desk chair in his darkened home office, monitoring the security footage—a *Clockwork Orange* character, his eyes pried open by fear rather than metal instruments. If she told him that she'd hid a threatening letter—even if she'd done so partly to protect him—he'd completely lose faith in her. He'd call off their engagement. He'd probably run back to his Connecticut wife and kids, his previously sheltered existence where thieves might steal money through trumped-up hedge funds, but they didn't beat people with crowbars or shoot strangers' children.

"My husband is in the hospital, undergoing a CT scan for his skull implant. He'll have surgery in a couple of days. They have to cut open his head again and fit a hunk of metal between his exposed brain and the thin layer of scalp that has re-formed."

Jade wanted to be as graphic as possible. If the detectives truly understood the extent of Greg's injuries, they'd understand why she couldn't discuss the threat (and her lie) with him now. "He's also suffering psychological aftershocks from his attack. I can't give him more reason to be paranoid. He can barely sleep as it is."

The other end of the line was silent for a moment. When Ricci finally spoke, she sounded resigned. "I appreciate why you wouldn't want to exacerbate any stress that Mr. Hamlin is under. We spoke with Greg's colleague, Marcel Bellamy. It seems that his concern about Mr. Bellamy was misplaced. The man competes for architectural projects with your husband, but we didn't get any sense that he wishes him ill. I think he actually admires him."

"So you understand why I can't tell him."

Ricci's sigh overwhelmed the speaker. "If you receive another threat, we have to tell him."

"Of course." The agreement came without hesitation, in part because Jade thought it the only way to guarantee Ricci wouldn't tell Greg, but also because she believed there might not be a second letter. The robbers had wanted her ring. The letter writer—Bernal—had wanted to celebrate karma coming full circle and pile onto her pain. He'd done that, and he knew the police were aware of him. Maybe that would be enough to get him to back off.

"Good." Ricci's voice softened. "And, Jade, Mr. Bernal gave me his email and phone number to pass along to you. I think that he feels badly about what he did in the past."

Jade struggled to respond. The idea of conversing with her harasser was ridiculous. He'd already gloated. Why should she let him do it over the phone?

"I realize you might not want to contact him, but I thought that I should give you the opportunity. I've found that sometimes talking to another victim of violence helps."

Though Jade knew Bernal was a victim, the things he'd written to her over the years precluded her from seeing him that way. However, Ricci didn't have that problem. If Jade didn't take the number, she would be the bad guy who couldn't let go of a grudge, while Bernal would appear the saint.

Jade muttered that Ricci could text her the contact before begging off to see Greg's scan. Instead of letting her go, Ricci said she had one more subject to discuss. "Have you had a chance to review all your blog comments and flag any that might seem suspicious?"

Jade's fear flipped to frustration. Ricci was just like her mother. The detective viewed the blog as nothing more than an invitation into Jade's private life. Neither woman could understand it was her business. "I read the comments all the time," Jade said. "They're all people sharing opinions on my designs or explaining how a recipe worked out for them. There's nothing like that letter."

"There's nothing like that letter," Ricci repeated, "but this one commenter, scenesetter2..."

The detective trailed off, apparently waiting for Jade to fill in the blanks. Jade couldn't recall the screen name, but that didn't mean the person wasn't a subscriber. She didn't pay much attention to her followers, aside from the few fans who shared photos and other content she could repost. Online media was all about the aggregate: how many people visited the site; how much time they spent on it as a whole; how many people engaged with her content. A follower was a number to her.

"Scenesetter2 doesn't seem too thrilled with your life," Ricci continued. "The person's comments are all pretty sarcastic."

"I don't recall any haters."

"Well, the meaning of the comments isn't always clear at first glance. I'll read a couple. Wait a second." Jade heard papers shuffle on Ricci's end. "Okay. Here's one: 'Must be nice to have a big house to decorate. The blog must be doing well!' There's a winking emoji after the exclamation point. And here's another: 'Beautiful table. It probably cost more than a month's rent.'"

If Jade had read such comments, she probably would have taken them as compliments. Ricci's acerbic tone made clear that they were anything but. "Here's another from before the break-in: 'Surprised you can lift a hammer with that rock.'" Ricci cleared her throat. "Your ring is in that picture."

Jade's stomach dropped somewhere between her knees. The snarky comments didn't cause the sinking feeling as much as Ricci's confirmation that strangers had noticed her ring in the blog. Perhaps Bernal had searched her name one day, stumbled upon the site, and become enraged by her "flaunting" her wealth, Jade thought.

"It might be nothing," Ricci said. "Maybe just a jealous housewife from the other side of the country. You never know though. In the meantime, try to keep any identifying information off the blog."

Jade murmured something affirmative and hung up. She managed a couple of steps back toward the CT viewing room before her vision blurred, forcing her to pivot toward the nearest bathroom. Greg couldn't see her like this. He had enough to worry about without taking on comforting her. Besides, it was all her fault. She'd apparently poked the bear with her aspirational-living blog posts, and the beast had nearly taken off her husband's head. Greg's job was to heal. Her new job was to fix this.

With the machines off, Jade was allowed into the radiation room. Greg sat on the slab attached to the scanner, his feet dangling above the floor like a toddler in a high chair. She hovered beside him, trying to project full confidence in his recovery while Greg's brain surgeon uttered scientific words that were over her head.

Hsu held an x-ray image that detailed, with painful clarity, the dent in Greg's head. He gave them both an overview of the surgery and then, at Greg's urging, began explaining the finer points of how he and his team would use the scan to create a 3-D-printed implant made from a variety of high-tech materials. Greg peppered the lecture with questions. He asked about the properties of the insert, how his cells would interact with the foreign object, what his risks of rejection were, whether there were alternative materials that needed to be considered... Question after question, as though he were taking a crash course in cranioplasty.

Jade limited herself to only two queries: What kind of recovery could they expect, and what did they have to do to make it optimal? She wanted Hsu to clarify that Greg should be on a limited-activity regimen. That way, when she reminded her security-crazed future husband of his need to nap and to stop staring at the camera feeds, she wouldn't be the bad guy.

"Most cranioplasty patients spend five to seven days in the hospital, to lower the risk of infection," Dr. Hsu explained. "Once a patient demonstrates that he can shower and dress himself, move around normally, then he can go home and begin the process of recovering there."

Greg grimaced as the doctor shared the part about showering himself. Jade caught Greg glance at her. She forced her expression to go slack. Her fiancé didn't need to see how afraid she was that the surgery might somehow go wrong, leaving Greg unable to perform routine tasks like bathing and dressing.

Dr. Hsu gave Greg a smile that adults usually reserved for children. "You'll be tired, and you might feel like you need an afternoon rest for a while as you heal. You should nap. Listen to your body."

A technician had brought Greg his helmet. Greg rotated the hard plastic in his hands, refusing to don it despite doctor's orders. Jade could tell from the speed with which he worried the hard hat that he desperately wanted to toss the thing before his surgeon found some way of affixing it to his head.

"I can't be napping all the time. I have to get back to work." Greg placed the helmet down beside him. "I have an important building project in Brooklyn, and I just want to resume my life, get back to my regular physical activities, not be stuck in the house all day."

Dr. Hsu glanced at Jade conspiratorially. The surgeon had to be gathering that Greg did not do well with others' orders. He returned his attention to his glowering patient. "I sympathize with your desire to return to normal, Mr. Hamlin. But you have to heal. I am sure your fiancée understands."

She squeezed Greg's hand. "I do."

"And I'm happy to call your office and explain the situation," Dr. Hsu continued. "Though I gather, given your position in the company and what happened, everyone is probably expecting you to be out for at least two months." Hsu lowered his voice. "You nearly died, Greg."

A gray pallor shaded Greg's fair skin. Jade forced a smile at him. "I have big plans for you, mister, and I need you healthy for them."

Greg squeezed her hand in return. Jade didn't sense any surrender in the gesture.

A real spring afternoon greeted them outside the building. Jade tilted her face up, basking in the blue sky that had replaced the slate gray expanses that had stretched into nightfall for several weeks. She filled her lungs with the perfumed air. As they waited for the valet to bring their car, she encouraged Greg to do the same.

"Just think, in a couple of months it will be summer, and we'll be sitting in lounge chairs on the back deck. I'll grill up some chicken." She rubbed Greg's shoulder. "Or maybe we'll jet off to some artsy city for design inspiration. Where did you want to go again? Colombia?"

Greg pulled at the chin strap securing his helmet. "I'll have to catch up on missed work. Marcel must be having a field day, jockeying for my projects. I'm sure he has an alternative proposal for the Brooklyn building already."

Jade considered what Ricci had said on the phone about Greg's rival. Though the guy vied for commissions with Greg (and perhaps other principal architects at the firm), the detective believed Greg had blown their competition out of proportion. Had he? Jade wondered. Or was Ricci easily swayed by men with good stories? Given that the detective was no longer even entertaining the possibility that Carlos Bernal had sent her the letter, Jade decided on the latter.

She grasped Greg's arm. "Even if Marcel is trying to take the Brooklyn building, he won't get it. You're a brilliant architect. Anyone interested in creating a work of art that will define their company forever knows that. Your résumé is imprinted on the New York City skyline."

Greg shrugged as if his famous tower in the garment district was no big deal. Critics said he'd designed the building's angles the way an expert jeweler cut a diamond, making it gleam and sparkle like a star over Penn Station, particularly at sunset. The tower had been one of Jade's favorite buildings in the city, even before she'd started dating Greg. It was original and yet reflective of its surroundings, futuristic and somehow a homage to all the skyscrapers that had come before it. When Greg told her that he'd designed it, she was immediately starstruck. The talent it must have taken to craft something like that, she'd thought. She'd wanted to understand the heart and mind that could create such a work. It flattered her that he'd been as interested in her.

"Clients will wait for you, honey."

"No one wants to wait for anyone, Jade."

The statement shut down any of the other encouraging messages she'd cued up. She kissed his cheek, letting her physical affection speak for her, and waited in silence for her car. It arrived a couple of quiet minutes later. The valet took one look at Greg's helmet-covered head and handed her the keys.

As she drove toward the highway, Greg fiddled with his phone. She wanted to quip that he'd had enough radiation for one day and should give the cellular waves a break. Instead, she repeated the doctor's advice about too much screen time exacerbating his headaches.

"I'm checking the security cameras," he snapped. He glanced up at her from the phone and softened his voice. "Those men are still out there."

He had a point. Jade concentrated on driving, though she glanced at Greg's cell with the same regularity with which she checked her rearview. She, too, wanted to be certain they were driving back to a secure house.

"Anything of interest?"

Greg clicked on a thumbnail. "Looks like the mailman came. More bills."

Jade made a mental note to check the mail before Greg had an opportunity. She didn't believe Bernal would send another note so soon after talking to the police. But she couldn't take any chances.

CHAPTER 11

A tremor ran down Greg's legs as he collapsed onto the sunroom couch. Walking to and from the car multiple times that day had exhausted him. He guessed that he shouldn't have been surprised given that everything drained him lately: thinking, standing, talking, even breathing. In the morning, he woke up tired. He retired to bed like the dead.

The incongruity of the man on the couch and the person he'd been before the attack did shock him though. It seemed impossible that a guy who, several months earlier, had run a half marathon from Brooklyn, over the Manhattan Bridge, up the FDR Drive, and then finished off with a loop around Central Park—in the cold, no less—could become fatigued by a jaunt up his own driveway. He couldn't even manage getting the mail.

He knew that his surgeon had said he would get better, that he should give himself time to heal, but patience was a trait he'd never considered particularly virtuous. For him, patience had always translated to submitting to someone else's schedule, an inability to effect change with the force of one's own ideas and ideals. He was supposed to be Ayn Rand's Howard Roark, not washed-up Peter Keating.

Slumped on the couch, his mental defiance seemed a feeble protest. In reality, he'd been robbed of his virility, rendered a retiree who required a cane to get around and napped in the middle of the day. His sexy, smart, and significantly younger fiancée was certainly taking so long in the bathroom to get a break from taking care of him.

The lack of a toilet flush as Jade emerged from the bathroom nearest the kitchen confirmed his suspicions. He strained to see her over his shoulder from his position two rooms away. Her dark hair cascaded down her shoulders. It appeared curlier than usual, perhaps because of the humidity.

Greg watched her enter the living room and head his way. Her eyes appeared browner, as though her pupils had shrunk to let in the least amount of light possible, to look into herself rather than at anything. Her expression seemed agitated. Seeing it scared him. Perhaps she'd had a long look in the mirror and decided that she couldn't take a life of putting a broken, old man back together. He couldn't fault her, he supposed. She hadn't signed up to be his nursemaid.

"Hey, can I get you anything?" The smile that followed was transparent. He could see right through it to the exhaustion underneath.

"No. I'll make myself a sandwich in a bit."

Jade glanced back at the kitchen without moving toward it. Instead, she hovered between the living room and the sunroom, biting her bottom lip. Chewing over her words. "Honey, listen."

Greg grasped the sofa arm, either bracing himself or preparing to shuffle from the room, he wasn't sure which. All he knew was that he couldn't hear Jade tell him she was leaving and just sit there. He had to stand up. Take it like a man. At the very least, he had to have the dignity to leave the room should he start to tear.

"Tomorrow, I really have to go into the city. I haven't been blogging like I should, and my traffic is sure to suffer." She walked toward the credenza on the half wall separating the living and sitting rooms and began fussing with the recycled glass balls she'd arranged in a wooden bowl on top. They were shades of teal and cerulean blue, reminiscent of the colors in the bathroom. Jade had a way of tying things together.

"I want to check out the Decoration and Design Building, blog about some pieces, take a break from photographing food and our home." She shook a hand through her spiral curls. "I've already done so many posts about incorporating island colors into white rooms."

The fist clenching Greg's heart relaxed its grip.

"I know it might seem selfish to leave you here." Jade continued fidgeting with the baubles, picking them up, rotating them, and placing them back in the bowl. "I won't be gone long. And—"

"It's okay, babe. I understand. You have an audience that you need to keep. I wouldn't want you to lose that because of me." His relief—or the adrenaline from his ebbing fear—gave him a sudden burst of energy. He pressed into the couch arm and stood. "In fact, it would be good for us both to go. I've been meaning to check in with the office, let them see that this whole head injury thing isn't some ploy to spend more time with my lovely fiancée."

Greg expected his compliment to elicit a smile from Jade. Instead, she looked stricken. "I was thinking I'd go alone. You're supposed to rest. Not work. You heard the doctor."

"It's not work to show my face. I need to remind people that I'm not dead."

Jade sliced the air with her hands. "You were nearly killed, Greg. They all know what happened. No one is expecting you in the damn office."

The sharpness of her gesture took Greg aback. Jade was a self-composed woman. Throughout their six-month relationship, he'd never heard her so much as raise her voice, let alone do it with accompanying hand signals. Greg wondered if she'd never yelled because he'd always been the kind of man to command respect. Perhaps his weakened state had made him seem like the type of person at whom Jade could rage.

"I'm expecting me in the damn office."

"You're being ridiculous." Jade pointed to the ceiling, a mom ordering a naughty child to their upstairs room. "You need to rest. Here. At home. And I need you to take care of yourself. You're still trying to act as though everything can go back to normal overnight."

"You just don't want me to go."

"Of course I don't want you to go!"

Jade's heightened volume started up the timpani in Greg's brain. He pressed his palm into the left side of his head, covering his ear like an obstinate child refusing to hear.

Her face fell. She lowered her voice. "You have to understand that your brain is vulnerable right now. I mean, you're supposed to wear a helmet, Greg, but you refuse to put it on in the house, so I highly doubt you'll wear it around your colleagues. You'll be putting yourself at risk for further injury if you go to the office before the plate is installed. And Dr. Hsu also said that you need to rest in the middle of the day. You heard him. If you come with me, I'll feel like I have to leave after a couple of hours and I won't get the work done that I need to do."

The pounding in Greg's head picked up its pace, drowning out the rational voice that sympathized with her dilemma. Obviously, she'd get more work done without worrying about dropping him off and picking him up. And yes, it made sense for her to fear that he might delay his recovery by pushing himself. Any trip to the office would surely end up with his commenting on architectural plans, if not sketching something in an attempt to get his team going on the proposal that Marcel was no doubt trying to co-opt. But Jade should also sympathize with his need for stimulation. What was he supposed to do all day until the surgery? Sit in the house? By himself?

"If you're nervous about being alone, I completely understand," Jade continued. "I'll call my mother. She's off tomorrow and would be—"

"Don't worry about it." He started past her, toward the living room. "I'll phone Leah."

"Leah?" Hurt pierced Jade's voice. Greg couldn't help but find the rise in tone satisfying. He could have said that he would call his daughter to keep him company. As an adult child without a steady job, still covered by his health insurance and living in the house that he'd built and paid for, Violet could be expected to stay with him for a few hours. In fact, given her opinion of Jade, she probably wanted permission to check on him. However, saying his daughter's name wouldn't have plucked his fiancée's insecurities, as Jade was doing by ordering him to stay in the house while she went to the city. He wanted Jade to feel some of what he felt, even if she didn't exactly deserve it.

"Leah lives ten minutes away. It's easy enough for her to check on me. Don't worry," Greg said. "I'll ask her to bring lunch."

He said the last part nonchalantly, as though he were trying to ease Jade's fears about his feeding himself. Really, he was twisting the knife. Jade prided herself on her cooking abilities and being the kind of woman who made meals for her man. It was a subtle theme in her blog, which didn't simply celebrate Caribbean style but also a kind of old-school dedication to matters of home and family that Jade told him was part of the culture. Greg's subtly equating Leah's "let's order in" chef skills with Jade's own was an attack on his fiancée's sense of self.

Greg strode cane-less through the living room, keeping his hands within reach of walls and furniture should he need to rebalance. He rounded the stairwell and headed into the office, where the dim natural light through the shutters would soothe his headache. By the time he reached his office chair, he was exhausted again. He slumped into the leather seat and pulled his cell from the front pocket of his jeans, the legs of which were considerably looser than fashionable because of the muscle mass he'd lost in the hospital.

The cell felt like a brick in his hands, something to chuck

at the home's omnipresent windows rather than a communication tool. He didn't know how to wield it. Speaking with Leah was a delicate matter. He couldn't simply call up his ex and say, *Hey, Jade will be out tomorrow; can you keep me company?* That would send the wrong message. Until the divorce finalized, he didn't want to give Leah false hope that they might rekindle their relationship.

Before he called, he jostled his computer mouse, waking the screen. The security app was already open. In the time it had taken him to cut across the house from the living room, Jade had started cooking. She leaned over a kitchen counter, dicing what appeared to be a red onion on one of her wooden boards. Every few cuts, she set the knife down and rubbed beneath her eyes with the back of her forearm. Greg told himself that the onion was making her tear. He'd meant to annoy her, not make her cry. Surely, she wasn't so bothered by his calling Leah that she'd become emotional?

He fought the urge to check on her in person. Any apology at this point would only emphasize that he'd brought up his ex to be petty. The last thing he needed was to appear any more insecure or weak than he already did.

He unlocked the phone with his thumbprint and hit the speed dial designated "home." At some point, he'd get around to changing the label in his contacts—though not today. He wasn't in the mood to distance himself from his prior household more than he already had.

Leah answered on the second ring with an immediate "How are you feeling?" Her voice had taken on a sexy rumble thanks to age (and likely wine). "Is everything okay?"

For once he found Leah's motherly concern soothing, probably because Jade had been yelling at him moments before. "Yeah. I'm calling because Jade has to go into the city tomorrow, and I'm going to be rattling around the house by myself. I thought maybe you'd like to come by for a friendly lunch. I'm not much for cooking at the moment—not that I ever was—but we could order. At the moment, I'm quite the conversationalist—or conversation piece, rather." Greg chuckled. "The things I can share about modern medicine."

Greg could sense Leah's confusion in the tense silence on the other end of the line. "Oh. Um. I'm sorry, but I can't tomorrow. I wish I could. I certainly don't think you should be alone while you're healing. But I have plans that I can't cancel."

"Cindy having a luncheon?" Leah's best friend in Greenwich, Cindy Brown, was a queen of the charity circuit. When Greg and Leah had been together, it seemed that the woman hosted a fund-raising event every month. Leah had hated missing them. For a stay-at-home mom surrounded by two young kids all day, Greg guessed that the luncheons had been a rare opportunity to get dolled up.

"What's the cause?" He tried to sound droll. "Neighborhood watch? I hear crime is running rampant these days. There was this guy I read about who was hit over the head with a crowbar. Nasty stuff."

Leah didn't laugh. "I'm sorry, Greg. I have a date. Matthew Grist. You might know him. He's the sports agent. Benjie's father. Remember little Benjamin? He was friends with Paul for a time. Anyway..." She giggled. Leah didn't giggle. "Funny thing, I ran into him, oddly enough, at a dinner party

at Cindy's house. Gail divorced him a few years back, and
she was actually the one to pick up and run to New York,
so Cindy and Jeff got to keep Matt as their friend after the
separation. I'm sure you two have met. He has dark hair,
green eyes. He played football once upon a time."

"I'm not sure."

"I guess you never paid much attention." Leah sighed.
"People in town have asked about you. Barb said to give you
her best. She was so sorry to hear what had happened. Jack,
her husband, is still working at Cedars-Sinai and told me to
relay that if there is anything he can do, he'd be happy to help.
David, Christine's husband, said the same thing. He . . ."

Leah continued rattling off names like a new contact who'd
learned she'd been in his graduating class. Greg listened
politely, not really caring about the stated sympathy of their
former friends. Most had never been more than acquaintances
to him anyway. Leah had been the one to concern herself
with forging real friendships in town. He'd simply adopted
whomever the partner of her friend had been, defaulting to
sports talk whenever he'd lacked anything in common with
the guy.

Strangely enough, he did care about Matthew Grist though.
The man had a salt-and-pepper goatee, if he remembered
correctly, and a full head of hair. Greg had noticed because
Matthew was a tall, broad guy whose size demanded a bit of
attention. Often, when his son hung out at the house with
Paul, Matthew had done pickup. In retrospect, Greg wondered
whether the guy had enjoyed checking out his wife.

His almost ex-wife, Greg reminded himself.

Greg put the phone on speaker and placed it on his desk.

He opened a web browser on his computer. Quietly, he typed "Matthew Grist" into the search box along with "Greenwich." The page populated with a row of images featuring a guy with salt-and-pepper facial hair and a broad body that advertised a certain vanity. In one photo, the guy had his arm around Eli Manning.

Greg closed the web page, admonishing himself for the pinch of jealousy in his gut. Leah deserved someone who would make her happy. His envy, he told himself, stemmed from frustration with his injury. He was simply resentful that he no longer looked healthy and fit.

"Violet? Violet!" Leah was shouting. At some point, she'd stopped listing his well-wishers and suggested that he ask Violet if she might want a daddy-daughter day.

"It would be good for you two to spend some time to-gether." Leah lowered her voice to a whisper. "You know the separation has been hard on her. She likes to think she came home to take care of me but, really, I think she delayed everything another year because the whole divorce shook her foundation and she wanted to be home."

It wasn't the first time his ex-wife had suggested their daughter's failure to launch was a result of his poor timing. When was there a good time to end a twenty-five-year rela-tionship? Clearly never.

"She's doing well," Leah whispered. "When she comes, ask her about school. Here, sweetheart. It's your father." Leah's voice was distant, as though she'd already begun to pass over her phone. "Be nice."

Static reverberated in the speaker as the receiver switched hands. Greg could sense his daughter's silent breathing on the other end of the line. The power struggle had already begun. She wanted him to say hi first.

Greg was too fatigued to play. "Hi, Violet." He forced a cheeriness into his tone that sounded false even to his own ears. "How are you?"

"Well, Dad. Thank you for asking." Violet coughed. "Of course, the real question is, how is the man recovering from a brain injury?"

Greg groaned. "I'm healing. In fact, that's kind of why I'm calling. I'm stuck at the house—apparently it's not a good thing to go traipsing around with part of your skull missing—and was hoping that you might keep me company tomorrow."

Violet hesitated a beat before replying, as though she had to check her busy schedule. She'd never reveal that she had nothing to do. "Sure. I'm free. Where will Jade be?"

Greg closed his eyes and tightened his stomach, readying for the inevitable. "She has to go into the city for work."

"Hmm. That's what she said, huh? I wonder what she's really up to."

Before he could retort, Violet added that she'd bring food and would see him at eleven. She hung up, leaving her unanswered question to putrefy. Greg tried to toss it aside, calling up his work email and scrolling through messages upon which he'd been cc'd as a matter of course. The question continued to fester, however, infecting him with doubts.

Jade was the Rumpelstiltskin of bloggers, regularly turning cheap bits of nothing into traffic gold. He'd read posts in which she'd put together a few colored pillows and used them as a jumping-off point to discuss color theory. Surely, she didn't really need to drive over an hour to the D&D Building on Third and Fifty-Ninth for inspiration. There had to be another reason that she wanted to be in Manhattan. The real question was what, and why didn't she want him to know?

CHAPTER 12

Eyes followed Jade into the kitchen. She sensed them as she removed the orange juice from the fridge, spurring her to whirl around, clenching the cardboard carton. The sight of the empty kitchen failed to exorcise the phantoms in her peripheral vision. Jade told herself the feeling of being watched stemmed from the letter she'd received and the knowledge that it had likely been hand-delivered. It was akin to the itchy awareness that people experienced after spotting a tick on a sock or a spider atop a friend's shoulder. Actually, no one was spying on her. At least, not at the moment.

Someone had been though. They'd tracked down her new address and traveled to her home just to let her know that she'd never escape from her past. How far away she moved, how much money she earned, how nice her house and community were, who her husband was—none of that mattered. She would always be Michael Thompson's daughter.

She filled two glasses of orange juice, leaving one for whenever Greg arrived downstairs. He'd stirred as she'd showered in the adjoining bathroom. However, when she'd approached to suggest eating together before she headed out, he'd been turned on his right side with his eyes shut tight.

He was upset about her leaving. Greg wanted her to hunker down in the house (or at his office), where he thought he could protect her. She found the desire admirable but not actionable. Greg needed all his energy to get better. If someone had an issue with her having a happy family because of her history, dealing with that person was her burden. Alone.

Still, she felt bad for lying to Greg. Breakfast would have to serve as her apology. She placed the homemade bread from the prior day in the center of the table, atop a wooden cutting board, and positioned the bread knife alongside it like a command: EAT. Beside it all, she left a small jar of strawberry-rhubarb jam and another of orange marmalade, along with two tasting spoons. The setup reminded Jade of what guests would wake up to at a bed-and-breakfast. She grabbed a pretty piece of stationery from a drawer and wrote a note in her most legible script telling Greg that she loved him and would be back later. To finish off the scene, she plucked a bright tiger lily from the living room vase and draped it over the note atop Greg's empty plate.

As she stepped back to admire her work, Jade got the distinct feeling that she wasn't the only one checking it out. For a second time, she shook off the skin-crawling sensation. The only people who would see her breakfast display would be Greg and perhaps Leah, if she arrived before he ate it all. There was no way whatever paper-bag lunch Greg's ex brought would look anywhere near as pretty or thoughtful as the quick breakfast she'd prepared.

Jade pulled her cell from her red bag atop the kitchen counter and snapped a photo of the scene. If she didn't have time to hit the Decoration and Design Building, she could post the image along with something about creating beautiful tablescapes. She could urge readers to submit their own "color-filled breakfasts" at the end. Participatory posts always drove traffic.

The time on her cell read ten after nine. Visitors weren't allowed in until one, and the drive wouldn't take more than an hour. However, there was always a painfully slow registration line. Eleven would be the ideal time to leave, she thought. Unfortunately, hanging around the house until then was certain to raise questions. The D&D Building opened at ten. Greg would wonder why she wasn't trying to beat the afternoon crowds.

Ten was a doable departure time, she decided. It would leave her an hour of sitting in that depressing parking lot; an hour of rehearsing what to say. It had been so long since she'd last seen her father. She had no idea what condition he would be in or what he knew of her life. Maybe he no longer cared what she was doing and dealing with. Life moved on for most people—even there.

Jade took her phone into the glass-walled sitting room. The view of the Long Island Sound would soothe her fried nerves, she figured. It would ease the sensation of someone staring.

But it didn't. As Jade settled onto the white couch, the prickle of attention grew more persistent. She found herself repeatedly glancing over her shoulder, certain Greg—or someone—stood right behind her.

Scrolling through her blog comments only intensified her discomfort. In her mind, she read everything with a sarcastic tone, trying to determine what could have been intended as a subtle dig. Most of the messages were undeniably positive statements from fans and friends. Some were neutral questions: "What is the purple flower in that bouquet called?"; "Would bright orange go with a gray wall?"

The posts from scenesetter2 were the only ones that seemed to possess a double meaning. In addition to the several quips that Detective Ricci had read to her, Jade found one more thanks to the comment search tool in her premium web page creator package. The message had been published about two and a half months earlier. Jade assumed she hadn't noticed it because it had been appended to a weeks-old post and the home invasion had occurred shortly after, pushing the blog to the back of Jade's mind.

The comment was under a photo of Jade's twelve-week ultrasound. Usually, she wouldn't have shared something so personal with her audience, but she'd been so excited by the sight of that glowing head and stubby limbs taking shape that she'd uploaded it along with a lengthy post about how her blog would soon include more kidcentric designs. Her audience had loved it. In fact, it had been her most engaging post all year. All her regular readers had chimed in with congratulations.

Everyone except scenesetter2. At the bottom of a list of nearly five hundred comments were four nasty little words: "Don't count your chickens."

The vague feeling of being watched suddenly exploded into a full-blown certainty. Jade shot up from the couch and moved to the narrow section of drywall connecting the glass windows to the rest of the house. She pressed her back against the firm surface and tried to steady her shaky breaths. Had scenesetter2 known what was coming? Had he or she been involved?

Jade swiped at the tears gathering in the corner of her eyes and forced herself to reconsider the comment. On second glance, the directive seemed more of a warning than a threat. It was the kind of statement a superstitious or religious woman like her mother might make just to emphasize that fate or God was in control. *Careful, Jade, the devil loves a party, and nothing tempts him like an early celebration.*

However, scenesetter2 was not her mother. It was too generous to assume that the comment's intent had simply been to caution her against prematurely announcing her good news. In light of the other backhanded compliments, the person had definitely been trying to dampen her celebration. Still, a desire to rain on her parade was different from plotting her baby's death. Most likely, scenesetter2 was a would-be designer resentful of Jade's relative success. Most likely.

Though the conclusion was logical, it didn't make Jade feel much better. The glass-walled room suddenly seemed too open, too exposed. She was an animal trapped in a zoo enclosure with anyone able to gaze inside and see exactly what she was doing and why. She needed to get out.

The sensation of someone staring persisted as Jade exited the back door and beelined to the garage. She backed out of the driveway without entering the address into her phone's map application, her sixth sense telling her that doing so would tip off the hovering ghost. It wasn't until she got on the interstate that she felt comfortable typing in her true destination.

CHAPTER 13

Violet stood on the curb, looking the house up and down like a jealous woman. A large black hobo bag dangled from her right shoulder, hitting the sliver of exposed skin where her cropped T-shirt met her cutoff jean shorts. In her left hand, she clutched a white paper bag with a stylized drawing of a slice of bread on the front. Greg zoomed into the live video on his phone and recognized the design as the logo of a favorite Greenwich brunch spot. The place made an avocado toast on sourdough with a perfectly fried egg, the salted yolk balanced atop the white like a bright sun through the clouds.

Seeing the package made him salivate. He enjoyed the Caribbean foods that Jade prepared, many of which paired ingredients he was accustomed to, like avocados, with things he'd never heard of—"johnnycakes," a kind of fish fritter that Jade served on paper towels to soak up all the excess oil; or breadfruit, a spiky melon-looking food that tasted like a potato roll. However, knowing that he would soon eat a classic American meal filled him with grateful nostalgia, like waking up to the scent of home.

Instead of coming straight into the house, Violet approached the mailbox. She glanced over her shoulder, as though she could sense him watching on his cell, before opening it up. When she turned back toward the house, letters and a magazine were gripped in her right hand.

Greg disarmed the alarm, set his phone on the kitchen table, and energetically hobbled to the entrance. Before he swung the door back, he was struck with a paralyzing fear. The brim of his baseball cap became damp with sweat. Was that truly his daughter he'd seen coming up the walk? Perhaps it had been the intruders and his mind had morphed them into a less-threatening image. He wanted to run back to his phone and double-check, though running anywhere was impossible, especially with the panic already seizing his chest.

Greg scolded himself aloud for being silly and unlocked the dead bolt. His heartbeat pounded in his head, slowing his hand. His throat became parched. He couldn't swallow. He couldn't breathe. Greg hung on to the door handle and forced himself to exhale for a full second, as Abigay had demonstrated. Inhale: one...two...three. Exhale: one...two...

Violet's voice sounded on the other side of the door. "Ding-dong, Dad." She rapped the door for emphasis. "Special delivery."

Greg's heart eased off the gas. He pulled back the door.

Violet was bent at an angle, staring into the doorbell camera as though it were a peephole. "You got one of these, huh?"

Greg stepped from the air-conditioning into the balmy spring day. The back of the house was several degrees cooler than the front because of the breeze off the water. Greg considered suggesting that they eat on the deck. It was shaded, which would appeal to his untannable child. Of course, it was also outdoors. Unprotected.

Greg pointed to the overhang, calming himself by focusing on what he'd done to secure his home. "I installed a bunch of outdoor cameras with intercoms too. There's one up there. You won't catch me opening doors for strange deliverymen again." Seeing Violet, in the flesh, returned some of the good feeling he'd enjoyed upon first seeing her through the cameras. "But a daughter bearing gifts is always welcome."

Violet stepped from beneath the canopy and scanned for the camera. Her nose wrinkled as she spotted it. "Tell me you hired someone. That thing is fifteen feet in the air. If you fell—"

"Jade did the drilling."

The smudged makeup around Violet's eyes underlined her concern. "You let her around you with power tools? That's hardly a smart idea."

There was more to Violet's comment than Jade's lack of familiarity with drills. Greg chose to ignore the implication. In response, his daughter gave him a half-embrace and then handed him a magazine and several legal envelopes, like a process server notifying him of a lawsuit. "Your mail."

He muttered a thank-you while ushering Violet past the threshold. There was little point to a man's fortifying his castle if he intended to stand outside it. "Come on. We'll eat in the kitchen."

Greg locked the dead bolt and then walked over to the

base station to hit a button re-arming the security system. Violet watched the procedure with a look of confusion.

"Once I tap my fob against this, it reactivates all the sensors, so I'm alerted to the doors jostling, windows opening, glass breaking. It allows motion on the floor though."

Violet turned her head from right to left, like a camera recording a panoramic image. "Are there lasers and trip wires too?"

As usual, his daughter found bemusing something that should have impressed her. "No." He covered his annoyance with a joke. "I don't take my design inspirations from Indiana Jones."

Greg dropped the mail on the entry table and returned his attention to Violet, deciding he could sort through the bills later. She was examining the motion sensor beyond the entrance above the main stairway. She shook her head and then turned into the dining room, taking time to check out the architectural details in the still-unfurnished area. She gestured toward the ceiling—a classic Tudor style divided by pale oak beams. "You kept some beautiful original features."

"I've always found the combination of heavy timber and plaster pleasing."

Violet pursed her lips, forcing him to consider how pretentious he'd sounded, and then turned her attention to the table in the neighboring room. The top was constructed of a slab of travertine marble cut with blue resin to imitate shallow water over a coral reef. It was supported by two carved-oak pedestals that were the same color as the overhead beams. The designer was from St. Martin, and Jade had fallen in love with what she'd called *the perfect marriage of his-and-her aesthetics*. He'd let her have it. Interior design was her thing. His forte was form and function, light and shade. The art of construction, not so much decoration.

"So you respected tradition." Violet pointed to the ceiling. "And then you completely broke with tradition." She let her arm fall in a hopeless gesture.

Greg picked up on the subtext of his daughter's criticism. Again, he chose not to engage. He didn't need to defend his choices, design or otherwise. "Kitchen's that way." He gestured with his chin for her to keep walking straight through the opening.

They entered the kitchen's breakfast nook. Violet dropped the take-out bag on the table. She began pulling plastic containers from the sack and placing them around the surface, pushing aside Jade's carefully arranged condiments. "It's only set for one," she grumbled.

Greg started toward the cabinets, using his cane to increase his speed. "Jade made me breakfast before she went out." He removed a plate from a cupboard and brought it toward the table. "I guess she didn't know when you would get here."

Violet waved him away. "No point in dirtying a dish." Greg thought it might be the first purely good-natured thing she'd said all morning.

He returned the plate to the cupboard and then moved back to the breakfast area, assuming the place that Jade had set for him. Violet took the seat diagonally across. She opened her plastic container, a BLT, from the smell of charred meat.

"Did you get me the avocado toast?"

Violet nodded as she took a large bite. "Mom ordered it." She spoke between mouthfuls. "She said it was your favorite."

Greg popped the clear lid off the untouched container. Lying in the center were two slices of bread, heaped with avocado and topped with a beautiful egg. Each looked as delicious as he remembered. He grabbed the cutlery atop his napkin and began carefully transferring one of the slices to his plate. "She was right," he said. "It is my favorite. Thank you."

Violet shrugged. "Thank Mom. I only picked it up."

Greg sliced across the center of the toast, breaking the jiggling yoke. It spread over the mountain of mashed avocado, spilling over the edge of the toast and onto the plate. "I will."

Violet gave him a dubious look. "It was nice of her to think of you, even though she had a date. It's her first, you know. She hasn't seen anyone this whole time."

Greg carved off a bite and aimed it for his mouth, intending to fill it rather than respond. What did Violet want him to say? He was sorry that Leah had taken the separation harder than he had? He was glad that she was dating? Perhaps he should have felt both things, but he knew he didn't. As much as he wanted Leah to be happy, he knew he would have been disappointed if she'd moved on before him. Deep down, he suspected that he'd been bold enough to date around only because he knew that she would pine for him at least a little, enabling him to retreat back home had things not worked out. Fortunately for him, they had—or at least they had until someone came at him with a crowbar.

He shoved the forkful of food inside his waiting mouth. Familiar flavors exploded on his tongue. He tasted the sweetness of the avocado mixed with the oily slick of the egg and the tang of salt and pepper. The bite brought back memories of Leah, Paul, Violet, and him crammed into a booth on Sunday afternoons, shouting to one another about their week over the din of clinking cutlery and drink orders. Their life had been chaotic sometimes, but Greg had thrived in that bustle: late nights in the office and the catch-up brunches with kids who were just as busy. He'd loved that. He'd wanted it again. Leah, however, had been looking forward to a quieter existence. She'd wanted easy social gatherings with neighborhood friends, watching late-night movies cuddled on the living room couch with glasses of chardonnay, and the enjoyment of a comfortable house that no longer required constant cleaning.

"You should have seen her before she went out. Hot." Violet took an aggressive bite of her sandwich. Bacon cracked beneath her molars. "She was wearing this white pantsuit and had her hair blown out. I helped with her makeup." Violet grabbed the purse that she'd slung over the back of a chair and pulled out her phone. "Here, look."

She fiddled with the screen for a moment and then pushed the cell toward Greg. He almost didn't want to see. He knew Violet wouldn't show him the picture if it was anything less than devastating. He took another silencing bite of his sandwich before accepting the phone.

Leah wore one of her trademark nervous smiles. A woman of the pre-selfie age, she'd never grown to love the camera, even though it had always loved her. Her golden hair fell in waves beside her delicately rouged cheeks, parting like a curtain to reveal her diamond jawline. Violet's influence could be seen in Leah's eye makeup. She'd outlined the wide-set eyes in the same black pencil that encircled Violet's own, making the blue irises pop from her pale skin. Leah appeared enigmatic and sexy, a noir heroine in daytime lighting. Matthew Grist was a lucky son of a bitch.

Greg forced the memory of his own fiancée into his head, reminding himself that he, too, was a lucky SOB. Jade hadn't left him, and he didn't want Leah. He just, selfishly, wanted to inhabit an alternative universe where he got Jade and Leah remained happy—and perhaps available—without ever replacing him.

He passed the phone back to Violet. "Your mother is a beautiful woman. You're lucky to take after her."

"She's a smart woman too," Violet added, ignoring the compliment. "And loyal."

Greg cut off another bite of his toast. "How have you been?"

Violet stopped chewing. "Good, I guess. I mean, what happened to you threw me a bit. For a minute, I thought you were going to die, and I'd have to live with the knowledge that I was busy hating you when it happened." She chuckled as though she were exaggerating for amusement's sake.

Greg remembered some of the things Violet had said when he'd filed the divorce papers. *Hate* probably wasn't that hyperbolic.

"Fortunately, you survived." Violet smirked at him. "So, second chance."

Greg smiled back. If he were to have a real second chance, he needed to keep the conversation far away from what had spurred him to leave Leah. "Your mom mentioned school?"

Violet looked down at her plate. "Oh, she did?"

"Yeah. Are you taking classes at the community college or—"

"I got into RISD."

A piece of avocado stuck in Greg's throat. He coughed as he tried to squeak out a clarification. "The Rhode Island School of Design?"

"The one and only." Violet glanced at him and then quickly returned her attention to her nearly finished breakfast, as if she didn't really want to see his reaction.

"How?" Greg grabbed the orange juice Jade had left for him and swallowed it down. It dislodged the stuck piece, enabling his voice to flow normally. "I mean, that's great. How?"

Violet stabbed at her breakfast, still avoiding eye contact. "I'd been working on a portfolio over the past year, and I guess they liked it. I also wrote an essay explaining my few years off as driven by a desire to develop my own aesthetic influences before anyone directed what they should be." She looked squarely at him—a challenge, albeit a weak one. "I think they appreciated that."

Greg reconsidered the young woman in his kitchen, this strange mix of goth-chic and prep school princess. Kate Moss without the cocaine—at least, he hoped. He'd always thought of Violet as confused and combative, determined to remain lost, perhaps until she found a spouse and had children to give her some structure. Did a deep talent lurk beneath the off-putting angst? Had he underestimated her? Clearly RISD thought so.

"What do you want to study?"

"Film." A pink flush glazed Violet's cheeks. "Maybe set design. I'll have to see."

"Well, that's great, hon. Just great." He forced a smile, knowing that he should feel pride—that he would, once the shock wore off and the news became real to him. "Who knows, maybe set design will whet your appetite for architecture and you'll go on to get your master's."

Violet's flush extended down to her neck. "It's okay, Dad. We don't all need degrees from Harvard. I'm happy seeing what RISD does for me."

"I didn't mean—"

"Yes, you did. You're a school snob who thinks Harvard is the be-all and end-all. The pinnacle of every stepping-stone school like—"

"I don't think of RISD as a stepping-stone."

"That's why Paul applied to Harvard early decision. He knew no other school would be good enough."

The pride Greg had felt moments before vanished. Violet wouldn't ever get through RISD, let alone go to Harvard, with such a thin skin. He'd only been trying to commiserate with her. "I am proud of your brother," Greg said. "He's smart, and he really applies himself. And I'm sure he went to Harvard not because of me, but because he thought it was the best place for him."

"Best place to become a speed freak," Violet muttered.

Quintessential Violet, Greg thought, tearing down whatever intimidated her. Surely she was poised to quote from some article she'd read recently about Adderall abuse in high schools to get into elite colleges or perhaps even such abuse in the Ivy League. Greg loaded up his fork, prepared to chew through the whole spiel. Instead, Violet simply looked at him with a mix of hurt and disappointment.

A small voice in his head, which sounded distinctly like Leah, told him to make nice. He knew that Violet got fired up whenever she felt he was unfavorably comparing her with her laser-focused younger brother. Rather than stoke her in-securities, he should try to soothe her.

"Perhaps I'm not putting things well. You'll have to excuse me." He took off his baseball cap and tipped it toward Violet. "I have a rather large dent in my head at the moment. It's possible that some of my missing gray matter contained neuropathways for tact. My point was that I am proud of you, Violet. It's quite an achievement, and I am sure you'll do very well there."

Violet transferred her glare to her plate. Her shoulders drooped. "Thanks. I'm looking forward to it, though it will be weird being one of the older kids in the school." She smirked as she continued examining the remnants of her sandwich. "I might have to date younger."

Greg laughed and picked up the last yoke-covered piece of his toast. "Well, that would be taking after the old man."

Violet seemed about to laugh but suppressed it. "I was kidding. I'm actually dating someone at the moment. Have been for nearly six months actually."

Greg's skin pulsed around his scar as his eyebrows abruptly retreated toward his hairline. His daughter had been working on a portfolio, applied to RISD, and had a boyfriend. They really had grown apart in the time that he'd been out of the house. Of course, he'd never really had conversations with his daughter about her life. His relationship with teenage Violet had been conducted via a game of telephone. She'd told her mother things, which Leah had then repeated with clear instructions about what he was supposed to know and what he could secretly know. That was how he had kept current with his daughter's life. With her mother no longer whispering in his ear, he'd been cut out of the loop.

"Are you going to be bringing this mystery man by for a meet and greet anytime soon?"

Violet picked up her fork and gestured to his head. "Well, I was waiting until you were a wee bit more presentable. And maybe less likely to have a stroke."

"This kid's that bad, huh?"

"He's not bad at all actually. He just has different priorities than you do. He's a musician. Plays guitar."

College? Greg wanted to ask but held his tongue. He needed to ask a few more questions first in order to counteract Violet's opinion of him as a school snob. Greg deliberately raised the pitch of his voice and wagged his brows. "Is he totally dreamy?"

Violet picked up her phone and hit some buttons. "See for yourself."

The young man on the screen would have been handsome, were it not for his neck tattoo. He had thick blond hair cut in a kind of shaggy seventies style that curled right below his ears. His eyes were deep-set and pale blue, similar to Greg's own, and he had a decidedly familiar roman nose that appeared extra prominent due to the angularity of his thin face. The boy might have passed for one of his children, Greg thought, provided he'd been wearing a turtleneck. No one who knew Greg would think he'd ever permit his progeny to scar themselves like that, especially not in such a prominent spot. Did the kid think he'd never have to apply for a normal job? Ever?

"What's with the ink?"

Violet snatched back her phone. "I knew you were going to ask that. It's related to his band and his name."

Below the kid's ear was a bright tattoo of an unwrapped candy bar, without the lettering. "Is his name Hershey?"

Annoyance flashed like lightning in Violet's blue eyes. "No, it's Heath. That's a Heath bar."

Greg struggled to keep his mouth from curling at the edges. The boy's name was Heath so he'd gotten a candy bar tattooed on his neck. What a genius! Did he think he might suddenly come down with amnesia and need a reminder? Greg imagined a humorous conversation between young Heath, suffering memory loss after a fall off his inevitable motorcycle, and his concerned doctor. *Wait, uh, I think my tattoo had something to do with my name. Uh, maybe the tattoo is a Baby Ruth. Ruth? Was that it?*

"And his band is O.K. Granola," Violet continued. "So it kind of looks like a granola bar."

A guffaw burbled from his belly, barreled up his esophagus, and exploded straight out of his mouth. Violet scowled at him. It wasn't fair. She wasn't being fair. How could she tell him something so ridiculous and expect him not to laugh?

"The band name is kind of ironic because music is criticized as being granola when it's bland, but sometimes simple music can be beautiful, right? It's okay to be granola. But he's also saying that granola isn't what someone might think it is."

Greg continued chortling. He held up a hand. "I'll never stop laughing if you continue to give me the kid's dissertation on his band name."

Violet folded her arms across her chest. "And this is why you'll never meet him, which is too bad. He's a great guy. Really supportive of me."

Greg sucked in a breath, held it for a moment, and then

exhaled. Laughing had felt good. It might have been the first time he'd done so since the attack. "I'm sorry. Come on, you have to introduce him to me if you like him. I introduced you to my girlfriend."

"Only because she was pregnant."

The comment opened an air lock that Greg hadn't even known existed, sucking the helium from the room along with the oxygen. He couldn't laugh. He wasn't sure he could breathe.

Regret wrenched Violet's mouth. "I'm sorry. I forgot that she . . ."

Greg swallowed whatever mean retort was forming in his throat. His daughter hadn't been happy that he'd gotten his girlfriend pregnant, but she wouldn't have wished for the baby to die, and certainly not so violently. "It's okay," he nearly whispered. "I forget sometimes too."

"Where is Jade again?"

A physical ache had accompanied the surge of sadness. Fatigue weighed on his mind. He suddenly wanted a nap. "The Decoration and Design Building. She needs inspiration for her blog."

Violet tilted her head as if to say, *You don't believe that, do you?* He looked at his two-thirds-finished breakfast rather than let his eyes betray the truth. No, he didn't. Jade had gone to New York to escape him. The design building, even if she went there, had been an excuse.

Violet glanced around the room, as though Jade might have left some prominent clue betraying her real whereabouts. Greg noticed her eyes land on the cell atop the kitchen table. "Did you check?"

"How am I going to check?"

For the second time in the same minute, Violet gave him her dubious head tilt. "Don't pretend you don't know how to use Find My iPhone. Thanks to that damn app, I think I'm technically still not allowed to drive the Audi."

Greg shrugged. "I don't need to spy on my fiancée."

"Yeah, you do." Violet pushed the plastic container from in front of her so that she could lean over the table. "Dad, you have to accept how little you know about this woman. You two dated all of six months before everything went down. Who have you even met in her family?"

"Her mother."

"The one person who'd lie for her no matter what."

"Her mother is a religious woman. She wouldn't—"

"Any of her friends?"

Early on, when he and Jade had first started dating, she'd invited him to a beer garden in Brooklyn to meet friends she said she'd known from college. The place had been unbearably loud, with some bearded DJ playing a guy who sounded like Michael Jackson but sang about expensive cars. After a brief round of introductions, he'd made clear that the place wasn't his scene and taken her out to dinner. He'd never really spoken with any of them.

"Sure. I've said hello."

Violet reached into the center of the table and snatched the phone. He extended his open palm and growled her name, the same way he had when she spent too long on her cell as a teen. *You've lost your privileges*, that growl said.

"I'm not going through your photos. I'm only looking to see where she is."

Greg kept his palm out for his device, but he stopped calling Violet's name. The truth was, part of him wanted verification that Jade had gone to the design building. Checking himself, though, would render him pathetic. He'd be the kind of insecure guy who went through his wife's emails and showed up at her girls' nights out. Of course, he'd been just such a guy. He'd surreptitiously installed the Find My iPhone app on his fiancée's phone when he'd downloaded the rest of the security camera software.

Violet tapped his screen. "Where is the design building?"

"Midtown East."

Violet pinched the screen and pulled her fingers apart, expanding the view of whatever was on it. She turned the device around to face him. "Why, then, is she on Rikers Island?"

Greg blinked at the small screen, not trusting the icon on the map. "She's not on Rikers Island. There's nothing there except a prison."

The last word died on his lips. In front of him was a clear image of a cell phone labeled "Jade." It hovered over a small island sandwiched between Queens and the Bronx, smack in the mouth of the East River. What would Jade be doing at a prison? Was she visiting a guard? She couldn't know anyone behind bars, could she?

"These things are more accurate than a CT scan, Dad. If the phone says she's at Rikers, she's at Rikers." Violet stood from the table. She shoved the plastic container with her lunch back into the paper bag and then grabbed his and tossed it inside. Her movements were jerky. Angry. "I can't believe this," she mumbled. "I can't believe this."

Greg patted the air, signaling Violet to calm down.

"You need to open your eyes, Dad." Violet's own eyes shivered with anger. She pointed aggressively toward his skull. "You have to start thinking with your head right now. NOT anything else. Why would Jade go to Rikers?"

Greg shrugged, as if there were a perfectly reasonable explanation that didn't involve visiting a dangerous criminal. He couldn't think of one. The prison guards certainly weren't listening to any interior design pitches.

Violet pointed a finger at him. "I'll tell you why she's there: She has criminal friends. Look at where she grew up. Bushwick, right? Come on. She must know gang members, robbers, dealers. Some of them must be on the outside. Probably some of them would be willing to do her a favor and get rid of her new, rich husband so she could collect on your life insurance policy and all the other assets that you carved out for her."

Greg looked at the phone again. The miniature cell marked "Jade" had not moved from atop the clearly labeled island. "Maybe someone stole her phone number and is using it in prison."

"Or maybe she's trying to kill you!" Violet's voice rose to a hysterical pitch. "What's more likely? You were nearly beaten to death in a nondescript rental house, in a safe neighborhood, while she escaped unscathed—"

"Not unscathed." Greg's voice dropped a decibel as it always did when Violet became loud. He could force her to listen by lowering his voice. "She lost our baby."

"How do you even know that? Did you go to the appointments with her? Because that would be a first. Mom said you never went for her."

Greg felt the blood rush to his head. "I went to some of them for you and your brother."

It was the truth. But it was also a fact that he hadn't gone to the appointments with Jade. When she'd told him that she'd missed a couple of periods, she'd offered to confirm things on her own since her cycle was often irregular and *there was no point worrying him if there was nothing to worry about.* That evening, she'd come back with a sonogram picture. He'd missed the second visit, too, because of work. He'd wanted to get a jump on the proposal for that building. He'd told Jade for weeks how important it was. He'd intended to go to the twenty-week visit—the one in which the ultrasound tech counted fingers and toes. But the baby hadn't made it.

"You don't know!" Violet's large eyes had taken on an anime quality. "You don't know. It could all have been an act. You don't even really remember what happened that day, do you? You've probably been relying on Jade to re-create it for you."

The egg and avocado were curdling in Greg's stomach. Violet couldn't be right. Jade loved him. They had chemistry. A shared love of design and art and travel. They'd had great sex, until the attack. She couldn't have been faking everything this whole time.

Violet squeezed the paper bag of garbage, breaking the plastic container tops inside. In Greg's mind, it sounded like the crack of a skull. "Listen to me, Daddy. You have to protect yourself." She stared straight into his eyes. "You have to get a gun."

CHAPTER 14

The prison was only forty-three minutes from her house without morning traffic. When she'd lived in Bushwick and needed to travel by bus, the trip had taken an hour longer. For the first ten years of her father's incarceration, she and her mom had suffered through the commute every Sunday after church.

In the beginning, she'd looked forward to the trips. Her father had never been that present during her childhood. He *had* bought her a bike and tried to teach her to ride it. But most often he'd ignored her, choosing to run with friends rather than eat family dinners at home and stomach her play-by-plays of kindergarten lessons. In prison, he'd had no choice but to listen to whatever was going on in her life. She could talk about anything: the art fair that she'd won, the book report that was taking her forever, the modeling scout who had found her at the mall and the subsequent catalog jobs she'd gotten. Jade even recalled her father sitting through her mother's rundowns of church services, which, not being a particularly religious man, he must have hated.

Her dad had been a literal captive audience. His choice was to either listen to them—taking pride in his daughter's accomplishments and the fact that his family visited each week—or go back to reading alone or working out solo, which were the only activities he'd ever mentioned.

Sometime around the eighth year of her father's incarceration, Jade had begun to lose her enthusiasm for the visits. She was a teenager with things to do on the weekends aside from traveling to a sad, smelly prison to cheer up a father who hadn't done the same for her when he was free. Moreover, she'd developed rather large breasts that she'd noticed the guards and other prisoners eyeing too frequently, despite the bulky button-down sweaters she'd always made sure to throw on over her black church pants. She kept going weekly for another five years, though, treating the visits as penance for whatever sins she'd committed during the prior seven days. Often, on the trip over she'd pick out some small offense—say, talking back to her mother—to justify the lines, and the pat-downs, and the *waiting*.

Nothing happened at Rikers without an excruciating test of patience. Jade suspected that enforcing sufferance, even for family members, was one of the ways guards kept prisoners in line. The whole island was dedicated to humbling folks and putting them in stasis.

Jade remembered all this and more as she walked toward the Rikers visitor center, confident in its location despite not having come in nearly a year. As the officers checked her driver's license against the list that she'd been added to the night before, she braced herself for the pat-down, recalling every embarrassing liberty that guards had taken over the years.

Adult Jade was smarter than her teenage self—or at least she had a bigger closet. As a result, she'd worn a pair of tailored slacks that didn't particularly show off her assets but were sufficiently tight to prevent the officers from needing to check between her thighs more than once. She'd also donned a fitted crewneck shirt with long sleeves, despite the warm weather outside, to guard against anyone seeing her exposed skin and wanting to see more. Her hair was pulled back in a no-nonsense bun that she hoped reminded everyone of the female corrections officers.

The guards still took their time with her. When she'd finally made it through the metal detectors and physical checks, it was a quarter to one. She was ushered into a large room with tables, two doors, and guards stationed at each point of egress. Despite the seriousness of his crime, her father was allowed to sit across from her without a glass partition. However, he was not permitted a hug or a handshake. Physical contact had never been sanctioned, even for her mother. Movies often showed prisoners receiving conjugal visits, but that didn't apply in maximum security prisons. As far as Jade knew, her mother took a vow of celibacy the day her dad had "gone away."

Jade picked a plastic chair at a table in a corner of the room. Under the blaring overhead lights, it didn't feel any more private than any other table. But it was a little farther away from the guards, which Jade thought might help her father be frank. As she sat, waiting for him to enter, she noticed the familiar smell of the jail, the stink of sewage lurking beneath industrial-strength cleaning products. Bleach and blood. Lemon-scented excrement. She cupped her hand over her nostrils and watched the door.

Her father entered in a long line of prisoners, all dressed in the grayish-green scrubs that were standard in the prison. As a child, Jade had once asked why he didn't have to wear an orange jumpsuit with D.O.C. stamped on the back, like on television. He'd explained that those colors were for when inmates were processed, in solitary, or in situations where they posed a flight risk. Everyone recognized prison orange. If they escaped, anyone outside would know they were dangerous. Such bright colors were unnecessary inside, however. Inside everyone knows that everyone is dangerous.

Prison had slowed the aging process for her dad. No matter how much time passed in between visits, he always looked the same: a six-foot-four giant with a commanding posture, unstooped by the nearly two and a half decades he'd spent in a facility designed to wear folks down. He had tawny brown skin, bleached yellow and unlined from the lack of sun. His nose was a bigger version of the one that Jade had inherited, and she'd gotten his expressive mahogany eyes.

They captured the light as he saw her, reflecting her own image. "Hi, Dad."

"Hello, Jade." The enthusiasm in his tone served as his embrace. "It's good to see you. It's been a while."

Hearing his voice stirred up suppressed feelings. Jade found that her chest felt tight. Tears filled her eyes. She ascribed the swell of emotion to the stress of the past couple of months. She had not suddenly been overcome by the presence of her father. She cared for him. Maybe she even loved him. But the affection wasn't anything close to what she felt for her mother or Greg. She hadn't known her father long enough to truly love him as an individual. If anything, she loved him as an idea.

She settled back into her chair as he took his seat. "I'm sorry it's been so long. I've been really busy."

"Your mother tells me. Engaged. Living in a big house in Rye." Michael smiled. Or rather he tried to. The expression displayed was an openmouthed smirk. Jade guessed he wasn't accustomed to smiling these days. "The fiancé's a famous architect, right? Greg Hamlet or Hamilton."

Jade didn't correct him. The amount her father already knew, despite her not visiting in nearly a year, was disconcerting. Of course she was aware that Abigay's prison visits often centered around discussion of what Jade was up to, probably because their daughter was one of the only subjects her parents still had in common. But she hadn't realized that her mother shared details such as where she lived or her significant other's name. Jade kept such things close to the vest whenever she visited. She and her mom might not believe that her father would ever do them any harm, but the man was still in prison.

"What else did Mom say?"

Michael's strange smile turned sheepish. "She doesn't like that he was married before, obviously, and she thinks that he believes he's made *a bit too much in the Lord's image*." He imitated her mother's accent. "But she says that he seems to really love you and want to take care of you." He chuckled. "I asked if he made you sign a prenup, and she told me that he was probably going to, because of his prior kids, but that he'd already set aside funds for you in the event that anything happened to him." Michael attempted his smile a second time. "I've heard a joint account is the new marriage."

"Did she tell you about what happened to him?"

Michael's face fell. "What happened?"

"He was attacked, Dad."

Michael's expression turned to cement. The impenetrable, blank look was one Jade had seen before on her father's face. She wondered if such hardening was Michael's way of protecting himself in a world where violence had to be the norm. A prisoner could not become emotional each time an attack was discussed. He'd seem weak. She'd gathered over the years that weakness was about the worst trait anyone could exhibit at Rikers.

"It happened a couple of months ago," Jade continued. "The robbers stole my engagement ring and beat Greg up pretty bad. They nearly killed him and..."

Her voice caught on what else they'd done. She took a breath and then continued laying out the facts. "Shortly after we came back from the hospital, a threatening note was placed in our mailbox essentially telling me that now I knew what it felt like to be attacked, and the past couldn't be forgotten."

Michael's mask didn't change. "You think it was the father. Bernal."

Jade had been about to say yes, but she didn't like the way her dad's voice had dropped a decibel on the man's name. No matter what Bernal wrote to her, Michael didn't get to retaliate.

"The police don't think so. They say he's moved on." Jade shook her head. "Is there anyone else you might have angered? In here, maybe? Anyone who might want to hurt me to get back at you?"

The questions seemed to break through Michael's stone face. He rubbed a hand over his mouth. "You know me. I keep to myself in here. I can't think of anyone except Carlos Bernal."

Jade nodded. She wasn't sure whether the confirmation of her suspicions relieved her or made her more afraid. "I don't understand why he'd become so vengeful all of a sudden."

Her father sat up a little straighter in his chair. "Maybe because I could get out soon."

The statement stopped Jade short. She'd nearly forgotten that her father's sentence had an end. In her youth, his remaining time had always been so long that neither she nor her mother had ever spoken of it. Counting down the years when Michael had fifteen or more to go seemed cruel.

"Wow." It was the wrong response to her father's admission, but Jade didn't have another one. She felt as though she'd dozed off on a long bus ride and been awakened by the conductor ordering everyone off.

"In a month, I'll have served twenty-five years. I'll be eligible for parole." Michael gave her the same awkward smile as before. "The parole board has to give victims' family members a heads-up. Maybe Bernal got a notice and went nuts."

In her mind's eye, Jade saw Bernal as he'd been that day in the courtroom, screaming that her father needed to go straight to the electric chair, that there was no justice in a world where he could someday be free. A vein in his neck had threatened to burst from his skin like the monster in *Alien*. He'd looked at her and her mother when he said it.

"Years ago, I wrote to him through the prosecutor. I told him how sorry I was for what I did." Michael grimaced. "He never responded. If you think it will help, I'll write him again."

"I think that might make him angrier."

Michael's head bobbed as though he were considering something. No matter what Carlos Bernal had done, she didn't want the man on her father's mind.

"So," she began, forcing a smile, "twenty-five years..."

"Feels longer."

"What will you do when you get out?"

Michael shrugged. "I don't know. Maybe try to get a job as a paralegal. I got the degree in here, and supposedly there are lawyers that hire ex-cons in exchange for tax relief or something."

Jade tried to picture her father in suit pants and a button-down. She'd seen him in a prison jumpsuit for so long that she couldn't fathom it. But she imagined she'd like the sight.

"So, what do you want to eat for your first meal out?"

Michael laughed. "Are you going to cook for me?"

"I can cook. Momma taught me."

"I've seen. Whenever I get computer time, I visit your blog."

Jade felt the shiver of being watched for the umpteenth time. Michael had been reading her blog around other prisoners. She'd unwittingly exposed her life—Greg's life—to criminals. Her ring was in one of the photographs.

"You read my blog in here?"

Michael beamed. "Yes. It's one of the ways I keep up with you."

"Do you clear the browser history after you're done?"

Michael's brow scrunched. "What?"

"The cache?" Jade still didn't see the reaction she was hoping for. "The record of what sites you visit."

He rubbed the wrinkles from his forehead with his finger-tips. "I don't know about any of that."

Jade stood. If Michael was keeping up with her on the prison computers, God only knew how many more convicts had seen her ring. "I'm sorry I have to cut our visit short, Dad. I have to make a phone call."

CHAPTER 15

Activity Detected! Greg moved his computer cursor over the alert and closed the message. The cameras didn't need to announce that they'd registered motion. He'd been monitoring the security feeds for hours, waiting for Jade to return home.

Her SUV rolled up the driveway, waking the camera mounted to the garage's exterior. Greg heard the automatic door's rumbling retreat through his desktop speakers. With a couple of mouse clicks, he switched to the grid view displaying all twenty live video feeds. He selected the garage's interior view. The setting sun backlit the image, casting Jade's face in shadow, rendering her expression unreadable.

Greg enlarged the video to full-screen. Had Jade brought company? Was anyone crouched in her vehicle's backseat?

As he squinted at the monitor, he tried to convince himself that such questions were ridiculous. His daughter's false accusations were making him paranoid. Violet despised his fiancée because she wished Greg would reunite with Leah.

It was as straightforward as that. Jade had done nothing to warrant suspicion. In fact, she'd diligently cared for him these past few weeks, chauffeuring him to the hospital, cooking for him, feeding him. She'd even helped him bathe and dress. Why would she do all that if she wanted him dead?

His mind answered the question in Violet's haughty tenor: *Duh, because she wants her cut of your multimillion-dollar life insurance policy, not to mention whatever you set aside for her in your will. If you leave her, no moola. It's not as if you two are married. She's not Mom. She's not entitled to half your assets. She can't sue for a share of your future income.*

Greg mentally countered the argument. Since coming home from the hospital, he'd been vulnerable. A quarter of his head lacked any protection. One hard push could result in a lethal fall, which could conceivably be attributed to his fainting from a panic attack or suddenly losing his balance. Yet Jade had never so much as bumped into him.

It would be too obvious to kill you now, his disembodied daughter argued. *Besides, you have cameras recording her every move.*

Greg zoomed into the video, highlighting the space between the driver and passenger seats. Though there didn't appear to be anyone sitting behind his fiancée, he couldn't be sure. Jade knew the location of the cameras. Her phone could display the same feeds currently on his computer screen. She'd know exactly how a person would need to hide in order not to be spotted.

But there wasn't anyone lurking because his fiancée loved him, Greg reminded himself. He knew that in his heart, didn't he? He was not an old fool who'd been manipulated by a beautiful, younger woman intent on stealing the wealth he'd amassed after decades of hard work. She loved him. She had to love him.

On-screen, the SUV's headlights shut off. Jade exited the driver's-side door. She slammed it behind her and then yanked open the rear passenger side. Greg's chest clenched as she leaned into the vehicle. He didn't hear voices. A moment later, she emerged cradling several phone-book-sized binders. Greg recognized the hefty items as sourcebooks containing wallpaper and fabric samples. Folks at his firm used them all the time with clients. Stores that primarily dealt with professional designers doled them out.

"See, she did go to the D&D Building," Greg whispered to himself. Violet retorted in his head: *Or she wants you to think she did.*

Greg switched back to the grid view. He tracked Jade's advance from the garage's interior to the north side of the house, where she was caught by the camera outside his office door. She turned east, rounded the house's rear corner, and stepped up onto the deck. Greg watched her pass the outdoor sectional and stone firepit, headed to the back door.

Her image soon overwhelmed the doorbell camera. Greg could see only her torso and the arm struggling to balance all the sourcebooks while she attempted to key in the door's unlock code. She hit several buttons and was met with silence. The system didn't notify anyone when a wrong code was entered. It simply didn't respond.

Jade tried the door handle. Greg heard it shake without jostling the bolt. He watched her attempt to enter the code a second time, bracing himself for the coming confrontation.

When she returned to the couch and set the books down, Greg knew it was time. Her next move would be to call him. There was no need to talk on their cells when they had the cameras' intercom system.

"You're home." Greg's voice echoed through his desktop speakers on a nanosecond delay. He watched Jade's lips relax from the tight, frustrated line they'd formed moments before.

"Honey, what's the door code? I must have forgotten."

"Where were you?"

It didn't seem that she'd heard the question. Rather than respond, she gathered the books and started toward the door a second time.

"Where did you go, Jade?" Greg enunciated each word, adjusting for the speaker reverb so she could better understand the question and perhaps even register the emotion fueling it.

"Sorry I spent so long at the D&D Building. Spring has really sprung there." Jade continued to walk as she talked. "There was a ton to see. I got ideas for the blog and the house, though I won't start on them until tomorrow. Tonight, I'm looking forward to lying down with you and maybe watching some television. We can order in."

She was lying, Greg realized. He'd finally discovered her tell—movement. When obfuscating, Jade became a flurry of activity. Greg recalled how she'd hurried around the kitchen after returning from the "library" when he first sensed something was off. Some folks couldn't make up stories with a straight face. His fiancée couldn't lie standing still.

Greg clicked the intercom icon on his screen. He leaned

forward so the computer's microphone would pick up his seething whisper. "You're not coming into this house until you tell me where you *really* were."

Jade halted her march to the door. She froze in front of the camera, visible from above her knees to her collarbone. Her chest rose and fell on his screen. She was breathing harder.

A sourcebook landed on the deck with a sudden thud. She crouched to retrieve it and then slowly returned to the couch. The books fell atop a cushion. Hands finally free, she rotated back toward the camera, facing him.

"I did go to the D&D Building." A loud sigh hissed through the speakers. Jade wiped beneath her eyes. The natural light was too dim for Greg to see if she was really crying. "But before, I went to Rikers Island correctional center. I'm guessing you know that."

Greg rotated his desk chair away from his screen. She'd admitted to lying with little effort. *Is that good or bad?* he wondered. Did Jade lie so frequently that it was easy for her to confess and move on? Or had she felt so guilty for hiding her real destination that the truth had been on the tip of her tongue, screaming to be released?

"I went to see my father." Jade's voice called Greg back to the screen. She was slumped atop the sectional's arm, still facing the camera. Her chin was tucked to her chest like a boxer guarding against a knockout. "I told you I didn't have a relationship with him, and that's pretty much the truth. He's been in prison for most of my life. Before today, I hadn't seen him in nearly a year."

Greg had imagined justifications for his fiancée's visiting a prison. He'd considered the possibility that Abigay had roped

Jade into participating in some kind of church prison out-reach, perhaps to show gratitude for all those prayer vigils on his behalf. He'd thought it possible that Jade received an anonymous tip from a convict about their attackers and had gone to check it out alone. He'd even pictured her tearfully telling him about an abusive ex-boyfriend whom she now suspected had been involved in the attack. Never had it occurred to him that his girlfriend might be visiting a loved one behind bars. Greg had never even known anyone who'd spent a night in county jail for driving buzzed.

For a second time, Jade ran a knuckle beneath each eye. "I'm sorry. I was going to tell you, but the timing just didn't seem right in the beginning and, next thing I knew, I was pregnant and we were trying to figure out the future. Then we were attacked, and I . . ."

A horrible thought materialized in Greg's mind. It flew from his mouth before he could process the consequences of letting it escape. "Did he do this?"

Jade's jaw dropped. "No. He's in prison."

"But he would know people, right? He could have hired someone."

She shook her head violently. "No. Greg, he's my father. He would never want to hurt me, or you. He loves me. And he's really tried to better himself, even in the worst conditions. He's gotten a paralegal degree. He's getting paroled in a month, and he wants to work—"

Greg barely registered any of Jade's words after "paroled." His criminal father-in-law-to-be was being released back into the world, into their lives. The man would see how much money Greg had and get ideas. He might give his daughter ideas.

If he hadn't already...Again, Greg imagined what Violet would say. *Do you really think it's a coincidence, Dad, that you were nearly beaten to death after proposing to a convict's daughter?*

Greg tried to shake off the question and listen through the speakers. His girlfriend was talking about her father's business prospects after his release. Clearly, she wanted him to like the guy.

He hit the intercom button. "Why did he go away?"

For a second, Jade looked like she'd been slapped rather than simply interrupted. She blinked at the camera. Her lips pulled back against her teeth. She covered the grimace by rubbing a palm across her mouth. When her hand dropped, it became clear she was crying. Tears streaked her cheeks. He could see their lines glistening in the last of the sunlight.

She looked so young and scared, Greg thought. Part of him wanted to rise from his desk chair, march across the house, fling back the door, and have her run into his arms. He wanted to let her cry into his shoulder and stroke her hair, to assure her that he'd love her no matter who her father was because he knew who she was, and he loved who she was. He wanted to promise to protect her and be there for her, to forever be her knight in shining armor.

But he didn't have any armor. He didn't even have an intact skull. "Jade, I need to know. What did your father do?"

CHAPTER 16

Felony murder. Jade had never repeated the actual charge aloud to another soul, not even her mother. Whenever they talked about Michael, they said he was serving time for *the mistakes that he'd made.* They never called him a "murderer."

Jade couldn't use that word with Greg, at least not now. The attack had made him paranoid. If she confessed that her father had gone away for killing a child, Greg would end things. It wouldn't matter that her dad had been defending himself from a rival gang's onslaught. Greg wouldn't care that Michael hadn't seen the boy on the sidewalk or that he'd been firing at a drive-by shooter in a moving vehicle. It wouldn't matter to Greg that the police had never definitely proven that the lethal bullet came from her dad's gun. Greg would care only that she was the daughter of a violent man, and he needed to be as far away from violence as possible.

Jade grabbed the couch arm. Every nerve in her body was demanding that she run, but she couldn't abandon her relationship. To do so would be to allow the men who'd robbed her child of any chance at life to also take her love. She and Greg were worth fighting for, she told herself. Besides, a lie of omission was different from a flat-out lie. One day, she would tell Greg the whole story—just not today.

"Drugs." Jade forced herself to look directly at the glistening lens affixed to the back door. "My dad was a dealer in my old neighborhood. I was seven when he went away."

Silence met her answer. Jade listened to the sad sound of the water at the edge of the property. It pulled back, rushed to the banks, and then pulled away again, an endless cycle of advance and retreat. After an agonizing minute, the intercom crackled to life. "Why didn't you just tell me?"

Jade was tempted to pose her own question: Why were they having this deep conversation through a locked door? This was not the way couples talked to one another, let alone those soon to be married. She stopped herself from counterattacking. She had lied, after all. He was entitled to an explanation.

"I was ashamed." Jade stared at the camera, hoping Greg would see the tears on her cheeks. She needed him to understand how difficult this conversation was for her. "I didn't want your family thinking any worse of me than they already do. I didn't want to be judged by my father's actions or to be stereotyped as ghetto trash." Her voice cracked. "Most of all, I didn't want to risk you changing your opinion of me..."

She trailed off. The intercom didn't allow two people to speak at the same time, and it was Greg's turn. Jade waited for his response. A cold breeze whipped off the water, pushing her hair into her face. Strands stuck to the wet spots on her cheeks. She peeled them back only to have the wind slap them forward again. It was a sign, just like the painful silence from the camera speaker. Greg wanted her gone. He was searching for the kindest words to break her heart.

"I should leave." Jade grabbed her purse and reached for the sample books. As she adjusted them beneath her arm, she realized the ridiculousness of carting around the superfluous "proof" of her visit to the D&D Building. For a moment, she considered leaving them. Then she thought of Greg, hobbling outside with his cane solely to pick them up, one by one, and put them in the garbage. She held them to her chest and started toward the garage.

The crack of a door stopped her. She whirled around, responding less to the prospect that Greg might be coming than her visceral fear of hearing a door open out of view. Before the attack, she'd been standing in front of the bathroom mirror with her side to the closed door. She'd heard a yell downstairs that she thought was Greg shouting at her to hurry up, followed by heavy footsteps and the opening of her bedroom door. By the time she'd realized what was going on, the skinny, ski-masked intruder was standing between her and the only way out of the room.

She remembered how her assailant had stared at her, his cold eyes examining her naked body. He hadn't said a word before punching her. He'd just charged forward and slammed his gloved fist into the lowest part of her abdomen. She'd doubled over, gasping, trying to explain her condition and simultaneously shield her belly with both hands. He'd grabbed her left wrist and wrested the engagement ring from her finger. After that he'd hit her again, right in the center of her unprotected pelvis. She'd fallen to the floor, writhing in pain as he rifled through her vanity and bedroom dressers, perhaps looking for drugs or more jewelry. She hadn't gotten up again until she heard the front door slam.

"Don't go."

Greg's voice brought her back to the present. She stood on the deck, and he leaned in the doorway, darkened by the light behind him. She could see his slanted posture and his cane, though not his facial expression. Maybe he wanted to break things off in person.

"Don't go," he repeated, stepping out onto the deck. The dark shading beneath the brim of his baseball cap obscured his eyes. "I love you."

Greg extended a hand. Jade wanted to fall into his arms and bury her face in his chest. But she couldn't. He wasn't well enough to absorb the force of her feelings. Instead, she approached him carefully, waiting for him to initiate an embrace.

Before she reached his open arm, he let it drop to his side. "I guess we both have to work on trusting each other," he said.

He turned and headed into the house, letting his words hang in the doorway. His statement was many things: an invitation inside, a promise to improve their relationship, and an admission that he no longer felt secure in her presence. Still, opening the door for her had been an act of faith. She had to walk through it.

Jade followed Greg into the sunroom and shut the door behind her. His hand clenched his cane at the sound of the lock engaging. "Maybe we should sleep in separate rooms, just until I get the plate put in. If you were to hit my head by accident..."

Jade murmured her agreement rather than call Greg on the real reason for his newfound concern. He didn't want to be vulnerable around her, given her history. She wondered if he would have reacted the same way had they not been attacked, and she'd been able to break the news the way she'd once intended—after they'd been married, had the baby, and been comfortable for a time in their new home. Perhaps after her father's release. Surely, Greg would have been understanding then.

The detectives had broken the news about her father at the worst time. Ricci had called him, Jade figured. She'd probably phoned right after Jade had dialed the station from the prison parking lot to tell her that Michael had unintentionally flaunted her good fortune to his fellow inmates. So much for the woman's promise to wait.

"The detectives called you." Jade let her voice fall at the end. She wasn't really asking so much as confirming.

"No. Have they called you?"

Jade stopped trailing Greg toward the stairs. "How did you know I went to the prison?"

He continued walking. "I was worried about whether you'd made it into the city, so I checked your phone location. You can do that on a family plan. There's an app you can download."

Jade had purchased her first cell phone in college with money from a recent catalog modeling job and a week's worth of bartender tips. She'd never been on a family plan. It hadn't occurred to her that signing up with Greg meant agreeing to a permanent tracking device in her purse. She'd thought they were simply saving a few dollars a month.

"Oh." Jade's head was pounding. The night had been too emotional. She needed an aspirin. "I'm going to get some water." She closed the gap between them to deliver a good-night kiss. Greg went still as she approached. His cheek felt cold against her lips. "Good night then. I love you."

Greg repeated the words, though he seemed to say them with resignation. She watched him ascend the stairs and safely make it onto the landing. A grunt echoed in the hall-way above as he presumably pulled back the heavy bedroom door. Jade wondered whether she should have run up to let him inside. She hadn't thought he'd want her opening the door to a room from which she'd just been banned.

Jade headed into the kitchen. Since moving in, she'd kept a first-aid kit in the pantry complete with aspirin and acet-aminophen. She hadn't wanted Greg to climb the stairs to the bathroom medicine cabinet if he was in pain.

She found the red bag on a shelf above the cereals and grabbed two Excedrin tablets. The medicine would zap the dull pounding in her temple, though the caffeine in it would keep her awake. Sometimes one had to choose the lesser of two evils, Jade thought. She filled a glass of water and popped both pills into her mouth. As she swallowed, she got the eerie sense that she had an audience. She glanced over her shoulder into the furniture-less dining room and through to the foyer. No one appeared to be there. Greg hadn't come downstairs. She'd have heard him.

She walked through both rooms to confirm, telling herself she was being silly. No one was in the foyer. However, a stack of mail lay on the entry table.

An icy fear filled Jade's insides as she approached the

letters. Had she gotten another threat? Had Greg seen? She glanced at her reflection in the large mirror above the table, forcing herself to relax her furrowed forehead before she moved any closer to the high-definition camera perched atop the counter.

Her trepidation dissipated as she sorted through the items. All the envelopes were addressed to her husband. Most appeared to be bills. There was one letter from a law office in Greenwich. An interior design magazine was the only item with her name on it. She picked up the glossy for bedtime reading and headed back up the stairs.

A nagging sense that she was being watched followed Jade to the second floor. She decided it stemmed from what Greg had done. It bothered her that he'd basically bugged her phone. He'd implied that he'd installed the app for her safety, but there had to be more to it than that. Sure, if she'd been attacked or kidnapped, the app would have enabled him to give the cops her last known location. But the police could obtain that information themselves from the phone company. They didn't need Greg to spy on her. He was watching her because he didn't trust her.

Was he watching her now?

The master bedroom and bathrooms didn't have a camera, but nearly all the other rooms did. As she entered the bedroom beside the master, she scanned for a device atop the windowsills or perched on the furniture. The room had been intended as a nursery. As a result, it had become a repository for all the unused items that Jade had purchased during her nesting phase: a daybed for napping in between breastfeeding sessions, a changing table, a rocking chair. A crib.

The stately piece was nestled in a corner of the room, its railing side facing the wall. The orientation was wrong for furniture meant to give a mother easy access to her child. But it was a fine, out-of-the-way spot for a wooden box that served no purpose.

Except it was serving a purpose. A camera sat atop the flat headboard. Its electrical cord snaked into the bed area and between two of the slats before connecting to a wall outlet.

Recommissioning their dead baby's crib as a camera mount smacked of callousness. Jade marched past the device and yanked the cord from the socket. Shaking from anger, she whacked the untethered device with the magazine. It tumbled onto a soft white rug that she'd bought for a someday-toddler, the rug's thick padding capable of cushioning any walking mishaps.

She slumped onto the floor beside it, tears boiling behind her eyes. Her phone buzzed in her purse. An alert shone on-screen: *Guest Camera Off-Line!*

Jade traded the magazine for her cell. She unlocked it and deleted the message. Then she paged through the apps for anything that appeared unusual. On the second screen, hidden between the icons for an art store and a home fashions site, she spotted the Find My iPhone app. She pressed her thumb into the icon until it began wiggling and an X appeared in the corner. She deleted it.

Never again would she give Greg her phone to install anything. He was her fiancé, not her father. And he definitely wasn't her jailer.

Her fury wouldn't let her settle down. Jade grabbed the magazine and began paging through it, mentally critiquing any design that was a reminder of her husband's minimalist, masculine aesthetic. The monochrome kitchen on page 15 with its handleless cabinets resembled the inside of a fridge. The Scandinavian-style white walls and wood bedroom on page 25 was too sterile to imagine intercourse ever taking place inside it. The concrete dining table on page 40 would be just the kind of thing Greg would buy, a commanding block of cement that looked about as appetizing to eat off of as a basement floor.

As Jade flipped pages, something hit her leg. She looked down to see a small card envelope about the same size of the subscription mailers normally stuck in magazines. Her full name and address were printed on the back. There was no return address. A stamp marked the top right corner.

Was this envelope actually mailed? Jade wondered. The police believed that the first note had been hand-delivered because its stamp hadn't been canceled. They'd hung Bernal's innocence on that fact. However, looking at the shiny USA flag on the envelope, Jade thought their justification for exonerating him seemed flimsy. Surely stamps slipped through the mail unmarked all the time. Whatever material made the stamp glossy and readable by scanning machines most likely made it difficult for the cancellation ink to stick. Bernal could have sent the first threat.

He could also have sent this.

Her hand trembled as she picked the card off her thigh. The spiky writing was familiar. She peeled back the envelope fold and then shook out its contents. The police might be able to lift fingerprints from the paper. She didn't want the oils on her skin obscuring any evidence.

A photo drifted to the floor. It was mostly black, except for the red marker redacting some text in a corner and an unmistakable x-ray image in the center. There was the bulbous skull nestled against the uterine wall, the stubby bent legs ending in the shadow of toes, the flash of white where the facial bones had formed. Jade had received a sonogram exactly like this one at her twelve-week scan. She'd printed it out for Greg.

But it couldn't be hers...Her ultrasound picture had been atop her dresser in the rental house. Surely, she or Greg had packed it.

Jade grabbed the photo and stared at the red lines, trying to read through the ink. The name of the hospital had not been hidden by the marker. Mount Sinai. She'd been going to Mount Sinai.

Jade scanned the rest of the information. The patient's name had been successfully blacked out, but there was writing left on the side: "GA=12w2d." Gestational age, twelve weeks and two days. Her baby had been twelve weeks and two days at the day of her appointment. It had been thirteen weeks and four days when it died.

The image in Jade's hand went blurry. She squeezed her eyes shut, forcing her vision to clear, and flipped over the picture. Written in red was a capitalized message:

SOME PEOPLE SHOULDN'T KEEP BREEDING.

A guttural sound escaped her lips, part scream, part groan. Her attackers had taken her sonogram. The punches to her stomach hadn't been meant only to immobilize her and steal her ring. They'd wanted to kill her baby. Carlos Bernal had paid them to kill her baby.

It was the only explanation, Jade thought. Bernal's prior letters had always lamented that she'd lived when his son had died. He wasn't going to let her father pass on his genes to yet another generation. He wouldn't allow his son's murderer to be released from prison and enjoy a grandkid's childhood.

Jade placed the picture on the edge of the crib and then grabbed her phone. She went to her text messages and scrolled down to Detective Ricci. That idiot officer had sent her Bernal's telephone number after deciding he'd had nothing to do with the first note or her attack.

The area code was 718. Bernal had stayed in Brooklyn to keep tabs on her mother and her, Jade decided. He'd been waiting all this time for the perfect moment to ruin their lives and make them feel the pain he'd suffered. Bernal had gone to her mother's church. He believed in biblical justice. "An eye for an eye, a tooth for a tooth, a hand for a hand," and a child for a child.

Jade clicked the telephone number. The blood rushing in her head nearly drowned out the sound of the cell ringing. She held the handset so tightly that it seemed the screen might crack.

The third ring was cut short by a male voice: "Bernal Plumbing and Maintenance."

It seemed she heard the greeting from underwater, that she had plunged into a deep pool and all noise had to break through the pressure engulfing her head. "Hi, is this Carlos Bernal?"

"Yes. With whom am I speaking?" His voice was the cheery

singsong of a salesman. *No wonder he duped the detectives,* Jade thought.

Her heart was hammering so hard it threatened to break her rib cage. She breathed in through clenched teeth, trying to slow its rhythm. "This is Jade Thompson."

There was a beat of silence, as if he were struggling to place her name, as if he hadn't been obsessing over it for years. "I was hoping you'd call," he said.

The phrase sounded menacing, a serial killer relishing the arrival of a new victim at his door. Jade's throat cinched. She swallowed hard to free her response. "I got your letter."

A sigh rumbled through the speaker. Jade couldn't pinpoint the emotion fueling the exhalation. Frustration? Satisfaction? It occurred to her that she should be recording the call. If Bernal admitted to sending her the ultrasound photo, she could play the tape for the police. She could tie Bernal to the break-in. But how to record a call already in progress?

"The police told me," he said.

It was a careful statement, Jade thought. Even if she recorded the call, Bernal was too smart to confess anything over the phone. She needed him to lower his guard.

"Let's meet." The suggestion was out of Jade's mouth before she fully understood how much it frightened her. Bernal was a man, and no doubt far bigger than she was. But that could be good, she told herself. His physical dominance would make him feel more at ease with voicing his threats and gloating about his actions. And she'd be ready with her cell videoing the whole exchange.

"Where?"

Jade thought she heard a smirk in his voice. Was he

thinking he'd show up at her house? Their conversation had to take place in the open—somewhere quiet enough to talk and for her phone to pick up what was said, yet with lots of witnesses. Jade recalled a coffee shop she'd passed earlier on her way to establishing an alibi at the D&D Building.

"There's a coffee bar on Fifty-Eighth between Third and Lexington."

Bernal repeated the address, as if he were writing it down. "When?"

Jade wanted to see him soon, before fear replaced the rage fueling her courage. It would need to be the next day, though, Friday. Greg's surgery was scheduled for the following Monday, and she had to be there. Some things were more important than justice. "Tomorrow."

"Unfortunately, I can't meet tomorrow or next week."

Was this a power move? Jade wondered. He would agree to meet, but only on his terms, at a time convenient for him. Or, did he need a week to set up whatever he had planned for her next?

"Maybe the following Monday?" Bernal cleared his throat. "One o'clock? Most of my jobs are in the morning." He coughed. "It will be good to speak in person. I've wanted to say some things for some time." His voice lowered. "I want to make things right."

Jade imagined by "right" he meant *even*. A horrifying thought occurred to her. Greg could be part of Bernal's revenge calculus. What better way to ensure she didn't have future children than to kill the man with whom she intended to conceive them?

"Okay, but don't get any ideas when I'm meeting with you,"

she said, keeping her voice as level as possible. "My house is being watched by the police." Nerves cracked the last word. Her anger was transforming to tears. She had to get off the phone before she lost it. "I'll make sure my husband won't be home while I'm meeting you at the coffee shop."

Bernal started to say something, but Jade hung up before she heard more than a syllable. Whatever he wanted to tell her needed to wait until their meeting. She had to record it for the cops.

CHAPTER 17

What was an excessive amount of time for a woman to spend in the bathroom? Greg pondered the answer as he glanced at the hour in the corner of his computer screen. Fifteen minutes earlier, he'd watched Jade abandon her laptop on the kitchen counter, cross through to the family room, and disappear behind a bathroom door. The red purse containing her makeup case and phone had been squeezed beneath her armpit. Applying lipstick took seconds. Conversing with criminals, on the other hand...

Greg kicked the attached cabinet of his protractor desk, sending him and his Eames chair rolling backward from the computer screen. His temples throbbed. Virtually stalking his girlfriend while she thought he checked email wasn't helping his recovery.

He'd been monitoring Jade ever since allowing her back into the house. She was hiding something about his attack and her involvement in it. He felt it in his lizard brain, the way a person senses when he's being eyed beyond his field of vision.

The prison visit had something to do with it. Jade's father was at Rikers, that much was true. Unbeknownst to his fiancée, Greg had called the correctional facility first thing in the morning and verified that a prisoner named Michael Thompson, age fifty-three, was in their custody. Jade's reluctant honesty about the reunion with her father, however, didn't mean she'd been forthright about her reasons for seeing the man.

Moreover, lying to keep her dad's drug conviction from him didn't make sense. He'd been honest with Jade about his own youthful dabbling with cocaine. On their second date, she'd asked him about the architecture business, and he'd responded with a series of rock 'n' roll anecdotes from his early days. He'd described the powder lunches split with fellow new hires so that they could continue drafting projects into the dark morning hours and the boozy client dinners that had always ended in backroom clubs. Sure, he'd emphasized that he was reformed and that attitudes about illegal drugs were different in the nineties. But given what he'd confessed, Jade should have assumed he'd be sympathetic to anyone suffering the consequences of the Rockefeller drug laws that he and so many others had skirted.

Nothing he'd seen on the monitors—so far—provided any clues to the real reason she'd tried to keep the visit secret. But she was being careful around the cameras. She'd removed the device from the guest room and spent the morning in semiblind spots around the house. She'd been hanging out a lot in the bathrooms.

An alert pinged on Greg's screen: *Motion Detected! Sunroom!* Greg scooted his chair back to the desk and clicked on the related video. Jade stood behind the white couch, squinting in the direction of the kitchen as though she might have seen something in the distance. A glance at the live feeds from the kitchen and the front yard revealed that whatever she'd detected had only been a shadow. No one was there.

Greg watched her walk through to the dining room, past the vestibule, and into the family room. Each new area that she entered resulted in a pleasant ding from his computer screen, like a video game character had successfully reached a checkpoint. Text messages piled up on the side of his screen: *New Activity Detected! Motion Entrance!*

"Greg?"

His name reverberated outside his office door. He brought the family room camera up to fill the screen. Her lips were painted a shade of rose, and it looked like she'd put on eye makeup. Perhaps she had been getting ready all this time. Leah would be at the hospital. No doubt Jade wanted to make sure she held up in comparison.

"Greg?"

He simultaneously heard the call echo in the neighboring room and from the computer speakers. Quickly, he closed the program. If Jade heard her voice through the door, she'd know he'd been watching.

"Be right out." Greg grabbed the helmet mocking him from the glass top of his protractor desk. He buckled it onto his head, grabbed the cane propped against a table leg, and hoisted himself from his favorite chair. He opened the door before she knocked. Jade hopped back with her hand in the air, lips parted as though she'd been about to say something, but his appearance had scared away the statement.

She ran her index finger along her clavicle. The bone

protruded above the boatneck of her tank like a hanger. She'd lost weight since the attack, he thought. Greg tried to recall if he'd seen her eat much on the monitors.

"The hospital wants you there by eleven. We should go."

Greg's stomach grumbled affirmatively. He hadn't eaten or had anything to drink all morning, as per the surgeon's orders. Not that he could fathom keeping down food knowing that in a few hours, his skull would be cut open for a second time. He limped into the family room, his balance affected by his concern about what was to come and his determination not to rely on Jade's help. As he passed her, Jade's arms flung toward his torso. Instinctively, he whipped the cane into her side.

She yelped like an injured puppy. "You looked like you were about to fall. I was trying to catch you."

Greg still wielded the cane like a baseball bat. He brought it back to the hardwood floor, trembling from the adrenaline that had propelled his knee-jerk response. "I lost my balance," he grumbled.

Jade blinked at him. He recognized the look on her face as one that had undoubtedly been on his own in the past twenty-four hours. She was struggling with whether or not to believe him. She rubbed her left flank. "I should get the car started."

The closest exit to the garage was behind him. Jade turned a hundred eighty degrees and retraced the path he'd monitored so carefully moments before, heading to the egress in the addition, he assumed. She favored her right leg as she speed walked. He'd hit her hip hard enough to cause a limp.

Leah and the kids were waiting in the neurosurgery ward. As Greg entered, they rushed him, driving Jade from his side with the force of their feelings. Leah's eyes darted from him to the kids and back to him. Concern twisted her mouth. Though his ex was still battling him in divorce court, she would never wish anything bad to happen to him. The night he'd left, she'd said as much: "I love our kids too much to hate you."

At some point in all the fussing, Jade sidled back beside him and announced that she wanted to find the doctor. Tears had carved their way down her cheeks. The sight of the tracks made some of Greg's worst suspicions seem foolish. Surely, Jade wouldn't weep over him as he headed into surgery if she only wanted him for his money or, worse, his life insurance policy, as Violet believed. Before he could suggest that Jade stay, his daughter caught his eye and rolled hers in his girlfriend's direction. Forcing a tear or two wasn't that hard, he decided. He told Jade that he'd see her in the recovery room.

Family time ended soon after she left. Nurses whisked him into a private room to prepare for his procedure. He changed out of his customary black T-shirt and dark slacks into a V-necked hospital gown with a garish blue pattern that Greg really hoped he didn't die in. At least he wouldn't be wearing the helmet.

From behind a curtain, a nurse instructed him to keep the gown open in the front and remove his underwear. Since the surgery would take several hours, the nurse explained, they'd have to insert a catheter. The idea of a tube being pushed into his urethra made Greg nearly more nervous than his skull being cut open a second time. He swallowed his concern though. The catheter wasn't optional, and whining about it would only demonstrate his out-of-whack priorities. *Mess with my head, fine, but please don't touch my penis.* Even thinking it made him sound like a character in a bro comedy.

A team of nurses set him up on a bed and wheeled him into the "operating theater," a term Greg found ill-fitting for the glaring white room with the pedestal table in the center. Disc-shaped lights hovered above the slab, recalling movie spaceships before CGI. Two large orderlies helped him from the rolling bed to the table and positioned him according to directions from the reconstructive surgeon.

Dr. Gordon Epps was a fair-skinned man with a square forehead and a widow's peak, both of which Greg noticed before any of Epps's more prominent facial features thanks to his newfound interest in head shapes. He also had the rumbling voice of a man who either drank too much whiskey or perhaps didn't speak often. Greg hoped it was the latter.

Through his mask, Epps explained what he would do while nurses applied local anesthetics to numb the areas where tubes would be inserted. Dr. Hsu was also present. Greg gathered that his neurosurgeon was on hand in case any of the lesser specialists in the room inadvertently damaged the brain that Hsu had previously saved from hemorrhaging.

Before the surgeons got to work, a smiling anesthesiologist explained that Greg would be asleep for the duration of the procedure. He expected her to place a mask over his face. Instead, she pointed to the IV in his hand and asked that he start counting down from twenty. Greg shut his eyes and started the sequence. To force himself to think positively, he paired each spoken number with the silent acknowledgment of something he still wanted to do with his life. "Nineteen." Put his stamp on the Brooklyn skyline. "Eighteen." Witness

Paul graduate from Harvard. "Seventeen." See Violet happy and settled at RISD. "Sixteen." Travel the world with a beautiful woman who loved him.

Was that woman Jade? He tried imagining her against a backdrop of brightly colored buildings. Her dark hair falling in loose curls to her breasts. Brown eyes shimmering with excitement and adoration. The picture wouldn't materialize. Instead, he saw her expression after he'd struck her with the cane, a mix of hurt and distrust wrenching her full mouth.

"Fifteen." The anesthesiologist urged him to resume the count.

"Fifteen." He searched for a goal to pair with the number. Walk Violet down the aisle? No. The last thing he wanted now that his daughter was headed to college was for the kid with the neck tattoo to propose and ruin everything. Moreover, he didn't want to vicariously live through his children's achievements. He still wanted to create and build and conquer, to make love in exotic locations, explore new territories, rage against the shrinking of his world and the dying of his soul—a soul that had died a bit each day that he'd been cooped up in the house, a prisoner of his own unprotected brain. He wanted so much, so much more than he could ever count.

"Four . . ."

A strange voice asked for clippers. Greg tried to finish the word but couldn't remember what he'd been doing. A warm stream of voices flowed around him, their utterances reduced to unintelligible bubbling and murmurs. He felt himself sink under the sounds. His grand ambitions dissolved in the silence.

* * *

Greg woke wanting to scream. The combination of anesthesia and anxiety had given him a nightmare worthy of Stanley Kubrick. A skinny blond doctor, face covered by a surgical mask, had held him down while a larger featureless man pried open his head with a crowbar. As Greg tried, and failed, to free himself, he'd seen Jade on a second-floor viewing platform, peering through the glass ceiling at his torture. Tears had tumbled down her face, but she'd never hit the glass. Never asked them to stop. *I'll be all right*, she'd mouthed instead, as though the assurance of her safety was enough for him. *Don't worry. I'll be fine.*

The sight of the blue hospital curtains did little to assure him that he was back in his own reality. Neither did the soft pressure of the bandages on his scalp. He reached up to pat his head but found there wasn't enough slack in the attached IV tube to accommodate the motion.

His monitors beeped as he jostled on the mattress. A skinny man in pale green scrubs peeled back the curtain. He introduced himself as the RN on duty and said that he would get his doctor for him. "I want my family." As he said the words, Greg realized that he hadn't asked specifically for Jade. He wasn't sure that he wanted her face to be the first one he saw.

"They're waiting outside. I'm sure that your surgeon wants to talk to you first. After he does, we'll send them all in." The nurse stepped back, pulling the curtain closed behind him.

"Um, how does it look?" Greg blurted out the question before the man could fully disappear. The nightmare had made him fear that his scalp deformity would be even worse than before. Perhaps he'd have a dent in his forehead or be missing a chunk of brain.

The nurse slipped back into Greg's tented area. "Well, it's nice and round." Puppet strings seemed to force the man's smile. "Hold on."

He disappeared behind the curtain. Greg heard footsteps against linoleum and a hushed conversation with a female voice. A minute later, the nurse returned with a large oval attached to a handle. Greg gathered that it was a mirror, even though the reflective side was turned toward the guy's torso.

"The staples can be a bit disconcerting but, as you know, they'll go away. You really have to look at the shape."

Greg sucked in his breath, bracing himself to see his face poorly sewn onto a Frankenstein head. He took the mirror, closed his eyes, counted to two, and then opened them. A ridge of stapled skin ran from his left ear to the top of his scalp. To Greg, the evenly positioned metal bars resembled a zipper. If he had a pull tab, it seemed that he'd be able to yank it across his head, releasing the teeth and peeling back the skin to uncover his brain. His intact brain, Greg reminded himself, in his now-intact skull. Greg forced himself to look beyond the garish staples to the shape of his head. It looked as it had pre-injury, he supposed. More importantly, the dented area was now filled out and symmetrical with the other side.

"Your doctor did a great job." The nurse sounded as though he was trying to convince both of them.

"He did." Greg passed back the mirror.

As the nurse took it, Dr. Hsu appeared behind him along with Dr. Epps. "So, you've been checking it out." The plastic surgeon held out his hand for the nurse's mirror and then held it up to Greg. "We totally reconstructed the missing piece, and I think the implant went in really beautifully. We still need to fully bandage you up obviously, but we wanted you to have a chance to see the skull for yourself. What we did was..."

Greg nodded along as the surgeons alternated explaining the techniques used during the surgery and why they had worked so well. He felt that he watched a badminton match with the doctors volleying compliments to one another. Occasionally, like a referee, Greg interrupted with a question such as how long he'd be in the hospital (five days to ensure the wounds healed without infection) and what he should expect in terms of recovery (barring unforeseen complications, they both expected a full one). Mostly, he simply watched the match. When it was over, he thanked them both, expecting them to leave to perform their next surgery of the day or perhaps relax at home with their respective spouses, enabling his family to come in.

The plastic surgeon did leave. Hsu, however, hovered by his bedside. "Greg, I know we will have another scan soon, but I wanted to ask how you are feeling."

Greg tried to crack a smile. "All things considered, pretty well, I guess."

"Headaches?" Hsu had pulled a notebook from the pocket of his white lab coat. A black pen hovered over the lined paper.

"Sometimes. They're not as bad as they were when I was first released."

Hsu wrote a short word on the pad. "How is your memory?"

"Good, as far as I know. I'm not forgetting anything that I'm aware of, save for the particulars of the attack."

Hsu scrawled what appeared to bc a full sentence. "How is the balance?"

Greg brought his legs up beneath the thin sheet covering them, testing his control of each limb. "It's coming along. I get light-headed if I stand up too fast or switch too quickly from bright light to something dimmer. But I feel more stable. I've been going up and down the stairs without help."

Hsu held up a hand, a crossing guard telling him to wait for passing traffic. "That's all good. But you have to remember to take it easy. Healing will take time."

"I know," Greg grumbled.

"And how are you feeling emotionally?"

Since the attack, he'd been riding a roller coaster of negative emotions, and he was all too aware that the ride was bound to push him out at his lowest point. But talking about it—hearing that those lows were normal after being hit in the head by crowbar-wielding robbers—wasn't going to make them go away. Besides, the anxiety and anger he felt were justified. He was living with a woman who lied to him, who might even have had something to do with his attack.

Greg forced what he hoped was a believably thankful expression. "I'm healing. It will take time."

CHAPTER 18

"The surgery was a true success."

Dr. Epps's announcement was for all of Greg's family gathered in the too-cold waiting room. But he'd stood in front of Leah as he made it, tacitly giving her first billing. Jade told herself he'd done so only because Greg's ex sat between their grown kids, at the center of the group, versus Jade's position on the periphery. However, she couldn't help thinking that the reconstructive surgeon's positioning had been more calculated than that. He'd faced Leah because she seemed more like a woman to whom Greg would be married. In comparison, Jade looked like a phase that would soon be over.

For all she knew, Greg was already done with their relationship and was just waiting until he felt strong enough to break the news. Not only had he insisted upon sleeping in separate rooms, but he'd barely spoken with her since her tearful confession. He'd said they both would have to work out how to trust one another better. But his figuring it out seemed to involve avoiding her. He'd spent much of that morning glued to his computer and the security monitors. What did he really think she was going to do? Jade wondered. More importantly, what did he believe she'd already done? And what might he do as a result?

Jade's upper thigh throbbed with the memory of the earlier strike. She tried to ignore it as Dr. Epps discussed how Greg's new head would be stronger than steel. She also tried to ignore Violet. For much of the time they'd been waiting, Greg's daughter had eyed Jade with apparent disgust. Violet shot her another disdainful look as the surgeon told them that a nurse would escort their group to Greg's private room once he was settled.

Jade avoided Violet's pointed stare by watching Epps head down the hallway. In the distance, she thought she saw Dr. Hsu's bald head. If anyone could explain to her what was going on in Greg's mind, it was his neurosurgeon.

She speed walked toward him, calling his name. Hsu turned around just before the elevator banks. He smiled when he saw her. "Everything went well, you must have heard."

"Yes. I wanted to thank you for all you've done." Jade shook his hand, trying to choose the best segue into her concerns.

"I wish he hadn't needed it, but I'm happy he is on the mend." Hsu withdrew his hand. His energy shifted toward the elevators.

"About being on the mend, does that mean he'll be more stable now that the plate is in?"

Hsu's expression lost some of its smugness. "His balance should improve, yes."

"I mean his mood. Since the attack, he's been different.

Anxious. Suspicious. He's installed security cameras all over our home—on the inside. He's constantly watching them. Watching me. He's lost weight. He's irritable."

"Violent?"

The spot below her hip seemed to pulse with her heartbeat. Greg couldn't have meant to hit her, Jade told herself. He'd been losing his balance. That's why she'd reached out for him in the first place. The cane had swung out.

"No, not violent."

Hsu regarded her like she was a patient with liver damage insisting that she only had a couple of drinks a week. "What you're describing sounds like post-traumatic stress disorder. It's not uncommon after a serious brain injury."

Jade felt a modicum of relief. "So it's something his brain will heal from then. And the plate will help?"

"Having his skull protected should make Greg feel less physically vulnerable. But what he's dealing with is mental." Dr. Hsu pointed to his forehead. The frontal lobe, as Jade had learned, not the parietal one where Greg had been hit. "He should really talk to a psychiatrist."

Jade couldn't picture Greg admitting to having a mental problem, let alone allowing a psychiatrist to examine him. He would think it a waste of money and time. He considered himself smart enough to know if his thoughts weren't logical.

"Oh." Jade couldn't manage more than the one word. She could feel tears building behind her eyes, pressing on her throat.

"I'll try to talk to him about it," Hsu said. "You should probably go see him."

Jade thanked the surgeon again and then retreated down

the hallway to the waiting area. As she drew closer to where they'd all been, she realized that Leah, Violet, and Paul weren't occupying their former seats. She sprinted toward the first person in scrubs that she could see, a thin nurse with bobbed brown hair.

"Hi, my fiancé, Greg Hamlin, just had surgery. Do you know where he is?" Jade couldn't keep the panic from her voice. She'd be late to see him. Again. God only knew what assumptions Greg would draw from that in his current state.

The woman's alarm at being accosted turned into mild confusion. "We sent the family in a minute ago. You're the wife?"

Jade didn't have time to erase the nurse's dubious expression. "What room is he in?"

The nurse led her down a corridor and then pointed to an open door at the end. Jade jogged most of the way, stopping right before the entrance to gather herself one last time. Leah's voice shot from the room. "Honestly, bald suits you. You need a good head to pull it off, and thanks to the miracle of plastic surgery, you now have one of the best."

"It's certainly head-turning." Violet said that. Even if Jade hadn't recognized her voice from hearing all the quips and wry comments to her brother in the waiting room, the dry sarcasm was a dead giveaway.

"Really, it's very Bruce Willis." Leah again.

"Who wants to look like Bruce Willis?" Violet.

"When we were a little older than you, every man wanted to be Bruce Willis." Greg's voice. It sounded stronger than Jade had expected and simultaneously lighter. He was talking about movies.

"And every woman wanted to be with him," Leah said.

"Well, I guess I have my Halloween costume if my hair doesn't grow in. *Die Hard*." Greg laughed. The sound lifted Jade's spirits as it simultaneously glued her feet to the floor. The return of his humor meant that Greg felt more like his former self. Though it didn't mean he'd act that way around her. No doubt it was easier for Greg to relax around the family that he didn't associate with his attack.

"Or didn't *die hard*." Violet chuckled. "Almost *died hard*."

Laughter erupted in the room, the relieved, rumbling belly kind that often follows tragedy. Jade wished she could join in. But the moment wasn't hers to share.

"Hey, where's Jade?" Paul's voice.

"Who knows?" Violet said. "She ran off right after the doctor said Dad had survived."

If she didn't enter, Jade realized, she might as well pack her things. Violet would portray her as a flighty young woman who had fled at the first sign that marriage wouldn't be all fancy restaurants and custom homes. There'd be no claiming that she'd wanted to give Greg time to enjoy his kids before showing up and reminding him of everything they'd lost.

"Is this it?" Jade called behind her as she entered, providing plausible deniability that she'd overheard Violet's comment.

Déjà vu was worse the second time around. Greg was so engulfed by family that she couldn't even see him without pushing through their force field of protective energy. She did it, though, sliding into the sliver of unwelcoming space between Leah and her slender son so that Paul had no choice but to move closer to the foot of Greg's bed.

A skullcap of bandages, similar to the one that had covered

Greg's head during his coma, hid where the surgeons had cut and stapled. However, these bandages were elastic and thinner than the prior coverings, enabling Jade to see the restored roundness of Greg's head. They were also a beige-toned white similar to Greg's skin color, giving the impression of baldness.

Below the bandages was the man for whom Jade had fallen. He looked as he had the day they'd met, blue eyes bright and alert. The smile that had lit them that first meeting faded when they focused on her. She smiled at him anyway, hoping the sight might remind him of the happiness they'd once shared. "I'm so relieved that you're all right."

"Glad you made it." Sarcasm saturated Violet's tone. "Where'd you go?"

"To talk to Dr. Hsu." Jade kept her focus on Greg. "About your recovery."

Violet rolled her eyes toward her father. "I thought maybe she'd needed to accept a collect call."

The dig wounded Jade, not because it referenced her dad's being in prison but because it made clear that Greg had told his daughter all about her big secret. Jade could only imagine all the gossiping that had been going on at Leah's house. The jokes at her expense.

As much as Jade wanted to confront Violet's quip head-on, making clear that she was aware of all the hurtful things Violet and her family had likely been saying, it wasn't the right time or place. Greg was in a hospital bed. "I intend to phone my mother later to relay the good news," Jade said, forging on as though she hadn't caught the prison reference. "She'll be relieved."

Violet folded her arms over her chest. Again Jade had the discomfiting sense of déjà vu. Violet had assumed the same position during their first meeting, directly across from her with Greg on a bed in between. "Will she? I think my mother would feel differently if I started dating a man my dad's age." Violet snorted. "I'm sure she'd think I was after his money."

"Violet." The humor had vanished from Greg's voice.

Leah stepped from the head of Greg's bed to stand beside her daughter, declaring her allegiance in any upcoming argument by her physical position. She draped an arm around Violet's shoulders and stared hard at Jade, warning against finishing the fight that her child had started.

Jade was tired of letting Leah assume the lead. She was not about to take orders from her fiancé's ex or let the implication that she was a gold digger go unchallenged. "My mother knows me better than to think such a thing, as does Greg. I work for my money, and I always have. I've never relied on my parents or a trust fund."

"Good." Violet's forced smile couldn't mask the sneer behind it. "Because there never will be any kind of trust fund for you."

"Violet." The warning in Greg's tone grew louder.

"The operative word in a trust fund is *trust*, Jade." Violet's raised voice drowned Greg out. "No matter what you say your reasons are for being with my dad, everyone here knows you can't be trusted. We're not fools. My father adds you into his will and armed robbers try to kill him within a month. Do you really think any of us believe that's a coincidence?"

"Violet, enough!" Greg roared the command. Though his tone seemed to defend her, Jade thought his lack of eye contact conveyed something else. She'd expected some kind of silent apology on behalf of his daughter, a *sorry this is happening* conveyed via a slight head shake or slow blink in her direction. The lack of it made Greg's objection about the *timing* of Violet's argument, not its content. It was as though he was embarrassed by Violet's choosing to accost Jade in front of them all, not the accusation itself.

Leah reacted to Greg's volume like a driver in a car crash. She placed an arm in front of Violet's chest and belted the other one around her shoulder, effectively holding her back. Again, she gave Jade a hard look.

"Why don't we all give Dad a rest?" The male voice startled Jade. Her head snapped to look over her shoulder at the open door. No one stood in the entryway to the room, but she caught Paul's narrow frame in her peripheral vision. He'd been so quiet that she'd forgotten he was there.

Violet stood straighter, apparently pleased with the possibility of taking the argument someplace where Greg couldn't object. Paul glanced at his fired-up sibling and then returned his attention to Jade, his intense stare urging her to be the reasonable one. "Second thought, we should get Dad something to eat. I'm sure he's starving after not having anything all day. The cafeteria won't be five-star, but I'm sure it has something edible. Jade, would you help me pick something out? You must know what he likes."

Paul hurried through each sentence, nearly releasing them all in the same breath. The speech pattern was sufficiently odd that Jade wondered if it was a strategy, an attempt to stifle the argument by smothering it with verbiage.

"Right. Dad, you're hungry?"

Greg murmured something affirmative. The grunt spurred Leah into action. She broke away from Violet and stepped toward her son, volunteering via body language to do the food run.

"We don't all need to go. You and Violet should keep Dad company. We don't want to leave him here with only cable news to watch." Paul directed Leah's attention toward Greg. "Ask the nurse for some pain medication, Mom. And if there's anything he's not allowed to have foodwise."

Greg's eyes were shut tight. Seeing him wince made Jade feel guilty for engaging with Violet. She was the older one, after all. More mature. She should have ignored the needling comments.

Paul led the way into the hallway. When they reached the T leading to the elevators and the first-floor cafeteria, Paul turned in the opposite direction. "I think the café is this way and down a few floors," Jade called out.

Paul continued his fast stride, as though he hadn't heard her. Jade couldn't understand why he wouldn't have been able to. Aside from the hiss of the central air and the hushed beep of in-room monitors, the floor was quiet. Their footsteps were the loudest sounds in the corridor.

As the hallway opened up to the surgical waiting room, Paul stopped. He faced Jade and gestured to one of the chairs. "Can we talk a minute?"

Paul bit the nail of his middle finger as he asked, an uncertain, boyish gesture that made Jade more comfortable with complying. She sat in the indicated chair, assuming that Paul would take a seat beside or across from her. Instead, he remained standing, lording over her reduced position with his considerable height. "My sister shouldn't have started that argument with you in front of my father. It upset him, and we want to see him recover as quickly as possible."

Opening with a concession was a debater's trick. Jade knew better than to assume it meant Paul was taking her side. "Of course. We *all* do."

Paul scratched at the light stubble on his chin. When they'd been waiting earlier, he'd regularly pawed at his invisible goatee. Jade had initially dismissed the fidgeting as discomfort at forgetting to shave. Such fussing, though, was more likely part of Paul's personality—or, at a minimum, one of the ways he handled stress. "You know, I believe that you really *do* love my dad, Jade." He shrugged. "I guess I get it. He's smart, accomplished, keeps himself in shape. I also know that when he wants something, he's relentless. I bet he worked really hard to sweep you off your feet."

Jade racked her brain for some PG-rated anecdote that would make it clear that Greg's appeal wasn't about his money, the house, or any of the lavish gifts he'd given her when they'd been dating. But she couldn't think of a story so much as a list of places where she and Greg had danced or drank or made love. None of that seemed appropriate to share with a kid under twenty-one.

Paul sighed. "Anyway, I really am sorry for Violet. She's concerned about our dad, but it's difficult for her to express that, so she takes it out on you."

The apology, as nice as it was for Paul to give, was a cop-out. Violet was not simply venting her frustrations, and they both knew it. "I think Violet has convinced herself that I'm out to get your father."

Paul rubbed the back of his neck as though the conversation was making him itch. "She took the divorce hard. I know that's not an excuse for her behavior. I'm just trying to explain. My dad left when I went off to college, you know? I guess he'd been feeling penned in for a while and, with me out of the house, he didn't feel a responsibility to keep staying for the kids."

Paul gave a sheepish smile that seemed to acknowledge he was a kid to Greg but not to Jade. She and Paul were only eleven years apart. Technically, Jade was closer in age to Paul than his dad.

"Anyway"—Paul's free hand clasped the back of his head—"Violet took Dad's leaving as him casting my mom aside because she was getting older. It made Violet hate him. But she doesn't want to hate him because he's our dad, you know?"

Jade did know. She had struggled with the same complicated mix of anger and love toward her own father. She hated what he did, but he'd still been responsible for her life. He was the man who'd watched over her while she'd learned to ride a bike, the guy with the infectious laugh who'd brought her "just because" gifts, including that first bicycle.

"Violet can't even be upset with my father now that he nearly died." Paul dropped one of his hands to his side, leaving the other draped behind his head. "So she's made you the bad guy. She's decided that our dad had a midlife crisis and would have come back—except that you came along, appreciated the lifestyle that he could provide, and got pregnant. And our dad is not the type of man to leave his kids, at least not when they're young."

Jade understood that Paul was simply explaining how his

sister saw things, but the characterization of her as a gold digger who'd used a baby to ensnare a wealthy man was completely unfair. Greg had decided to forgo protection. Why did no one think that he'd trapped her? Moreover, he'd told her that he wanted to spend their lives together mere weeks into dating. She might not have been sure about the relationship until she'd gotten pregnant, but Greg had been absolutely positive.

"I am only trying to explain the narrative Violet has created," Paul said, perhaps reading the objection on Jade's face. "You're her scapegoat."

Jade stopped bracing herself for a blow. Instead of hurting her, Paul had made Jade empathize with his sister. If anyone knew what it was like to create a story about someone to justify loving them, it was her. Over the years, she'd created her own tragic hero tale about her father. He'd been a poor guy struggling to support a family in a depressed, violent area. She'd blamed the rival gang for the murder, the police for not trying hard enough to find the other shooters, even "the system" for locking up a young man for twenty-five years for a "horrific accident." However, deep down, she'd always known that the person at fault was Michael Thompson. Lots of people grew up in the projects and didn't wear colored bandannas or carry guns.

"I get it," Jade said as she looked up into Paul's pale blue eyes. They reminded her of Greg's own. "I love your father. I hope someday Violet will be able to see that and not think of me as the reason your parents aren't together."

Paul shrugged his eyebrows. "To be honest, I actually think my mom is better off without my dad. Don't get me wrong, I love him. But he's a complicated guy."

He scratched the side of his jaw. Jade wondered whether all the fidgeting was because he feared his mother or sister learning of their friendly conversation. The Hamlin women certainly did not want peace between their houses.

"When it comes to architecture, he's a true genius," Paul continued, covering his mild criticism with praise. "Dad can see things that aren't there, the potential in spaces and materials, the beauty in what's possible. But when it comes to people, he has blind spots. He has a tendency to see what he wants to see, rather than what's really in front of him. It can be hard living up to whatever image he has of you, and he's not always..." Paul trailed off, searching for the right word.

"He's not..."

Paul exhaled loudly. "He's not always kind when people fall short." He lowered his voice, as though Greg might hear him in his room down the hall. "But who is, right? No one likes to be disappointed."

Jade considered his last statement. Could Greg's *disappointment* be to blame for his anger toward her? Had she fallen off some lofty perch, and he'd become furious and distrustful as a result? Or was it all the PTSD? And what exactly did Paul mean when he said Greg was not always kind? Did he lash out? Yell? Hit?

Paul looked over his shoulder, perhaps checking to see if there were any witnesses to his small betrayal. No one walked down the hall. He turned back toward Jade and offered a conspiratorial smile. "Anyway, we should probably get my father that food I suggested. We can't have my sister thinking we were actually having a nice chat."

Jade stood from the chair. She was so grateful to Paul for

extending an olive branch that she could have hugged him. However, the way he stiffened as she rose made it clear that any physical contact would be too much. He'd taken the first step to having a civil relationship with her, but that didn't mean he intended on calling her *Mom* anytime soon.

"Thanks, Paul."

"Don't mention it." He chuckled and scratched the side of his head. "Really, don't. Violet would kill me."

CHAPTER 19

He was finally getting out. Greg's latest hospital stint had been five days, which should have been a walk in the park compared to the two weeks he'd spent haunting the halls of the rehabilitative care ward in a bike helmet after waking from his coma. But his improved health had rendered it excruciating. The knowledge that he had an intact skull—even better, an enhanced titanium cranium—had reenergized him. Twenty-four hours postsurgery, he'd been up and about, employing his cane as a sort of spotter rather than a tool to support his weight. Within forty-eight hours, he'd ditched the cane completely. By the time seventy-two hours passed, he'd felt ready to return home and resume his life.

What that life would look like, he no longer knew. As he packed the framed photos of him and his kids, left by Leah to spruce up his room, it seemed the happily-ever-after he'd imagined with Jade had been a dream. Its logic didn't make sense in the light of day. He'd thought Jade his perfect match: a designer who, like him, wished to create beautiful spaces, and an adventurer forever searching for inspiration in new cultures and places. But perhaps he'd only projected his own desires onto her. Had their baby lived, Jade might have become like Leah—a homebody immersed in the lives of their children and local gossip, fixated on securing the best fourth-grade teacher for Violet or deciding what she'd wear to the Cipriani charity function in order to end up splashed on the cover of the local magazine.

Jade becoming boring might have been the best Greg could have hoped for. As it was, part of him feared the woman he'd fallen for was someone whose real desires were far darker than he could have fathomed.

He watched Jade fold the last of his clothing into his leather suitcase, taking care to separate the items that needed washing from those he'd never worn. She zipped it up and then gave him one of her trademark close-lipped smiles, an expression capable of hiding her true feelings. He had to give credit to her poker face. Looking at her, he couldn't discern whether she loved him or was simply counting down the days until she could again attempt to have him killed without arousing suspicion.

"I'll take this down and then have the valet bring the car around so you don't have to wait."

Playing the good wife, as always, Greg thought. Jade was constantly feeding him and getting things for him, making sure she appeared doting to strangers. If he died, the insurance investigator would be hard-pressed to find anyone who would accuse her except for Violet. *She was always so kind*, the doctors and nurses would say. *Always so patient.*

Greg grunted his thanks without looking up from his duffel.

He listened to wheels rolling on the linoleum floor, the sound becoming fainter as Jade likely rounded the hallway. With her gone, the tension in his chest—a pain he'd once associated with longing—released.

He zipped up his smaller bag, slung it over his shoulder, and grabbed his cane. Though it had ceased being necessary a few days after his surgery, he couldn't trash it at the hospital. He'd have to drop it off at a local Goodwill or maybe a community for indigent seniors. Fortunately, his rehabilitation specialist had happily taken back his helmet.

"You about to take off?"

Footsteps followed up the question. Dr. Hsu entered his room, looking like he'd spent the past week in the Caribbean. He had a ruddy tan and the relaxed look of a man who had been doing nothing more strenuous than soaking up vitamin D.

"I am, thanks to you."

His surgeon gave him a tight smile. "Before you go, I was hoping we could chat." He gestured toward a chair in the corner of the room. Whatever Hsu wanted to discuss, he thought Greg should sit down for it.

Greg remained standing. He forced a chuckle. "Don't tell me. My insurance company is fighting the charges."

Hsu's smile loosened a bit. "They all do. It's part of the negotiation process. But that's not it. I wanted to ask how you're feeling—emotionally."

The surgeon had tried to have this conversation with him before, Greg realized. He'd avoided it then, impatient to see his family postsurgery. Now that he was getting out, there seemed to be little harm in elaborating a bit on his blanket

I'm fine, especially because he wasn't sure he was fine. He was returning to a house with a woman who might want him dead. He needed to at least tip people off that his fiancée might not be taking the best care of him.

"It's been difficult." Greg set his bag down on the bed, indicating that he would stay awhile. "As I'm sure you can imagine, the attack heightened my concerns about securing the house and protecting my family. And that brought certain things to light about my fiancée that have been disturbing."

Hsu raised his brows, crinkling the perfect arch of his forehead. "Like what?"

"She'd been hiding some things. Her father has been in prison. She'd only said they were estranged until I caught her visiting him."

"You caught her?"

"I tracked her phone."

"You'd been tracking her phone?" Hsu's eyebrows ticked up another centimeter. The surgeon seemed more concerned with Greg's actions than Jade's secrets.

"Yeah, she was going to Manhattan." Greg's hands landed on his hips. Whenever he felt defensive, he assumed power positions. It helped him regain control. "The men who broke in are still out there, and I was trying to protect her."

"How would that protect her?"

"I could call the cops if something happened, tell them where she'd been last."

"But then whatever was going to happen to her would have already happened."

"Well, if she was kidnapped..." Saying it aloud made Greg realize the silliness of it. A runaway or a child might be lured into a dangerous situation, but grown women were not nabbed off of New York City streets. "And I have to protect myself too," Greg continued. "As my daughter points out, it's not often that people are the victims of near-deadly home invasions. It had never happened to me before Jade. I'd proposed, written her into my will, and then—"

"Greg, you suffered a real trauma. That kind of an attack is bound to have both physiological and psychological impacts. Anxiety, paranoia, mistrust of those closest to you—these are common symptoms of post-traumatic stress."

"I have reasons for my mistrust."

The waves in Hsu's brow changed direction. "Because your fiancée didn't share what I imagine could be a source of extreme embarrassment for her: a father in prison. Not the kind of thing people like to brag about, right?"

"We'd been together six months before the break-in."

Hsu tilted his head from side to side, a noncommittal gesture. "I understand why trust would be difficult for you given what happened. In addition to the trust we put in our loved ones to treat us with a measure of affection and respect, we anticipate that strangers will follow certain rules. We expect to pass people on the street without them becoming violent toward us, and to safely open the door to an apparent deliveryman and receive a package. This is part of the social contract in which we all put our faith. It's what allows us all to live in this world."

Hsu scratched his laurel wreath of gray hair. "When there's a violation of that basic trust, it can be difficult for the mind to compartmentalize the trauma and continue to believe that the other patterns will hold. That results in confusion. Anxiety.

Suspicion. In some cases, people project their fears about strangers onto their loved ones."

Greg eyed the surgeon. "I see you've talked to my fiancée."

"You just told me that you were tracking the movements of the woman you'd intended to marry before the break-in. You implied that she might have been involved in an attack against the both of you." Hsu shook his head, a professor disappointed in his student's conclusions. "PTSD is a serious consequence of this kind of trauma, and it should be treated with therapy."

"I have my family to talk to."

"A sympathetic ear isn't the same as a licensed psychiatrist, a doctor trained to recognize when the mind is playing tricks and—"

"I'll take it under advisement, Doctor." Greg knew his tone indicated that he'd do no such thing. When someone broke an arm, they saw an orthopedist. He'd suffered a broken skull and had seen a neurosurgeon and a reconstructive surgeon. Hsu had previously assured him that his scans showed no significant impact to his brain function. His mental processes were fine.

Hsu fixed him with a stare that Greg could only assume was the same look the man had when operating. The focus was so precise that Greg felt sliced by it.

"Unaddressed, these symptoms fester. People can become depressed. Extremely paranoid. Sometimes furious. They overreact." Hsu took a step closer. "They hurt people."

Greg let the doctor's words penetrate his reconstructed skull. He didn't think of himself as capable of hurting anyone. However, he had to admit he'd struck Jade with his cane.

And why had he done that? Because he'd stumbled and then assumed that her reaching out had been an attempt to throw him to the ground.

The memory made Greg sick with himself. Since learning about Jade's incarcerated father, he'd treated her with extreme distrust. But was it really warranted? She'd committed a lie of omission, avoiding telling him the whole story about her father because, as Hsu and Jade said, she was embarrassed by it. Possibly she'd visited her father for the first time in nearly a year only to make certain that he wouldn't attempt to see her until her fiancé had healed and she'd had time to properly explain the circumstances. Insulating a spouse from family drama while he recovered from a brain injury was what a good wife would do, wasn't it? And Jade might have succeeded, too, had he not let Violet rile up his already-stressed mind about Jade's ulterior motives.

"The brain can start to feel mistrustful of everyone, huh? Because it doesn't know which of its previously made assumptions about human behavior still hold." Greg looked at Dr. Hsu for confirmation that he'd correctly understood.

The surgeon returned one of his tense smiles, a reward for Greg's coming around. "I'm afraid so. That's why it's important to talk to a professional. We need to make sure that your brain connects the right emotions to the right people while it's still reeling from all of this. I can email you some recommendations."

Greg nodded. He still had no intention of lying on a couch discussing his dreams with a stranger, but Hsu knew the workings of the brain and he'd made a good case that Greg had been misinterpreting its signals. Meanwhile, his fiancée had been stomaching his suspicion and dutifully caring for him. He owed Jade an apology. A big one. He just hoped it wouldn't be too late for her to accept it.

Greg saw Jade anew as he joined her outside the hospital entrance. She sat on a bench just beyond the vestibule, staring off at a point in space. She looked beautiful, as always, but also sad. Greg considered that he'd made her that way.

He approached slowly, not because he didn't have the cane but because he didn't want her to bolt upright with that brave smile she'd been putting on for his benefit. He needed her to sense from the way he joined her on the bench and patted her hand that he was not the same man for whom she'd had to keep her guard up. "I'm sorry, honey."

Jade turned toward him. The caramel shades in her eyes emerged in the bright sunlight. "Sorry?"

"I shouldn't have gotten so upset with you for visiting your father without telling me. Our relationship has moved fast. Love at first sight does that, I guess. I get that there are some things you need to tell me in your own time."

Jade's bottom lip trembled. "No. It's my fault. I should have explained everything earlier." She looked down at her hands clasped in her lap. Her thumb worried the back of her knuckles. "I need to tell you—"

"You don't have to tell me everything, and you don't have to apologize." He pulled one of her palms away from the knot it had formed with her other hand. It was clammy, the way his own hands became after a panic attack. "It was me. Dr. Hsu and I discussed it. I needed to hear again that it's common after a traumatic brain injury for the mind to kind of overload on fear and send out warning signals over nothing. Maybe it's some instinctual way of making a person hide out and heal. Point is, my mind was misfiring and making me overly suspicious, and since you've been with me—day in and day out—you've borne the brunt of that."

"But I—"

"I understand what's going on now. My brain's been pounding the panic button. That day when you came back from visiting your father, Violet had been with me, filling my head with crazy theories about you wanting to get rid of me for my money."

Anger flashed in Jade's eyes. Greg immediately regretted mentioning his daughter. Holidays were already destined to be hell without him giving them more reasons to dislike one another.

"Greg, I'd never hurt you. I—"

"I know that. I do." He cradled her face in his hands, lacing his fingers through her thick hair. "And I know something else. My biggest fear is losing you." Emotion squeezed his larynx. He gasped, loosening his throat just enough to squeeze out the most important part. "I love you. I love you so much. And I'm going to be better. I promise to stop obsessing with the security cameras. What happened was horrible. But I want to move on and live my life—our life."

Jade threw her arms around him and sobbed into his shoulder. Greg felt a wetness on his neck and cheeks. "I love you too," she said. "Let's go home."

His house was even more beautiful than he remembered. The large magnolia in the front yard had erupted in pink and white, a thank-you for his insistence that the bulldozers leave it alone. It framed the right side of his understated master-piece, his perfect blend of old and new, established aesthetics merged with contemporary architectural principles. He loved this house. He loved the woman with whom he would share it. His life was back on track.

Greg was out of the car before Jade could shut off the engine. He exited the garage and hurried to the back deck, admonishing her to leave the luggage and join him. The willow waved a welcome from beside the water, which sparkled in the bright afternoon like a toothy grin. In the week he'd been gone, the calendar had turned over. May had brought flowers, seventy-plus temperatures, and the caress of a warm breeze off the water. Greg filled his lungs with it all.

Jade's footsteps sounded on the patio. One of his bags pulled down her left shoulder; her purse dangled from her right. She headed toward the door to the sunroom. "Do you want to relax out here? I'll put—"

His lips were on hers before she could finish the sentence. He pulled off her purse without breaking contact and tossed it on the wicker coffee table. With his right hand, he pushed the other bag from her shoulder. Greg heard glass shatter as it hit the deck.

"The frames." Jade barely got the words out before he silenced her with more kisses.

"It doesn't matter." He brought both of his hands just above her breasts and began undoing the buttons on her denim shirtdress, kissing each new inch of revealed skin as he went along. When he reached her naval, she tried to pull back from him, but he quickly transferred his hands to the sleeves clinging to her shoulders and yanked them to her bent elbows.

"Greg, the neighbors."

The back deck was partially hidden by the detached garage and the willow. But Greg wouldn't have cared if it had been encased in glass. Jade's breasts swelled from a lacy black bra. The dress was barely holding on to her hips. He pushed it past the bone. "Fuck 'em."

Jade stopped protesting as fabric pooled by her ankles. He guided her to the wide chaise on the far side of the L-shaped sectional. She stood still for a moment, a lingerie model waiting for the photographer to dictate a pose. A yellow swath shone on her left thigh, just below her pelvic bone—the remnants of the bruise he'd inflicted.

The sight of it made him want to beg forgiveness. He dropped to his knees. Instead of apologizing, he embraced her waist and pulled her toward him. He kissed her outer thigh and then traced his lips over the bruise toward her inner thigh. He pushed aside her underwear and pressed his mouth to her crotch.

Jade moaned. Her hands went to the sides of his head before jerking back, as if she'd been scalded. "Don't you want to lie down first?"

Greg understood why his fiancée would suggest he assume the submissive position. Her fingers had grazed the crescent-shaped scar running from an inch above his left ear to the center of his skull. With the right care, the line would flatten and fade over time. The silvery prickles covering much of his scalp would never grow on the follicle-free scar tissue but hair would sprout everywhere else, enabling him to eventually cover the problem with the right cut. In a few months, he'd again look like the virile man that he'd once been—that he still was, dammit.

He stood and shoved her backward onto the couch cushion. "Not tonight."

The sex didn't last long. He'd wanted it to be a victory lap, a slow advance to the finish amid the deafening sound of Jade's appreciation. Instead it had been more like a first time, the torturous anticipation resulting in a quick climax. Even so, he was pleased with himself. Hsu had cautioned that sex could be "challenging" for a while. The increased blood pressure and jarring motions could trigger an erection-killing migraine. That hadn't happened.

Greg lay on his side atop the chaise, still naked. Jade's bare bottom pressed against his pelvis. Her perfect head rested on his forearm. She smelled like coconut oil and fresh linen. He wanted her to stay like this, wrapped in his arms. But she wanted to go. He could feel her back tensing against his chest, her energy pulling away. He buried his nose in the crook of her neck and kissed her clavicle. "I love you."

The three little words weren't enough for her to settle into his embrace. She wriggled beneath his right arm, trying to free herself from his stubborn hold. "I love you, too, but we can't spend all afternoon naked in the backyard. We've already been out here an hour. There are boats..."

He nuzzled the dark hair away from her neck to kiss beneath her earlobe. "So?"

"So, someone will see us."

Her concern wasn't entirely irrational. Though the deck

was set back from the shoreline and partially hidden by the willow, he had an unobstructed view of the water, which meant that anything in his line of sight had a clear view of him. Everything in the sound, however, was far, far away. The few visible boats were sufficiently distant to recall toy ships bobbing in a lake. "Someone would need binoculars."

Jade peeled off his hand and hurried to her puddle of a dress. "Maybe someone has them."

Greg sat up on the couch and clapped his hands onto his thighs. "Well, if they're going through all that trouble, perhaps we should give them another show."

Jade slipped her arms into her dress sleeves and began furiously buttoning. "I don't want to take another chance. The cops haven't caught anyone yet. We still don't know if it was about more than just the ring. There could be people out there with some kind of a vendetta."

Greg's internal alpha male wanted to beat his chest and brag that he'd take care of any intruder, to assure "his woman" that she was safe with him. But he knew such posturing was pointless. He hadn't been able to scare off two men when he'd been an athletic, fifty-two-year-old runner who regularly lifted weights. He certainly wouldn't intimidate anyone in his current state—and Jade knew it.

He hated that she knew it. He hated more that she'd reminded him.

His deck no longer seemed an idyllic extension of his home. Intruders could come by land or sea. Greg shuddered. The agreement on Jade's face made clear that she'd seen.

He overcompensated for the involuntary reaction with

brazenness, stretching in front of the couch and then swaggering to the back door. The doorbell camera would capture his skinny nakedness topped by the bald head and raised scar. It wouldn't be a pretty picture. But he supposed it didn't matter. Jade didn't seem to use the security app much. He doubted she ever looked at the video history. And he was going to stop looking at it so much. He'd promised.

They entered the glass-walled sunroom. Jade hurried to the credenza on the far wall, silencing the alarm with her key fob before it had a chance to beep more than twice. Standing in the center of the room with glass to his back and both sides, the alarm seemed silly. It took time to call the police. Time for the officers to respond. Probably more time than it would take for attackers to break the glass and put a bullet in his head.

Greg continued on into the adjacent living room. It was also too exposed for comfort. In an effort to extend the water views to every room of the house, he'd designed the addition with an open layout and removed every non-load-bearing wall in the original structure. The concept was perfect for a man with nothing to fear. He wasn't that man anymore.

The bedroom was the one exception to the home's openness. He extended his hand to Jade, who had returned to her hospital-visit state, completely buttoned up with her hair smoothed down and purse slung over her arm. He pulled her into him and planted a kiss on her lips. "One more go? Inside?"

She giggled. "Are you trying to get me pregnant again?"

As soon as she said it, her smile vanished, as if she hadn't realized the quip would cut so deep. Greg hugged her tight to his chest. He held her like that for a full minute, observing a moment of silence for what they'd lost. After, he whispered into her ear: "I want what we had, baby."

"Me too." She tried to smile again. The expression appeared pained. "I want a baby."

CHAPTER 20

Someone was watching. The baby hairs on Jade's neck prickled from a predatory stare. She could feel unseen eyes tracking her descent from the second-floor hallway into the foyer, waiting for her to make a mistake.

Her first instinct was to blame Greg. In spite of his promises to cease obsessing over the security cameras, Jade figured he'd returned to watching the live feeds. Avoiding the footage for a weekend had been as long as he could last, she thought. He was in his office, monitoring her movements as he'd done for weeks.

As she approached the front door, she realized that Greg hadn't resorted to old habits. Her fiancé stood before the entryway mirror, adjusting a heather newsboy cap atop his head. He pulled it low on his brow and then examined his reflection at a three-quarter profile. Raised, stapled skin peeked from beneath the hat, the spiny tail of some parasite trying to worm its way into his brain. He removed the cap, revealing the entire sickle-shaped scar, and then placed it back on his head askew, as if it were a beret.

Greg must have sensed her eyes on him. He looked over his shoulder and then turned to face her. "Better than the ball cap, right?"

The hat didn't cover Greg's head quite as well as his oversized college cap, but Jade thought the color much more flattering on him than crimson. The blue threads running through the fabric brought out his eyes and went well with the navy blazer adding needed weight to his frame. "You look great."

"Well, *great* might be too strong a word. You look great." He angled his head back to the mirror and checked out the now-hidden scar. "I just don't want to seem too frail to work. Can't have the big bosses seeing me and thinking they better put one of the other principals on my projects."

Jade approached the entry table. She patted Greg's back with one hand while deactivating the alarm with the other. "We should get on the road."

Greg had told his office he'd be in around nine thirty or ten so they had time. However, Jade couldn't stand being in the house any longer. She needed the distraction of driving and, eventually, Greg's colleagues. Every moment that she lingered reminded her of what she intended to do in a few short hours and sapped some of the courage required to do it. Had she not spent so much of the prior week at the hospital, Jade suspected she might have already canceled her meeting with Bernal.

Her feeling of being watched stemmed from stress about the upcoming meeting, she decided. Jade grabbed her purse from the entry table and slipped her cell into the change pocket. Earlier, she'd turned off its passcode so that she could activate the device simply by brushing a finger against the screen. Another tap would start the video camera recording.

She extended her hand to Greg. Adrenaline made it shake. "Shall we?"

Fortunately, Greg didn't seem to notice the tremble as he laced his fingers between her own. She supposed he was too preoccupied with his imminent return to work. For weeks, he'd been fighting to show up at the office and defend his territory against circling hyenas. Greg was a lion at heart, Jade thought. He relished confrontation while she wanted nothing more than to run away.

The trip into the city could take over an hour during the morning traffic rush. Jade made it within forty minutes. Some of her speed stemmed from the lack of bumper-to-bumper traffic after nine o'clock. However, much of it was owed to her driving. Nerves leaded her foot as she headed down Interstate 95 into Midtown. She'd navigated across the island with the aggression of a bike messenger, following vehicles inches from their back bumpers and weaving around double-parked taxis.

As she handed her keys to a parking attendant, Jade noticed that Greg looked relieved to be exiting the car. He shut the door behind him and then lifted the top of his hat, as if to air out the sweat on his brow. Jade caught the attendant's glance at Greg's scar. Thankfully, the guy averted his eyes before her fiancé realized he was being gawked at.

Jade accepted the garage ticket and then turned her attention to Greg. "So, we'll head into your office and then, while you get reacquainted with everything, I'll duck out to the Decoration and Design Building to get out of your hair."

Greg adjusted the angle of his hat so that it again dipped low over the scar. "I don't want you to feel like you have to leave. You're welcome to hang out in my office."

"Oh. Thanks." Jade started toward the exit, not wanting Greg to see how she really felt about his offer. She needed him to stay safe in his building while she talked to Bernal— alone. "I'm sure you'll have a ton of people waiting to catch up with you. I wouldn't want to be in the way."

If Greg responded, she didn't hear him. Her pace, at a couple of feet in front of him, was designed to discourage discussion. She maintained it until she reached the street and could be confident that the din of crosstown traffic would quell any further conversation about her plans for the day.

Greg's office was right beside the garage. As Manhattan sky-scrapers went, the building wasn't that impressive—certainly nothing like the innovative structures designed by Greg and others at his firm. It was an average-sized tower surrounded by a wide base that spanned a city block. However, the entrance made up for the plain exterior. A massive mural covered one wall of the marble-encased space. The opposite wall was lined with potted ficuses. Taken together, the decoration gave the impression that the building tenants cared as much about art and nature as they did about money.

A long marble reception desk sat at the back of the room. Two security officers loomed behind it, each looking very authoritative in his dark blue uniform. Jade wondered if they carried guns. Even if they didn't, Bernal couldn't get to Greg in his office, she thought. He wouldn't even know for sure that Greg had gone to work.

Her fiancé flashed his key card at one guard and then

signed her in. She had to show her license before they would allow her to pass through the turnstiles—another good safety measure. Surely Bernal wouldn't want a record that he'd ever visited Greg's building.

Jade followed Greg to the closest elevator and watched as he pressed the button for the fourth floor. She expected the doors to open into a hallway that would then lead to Greg's firm so she was surprised when it retracted to reveal an atrium filled with people. At least three hundred coworkers stood in the open space between two grand staircases, both of which apparently led to the glass-walled offices overlooking the main floor. As soon as they stepped from the elevator bank, the crowd began clapping.

Greg's body went rigid. Jade turned to see a red flush creeping up his neck toward his tilted cap. The little she could see of his scar appeared to throb.

Two figures stepped forward from the crowd. One was a man in a staid charcoal suit and wearing round, black-framed glasses seemingly stolen from the famous Swiss architect Le Corbusier. The other person was a woman in a cherry-red pantsuit with auburn hair, worn curly.

"Richard Lee and Dana Covitz," Greg whispered. "Co-CEOs."

Richard reached them first. He clapped Greg loudly on the back in front of the audience. At the same time, Dana sidled between Jade and Greg to pat his bicep. "We all wanted to tell you how happy and relieved we are to have you back," Richard said.

"As many of you know, what happened to Greg is the stuff of nightmares," Dana added, speaking more to the crowd gathered than to either of them.

"Masked men broke into his home and attacked him with a crowbar," Richard continued.

"But Greg, as we all know, is a fighter." Dana's exclamation was met with applause.

"He's here, less than a week after brain surgery. Brain surgery!" Richard squeezed Greg's shoulder and grinned at him before turning back to the crowd. "Because he is dedicated to his vision."

"His passion," Dana added.

"And this firm." Richard cleared his throat, as though choked up by the thought. Jade saw a shine in his eye. The man was near tears over Greg's dedication, yet her fiancé had been worried that the firm's higher-ups would give away his projects. Perhaps his PTSD had been even worse than she'd realized.

"That is why he is a principal," Dana added.

"That's why his buildings define skylines," Richard said.

"And that's why we are all so very fortunate to have you with us," Dana finished.

The crowd erupted in cheers and then quickly hushed, responding to some unseen item clinking against a glass. Everyone was watching Greg, waiting for some inspirational words. Jade wondered what they expected from him. Wasn't it enough that he'd returned to work?

A small gasp brought her attention back to Greg. His eyes were tight, and his lips were pressed together. He seemed flushed. Jade knew that look. He was trying not to cry.

She stepped in front of Dana, grabbed Greg's hand, and squeezed. The pressure seemed to relax his face. He flashed a grateful smile before returning his attention toward his expectant colleagues. "Thank you all. I'm very grateful to be alive, and to be here."

The last word garnered hoots and hollers. After they died down, the crowd still didn't disperse. Jade followed close behind as Greg made his way to the right staircase, stopping every few seconds to assure some well-wisher that his surgery had gone well, his brain was intact, and his hair would grow back.

It took nearly thirty minutes to traverse the several yards to the stairs and ascend to Greg's fishbowl office. As soon as they entered, Greg walked to his desk and slumped in the chair behind it. All the emotion and talking had clearly exhausted him. Jade feared he would want to go home. She needed him to stay at least until her meeting had ended.

"That was some welcome back!" she exclaimed, trying to inject him with excitement as she dropped her bag on his desk. "They must really love you here."

Greg pulled back his hat to rub his forehead. "Yeah. That was unexpected." He sighed. "Do me a favor? Shut the door and pull the shades."

Jade closed the glass office door. As she began lowering the cream-colored window treatments, she noticed a tall man heading toward them. If the stranger had looked more like a member of the mostly white male crowd below, Jade might have continued to close the blinds. But the sight of the guy's deep brown skin and shaved head stopped her. Someone in Greg's office was Black like her, and he appeared to be around her age.

She gave him a smile, acknowledging his presence, before turning to Greg. "Babe, I think someone is coming to see you."

Greg sat straighter in his chair. His mouth retracted into a terse line. "Marcel."

CHAPTER 21

His fiancée was attracted to his enemy. Greg supposed he shouldn't have been surprised by Jade's grin upon seeing Marcel. His colleague elicited the same wide-eyed welcome from many in the office, particularly the young single women. Marcel was thirty-eight years old with broad shoulders and a posture unbent by age. He possessed a rich brown complexion that didn't require a tan to appear healthy and a head shaved by choice, probably just to prove that he could pull off what other men feared.

To Jade's credit, her smile reversed course as soon as he uttered Marcel's name. She knew the guy had been gunning for his projects. Marcel's presence was the real reason he'd been anxious to return to work, hurrying back the Monday after his hospital release despite the throb in his temples.

Greg asked Jade to let in his would-be usurper, wanting to display the slight contempt of not getting up himself. While the rest of the firm may have been praying for Greg to have a speedy recovery, he was sure Marcel had been hoping for permanent brain damage.

"The head is back in shape, I see." Marcel said it as if he were pleased, though his statement was merely an observation. Greg appreciated the careful wording. Marcel was not explicitly claiming that he was overjoyed at the turn of events.

"It's round again." Greg deepened his voice in an effort to sound robust. He gestured to Jade with a broad smile. "This is my fiancée, Jade."

Marcel offered a respectful hello along with an obligatory sentence about having heard a lot about her. The latter implied that Greg actually chatted with Marcel, even though whatever Marcel had picked up about Greg's personal life had to have come secondhand. As Marcel spoke, Greg caught him subtly taking in Jade's full chest, covered by a white silk blouse, and the curves that her wide-leg pants couldn't hide.

Pleasantries over with, Marcel turned to Greg with a look like he'd smelled something offensive. "I wanted to let you know that the police came to my house. They were asking about you and work." He scratched the back of his neck. "I think they were under the impression that we had a bitter rivalry that could have turned violent. Michelangelo versus da Vinci." Marcel chuckled, a dry laugh that failed to dilute any of the tension in the room. "Though I don't understand where they might have gotten that impression."

Greg considered pretending that he had no idea what Marcel was talking about. The police could have asked around at the office and heard that he and Marcel were professional rivals who didn't care for one another personally. But Jade was present, and she'd heard him name Marcel as a person of interest in the hospital. Lying would make it seem that Marcel intimidated him when, really, he simply didn't want to bother with any headache-stirring conversations.

He twisted the band of the Apple smartwatch on his wrist and turned the device to silent. It monitored his heart rate, and Greg was sure that any exchange between them was sure to make it pick up. He didn't want to alert Marcel to his nerves or frustration by announcing he'd met some beats-per-minute exercise goal.

"The detectives came to me, moments after I woke from a coma with my head bashed in, to ask if I could think of anyone—*anyone at all*—who might want to hurt me." Greg waved a hand, dismissing what he was about to say before he verbalized it. "I said your name because, as you're aware, we've jockeyed for some of the same projects, and it was the only one I could think of."

Marcel scratched at his temple. "Listen, Greg, I wanted the Brooklyn Bay Building, obviously. Who here didn't?" Marcel smirked. "But not enough to . . . What do the Mafia guys say?"

Greg gave Marcel a measured look. "Take me out."

Marcel chuckled. The laugh sounded forced. "Or bump you off, I guess."

"Right." Greg forced a smile. "I don't think that."

Greg didn't add the operative word: *anymore.* Greg *did* think Marcel the kind of man to capitalize on a competitor's misfortune and even slyly attempt to bring it about. He'd personally witnessed Marcel engage in verbal sabotage of other principals, casually criticizing their work in an effort to make it seem as though he could have done a better job and should get the nod for the next proposal. For the right project, he could imagine Marcel doing more than talking. The big sky-scrapers brought in hundreds of millions, sometimes billions, to the firm, with the principal architects receiving sizable cuts of the total design fees. Santiago Calatrava, the architect of the World Trade Center Transit Hub, had received 20 percent of the four hundred and some-odd million that the city paid for the building's creation. Getting rid of Greg, of course, wouldn't move Marcel to that level. Greg wasn't at *that* level. But it would remove one rung on the ladder.

In his coma haze, however, Greg hadn't considered the difficulty of having someone killed. Normal people didn't meet the kind of folks who hired out their brawn, nor have accounts from which a hundred grand or so could go miss-ing without records. Marcel was a political predator. Greg doubted he possessed the connections to hire a real killer. The police had said as much.

"What are you working on these days?" Greg folded his hands atop his desk and stared at Marcel, making clear the pointedness of his question. He knew that his colleague would be crashing on his own proposal for the building that Greg had been tapped to create—in case Greg didn't return to the office in a timely fashion.

Marcel walked over to a white bookcase with Greg's various crystal awards. "Oh, you know, a little of this, then a permit comes through and it's a little of that. There's that café on Eighth Avenue." Marcel turned to face him again with a sigh. Greg braced for some "let's bury the hatchet" speech. "I've been having fun playing with the company's new tech."

Greg perked up. Marcel's version of bygones was to discuss something that actually interested both of them. "What do they have?"

"Well, there's some new CAD software that makes it much easier to model in 3-D. Autodesk is still superior when it comes to drafting in two dimensions, but some of the features on this new program you just have to see to believe. We got a demonstration. And there's a new toy to play with too." Marcel flushed, either from excitement or, perhaps, the realization that he sounded like a little boy who'd spied his birthday present in the closet and couldn't wait to brag about it. He pointed to Greg's Apple Watch. "I know you appreciate technology."

"I do."

Jade walked over to Greg and rubbed his shoulders. "You should have Marcel give you a demonstration of the new stuff. Don't worry about me. I was thinking of heading over to the D&D Building again, like I'd said. It's only a couple of blocks away. I can get some ideas."

The prospect of Jade leaving triggered a dual fight-or-flight instinct inside Greg. He had the urge to run after and then away with her, squirreling her into some safe house where he could protect her even in his weakened state. Thanks to Dr. Hsu, he was aware of the PTSD-fueled insanity of his desire. He obviously couldn't expect Jade or himself to remain behind closed doors until the police caught their attackers—if they ever did. But, given the circumstances, he also thought even his irrational fears could be indulged for a few days. She didn't *need* to go to the Decoration and Design Building. Nothing she'd picked up had made the blog the last time. He'd checked.

"I don't have to spend too long here and bore you, honey," Greg said. "I only have to check in with my team, really. If you wait, I'll come with you."

"No!"

The rejection came out like a slap, causing even Marcel to regard Jade with a wrinkled brow. She was acting strange, Greg realized. She'd been distracted all morning, and she'd driven in as though they'd been late for an appointment. Maybe she had somewhere to be, Greg thought. She'd been the one to suggest they head into the city, after weeks of encouraging him to concentrate on healing.

Greg reminded himself of what Dr. Hsu had said about misplaced paranoia. But his assessment of Jade wasn't based on a feeling. Her behavior was demonstrably off. Marcel's quizzical expression confirmed it.

"You should stay here. You've been gone for a while and need to catch up with people." Jade softened her tone. "I should only be a couple of hours."

The prior time she'd gone to the D&D Building had been a cover. Greg wished that he could track her phone to see whether or not she made another pit stop before window-shopping. But he couldn't. Jade had turned off her location sharing. The Find My iPhone app now showed only his iPad, phone, and watch.

Greg glanced at Jade's purse on his desk and began fiddling with his watchband. "Marcel, Jade is a designer. She has a blog on incorporating Caribbean culture into interiors, among other things. I bet she'd have some ideas about how to make the café a bit different from the ubiquitous industrial-chic coffee bars in town. When Starbucks starts building spaces with concrete floors, whitewashed brick, and casement windows, the trend is done, huh?"

Greg knew that Marcel wouldn't really care to hear the thoughts of another interior designer, given all those already at the firm. But he assumed his colleague would be too courteous to not ask Jade a question or two. And Jade was too passionate about her aesthetic not to share some thoughts.

Greg watched as the scene played out as he expected, with Marcel inquiring about the hallmarks of Caribbean design and Jade responding—though not as enthusiastically as Greg had anticipated. Still, she made mention of the materials and color schemes involved in island decor and the stark contrast of the Caribbean's colorful Afro-Indian-inspired palate to the Nordic norm of blond woods and white walls. As she talked, Greg removed the watch from his wrist. He stood, as though to stretch, and dropped it into the wallet flap inside her tote.

Jade finished answering Marcel's question as Greg's hand still hovered above her purse. She turned to grab it, thankfully too distracted by Marcel's promise to "consider some of that" to appreciate Greg's awkward arm position. "I should really leave you to your work, honey."

Greg rounded the desk to see her out. "I'll see you later," he said, planting a hard kiss on her lips to both mask his suspicions and stake his claim. He watched her go and then turned abruptly to his colleague. "So, Marcel, how about showing me this new tech?"

CHAPTER 22

Jade didn't know what Carlos Bernal would look like. When she'd been a child, he'd cut a ferocious figure with a thick neck, heavy cheeks, and burning black eyes. She'd believed him capable of lunging from the courtroom audience and beating her father to death before all the officers could react. The reality was that he couldn't have been as huge or intimidating as she remembered though. All angry adults appeared overwhelming to a skinny kindergartner.

As she jaywalked across the midtown street to the café, she tried to age the man in her memory, thinning his dark hair, adding weight to his jowls, reddening his cheeks with an alcohol flush. The result was a composite of her childhood recollections and every mug shot of a mass shooter. She couldn't control her shudder as she arrived at the coffee shop entrance.

The establishment was smaller than Jade had thought, with a single seating area overwhelmed by a farmhouse table. The furniture was pressed against an accordion-style wall of windows, fully retracted to let in the day's hot air. Behind the table, an androgynous barista served coffee at a wooden bar constructed from recycled shipping pallets.

Two suited men meandered inside, waiting for coffees. The first was stocky with a mahogany neck that protruded like a tree trunk from the fence of his buttoned shirt collar. The other was fair and lanky with curly light brown hair cut at his cheekbones and wire-framed glasses. Neither was old enough to be Bernal.

Jade shuffled in line behind the brunette and listened as he ordered an iced latte. Her nerve-cinched throat felt incapable of swallowing anything, let alone something as bitter as black coffee. Still, she ordered a small regular cup to give herself an excuse to loiter. She claimed one of the four empty stools and then set her bag on the table against the window.

Her coffee cup rattled each time she brought it to her mouth, threatening to spill its contents on her clothing. Every muscle was begging her to leave. Run. It occurred to her that she should have suggested talking outside on the sidewalk where it would be easier for her to sprint away. She'd chosen flat shoes precisely for that purpose.

The other two men received their more complicated orders and exited the shop. They glanced at her as they left. Reflexively, she looked to her cell phone screen, as if engrossed in some online article or text exchange. Sustained eye contact was an invitation for conversation. As the guys walked down the street, she cursed herself for not smiling, encouraging them to stick around. Two grown men were much more of a deterrent to Bernal lashing out than the thin teenager behind the coffee bar.

Jade was still watching the men out the open window when she thought she saw him coming from the opposite direction. The approaching guy was thinner than she remembered. His stomach didn't swell over the waistband of his belted slacks or puff out the short-sleeved button-down with a company logo on the chest. However, he possessed the square wrestler's jaw and heavy cheeks that she recalled from her childhood, although the lost weight and neatly trimmed pewter beard had altered the overall picture. Gone was the vicious troll imprinted on Jade's young brain. If this was Bernal, he'd become regrettably handsome.

Good-looking people had an easier time convincing others of their sincerity, Jade thought. If this man was her attacker, it was little wonder that Detective Ricci had fallen for his innocent act. Who wouldn't want to think the best of an attractive man who'd tragically lost his son to violence?

Jade's back stiffened as the guy approached the door. She glanced outside, wishing that there were more people passing by. Her chosen time had been a mistake, she realized. Prime time for coffee was in the morning and late afternoon when folks needed a break from hours in the office. Lunch was when workers either held business meetings at restaurants or ate their online deliveries at their desks.

It was too late to change plans now. She snatched the sonogram from her bag and slipped it behind her coffee cup. Almost simultaneously, she tapped the camera icon on her cell screen, switched to video recording, and hit the red button. The phone was back in her purse, peeking from the unzipped opening, before the man entered the coffee shop.

As the door shut behind him, he looked right and left,

as if he didn't know who he was searching for. His brow lowered when he saw her and then rose in recognition. "Jade Thompson?"

Her confusion made sense, Jade thought, but his had to be an act. Obviously, he'd seen her blog. How else could he have tracked her down? He knew what she looked like. He knew where she lived. Perhaps he'd agreed to meet as some kind of performance to keep the police on his side. *I tried talking to her, but she kept accusing me. She's crazy. Ask the barista.*

Jade reclaimed her coffee cup. The liquid inside was still hot enough to sting if she needed to throw it in his face. "Mr. Bernal." She hated to use a title next to his name, but she thought it might remind him that she'd been his son's peer once. She'd been innocent.

He pulled out the stool two seats away. As much as she didn't want to be near him, Jade wished he'd taken the vacant seat right beside her. It would have made it easier for her cell phone to pick up his voice.

"I wasn't sure that I'd recognize you." He rubbed his palms over his bent thighs, perhaps pretending to be nervous to throw her off guard. "You look like him a bit."

The statement could be both accusation and justification. Bernal was confirming his belief that she needed to pay for the sins of her father because of the blood in her veins. And there was no denying that blood. Michael's genes had elongated her limbs and drawn the damning shape of her nose. They'd stripped away the red bark of her mother's skin and slivered her round brown eyes when she smiled. To anyone that knew him, she was Michael Thompson's daughter—at least on the outside. People pretended the inside mattered more, but Jade knew as well as any adult that nearly all judgments were made in seconds based on what was visible.

"I don't believe my father intended to kill your son, but—"

"His intent doesn't matter," Bernal snapped. "He was dealing drugs and making the neighborhood dangerous, turning it into a place for gang violence, drive-by shootings, and kids getting caught by stray bullets."

The rage in Bernal's voice was below the surface. Still, she heard it, the crackle in smoking firewood. She needed to stoke his anger, make him careless enough to erupt with the truth. "My dad has served twenty-five years. He's been punished."

"There's no punishment that can bring my son back." A mist formed over Bernal's eyes, which he promptly wiped away. Fury, Jade knew, could also form tears.

"But revenge makes the pain a bit easier to bear, huh?" She plucked the photo from behind her coffee cup, flipped it to the back side, and slid it in front of him, refusing to take her finger from the corner. "Did killing my baby make it easier to bear?"

He stared at the message while his top lip curled. His palm wiped away the expression before Jade could figure it out.

"I don't know what you're talking about." Bernal glanced behind him, perhaps checking to see if the barista had heard her accusation. "Look." He leaned forward.

In her mind, Jade had planned for just such a scenario. She'd intended to push her bag toward him, enabling her cell to pick up any whispered gloats or threats. But her body did not respond to her brain's orders to stay still. As Bernal's thick form invaded her space, she lurched backward, destabilizing the stool beneath her. She jumped off as it crashed onto the hardwood.

Bernal rose from his seat and grabbed one of the stool's metal legs. One swift motion would send the chair crashing into her face. Jade retreated into the corner with her palm turned out above her forehead, ready to block a blow.

Her reaction seemed to shock Bernal. He winced as he righted the stool. "The police told me about the letters and your assault. I had nothing to do with them." He resumed his seat. "As I told the detectives, I was with my sons. I don't know where you live. I gather that your mother—Abigay, right—is still in Brooklyn—"

The denial didn't register over the pulse in Jade's ears. She heard only her mother's name, spoken offhand as though Bernal had obsessed about it so much that he and Abigay were on a first-name basis. "My mother prays for your family and your son every day," Jade said. "Her only fault is taking the gospel too literally. She believes everyone can be saved as long as he repents. What happened is not her fault. She doesn't deserve to be punished. I don't deserve to be punished. I was a kid too."

Jade was pleading. She realized it, not from any aware-ness of her imploring pitch or the tears filling her eyes, but because of the look of mortification on Bernal's face and his pupils, swinging between her and the wary barista like a pendulum.

"I know, Jade." Bernal's eyes retreated to his lap.

"Then why are you still sending them?"

His face reddened, perhaps from the difficulty of restraining his anger. "I understand that you believe I had something to do with the recent attack on you, and I guess I can comprehend why. We all want someone to blame when something horrific happens so that we can feel our pain has a purpose."

He met her gaze, waiting for some sort of agreement. Jade maintained eye contact. She wasn't hoping for a confession anymore, only that he'd perhaps see her as a person and not an extension of her dad—that he'd sympathize with the human he was hurting and leave her alone.

"After Mateo died, blaming his killer wasn't enough for me. Michael Thompson being in jail wasn't going to bring my son back. Even your father's death, which I wanted so badly for so long, which I prayed for at night before drinking myself to sleep—it wouldn't bring me justice. He would never hurt like my wife and I hurt." Bernal kept his voice level, but his tone assumed a growling quality. "The only way your dad would come close to feeling my pain was if something horrible happened to his child. Only then would he suffer some degree of what I was suffering. Only then would your mother suffer like my wife was suffering."

Bernal rubbed the heel of his hand over one eye. Jade realized that they'd grown bloodshot since he'd been talking. He wasn't crying. But he was close. "I sent you those notes on Mateo's birthday all those years to try to spread my suffering. I thought if I could make your parents fear for their child, even a little, that was some measure of justice."

A buzzing sound, like a fly but at the volume of a drill, overwhelmed Bernal's last word. Jade didn't dare take her eyes off the man for fear of shutting down his confession. "And so when you learned he would be getting out..."

Bernal turned toward the coffee bar, perhaps wondering

whether the racket emanated from one of the machines. Jade couldn't let him get distracted by the electronic humming. She inclined farther into his space, demanding his attention with her uncomfortable closeness. "You realized you needed more justice..."

Bernal shifted in his seat, widening the space between them. "I got the court notice earlier this year. But I stopped sending the letters more than a decade ago." A smile relaxed his mouth. "My wife saved me. She got me into AA before drinking cost me my business. The program helped me see that my anger wasn't doing anything but eating me alive, enlarging the hole left by Mateo and encouraging me to fill it with liquor."

The smile grew. "I got sober. My wife and I had the twins. They're nine." Teeth glistened as Bernal's lips parted. "My boys, they have this love for me. It's pure and nonjudgmental. Maybe that will change when they're teenagers." He chuckled. "But I'll take it as long as I can get it. We went on vacation to Cooperstown just last week. Kids wanted to visit the Baseball Hall of Fame."

His focus shifted from inward to her again. "Ten years ago, when my wife got pregnant and I'd had my first year sober, I realized that the love she had for me when I was drowning myself in alcohol was what I really needed—not some warped idea of justice or retribution. I realized it wasn't justice to spread my pain to you."

Bernal reached both palms toward her, as though holding an invisible gift. "I didn't send those new letters, and I apologize for those I sent years ago. I'm sorry that you, too, have been victimized by violence. I don't wish you ill."

Jade felt like she'd been on a roller coaster that had sped toward the apex of a dead-end track. Instead of jumping the rails, it now careened backward. Bernal had detailed every reason for harboring his hate toward her only to swear that he no longer bore her any anger. It didn't make sense.

And yet Jade believed him. Apologizing had loosened a vise around his neck, releasing the pressure that had reddened his face and shot lines across the whites of his eyes. He was relaxed. Relieved. Happy, even. His revenge was his happiness, Jade thought. He'd wanted to apologize, perhaps. But he'd also wanted to show her that Michael Thompson had not destroyed him.

Bernal slipped off the seat.. He stood in front of her, arms extended a couple of inches from his sides as though he might accept a hug. "I hope the police find out who is harassing you. And I sincerely hope that you and your fiancé can help one another heal the way my wife helped me."

The kind words pulled some drain deep inside Jade's chest, releasing the fear that had filled her all morning, overflowing the reservoir that had been collecting since the day of her father's arrest. Jade found herself standing in front of Bernal, shaking. Tears were slipping down her cheeks. "I didn't know how much I needed to hear that until now." She sniffed. "Thank you."

Since Bernal had started talking, several other patrons had entered the store. More than a couple were looking at them as if they were watching a reality show. Bernal suggested that they go outside.

Jade picked up the ultrasound photo and placed it back in her bag. They headed out the door and onto the sidewalk.

After spending so much of the conversation braced for an attack, Jade couldn't completely accept that it had ended with an apology. A small part of her worried that the whole inter-action had been a figment of her imagination, fueled by her subconscious desire to be absolved of her childhood guilt. But Bernal was there, dark hair glistening in the sunlight. He outstretched his arms. "Take care of yourself, Jade."

She leaned into his hug, sniffling and thanking him. After a moment, she started to pull away. She was so desperate for compassion that she was crying into the chest of the man whom her father had nearly destroyed. It wasn't fair to dump her burden on Bernal.

He gave her a small smile and then headed down the street. As Jade watched him leave, she realized the buzzing noise was deafening. She scanned for the temporary plywood walls of a construction site. Instead she saw what appeared, at first glance, to be a giant white dove hovering across the street— the Holy Spirit to whom her mother prayed, vibrating the air with its divine love.

Jade no longer put stock in such symbols. Yet, like any child raised in the church, part of her still hoped that maybe the Bible's miracles had been more than stories embellished to deliver moral lessons. She wanted to believe that suffering had a reason, that the Lord worked in mysterious ways, and that perhaps losing her child had been a step toward some moment of grace.

The skeptic in her demanded she look harder. She rubbed her eyes, forcing them to adjust to the brighter light outside, and zeroed in on the humming object. The bird's square body became visible beneath its four whirling propellers. Not a dove, a drone.

Someone was filming the street. Jade turned away from it and toward the Decoration and Design Building. Her forgiveness had been orchestrated by the power of Bernal's wife and Alcoholics Anonymous's twelve steps, not divine intervention. No higher power was protecting her from her harasser.

Jade removed the sonogram and reread the message on the back: SOME PEOPLE SHOULDN'T KEEP BREEDING. Knowing Bernal hadn't written the note changed her interpretation of it. Before she'd assumed that "some people" had referred to her and her father, and "keep breeding" had meant passing on her father's genes. But the latter phrase actually suggested that "some people" had already birthed a child.

Jade slipped the image of her one and only pregnancy back into her purse. She was not "some people," Jade realized. Greg was.

CHAPTER 23

The firm's new toy was a drone. *And not just any drone*, according to Marcel. Management had splurged for a Specter Pro, a top-of-the-line "intelligent" flying machine capable of semiautonomously traveling to any GPS coordinate within twenty miles while simultaneously livestreaming high-definition video. Its operator needed to worry about only the altitude and the route.

And apparently the cops. Marcel had explained that city law forbade piloting above Manhattan streets where passersby might be photographed without consent. However, he'd added with a wink that the NYPD was *probably* too busy with "real crime" to bother with mere privacy violations.

As soon as Greg had seen the drone's HD control panel, he'd wanted to pilot it to one specific point of interest: a café two in from the intersection of Fifty-Eighth and Third Avenue at 40.7497 degrees north and 73.9755 degrees west, according to text tucked in the corner of the map on his Find My iPhone app. The spot was about a block west from the Decoration and Design Building's well-known location. It was where his "watch" icon had been stamped for twenty minutes.

Coffee shops didn't last long in Manhattan if they failed to operate with the efficiency of an Indy 500 pit crew. If Jade had stopped for a cup, or even a quick bite, Greg figured that she would have had her order almost immediately and certainly under five minutes. Why nurse a drink by herself for that long? Unless she wasn't alone.

"I've been wanting to check out this spot," Greg had told Marcel, implying that he had his eye on a prospective building site. "It's inland."

When his colleague hadn't immediately relinquished his hold on the drone controller, Greg removed his cap and tilted his chin to his chest, showing off the ugly reminder of his brush with death. "I think this is worth at least one get-out-of-jail-free card."

Marcel had given him a pity chuckle and handed over the device. "When you're done, put it at five hundred feet and select the home button. It'll hover above the building until I return to guide it through the window." He coughed. "I'm going to grab a coffee from the break room. Plausible deniability if you crash it into the Chrysler Building."

Greg had laughed as if such an accident was beyond the realm of possibility, even though he feared it wouldn't be. As soon as Marcel closed the door behind him, he'd clutched the controller and entered in the coordinates, praying that it was as easy to operate as Marcel had made it seem during his demonstration.

He'd kept the device at five hundred feet, far above the water towers atop Fifty-Eighth Street's skyscrapers. As the drone neared his coordinates, he'd dropped it to one story above street level and then struggled before rotating the vessel to face the desired building. After a few tries, he'd successfully angled its camera down to the street.

The video had immediately caught Jade. She'd been sitting in a coffee shop, framed by black-painted brick walls in a glassless expanse. The drone's elevated vantage point had filmed her from the top down and in profile, the way the dead might view the living. Greg had seen the dark crown of her head and the bronze of her skin. He'd recognized the white top that she'd been wearing all morning.

He'd also seen the man beside her. The guy had appeared younger than Greg, though older than Jade. He'd possessed the broad shoulders of a college quarterback and thick arms that Greg suspected could do some damage. The stranger's skin tone was roughly the same color as Greg's, rather than any brown shade similar to Jade's complexion. This was not her father, he'd thought.

The man had been talking to his fiancée, delivering some long soliloquy that appeared to have her rapt attention. Greg hadn't seen the guy's lips moving, but the changing inclination of the stranger's head indicated that he'd been the one holding court. Jade had moved closer at something he'd said. His hands had been beneath the table, perhaps on his lap. Perhaps on Jade's knee. Greg had no way of knowing.

"She could have sat down, and some man just started flirting with her." Greg had said the words aloud, hoping they'd ring true. But he hadn't believed them, just as he hadn't bought the flurry of other explanations that he'd come up with to excuse her lengthy stay at a coffee shop: She'd called a friend or decided to check in with her mother; an item in the store had presented itself as good blog material.

His gut had told him to go with his first suspicious instinct. And though he knew he wasn't supposed to trust it—knew that it had been compromised by postattack paranoia—he'd had no choice but to react to the hollow feeling in his stomach demanding to be filled with the truth.

Ultimately, the stranger had slipped off the seat, apparently saying good-bye, and Jade followed him outside the coffee shop. Greg had rotated the drone to face her just in time to see his girlfriend fall into the stranger's arms.

Greg braced himself for the shallow breaths, blurred vision, and sudden sweats of a panic attack. Instead, his breathing smoothed. His eyes focused on the screen. Seeing Jade embracing this other man—a man she'd planned to see behind his back and lied to him about—didn't scare him. It enraged him.

The stranger patted her shoulder and pulled away. She stood on the street, watching him leave like an abandoned lover. Suddenly, as if she could sense Greg's gaze, she looked up and stared directly at the drone. Even at this distance, Greg could see the wonder and joy parting her lips. She was radiant. Beatific.

A moment later, she was walking down the street, probably heading toward the D&D Building for some trifle she undoubtedly believed adequate to trick the rich old fool whom she pretended to adore but had never once looked at with such rapture. Violet had been right all along. A beautiful, smart woman wouldn't date a man twenty years her senior without an angle. Jade wanted his money. She and her boyfriend might even kill to get it.

Greg brought the device back up to five hundred feet and selected the home coordinates. The drone began speeding over the city toward its home base, like Jade rushing to establish her alibi before she returned to him. He exited Marcel's office and headed for the safety of his own war room.

Once inside the fishbowl office, he pulled all the shades, preventing his team from seeing inside while simultaneously signaling that he should not be disturbed. He locked the door and then leaned back in his power chair, Pacino in *The Godfather* contemplating his next move. Calling the police would make him seem like a crazy person. He'd followed his girlfriend with a drone—an illegal act to begin with—and watched her have coffee with a man and then hug him goodbye. There was nothing unlawful about her actions. There wasn't even any moral offense since a hug couldn't exactly be construed as cheating.

She'd lied about their meeting, of course. But Jade would easily spin some story about the man being an old friend from her Brooklyn neighborhood whom she'd run into by chance and caught up with over a coffee. Any talk of her earlier nervous demeanor would be dismissed as the paranoid ravings of a traumatic brain injury victim.

No. He couldn't go to the detectives with this, Greg decided. But he had to call someone.

He pulled his cell from his pants pocket and hit the speed dial. Five contacts showed on-screen: Jade, Leah, Paul, Violet, and Work.

Greg paused over Jade's name. Part of him wanted to call solely to scream obscenities at her. He wanted to tell Jade that she was a liar and a cheat. He wanted to brag that he'd spied on her because—unlike the sucker that she thought he was—he'd known all along that she couldn't be trusted. He wanted to assure her that she'd never get a dime from him and pledge to spend every cent that he'd promised her on tracking down her boyfriend. Most of all, he wanted to swear on the Bible, and every other good book ever written, that he would make certain she went down for conspiracy to commit murder, spending every last day of her pretty youth locked away just like her low-life father.

Greg hit the selected number and listened to the rings.

"Hi, Dad." The worry in Violet's voice seemed prescient. "Is everything okay?"

"You were right." He was raspy with rage.

"Aren't I always?"

"I have to break it off with Jade. But before I do, I need a gun."

CHAPTER 24

Gunfire. Jade struggled to see something less violent in the abstract mural dominating the wall across from the reception desk. Nonrepresentational art was always subject to subconscious interpretation. She knew a different woman would see a twinkling night in the starbursts. She could imagine a kindergarten teacher relating the layers of bright, irregular shapes to the construction paper littering her classroom floor. Greg would discover something profound in the frenzied charcoal lines that alternatively asserted themselves in the foreground and shrank behind slashes of primary colors.

But Jade was the daughter of a man about to be released for shooting a child. To her mind, the starbursts were shattered glass around 9-millimeter-sized holes. The irregular shapes resembled chalk outlines of fallen victims. The gray lines evoked the wisps of smoke that lingered after a blaze of bullets.

She turned her attention from the contemporary art back to the large male security guard who wouldn't allow her up to

Greg's floor. He hunched behind his marble reception desk, avoiding eye contact. Twenty minutes earlier, he'd called Greg with news that his fiancée was in the lobby. Rather than instruct him to let her through, Greg had said that she should wait downstairs.

Jade supposed that he'd gotten waylaid on his way out by a fellow principal or perhaps some junior member of his team in desperate need of direction. He wasn't answering her texts requesting an ETA so she didn't know for sure. She'd have to call him, she decided. As much as she didn't want to interrupt an important meeting, her legs were tired from all the walking, first to the coffee shop and then around the design building for over an hour before hiking back to Greg. If he didn't want her to wait in his office, she could grab a coffee at the Starbucks next door and sit for a few minutes.

Her phone lay in the front pocket of her purse. She pulled it out and unlocked the home screen. A selfie of her and Greg at the new house greeted her. They'd taken it shortly after the addition's exterior had been constructed but well before the interior had been finished. She was laughing, and he was smiling at their mirror image on the screen. It wasn't a great photo. Greg's neck was cut off, leaving a grinning face and the side of his extended left arm, like the Cheshire cat after his body began disappearing. Her mouth was open too wide and showing too many teeth. Jade liked it, though, because the shot reminded her of that night—before the attack—when they'd burned birch logs in the outdoor fireplace and slow-danced to love ballads popular before either of their times. The memory stirred a smile, as it always did. She felt it as she waited for Greg to pick up his phone.

As the cell rang, Jade felt something else—a strange vibration by her ribs, emanating from the purse at her side. She tossed the bag from her shoulder onto the floor, her skin crawling with the thought of the roach or confused bee wriggling by her wallet. The bag continued to buzz on the ground, its motion tapping the metal clasp against the ceramic tile.

Jade considered kicking the purse in hopes of scaring the insect into leaving. Before she could, the vibration stopped. At the same time, Greg's voice mail answered. Jade sensed it wasn't a coincidence.

She reclaimed her bag and began going through the zippered exterior pocket, unsure what she was looking for but certain that it had to do with Greg. Her probing fingers hit the slick face of something. She snagged it by the attached strap, recognizing what it was before removing it from her purse. Greg's Apple watch.

Had he tired of fidgeting with it and slipped it into her bag for safekeeping? Jade tried to convince herself that the answer was yes. Her bag was coming home with them, after all. Greg could have worried that he'd forget his gadget on his desk or in a drawer and then be without it until he returned to work. Depending on how his short day had gone, that could be the next day or the next month.

Her justifications churned in her belly like a bad meal. It wasn't in Greg's careful, controlling nature to hand over his watch without at least a warning to be cautious with it. But it was like him to spy on her. She knew the real reason the watch was in her bag. Greg had used it to track her.

The discovery multiplied her annoyance at his refusal to let her up to his office. She dialed him again. The watch responded by vibrating in her clenched fist. For the second time, his voice mail picked up. "I found your watch, honey. I don't know how it ended up in my purse. Anyway, if you're looking for it, guess you know where to find me."

Her dry delivery conveyed the double message. She dropped both her phone and the watch back into her bag and returned to considering the mural. The shape spatter was densest on the right side and became gradually thinner toward the left. Again, Jade thought of a bullet exploding from a muzzle in a rush of smoke and fire. But this time, she also saw a scream.

She paced for another five minutes before realizing that she could use the idle time in the echoey lobby to tell her mother about Carlos Bernal without fear of Greg listening in through the security cameras. Abigay answered her call on the first ring, like she'd been waiting for it. Her mother swore she could sense when Jade needed her, even claiming to have suffered an excruciating stomach cramp around the time Jade would have been miscarrying.

Not knowing how long she had before Greg's arrival, Jade launched right into her story, rushing through her discovery of the hand-delivered threats, her reasons for believing Bernal had sent them despite the detectives' disagreement, her decision to meet with him in hopes of taping a confession, and his surprising, healing kindness. During her recap, Abigay was at turns hostile (*Jade, you nuh have sense? Meeting with a man you thought might have attacked you!*); thankful (*Praise God, he found peace. His son can rest*); and defensive (*Forgiveness? For what? There's no shame in speaking for a sinner. I'm not to tell the truth that Michael was a good man who made a mistake dealing drugs?*).

After Jade had finished, Abigay exhaled loudly through the speaker and asked whether she was sitting down. The lobby lacked so much as a covered radiator to rest upon. Rather than explain that she was, actually, leaning in a corner by the revolving doors, Jade murmured something affirmative and asked that Abigay stop making her nervous.

"Your father is getting out of prison." Jade heard the smile in her voice. "He served his twenty-five years, and no one objected at the parole hearing. He's coming home."

"To your apartment?" Jade didn't think of the rent-controlled unit as her father's *home*. Her mother had paid the rent on it for two and a half decades, some of those while putting herself through community college and then nursing school. Even when Michael had been free and probably covering the rent, he'd been a sporadic presence.

"Not right away." Abigay sounded uncomfortable. "I fell in love with your father as a girl. I still love him—in a way. He gave me you." She sniffed. "Your father was the only man I'd *known*. After he went away, I kinda shut down that part of myself completely, maybe as punishment for that little boy, you know? How could I go carrying on with anyone when my husband had taken someone's child?"

Jade heard the sharp sound of a sob. Was her mother crying? "Sometimes I think, though he's my husband, the love I have for him is brotherly," Abigay said. "I can't love the other way anymore."

Jade didn't know what to say other than "sorry." But she held back even that word. It felt cheaper than any platitude, given what her mother had just confessed. Michael's actions had robbed a family of their son, a boy of his life, and her of a dad. But they'd also stolen a young woman's ability to love romantically and experience physical intimacy. Her mother had turned to God to occupy that space in her life, Jade realized. But even the Almighty might never have filled it.

"You have to be so careful who you fall for, honey. The wrong man—" Abigay cleared her throat, either to stop herself from crying or to definitively change the subject. "My church will help him get settled in a three-quarter house in the neighborhood. The owner is a former addict who regularly attends service, so he's going to do right by him. It won't be like those stories where ten men are shoved into a room of bunk beds like a bunch of sailors. It's a nice place. Better than he's used to..."

Jade couldn't imagine the statement being false. Though she'd never seen a prison cell, she'd searched for online images of Rikers accommodations when her father was first sent there. She'd seen cells hardly bigger than a city bathroom, outfitted with narrow beds that would have required larger men, like her father, to sleep in a fetal position, and combination sinks/toilets that she hadn't realized existed.

"A so di ting set," Abigay said, slipping into Patois. Emotional conversations always brought back her mother's native dialect. "It's a blessing anyway. A second chance is always a blessing."

Jade agreed, told her mother she loved her, and hung up the phone. She then meandered back to the mural and gave it another look, her mother's confession still weighing on her shoulders. The gun symbolism remained there for her—unable to be erased once seen—but she could also appreciate the art for what it was: a celebration of color and shape and light. With her father's sentence served, perhaps her mother could regain some of the joy she'd kept from herself over the years.

Jade was still admiring the painting when she heard a gruff male voice behind her.

"Let's go."

Greg looked the same as when she'd left him, up to the heather gray cap topping his head. But his expression was different. Harder. And his voice had dropped a decibel, rendering it foreign to her ears. Something unfortunate had happened at the office, Jade guessed. Marcel was the likely culprit. Maybe Greg's first instinct had been correct, and the guy had been trying to steal Greg's projects, one way or another. Perhaps he'd even been successful.

"How was your day?" she asked warily.

Greg stormed past her toward the exit. "I want to get home."

Anger improved Greg's balance. He strode toward the garage, weaving through workers meandering back from their coffee breaks like a car trying to lose a tail. Jade found herself stuttering apologies and pardons as she bumped into strangers while trying to catch up.

She reached the garage less than a minute after him. In those short seconds, however, Greg had started an argument with the parking attendant. He was yelling at the guy, insisting that the young man had to recognize him from earlier and that he wanted his car immediately. Thankfully the attendant—likely no older than Greg's son—wasn't engaging. He pointed at a large sign indicating the rates per hour and the not-so-fine print explaining that lost tickets would result in a charge of the daily maximum.

"Honey, it's okay." Jade fished her wallet from her purse as she hurried over. "I have the ticket."

Greg glared at her as she pulled the paper square from behind her license, as though she'd undermined his argument by guarding the receipt. The young man rang her up with a broad smile that Jade interpreted as relief before hurrying down the ramp for their vehicle.

"How much are you planning on tipping your new boyfriend?" Greg spit.

Had his tone teased, she would have immediately understood that he referred to the parking attendant. However, the venom in the question kept her from processing it. "Sorry?"

"How much of my money are you going to give the parking attendant?"

Jade was tempted to tell Greg that she made her own money and would be giving the customary "couple of bucks" to the man. But she didn't want to court an argument, particularly one about finances. Jade had her own cash because Greg paid for their essentials. Her entire pretax income couldn't cover their yearly mortgage.

"Did something happen at work?" She reached for his arm. "We can talk about it."

Greg recoiled like she'd moved to strike him. "Work is fine."

"Are you feeling all right?"

"Fine."

The car screeched up the ramp. Greg yanked open the passenger door before the vehicle came to a complete stop and then slammed it behind him, broadcasting his annoyance to anyone in the vicinity. Through the windshield, Jade caught the attendant wince. As he handed her the keys, he told her to have a nice evening with an expression that read *good luck with that.*

Anger wafted from Greg like steam from a covered manhole, clouding the air between them as she inched the SUV across the sidewalk. She merged into the sluggish crosstown traffic and opened the back windows, hoping a fresh breeze might blow away some of the bad energy. Instead, it increased it, inviting in the offensive car horns, blaring music, and collective frustration of all the workers who had left by four to beat rush hour only to find themselves in the thick of it.

Jade raised the windows and turned on the climate control. The hissing air emphasized the heavy silence. "I had a good day," she volunteered. "Talking about that coffee shop with Marcel gave me the idea to take photos of items that would bring Caribbean vibes to work environments. I'm thinking of collaging them in a post: 'Ten ways to cool out your high-stress space.' What do you think?"

Greg didn't answer, but the energy between them took on a charge. Jade reminded herself that he'd taken pains to keep tabs on her location. He knew his Apple Watch had been loitering at the coffee shop. Her not mentioning it probably seemed suspicious.

"The shots are on my phone." Jade gestured with her head toward her bag atop the console between them. She cleared her throat. "Before I headed over to the D&D Building, I also went to this cute coffee shop around the corner. I spent some time there thinking, and I realized that I should be reaching out to designers to sell their stuff on my site."

Greg's breathing grew louder. A side glance revealed his

nostrils were flared. "You were *thinking* at the coffee shop the whole time?"

The meeting had been at least thirty minutes. That was a while to sit and think, especially for a doer like herself. "Well, I was looking up different designers too. Trying to get ideas of whom I might like to approach."

Her chatter wasn't clearing the air. In Jade's peripheral vision, she saw Greg fidgeting. He opened and closed his fists and dragged the heels of his hands across his thighs, moving for the sake of not sitting still. The jittering was a sure sign of his anxiety over whatever had happened at the office. If Greg didn't discuss what bothered him, Jade feared he'd blow like a high-pressure pipe.

She tried a more direct question. "So, did you talk to your team? Were they moving along in your absence, or did you feel like things had stalled?"

"They're fine."

"And Marcel? Is he staying on his side of the playground?"

Greg glared at her as though she'd grossly insulted a personal friend. "He's a good guy."

"Oh. Really?" Jade revised her theory about Marcel's involvement. Greg must have overreacted to their competition, as he'd said. "Well, he seemed nice today. I'm glad you two resolved some—"

"What happened to the baby?"

The question came at her like a speeding vehicle running a red light. She'd been obeying the rules of conversation, asking about his day and inching toward what might be bothering him, and he'd T-boned her in the intersection, spinning her around into oncoming traffic.

Jade gripped the steering wheel and tried to figure out which way to turn. Someone at work must have brought up the pregnancy, forcing him to explain that she'd miscarried during the attack. But why the sudden anger over it? Did he blame her for not saving the fourteen-week-old fetus and allowing them to have a funeral?

"Like I told you, I miscarried." Jade choked on the word, forcing her to cough and repeat herself. "The punches to the stomach, or maybe the stress of everything, started labor. I was bleeding. The cops took me to the hospital..."

Jade focused on the red taillights in front of her, trying to keep her mind from accessing the image. It came anyway, her consciousness falling to it like a marked page in a book. She saw "it" in the palm of her hand. The gelatinous skin, translucent and blood red, pulled like a mask over the distinct shape of a human skull. The dark impressions of eyes. Feet and hands tinier than a Barbie doll's. Too small to become a baby. But too big, she thought, to be dismissed as anything else in the animal kingdom. Her little fairy.

The image would forever be with her. Sometimes she wished she'd never seen it.

The traffic blurred ahead. She glanced at Greg, wondering if he, too, was becoming wistful. His icy stare had not melted at all, despite her own watery vision. "Does the hospital keep records?"

Greg's question didn't directly accuse her of anything, but she sensed the blame in it—possibly because she didn't know the answer. When everything had happened, she'd been hysterical from the attack and seeing Greg on the floor with blood pouring from his bashed skull. The blood running down her thighs hadn't even registered until a female paramedic asked if she'd been raped. Jade remembered telling her *No, I'm pregnant*, with a kind of shock, as though carrying a child created a magical barrier against sexual assault. The woman's grim expression had said *Not anymore*.

"The hospital only reports a death at twenty weeks gestation," Jade said, repeating the exact sentence from the miscarriage pamphlets she'd received when the hospital discharged her. "Legal viability is at twenty-four weeks. You can't get a death certificate until then."

Greg coughed. "No record then. No evidence that you were even pregnant."

Jade reflexively pulled a hand from the wheel to touch her belly. "I have that ultrasound picture."

"I didn't go to that appointment," Greg mumbled.

The light up ahead turned red. Jade reacted late, distracted by her raw emotion to Greg's clinical questions. She slammed on the brakes, causing her tires to screech as the SUV skidded toward the vehicle in front of her. The accident avoidance system began beeping loud and fast, like the car itself was having a heart attack.

Jade tucked her chin to her neck and closed her eyes, bracing for impact. The SUV came to a stop without the accompanying crunch of metal on metal. A glance at the front camera in her console showed a mere inch between her front grille and the lead car's bumper. The driver she'd almost hit casually raised a middle finger to his rearview. Horns blasted behind her. Jade heard a male voice shout, "Pay attention, bitch!"

The common epithet shouldn't have been what broke her. But she suddenly couldn't take any more anger. She was back in the room, seeing her attacker drive his fist into her abdomen. She started crying.

"Pull over."

Jade didn't hear compassion in Greg's command. She obeyed without speaking, putting on her blinker and moving toward the idling vehicles on the side of the avenue. Safely at the curb, she let loose, releasing the menagerie of caged emotions. Saltwater tears blinded her. She heard a door slam, followed by the sucking sound of her own door flinging open.

Greg loomed over her, his nose wrinkled in disgust. "I'll drive. I don't want you to kill me."

CHAPTER 25

Violet approached the house like she intended to rob it. Mirrored sunglasses hid her face behind a distorted reflection. A weathered Yankees cap covered her blond bob. She marched up the walk with her head angled down and her back hunched, shielding whatever she carried from the outdoor cameras.

As she hit the steps beneath the portico, Greg switched from the front camera feed to the doorbell's view. It took only a second to bring up the new video full-screen. In that short time, however, Violet transferred the item she'd held outside the frame. She leaned toward the buzzer, giving Greg an uncomfortable close-up of his daughter's breasts in a too-tight tank.

Greg stood from his desk chair and palmed his cell. Before Violet could ring, he clicked the microphone icon on his monitor. "Hey, I'll be right there," he whispered. "I think Jade's still sleeping."

He crossed through the family room to the foyer and front

door. Unlike after their other arguments, he hadn't needed to suggest to Jade that they sleep apart. She'd spared him the trouble, grabbing some blankets and storming into the spare bedroom. Whether she'd gone to sleep or passed the evening plotting against him with her boyfriend, Greg didn't know. She'd deactivated the camera.

He turned off the alarm before opening the door so the sound wouldn't wake his soon-to-be ex-girlfriend. Violet entered as though she were being timed anyway, rushing into the foyer, her arms crossed over what Greg could finally identify as a black case. As he shut the door, Violet cut a jagged path around the vestibule, peering into the open mudroom, family room, dining room, and what was visible of the kitchen beyond.

Violet whirled around, clutching the case like a sleeping baby. "How do you know she's still upstairs?"

Greg brandished his cell. "I'll get an alert if she comes down to the first floor."

The safety measure didn't appear to impress his daughter. "Can she see the same cameras?"

To his knowledge, Jade didn't use the app. He'd never seen her check her cell before opening a door or witnessed her scrolling through saved videos. But she had the same access to the system he did. When he'd installed the app on her phone, he'd only been thinking about keeping her safe.

His daughter frowned, deriving his answer from his silence or some stricken look on his face. Greg patted Violet's bicep, a fatherly welcome gesture for anyone watching. "Let's go to the office." He mouthed the words "No camera."

Violet followed him through the family room, resuming her

hunched walk to hide her package. When she entered the office, she immediately shut the door and asked if it locked. Greg told her to push in the button at the center of the knob. The lock could be disabled by simply jabbing a straightened paper clip through the pinhole on the other side. But it was better than nothing.

Door secure as possible, Violet brought the case down from her chest. It was constructed of a hard plastic, like the container for his cordless drill in the garage. However, the combination lock beneath its handle suggested that it held something more important.

She carried it not to the desk, but to a wooden drafting table pressed against the wall shared with the family room. Greg had salvaged the piece from his former house. When Violet was growing up, the top had often been raised to a forty-degree angle, displaying the latest printout of whatever he'd been drafting on the computer. Since he'd always worked for his large firm, Greg had never suffered through the laborious process of hand-drawing blueprints. But something about seeing a plan on paper excited the artist in him.

The drafting table was bare at the moment. Violet placed the case in the center and then keyed in a three-digit code, which she announced to Greg number by number. He heard a loud click, similar to a retracting dead bolt.

Violet smiled for the first time since arriving. "Dad needs a gun; I pack the heat."

She stepped to the side, gesturing like a magician to the open case. Nestled inside thick black foam was an even blacker handgun. Greg recognized the weapon from action movies, though he had no idea what it was called. Inside the same case was a black cartridge. Beside that were empty cutouts for two more.

Greg felt the strange sensation of standing on a cliff edge, when the body wants to bolt backward but a small voice in the mind says jump. Forces of creation and destruction pulled his insides in opposite directions. Overriding them both was an instinct of self-preservation. It told him to pick up the gun.

He reached for the pistol, pushing his fingers into the space between the foam and the plastic handle. "Is it loaded?"

"No. You only want to scare her, right? Make sure she leaves the house without a fight."

Greg wasn't exactly sure what he wanted. Jade had lied to him. *Cheated* on him. For all he knew, she'd plotted to have him murdered with her boyfriend for his money. He wanted her out of his house. He also wanted her to pay.

Greg withdrew the pistol from its case and wrapped his right hand around the grip, fitting his fingers into the molded grooves. His index was naturally left out. Rather than put it on the trigger, he extended it below the barrel.

"It's a Glock 19—one of the simpler Lugers to shoot because it's relatively compact and light, but has a good-sized barrel, making it easier to aim."

Violet sounded like a card-carrying NRA member, though Greg didn't understand how she could be. She was the daughter of two gun-abhorring liberals who had screened her friends by asking parents whether or not they had weapons in the house. They'd never hunted. Never gone to a range. He and Leah had shown the kids the film *Bambi*.

"Is this yours?"

Violet scrunched her nose. "Heck no." She chuckled. "I don't need any temptation when I'm angry."

"Where did you get this?"

Violet chewed her bottom lip. "Let's say a friend."

"Is it from a friend?"

Violet shrugged in the way she always did when she suspected a scolding. *It's no big deal, Dad. Chill.* But it was a big deal. He'd said that he needed a gun, and his daughter had shown up with one the next day as though she had an arsenal in the closet of her lilac-painted bedroom.

"Isn't it against the law to transport firearms across state lines? And don't you need a permit? Do you have a permit? Is this registered?"

Violet raised both hands in surrender. "You shouldn't wave a gun around like that. Even when you think it's not loaded."

Greg realized he'd been gesturing emphatically with the weapon as he rattled off questions. He placed the Glock back in its case, though not inside the designated cutout. Whether he liked it or not, he knew he wasn't done with it.

"Is it even legal?"

Violet raised one shoulder before answering. "It's registered in Vermont. It's legal to transport a gun across state lines as long as the gun is unloaded and locked up while you're driving—or so I've been told. If you don't like that, you can take it up with your federal legislator."

Greg put his hands on his hips, wanting to scold someone. He did not live in the Wild Wild West; he lived in New York State. It couldn't possibly be so simple for him to have a weapon. "Who is this licensed to?"

Violet removed her sunglasses, placed them on the table,

and picked up the Glock with one fluid motion. She held it the same way Greg had, though her face didn't appear to show any of the conflicting emotions that had racked him moments before. "Don't worry about it, Dad. No one who will get you in trouble." She grimaced. "You just need it to threaten her anyway. It's not like you're going to shoot it."

She took a few steps to the side and widened her stance. "You've got to be believable though." Her left hand clasped over her right. She kept her arms extended as she raised the barrel. The muzzle pointed at Greg's chest. "So, this is how you hold it." Her index finger rested on the trigger. She stepped her right leg back.

Greg watched, so horrified at the sight of the weapon and his daughter's seeming familiarity with it that it didn't occur to him to get out of the way. Violet seemed to move in slow motion. Her left arm bent slightly. Her blue irises flashed like gas flames. The left eye squinted, blocking the bright bar of sunlight slipping through the shuttered window. "This is how you aim."

She pivoted toward the wall. Greg heard a sharp click.

He realized that he'd been holding his breath, braced for an explosion. He exhaled as Violet turned back toward him. "And that is how you shoot." She grinned and lowered the gun. "You should never really aim it at anyone you don't intend to kill, even if it's not loaded. You don't want to find out that there was one in the chamber."

Greg started to breathe normally again. "How did you learn all this?"

Violet smirked. "Mom and I went to a shooting range. I thought it would be a good way for her to get out her suppressed aggression."

"That gun isn't Leah's." Greg said it like a statement instead of a question. Country clubs were his ex's domain. He couldn't picture prim Leah in her cashmere sweaters firing at paper silhouettes.

His daughter's wry smile twisted a bit more. "Why would Mom need a gun? She has her lawyers."

Violet passed the Glock to him like a knife, turning her hand so that the dangerous end faced the floor. Greg accepted the weapon. Holding it failed to fill him with any of the pride evident on Violet's face. If anything, he felt disappointed in himself. Before the attack, he'd often cited statistics showing that gun owners were more likely to injure themselves or a family member than to protect their household. He still knew that to be true. But he was also living in a house with a woman who had criminal connections, another boyfriend, and had been lying to him since their attack. He had to be prepared when he broke it off with her. Knowing she would soon be cut from his life insurance policy would surely speed up whatever timetable she and her boyfriend were working with.

He turned toward the wall, copied Violet's former stance, extended his arms, and aimed with his finger on the trigger. *Click.* He had never thought it would come to this. *Click.* He'd loved her. *Click.* But he would protect himself. *Click.* Jade wouldn't get away with murder. *Click. Click. Click.*

"Look at Scarface!" Violet chuckled.

Greg turned toward his daughter. He wasn't wearing a hat so the scar atop his spiky-haired head was visible in all its red, raised glory. The thought made him self-conscious enough without her rubbing it in.

"Sorry, too soon? I didn't say Scarhead." She stifled another chuckle by clearing her throat. "Don't dry-fire it too much; apparently it can damage the gun."

Greg dry-fired the Glock one last time and then fit it back into the gun-shaped hole in the foam. He closed the case and turned the dials of the combination lock, hiding the code.

"So." Violet clapped him on his shooting arm. "After all that, I'd say you owe me breakfast."

Greg told Violet that he'd take her to a pancake place in town. As she listed all the "far superior brunch spots" in Greenwich, he heard a soft ding from his computer. He rounded the desk and woke up the sleeping monitor. An alert obscured the full-screen image of the front lawn: *Motion Detected!*

He clicked on the warning. The image of the silent street was replaced by a view of the foyer. Jade headed down the stairs. She was dressed to seduce in a pretty white outfit that showed off her sculpted legs and a touch of cleavage. Her hair had been washed and fell in natural curls over her exposed shoulders. Greg couldn't tell exactly if she'd applied makeup, but her lips appeared full and shiny, and her skin was flawless.

"Jade's up and dressed."

Greg switched to the grid view as Jade walked into the vestibule and toward the kitchen.

"Let's go. Before she realizes we're here."

The idea of running from Jade's presence made Greg want to unlock the gun case. This was his home. He'd owned it before his fiancée had ever been in the picture. He'd invited her to share it with him because she'd tricked him into believing that she'd be a loving wife and mother. She'd never filled either role. She wasn't getting the house.

"No. We're not hiding from her."

"You're not going to threaten her with me here? If something happens, I don't want—"

"I'm not going to order her from the house at gunpoint at the moment." He intended to confront Jade later, after Violet had left and he could speak freely about the affair. He'd told Violet only that Jade had been lying about her whereabouts and that he wanted out of the relationship. Suggesting to his daughter that his girlfriend might have wanted to kill him for his money was somehow less humiliating than admitting Jade had been sleeping around. "But I am going to make clear that she's not invited to breakfast."

He strode through the house toward the kitchen. Violet followed close behind, seemingly eager for the confrontation now that she'd resigned herself to one. By the time they'd crossed through the dining room and entered the kitchen, his daughter was at his side.

Jade stood at the range with her back to them. From the sweet smell wafting from the stove, Greg guessed she was melting butter for eggs.

"Good morning." Violet's tone made clear that there was nothing good about it.

Jade spun to face them. Her palm pressed between her breasts. "Oh. Violet. I didn't realize you were coming over." Her dark eyes zeroed in on Greg for an explanation—as if he owed her anything.

"I came for breakfast," Violet volunteered.

Jade smiled. The expression was clearly fake, a tic of her

mouth muscles triggered by a pathological need for polite-ness. Greg wondered whether Jade's smiles had always been like that and he was only now noticing.

"I'm cooking eggs and would be happy to make some more," Jade said.

Violet rolled her eyes in Greg's direction. "I don't really trust your food."

Jade's eyes narrowed. She put her hands on her hips, a sitcom mom about to admonish a rambunctious child. "I know that the *ethnic* dishes I cook for your father aren't what you're used to, Violet. But that doesn't mean they're not good or are poisonous. Besides, I'm making these hard-scrambled. American-style."

Violet turned to face Greg. "I wouldn't eat anything from her."

Jade stepped toward Violet, perhaps emboldened because she was being disrespected in what she considered to be her home. "You know, I don't understand why you feel the need to be so rude to me. I'd get it if I was a homewrecker who'd broken up your parents' marriage. I'd accept you being nasty. Maybe I'd deserve it. But I didn't do—"

"Are you kidding me?" Violet threw up her hands as she yelled the question. "How can you stand there and play innocent? Are you some kind of sociopath?"

Jade blinked rapid-fire. "What? I am not a cheat. I met your dad—"

"Just remember, the past won't be forgotten."

Smoke rose from the pan atop the stove. Greg hurried to the range as Jade continued to stand there, a look of horror on her face.

"There won't be any forgiveness for what you did," Violet continued. "I'll keep going to the—"

"We can't burn down the house." Greg nudged Jade out of the way and shut off the burner. A haze filled the room. Any more smoke and the detectors would surely have gone off.

Jade faced him with her mouth still open, a fish shocked to be yanked from the water after nabbing its meal. She turned back toward Violet. "Wait. It was you."

Jade stormed over to the counter. For a petrifying second, Greg thought she was headed for the knife block. He was about to shout for Violet to run when he saw Jade grab her purse. She pulled out a square piece of paper. "Violet sent me this." She waved what was perhaps a Polaroid, a lawyer brandishing an exhibit for the jury.

"This is our sonogram. It had gone missing after the attack and then was mailed back to me with a message." She shot Violet a hateful stare. "She wrote that some people shouldn't keep breeding."

"What?" Violet's surprise was different from Jade's faked emotion. His daughter looked genuinely flabbergasted.

Jade shoved the photo at Greg, demanding he take it. It was a printout of an ultrasound, as Jade had said. In the center was the blurry white image of a baby floating in a black void.

"Flip it," Jade instructed.

Greg turned the image over. In red ink was the message to which Jade had referred. The handwriting was spiky and in all caps. Greg remembered Violet's youthful handwriting, a tight cursive that had tested the reader's resolve. This writing was not like that.

"She meant you," Jade continued. "Violet doesn't want you to keep having children and diluting her share of your fortune."

"You're the one after my father's money," Violet shouted. "You're the one lying—"

"You got this in the mail?" Greg interrupted.

"This was the second one. The first said the past can't be forgotten, exactly what Violet just said." Jade faced his daughter a second time. "Who did you get to kill the baby? A boyfriend? A couple of guys from town? Did you mean to nearly kill your father, too, or was that an accident?"

"You're insane," Violet shouted. Horror widened her eyes into a cartoon character's. "Dad, she's making all this up. The most I have ever done is write a few snarky comments on her ridiculous blog posts. I've never mailed her anything."

"Please, Greg." Jade's voice cracked. "You have to believe me. I didn't want to tell you about the messages because you were healing, but she's been sending them. The police have the first one."

Violet aimed her finger at Jade's chest. "You probably wrote them yourself to garner sympathy or to try and drive a wedge between me and my father so you could continue to manipulate him."

Greg closed his eyes and reminded himself that the shortest distance between two points was a straight line. Jade was a proven liar and cheat. It wasn't an illogical leap to assume that even if there were letters, she'd written them in hopes of deflecting police suspicion that she'd had anything to do with his attack.

He placed the ultrasound picture on the counter and

turned away from it. The baby, if there had ever been one, probably hadn't even been his. "I'm taking my daughter out to breakfast," he said.

Jade covered her mouth with both hands, playing the role of the wronged woman. After a beat, she snatched the photo and her purse from the counter. "Do whatever you want. I'm going to the cops."

The door slam shook the house. Greg caught Violet's wince at the sound. She looked up at him, blue eyes like proverbial saucers. "She's crazy, Daddy. I mean certi-freakin'-fiable." Violet mashed her lips together. "There's a cartridge in the case with fifteen 9-millimeter bullets. You should load the gun."

CHAPTER 26

Jade peeled out of the driveway with the SUV's windows all the way up. In the privacy of her car, she shouted every obscenity that she knew. She cursed in both American English and Jamaican Patois, combining the dialects to create new epithets. "Ras asshole! Bumba bitch!" She said things that would have earned her a beating as a child. Words outlawed in her mother's home country.

Fury weighed down her foot on the gas. Twelve minutes after storming from the house, she was marching up the steps to the local police station. As before, she announced her name and case number to the desk officer, handed over her "evidence" through a retractable glass partition, and then followed him to the interview rooms.

The comfortable room must have been in use. Jade waited for the detectives in a space akin to the interrogation rooms she'd seen on police television shows. Gray walls met gray floor tiles. A table was wedged between two plastic chairs. The furniture appeared bolted to the ground.

After twenty minutes, a door retracted with a loud click, revealing that Jade had unknowingly been locked inside. Detective Ricci entered first, followed by McCrory. As was the case the first time they'd talked, Ricci took the seat while McCrory manned the door.

"So, you get this second note nearly two weeks ago." Ricci set a manila folder on the tabletop and opened it. Both messages sat inside clear plastic sheaths, along with their respective envelopes. "Yet you don't let us know about it until now."

Ricci's demeanor seemed different than at their prior meeting. Gone was the sympathetic smile and concerned eyes. The woman sitting across from her had a tight jaw, emphasized by a downturned mouth. She pushed the plastic envelope containing the sonogram picture across to Jade, like she was passing exhibits to a defendant.

"I thought Bernal had sent it," Jade explained. "I knew you didn't, so I figured what was the point in telling you?"

Ricci placed an elbow on the table. She propped her forehead against her spread fingers. "As I've said, we talked to Mr. Bernal. He didn't—"

"I know." Jade flashed both palms in surrender and then folded her hands atop the table. "You were right. I spoke with him."

The detective raised her head. It occurred to Jade that Ricci had been braced for her to accuse Bernal again. "Good."

Jade took a deep breath. "I know who did it now."

A cough erupted by the door. Ricci shot McCrory an admonishing look. She turned back to Jade with a sigh and then positioned the first encased note near the second, as if adding a suspect to a lineup. "Who would write these, Jade?"

Though Jade had both messages memorized, she read them afresh, trying to view each from Violet's perspective rather than that of a man whose child had been killed by her father.

NOW YOU KNOW HOW IT FEELS. THE PAST CAN'T BE FORGOTTEN.
SOME PEOPLE SHOULDN'T KEEP BREEDING.

The first note easily fit with Violet's well-known feelings. Greg's daughter believed that her dad was abandoning his former family for his younger wife, *forgetting the past*. She wanted Jade to know that neither she nor her mother would be relegated to the background. The second note was a justification for killing their baby. In Violet's mind, Greg had birthed two kids. He wasn't allowed any more. If Jade wanted children, she should find another man.

"It's Violet, Greg's daughter." Jade stared into Ricci's dark eyes, trying to detect some reaction to her big reveal. The detective's expression betrayed nothing but fatigue. "She doesn't want us to get married because any kids that we have will share in Greg's estate, meaning less money for her," Jade continued. "Violet must have paid someone to break in and attack me, hoping I'd lose the baby."

McCrory stepped farther into the room. "But your assailants stole your engagement ring."

"Maybe that was a cover." Jade tossed up a hand. "Or it was how they got paid."

For the second time, Ricci looked over her shoulder at her partner. Some silent signal passed between the two of them.

She turned her attention back to Jade. "We have a couple of other theories."

Ricci leaned forward across the table, reducing the distance between them to a nearly intimate level. "What happened to you and your fiancé was horrible. Anyone going through that could be expected to have some PTSD. You must feel scared. Threatened. You probably can't sleep. You want to make sure the police are protecting you and Greg, that we're keeping your case at the top of the pile even as it grows colder. Fear makes people act out of character. I understand."

Jade heard the accusation in Ricci's *understanding*. "You think I wrote these?"

"I think that you're feeling vulnerable and neglected."

Jade vibrated with indignation and, she realized, a small measure of guilt. Her keeping the second note quiet had made the detectives believe she didn't view the messages as real threats. That had them thinking she'd penned them herself.

"I did *not* do this." Jade raised her voice on the operative word. Her heart was hammering inside her chest, demanding that she either run from the police station or defend herself. "You have to believe me."

Ricci nodded. The head movement didn't convey agreement as much as condescension. It was the nod people gave a crazy person who wasn't making sense.

Jade searched her brain for some evidence that could prove she hadn't written the messages. A handwriting test? Did real police officers even do those, or was it something only for TV shows? Would her recorded conversation with Bernal work?

She decided that the recording wouldn't help. It would only prove that she'd accused someone with little evidence—

after being told by the cops that he hadn't done anything—
and then illegally videotaped their meeting. If only there was
video of the mail...

But there was! Jade began rifling through her purse for her
cell. "You can check the security tapes for this last message.
I think the app saves clips for a month." Jade pulled out
her phone and clicked on the program's icon. She selected
the street-facing outdoor camera. "I'd gone to see my father
that day. When I got back, the sonogram was in a stamped
envelope tucked into a magazine. It was with the rest of the
mail. I'm sure we'll see the carrier drop it off."

McCrory made a throat-clearing noise. "If the letter even
made it through the post office. The last one didn't."

Jade ignored his quip. She clicked on the correct date and
began scrolling through the day's events in reverse. "Okay. So
here I am returning home and here is... Wait a second."

There, standing at her mailbox, was Violet. Jade dragged
the cursor back through the timeline and then double-clicked
to play the video, angling the screen so that both she and
Ricci could watch. A Mercedes pulled up in front of the
house. Violet exited the driver's-side door, carrying a bag.
She stopped, suddenly, at the mailbox beside the curb. Her
head turned over her shoulder to examine the street and then
rotated toward the house. Apparently seeing no one, she
pulled open the lid and shoved her hand inside.

"See." Jade rewound the video a second time and passed
the phone to Ricci. "There she is, slipping in the note."

Ricci squinted at the screen. "I don't know if I see anything in her hand before she gets the mail. The image is
too small."

"You can zoom in." Jade reached over Ricci's shoulder to touch her cell screen. She pinched her fingers together and separated them, demonstrating the enlarging technique.

Ricci held the phone close to her face, as if she were near-sighted. She shook her head. "It's still too tiny. Her hands are the size of a few pixels."

Jade reached for her phone. She stared at the blurry image of Violet. Ricci was right. The image was too minuscule to discern what—if anything—was in Violet's right hand. Greg would have gone blind staring at such small thumbnails. It was no wonder he watched mostly on his desktop.

"You can bring up the same security app on a computer screen," Jade said. "Greg always watches the footage on his office monitor. You probably just need to log in as me or something."

Ricci gave McCrory another meaningful look that couldn't be translated by Jade. "Okay." She reached into her blazer and withdrew a notebook from an interior pocket. "Why don't you give us your log-in info?" Her hand ducked back into the jacket, reemerging with a pen. "We'll check it out."

Jade considered the app on her screen. She was sure that the user name was Greg's email. However, the passcode was more difficult to guess. Jade was tempted to call Greg and ask, but she couldn't imagine him handing over the code with Violet around. His daughter would convince him that she wanted it only for some nefarious reason. He probably wouldn't even answer the phone.

"I need to figure it out first."

Ricci visibly stiffened. The detective had her preferred theory: The victim was sending the messages to herself to

keep the case at the forefront and was now throwing a hated
stepchild-to-be under the bus in order to cover her misdeeds.
In Ricci's version of the story, Jade was the wicked queen.
Violet was Snow White.

Jade logged out of the app. Moments later, she entered
Greg's email in the username field. For the password, she
typed his birth date. The phone vibrated in her hand. Apparently, wrong guesses elicited a buzz. She shot Ricci a sheepish
look. "Greg has a few codes that he uses all the time. I'm sure
it's one of them."

Jade could feel her audience losing patience. Neither the
detectives nor the app would allow her several failed attempts.
The code to the house's locks was a date, Jade knew. It wasn't
Greg's birthday or something romantic like the anniversary
of their meeting. The year was '01. December 8, 2001, to be
exact. Paul's birthday, probably. The math was right for it.

She tried the numbers. The security application opened.
Jade nearly groaned with relief. She rattled off the passcode
to Ricci.

"Just look at the footage." Jade stood from the table. "You'll
see I didn't do this. It's all Violet. She wants me out of the
picture—maybe for good."

CHAPTER 27

Jade's SUV turned into the driveway. Greg tracked its advance toward the house, zooming in to reveal her in the driver's seat. As the garage door opened, he dragged his cursor back over the video's progress bar, reversing the vehicle onto the street. He then played the tape forward in slow motion, examining each frame and the changing sunlight reflecting off the vehicle's metallic paint.

He stopped the footage on a clear shot of the side window. The untinted backseats were empty. If Jade had brought company, he was hiding in the back.

Greg switched back to the grid view. The SUV was in the garage with its lights off. He enlarged the live video, revealing Jade leaned back in her seat with her eyes closed and hands pressed against the steering wheel. Greg activated the intercom. "Come inside. We need to talk."

Jade snapped to attention. She leaned over the steering wheel, turning her head sideways to eye the camera.

"I'm in the office," he continued. "Use the side door."

Greg didn't add that Jade could come in *only* through the side door. At Violet's suggestion, he'd changed the codes at the other entrances, ensuring that Jade, and whoever she might bring with her, couldn't get the jump on him. Not defending her against his daughter's verbal onslaught would have put any girlfriend on guard. He and Violet had both agreed that Jade might decide that tonight was her last chance at him before he broke things off and changed his will.

Jade exited her vehicle's driver's side. She looked directly at the camera again, as though she could see him watching through the lens. She stuck out her chin, a show of bravery or perhaps defiance. "We do need to talk, Greg."

He switched back to the grid view. His eyes darted to different camera feeds, monitoring Jade's walk toward the door while also checking for other uninvited guests. As he watched, he stroked the Glock's grip. He'd gotten over feeling disappointed with himself for the weapon. The gun was power. After everything that had happened to him, he needed to take his power back.

On-screen, Jade was nearly at the side door. Her footsteps, audible through the office's two shuttered glass walls, echoed on a nanosecond delay from the computer speakers. He lowered the gun to his side, squeezing it and his bent right arm onto the seat. The chair's plush black leather partially camouflaged what wasn't hidden by the sloping armrests on either side.

Jade entered the room, backlit by the orange glow of the sunset behind her. The strap of Greg's baseball cap became instantly damp. She hadn't been holding a weapon. He'd just seen her. But he could no longer see her clearly. She knew about the cameras. What if, like him, she'd been hiding a gun out of view?

She came into focus as she shut the door. Her empty hands dropped to just above her knees. However, a purse hung from a shoulder strap and dangled beside her ribs. What could it contain?

"Greg." Her bottom lip trembled before firming into an expression of resolve and regret. For a moment, he saw Jade as he had in the beginning: a beautiful blend of determined woman and undecided girl, ready to conquer the world but willing to be led to the battle. The contrast had drawn him to her. When they'd first started dating, he'd thought of her as an unfired clay vase, previously sculpted into a magnificent shape, though still able to be molded around the edges without chipping. In retrospect, he'd been fooled by her youth, projecting an innocence onto her that a sociopath could never have possessed.

With his left hand, Greg gestured to the kitchen chair he'd set in the room earlier, across from his desk chair yet sufficiently far away to deter physical contact. A look of resignation descended upon Jade's face at the sight. The seat was like the surprise presence of a human resources manager in a meeting with the boss. She knew what it meant.

Jade folded her arms across her chest. The barred light from the shutters colored her in stripes of light and dark. "I'd rather stand."

It was probably better that she did, Greg decided. Leaving was easier when already hovering by the door. "You're having an affair. I caught you, and I want you out of the house."

Jade tilted her head back as she shook it, simultaneously

saying no and appealing to a higher power. "I am NOT having an affair, Greg. Violet is filling your head with nonsense."

Calling his daughter a liar when denying the truth to his face took gall. But then he knew Jade had it. She was a cheater—possibly an attempted murderer.

He rubbed his thumb against the Glock's rough grip. "I saw him, Jade. Yesterday, when you were *thinking* at the coffee shop, you met with him and talked. You embraced him. You probably would have done more if you hadn't been in public."

Jade's mouth dropped open. "But how?" She seemed to realize the answer before the question fully left her lips. "The drone."

"I followed you with it. You were acting odd. I suspected that you were using the D&D Building as an excuse to keep me in the dark about something, again."

"Greg, you don't understand. That meeting was about my father."

Her father was Jade's excuse for everything. If her hired murderers had killed him, Greg supposed Jade would have sent the cops in the poor man's direction. Or perhaps her convict father had orchestrated the whole thing, directing his seductress daughter from prison.

"I am not having an affair," Jade continued. "I'm absolutely not. I love you. I've loved you since—"

"Liar!" Greg curled his fingers around the weapon.

Jade wiped beneath her eyes. If she was crying, Greg couldn't see the tears.

"You're right. I wasn't completely honest with you when I said my dad was serving time for drugs. It's more complicated than that." She sucked in a breath and then let it out in a rush, like the air had been knocked out of her. "When he was dealing, he got involved in a shoot-out. A young boy was killed in the cross fire. That man I met was the boy's father."

Lies were usually kept to simple denials or one-sentence explanations, such as *I unexpectedly ran into an old family friend*. Jade's tale seemed too elaborate and nonsensical to be completely false. But she might have known he'd think that. She'd had all day to make up the perfect story to sucker him in.

"Why would you meet with the victim's father?"

Jade sniffed. "For years, he'd sent my family threatening letters. With my father getting out, I'd thought maybe he was responsible for the new messages and our attack. The police didn't believe he'd had anything to do with it, though, so I asked to meet with him in hopes of getting a confession. It was stupid. But I was scared he wasn't done with us."

Greg felt tears building behind his eyes. The desperation on Jade's face, coupled with her detailed explanation, was drawing him in, giving him hope that she might actually love him and that everything had been a misunderstanding. But *everything* could not be a misunderstanding. What had happened to him had been a calculated, deliberate act—the kind committed by an accomplished liar.

"You want me to believe that you embraced the man sending you threats?"

Jade pressed her palms together as if praying. "The police were right. He hadn't sent them. He's moved on and forgiven my family. That's why we hugged. I was grateful. You can ask the cops. Detective Ricci, the female officer you met in the hospital, she put me in touch with him."

Greg's hand loosened on the hidden gun. Surely, Jade wouldn't urge him to verify her story with the police if she were lying. "But if you're not cheating, why wouldn't you tell me you were meeting this guy? Why wouldn't you have explained all this before?"

Jade chewed her bottom lip. "You were sick. I—"

"No!" His anger exploded. He would not let her use him as an excuse. Lies were not told to protect anyone other than the liar. "You knew how upset I'd been after finding out about your first *omission*, and yet you continued to hide things from me."

She made a tortured noise, somewhere between a whispered scream and an anguished groan. Perhaps to keep from repeating the sound, she covered her face with both hands and shook her head, arguing with herself about something. Finally, she let her arms fall to her sides.

"When you walk into a room, Greg, people see you. They look at the way you carry yourself, they listen to you speak, they watch your actions, and *then* they form opinions. When I walk into a room, it's different. Folks make immediate assumptions, negative assumptions, at a glance. Take your kids. Violet can't look at me without seeing a gold digger. And what have I done to earn that opinion? I don't ask you to buy me expensive things. I didn't quit my job when I got pregnant." Jade gestured as she spoke, alternately begging with folded hands or throwing her arms up in frustration. "Every day, I am fighting to be seen and judged for my actions—not for my race, or my gender, or my youth, or, least of all, my father. When we met, I felt that you saw me. You recognized my interests and desires and talents. And I wanted you to continue to see me that way.

"After everything that happened, I feared that knowing I was a convict's daughter would distort your view of me forever. You'd stop looking at me as a hardworking, dedicated woman who loves art and culture and wants to explore this world with you—to have this big, full life with you—and you'd start seeing me as an extension of my father's violence."

Jade's shoulders shuddered. Seeing her cry, Greg wanted to hold her, tell her he understood, promise that they could move past all the deceit and mistrust that had driven them apart these past few months. But he knew he had to fight that instinct. Jade was using her race and youth to make him feel guilty for his family's legitimate suspicions about her. His legitimate distrust.

"How can I believe you?"

"I have something." Jade pulled her purse in front of her chest like a bulletproof vest. She reached into the bag.

Greg jumped from his chair. "Wait."

Jade stumbled back. Unspent tears froze in her eyes. She was holding her cell phone.

"Why do you have that?" Her voice trembled.

He was pointing the gun directly at her, Greg realized. Some combination of fear and self-preservation had made him raise the weapon.

"Did Violet give that to you?" Jade asked. "The guys she hired didn't finish the job, so she's convinced you to do it?"

Jade's accusation stopped Greg from lowering the weapon. His daughter loved him. She'd been trying to protect him from his girlfriend's manipulation all this time, telling him truths he'd refused to hear about what a young, beautiful Black woman really wanted from a guy like him. She'd warned him that Jade would try to turn him against his real family, make it seem that his own flesh and blood had it in for him despite Jade's being the one with criminal connections and the one caught in lie after lie.

"You're pathological." Greg wrapped his free hand around the grip, bracing himself as Violet had shown him. "First you tell me your dad's in jail for drugs, and now he's in for, what, manslaughter? Murder? Do you make this shit up on the fly?"

Jade raised her hands in a don't shoot gesture. "Greg, please." She lowered the hand with the cell. "I recorded the conversation. It's on my phone. I'm disabling the passcode." She swiped across the screen and then hit a couple of buttons. She extended the device toward him, a peace offering or maybe a white flag. "You can hear the whole conversation. You'll see that I was trying to protect us. Violet is behind all of this."

Rage shook the Glock in Greg's fist. He walked to the door, stepping sideways to keep the gun trained on Jade's torso. "I'll ship your things."

Keeping her free hand in the air, Jade slowly lowered the other to drop the phone onto the floor. "Just listen to it, please."

Greg gestured with the gun barrel. He yanked back the door. "Get out."

She didn't need to be told twice. Before he could blink, Jade was running past him into the darkening evening. He could hear her sobs over the pounding of her footsteps.

Greg stood in the doorway, hand still on the weapon, and watched the garage bay door retract. He kept holding the gun, guarding his castle, until her car disappeared down the street. Only when he was sure she wouldn't return did he close the door, press his back against it, and break down.

CHAPTER 28

The apartment smelled of corn and coconut milk. Rather than cook, Abigay had wanted to call the cops, but Jade convinced her to retreat into the kitchen. The police would only escalate the situation, encouraging her to press assault charges and make Greg pay for the violent end to their engagement. Jade didn't have the energy. She wanted only to curl up on her mother's couch and cry.

Abigay entered the living room carrying a steaming bowl of yellow cream. She passed it to Jade, apologizing for the lack of cinnamon sprinkles on top. "I was surprised I had cornmeal," Abigay said. "I haven't made this since you were a child."

Jade held the warm bowl between her hands and breathed in the sweet aroma. Her eyes welled for the umpteenth time since fleeing her home the prior night. Months earlier, she'd mused about making cornmeal porridge for her own son or daughter. She'd imagined the child's face, some blend of her and Greg's colorings and features, sitting down on a cold day to the thick, warm concoction. The ultimate comfort food.

That child would never exist. That life had been ripped away. And here she was, sitting back on her mother's couch as if all the progress she'd made in her thirty-two years had never happened.

A sharp buzz resounded in the apartment. Abigay's expression morphed from motherly to momma bear. Jade knew what she was thinking. Greg had come. Perhaps he'd listened to the recording after all and realized she'd been telling the truth. Maybe he'd even confronted his daughter and received a confession.

"It better not be," Abigay said with a sneer in her voice before marching over to the call box.

Jade rose from the couch to set her porridge on the dining table. "Momma, don't turn him away."

"I could do plenty worse than that." Abigay hit the intercom button. "What do you want?"

"Mrs. Thompson?"

Jade immediately recognized the speaker's identity. Her voice had become all too familiar. "It's the police."

Abigay again pressed the intercom. "This is she."

The ferocity vanished from her mother's tone. Abigay was now back to being the polite and proper churchgoing woman whom most would recognize as Mrs. Thompson. "And who, may I ask, is this?"

"This is Detective Ricci. I'm one of the police officers working on your daughter's case. I don't want to worry you, ma'am, but we've been trying to get in contact with Jade and she hasn't been answering her cell. She gave us access to her security cameras. We saw her leave her house yesterday in a bit of a state."

Abigay leaned into the intercom. "She's here and safe. I'm sorry to say with no thanks to you."

She'd been wrong, Jade realized. Her mother had *not* returned to her church lady persona. Though she'd toned down the attitude, Abigay was still in protective mode.

"I understand, ma'am. My partner and I would very much like to speak with her. There have been some important developments."

Abigay looked to her daughter for guidance. Jade shrugged. If she denied the detectives a chance to question her today, they'd only return in the morning. "It's all right, Momma. Better to get it over with."

Abigay's index finger hesitated above the buzzer before finally depressing the button. The speaker echoed with the sound of a door cracking open and then crashing shut. Her mother gave her a look that said she didn't agree with Jade's course of action before moving toward the apartment door.

Jade returned to the living room couch to wait for the detectives. She sat on the edge of a cushion, holding her spine rigid and away from the backrest. Part of her hoped that the cops had come to say they'd caught Violet on video delivering the note. But a larger part of her believed that they'd ventured to Brooklyn at Greg's request.

Heavy footsteps sounded outside the door. Abigay waited for the officers to knock and identify themselves before opening it. In lieu of a welcome, she crossed her arms over her chest. "My daughter has been through a lot."

Ricci murmured something in agreement. She entered first with her head bowed, as if walking into a church. McCrory followed, carrying a plastic folder.

Jade felt a flutter of hope at their deference. Maybe the cops really had come with evidence against Violet. Perhaps they were here to let her know that they intended to file charges against Greg's daughter—if not for attempted murder, then at least harassment.

"Hello, Ms. Thompson," Ricci said, focusing her attention on Jade. "As I mentioned to your mother, we've been looking at the security footage that you gave us access to. We've noticed something of interest."

"You saw Violet deliver that message?" Jade asked.

Ricci sat on the opposite couch cushion, bringing herself to Jade's level. "No. We brought up the footage on a much larger screen and even had our tech guys clean things up. It doesn't appear that she dropped anything into your mailbox."

Jade eyed Ricci warily. "I guess she mailed it then."

"We don't believe so," Ricci said.

In her peripheral vision, Jade saw her mother step closer to the armrest beside her. She reached behind her for Abigay's hand and gave it a squeeze. If the cops arrested her because of Greg's accusations, she needed her mother to remain calm.

"A car came by around 4:00 a.m. earlier that same day," McCrory said as he opened the folder. He passed Jade a plastic-encased computer printout.

The enlarged photo was a grayish green due to the security camera's night-vision setting. Even so, Jade could tell that the vehicle in front of her mailbox was dark, perhaps even black. The car was parked facing the wrong direction. A gloved hand extended out of the driver's-side window and reached into the mailbox at the curb.

"Do you recognize this vehicle at all?" Ricci asked.

Jade squinted at the front grille. Three silver rings seemed to glint in the light, three-fourths of the Audi symbol. Jade assumed there was another circle just beyond the camera's view. "I don't know anyone with an Audi."

"We were able to make out most of the plate," McCrory said. "It appears to be registered to Mr. Hamlin."

Jade felt a burst of hope. The officers didn't have definitive evidence that Violet had sent the notes. But they were getting closer. "Greg has a Tesla. I've never seen that car, but maybe it's old." She passed the photo back to McCrory. "Greg could have given it to Violet."

McCrory put the item back in the manila envelope. "Did you know that your fiancé had a life insurance policy?"

Whatever Jade had felt bubbled to the surface, fizzled and blackened, like oil left in a too-hot pan. McCrory had to be asking because of Greg's accusations. "Yeah. It's why he's convinced that I was trying to kill him." Jade snorted. "It's all nonsense. Since he's not officially divorced from Leah, his ex would have gotten half of everything off the top, including the half a million he set aside for me in his will and insurance policy. There's no way I would have even been able to keep the house with that."

Ricci made a grumbling noise. For most people, Jade realized, even a $250,000 windfall would be a life-changing amount of money. "Did you know he'd taken out a policy on you?"

Jade realized that her face must have betrayed her shock because her mom was violating all tacit rules about personal space. She'd taken a seat on the couch arm and was leaning over Jade's shoulder. Her breath steamed against Jade's neck.

"There's a two-million-dollar policy in your name," Ricci said.

"No there's not." Jade shook her head for her mother's benefit. "I'd know, wouldn't I? I would have had to have a medical exam or signed something."

"Not necessarily." Ricci's face brightened like she'd just confirmed some awful theory that had been batted around the station. "For the right premium, Mr. Hamlin could take out a policy on anyone he has a demonstrable insurable interest in—anyone whose death would cause him financial or emotional harm. You're his fiancée, and you were pregnant."

Abigay stood and raked her hands down her cheeks. Her lips were mouthing prayers—or obscenities. Jade couldn't tell.

"Greg didn't need money," Jade protested.

"Everyone can always use more money." Ricci glanced from Jade to her mother. "Mr. Hamlin's life was expensive. He had a soon-to-be ex-wife entitled to half his assets who'd already received the marital residence and was demanding hundreds of thousands in annual alimony to maintain her standard of living. He had two kids whom he was supporting, one at Harvard. He had the new house, which had cost eight hundred thousand in renovations."

"You think he set up the home invasion to hurt my daughter." Fury raised Abigay's voice.

"We don't know anything definitive," Ricci cautioned. "We're investigating. We'd like to know what Jade knew."

Jade bolted upright, matching her mother's rage, though for a different reason. The police were doing the same thing that Violet had done to her father, filling her head with suspicions. "I know Greg was nearly beaten to death."

Abigay grabbed her arm and shook it, the way she had

when Jade was young and not listening. "He could have intended for the robbers to only go after you. They might have planned to knock him out in order to deflect suspicion. Maybe one of them did it too hard."

Jade noticed McCrory's subtle nod, indicating he shared Abigay's suspicions. Jade pulled away from her mother's grip. "An insurance policy isn't proof of anything."

She tried to say it with resolve, for her mom's sake. Abigay had been upset enough when Jade described how Greg ordered her from their house at gunpoint. She didn't need her mother dwelling on how close he might have come to actually firing.

Her tone wasn't completely convincing. Jade had never been a good actress, and the truth was that she felt sick with doubts. Questions roiled in her mind and gut. Had Greg really accused her of setting up his attempted murder because he'd been hoping to claim self-defense when he killed her? And if that was his plan, why hadn't he done it? Had he simply chickened out?

She needed to lie down. Her head pounded from stress. Her chest hurt from heaving. Her eyes were sore. She felt as though she'd aged several decades in a day. Was this how Greg felt after waking most mornings? Did everything feel overwhelming to him?

She moved to the door and opened it wide. "Call me when you have something concrete, Detectives. Until then, I'd like to be left alone."

CHAPTER 29

A peach, silken something landed on the edge of the giant cardboard box beside the master bed. Greg thought it might be the outfit Jade had worn to the Four Seasons restaurant when he'd taken her on a quick jaunt to the Bahamas. She'd been complaining about the prematurely cold November, and he'd surprised her with tickets for a long weekend. He'd taken the fabric off of her in their villa, the silk ending up in a pastel pile on the floor. They'd made love by the plunge pool and then again in the hammock. Afterward, they'd looked at the stars, marveling about how many they could see without Manhattan's omnipresent light pollution. They'd mused about the importance of seeing real stars in one's life, of getting away from big cities to appreciate "God's architecture." Jade had said the latter. She had a way of phrasing things.

Violet had crumpled the fabric before tossing it in the wardrobe box. His daughter seemed determined to ship Jade's items back to her in the most disheveled state possible. The added meanness wasn't necessary, but Greg didn't feel up to stopping her. Sitting on his bed, staring into space without tearing up, was taking all his effort.

Another fabric ball, this one blue, bounced off the cardboard rim and landed inside the box. "Well, that's it!" Violet sounded triumphant. "Only hangers left, and you should keep those. You can never have too many hangers."

"Toss them in the box, Violet."

"They're felt." She poked her head from the closet. "I'll take them if you don't want them. Save me a trip to HomeGoods."

"I want her to have everything she's entitled to."

Violet stepped into the room, hands gripping her hips like she was the adult between them. "She's not *entitled* to anything. She lied about being pregnant to force you into proposing and then set up a break-in that nearly killed you. We shouldn't be mailing back her shit; we should be burning it."

Greg rubbed his hands over his face, staving off his tears. Jade had lied to him and cheated on him, so logically it followed that she might have also had something to do with the break-in. He'd accused her of as much when kicking her out. But his heart was refusing to accept the truth that his head had already absorbed.

Violet kicked the box, hard enough to create a dent, though not to break it. "She won't be able to wear any of this in prison anyway."

Greg stood and pushed down one of the cardboard flaps. "She probably won't go to prison. The police haven't found anything tying her to the crime. Unless she suddenly shows up with her engagement ring on—or with the cash equivalent in her bank account—they won't arrest her."

Violet pouted. "Well, she's not getting the fucking hangers."

The comment was meant as a joke. Greg tried to crack a smile but found he couldn't compel his facial muscles to play along. A buzzing from his phone saved him from a second attempt and potentially squeezing out a tear.

A motion alert dominated his home screen. Greg clicked on the video to see a police car pulling up to the house. A young female detective and her larger male counterpart exited the vehicle and headed up the walk.

As Greg watched the screen, Violet exited the room. He heard her hurry down the stairs. "Dad, the police are here."

Greg slowly rose from the bed and headed to the hallway. From his position on the landing, he saw Violet allow them into the foyer and then shut off the beeping alarm with the key fob he'd left by the base station. He'd deactivated Jade's old one.

The detectives were dressed like office workers rather than cops. But they each held badges up for identification.

"Why are you here?" Violet folded her arms over her chest, assuming a guarded position. She likely figured they'd come to question him about ordering Jade from the house at gunpoint.

"We're here about your father's case," the female detective answered. Greg vaguely remembered her from the hospital.

"Whose car is that out there?" the male detective asked. "The Mercedes."

"It's my ex-wife's," Greg shouted down the stairs, making clear that he would answer for Violet. God only knew what the cops thought of his daughter thanks to all Jade's lies. "She lets Violet borrow it."

"Do you have a car?" Again the female detective addressed his daughter directly.

"No. I have a motorcycle, actually. But it freaks my father out to see me on it."

Greg hustled down the last few steps, wanting to get between his daughter and the police before she could say anything else. It didn't occur to Violet that they could actually suspect her of anything and that her best course of action was to keep her mouth shut. She was a suburban kid, raised to think the cops were always on her side.

Greg inserted himself between Violet and the female officer. "What is this about, Detectives?"

The larger male officer stepped forward. "Some information has come to light in the course of our investigation, and we wanted to ask you some questions."

Greg wasn't sure he liked the way the man regarded him as he said it. The guy hadn't offered a friendly smile, or even a sympathetic one. He was used to the police looking at him like he was a victim.

He led them into the family room beside his office. It wasn't as nice as the sunroom, but it got less glare off the water in the afternoon. Glare sometimes made the security camera images less sharp. He wanted to be able to scrutinize the recording of their conversation later.

He took a seat on the chaise at the end of the couch. Violet stood beside him, arms folded across her chest. He guessed she'd sensed his lack of welcoming demeanor.

"You have a life insurance policy, yes?"

The question indicated that they were following up on Violet's suspicions about Jade. Greg sat back into the couch.

"I've had one since Violet was born. About a month before I was attacked, I amended it to include Jade and any future children with her."

"He also set aside money for Jade in his will." Violet walked around him, positioning herself closer to the standing detectives. "How much did she stand to gain, Dad?"

The detectives' stoic expressions indicated that they already knew. And they weren't impressed.

"Dad," Violet urged.

"About half a million."

The female detective pulled a notebook from inside her jacket pocket. She flipped back a few pages. "But your soon-to-be ex-wife, Leah Hamlin, is asking for half of your estate in the divorce."

"Yes."

"It's a safe assumption that Ms. Thompson wouldn't have gotten that amount," McCrory said.

Greg didn't believe in *safe assumptions* anymore. "That's for the lawyers to figure out. I was only making sure that if anything happened to me before the divorce was finalized, Jade and the baby would be taken care of." He glanced at Violet. "I didn't want her to be forced to take your sibling and move into some apartment in a bad area."

"And Ms. Thompson knew the terms of your will and life insurance policy?" McCrory asked.

"Sure."

"Did she also know about the life insurance policy you'd taken out on her?"

The temperature in the room changed. Whereas before the air had felt warm, even muggy, it now felt cool and charged. Goose bumps emerged on Greg's forearms. "I probably mentioned it."

"Really?" Ricci's exaggerated surprise reminded him of Violet playing dumb as a kid. "I spoke with Ms. Thompson earlier. She said she didn't know anything about the two million you'd taken out on her."

Violet, always the protector, sidestepped closer to him. "I knew about it. My father mentioned it in the hospital after he woke from his coma. I told him putting Jade into the will a month before he was nearly killed couldn't be a coincidence. But he said that they'd both been getting their financial houses in order for the baby."

Ricci pursed her lips and nodded in another over-the-top display. This one conveyed doubt through pretend agreement.

"When I amended my life insurance policy, my financial adviser suggested that I also take one out on Jade."

"In case your healthy, thirty-two-year-old wife suddenly died?" Ricci's tone underscored the irony of her question.

"Yes. In case of a freak accident or tragedy that left me a single father of a young child. That's what insurance is for." Greg glanced at Violet. He wished he could send her from the room for what he needed to say next, but he knew asking her to leave would only increase her resolve to stay. "It was also a way to keep more of my money. It was a whole-life plan. I pay into it, it accrues interest, and that interest can't be taxed by the government. The eventual payout isn't taxed either."

McCrory's brow furrowed. "But it only pays when Jade dies."

Greg gave him a hard look. He knew when he was being accused of something. "As my financial adviser explained it, you can borrow against the value of the plan. If I needed to, I could take out a two-million-dollar loan and use the policy as collateral. The bank would get paid back in the end, whenever that *naturally* occurred."

McCrory crossed his arms over his chest. "So you're saying it was *just* a tax shelter..."

"He was trying to keep money from my mom." Disgust curled the edges of Violet's mouth. As Greg feared, his daughter had not only followed along with his financial lesson, but she'd also successfully read between the lines. While the policy did shield money from Uncle Sam, its main purpose had been to limit the assets that Leah could claim as communal property. His ex would have had a difficult time arguing that she was entitled to a life insurance policy for his new wife—even if it had been bought with money he'd earned while they were married.

"I was only following financial advice."

"I bet you were." Violet pivoted toward the foyer. "If you'll excuse me, Detectives. I should get back home."

She stepped around McCrory's broad figure, like he was a column or a half wall and not a person clearly trying to make eye contact with her. When Violet was upset, she put on blinders. "One more thing, Ms. Hamlin," McCrory called after her. "Do you ever drive an Audi?"

"No." Violet maintained her march to the door, too angry to find anything suspicious in the question.

Greg, however, understood that the vehicle was important. They'd asked Violet what she usually drove earlier. "What is this about an Audi?"

McCrory ignored the question. "Ms. Hamlin." He jogged

into the neighboring room as Violet collected a light jacket that was half hanging off the entry table. "Does your mother drive an Audi?"

Violet slipped her arms into the jacket sleeves. "No. The Audi was my dad's old car. It's not even here."

"Where is it?"

Greg wasn't positive where the detective was going with his line of questioning, but he gathered it was nowhere that he wanted to end up. He stood from the couch. "Don't answer that, Violet."

Violet's eyes widened beneath their heavy kohl lids. Her red lips pressed together. Though she might not like what her father had done, she knew better than to try to stick it to him by disobeying a direct order in his emergency tone. All parents had some combination of volume and pitch that made their kids immediately understand that what was being asked wasn't subject to debate.

McCrory looked at Greg with a terse expression. "It's related to your case."

"I understand that," Greg snapped. "I also understand that your questions today haven't been so much about finding the men who bashed in my head as they've been about uncovering motives that I might have to hurt my loved ones."

"Mr. Hamlin." Ricci took a step toward him. The sympathy was back in her pained smile. "This is about finding the men who hurt you *and your fiancée*. It's about the notes in your mailbox, addressed to Jade."

Violet transferred the furious look she'd given Greg earlier to McCrory. "The letters she accused me of writing that she probably wrote herself."

"We're trying to determine who wrote them and if they are at all related to the break-in." Ricci rotated back to face Greg. "Ms. Thompson had asked that we refrain from telling you until you'd finished with your surgery and would be more up to hearing the news."

. The confirmation surprised Greg. He'd been listening to Violet's opinions on Jade for so long that he'd begun interpreting them as facts. He recalled what Jade had said the prior night before leaving her phone with her supposed proof. He'd refused to listen to any recording lest he be taken in by more lies.

"Did she believe the messages were related to her father?" Greg asked. "And you put her in touch with someone?"

Ricci's sympathetic expression reverted to suspicion. "Yes. A Mr. Carlos Bernal. She told you the story?"

Greg ignored Ricci's incredulous look. He wasn't about to explain the gun-wielding altercation that had forced Jade to spill the details. "And you talked to this guy?" he asked.

"Yes . . ."

"Is he about my age? Dark hair. Gray beard. Fit."

"That sounds like him." Ricci's eyes narrowed. "Have you met him?"

Greg's stomach dropped into his bowels. Jade had been telling the truth. All that time when she'd been pleading with him to listen, she'd been speaking honestly—and he'd been waving a gun.

"When is Ms. Thompson coming back from her mother's?"

The question, or maybe the lines between Ricci's brow as she asked, made Greg think she already suspected the answer. Her curiosity about Jade's life insurance policy indicated that they considered him a suspect in his own beating. He wasn't about to give them more reason to doubt his intentions.

"I think you should leave now, Detectives." Greg pointed to the exit. "Violet, let them out."

Violet didn't hesitate. She opened the door, giving both officers a taste of their own glares on their way out. After she slammed it behind them, she turned her piercing stare back on its original target. "What was that about?"

"I'm not sure," Greg said. "I need to talk to Jade."

CHAPTER 30

"I didn't tell you, Jade? Nuh ev'ryting soak up wata a sponge. Wha mi seh? Oily tung nuh mus tell di truth. Nuh all roof a shelta." Abigay was so angry that she'd switched from biblical proverbs to ones in Patois. She paced back and forth in front of the living room couch, exclaiming in dialect about not believing everything people say and falling for Greg's sweet words and professions of love.

Jade could do little but nod in agreement. Her fiancé had put a secret two-million-dollar bounty on her head. As much as she wanted to excuse his actions, she couldn't fathom why he'd have done such a thing—unless her mother was right. Greg had never really loved her. Struggling under the weight of his debts to his ex-wife and wanting to maintain his social status, he'd decided to seduce a young woman capable of qualifying for a hefty life insurance policy. He'd always planned to kill her. Thanks to some miracle—no doubt brought about by her mother's constant prayer—the men Greg had hired to murder her and make it look like a home invasion had hit him too hard. Knowing they wouldn't be paid by a dead man, the thugs had taken her ring and aborted the rest of the job.

Though she could wrap her head around the theory's logic, her heart still refused to embrace it. She knew how Greg had looked at her. How he'd held her. How he'd made love to her. How could he fake all those emotions? And for months?

And if her death had been the end game of their relationship, then why hadn't he killed her in his home office the prior night—or any of the other million times they'd been together, without witnesses, in the house? Surely, he could have invented a believable story for shooting her. He'd thought she was an intruder perhaps. Or, she'd tried to attack him, forcing him to fire in self-defense.

The questions rattled around Jade's brain—the hope left in Pandora's box after all the demons had been released to rage. "He could have just killed me." She whispered the words. "Why wouldn't he have killed me?"

"Because life insurance policies don't pay out to murderers, Jade."

Abigay believed that hard truths were blessings. Better to see people for who they were and react accordingly than to romanticize them. Though Jade could understand how her mother had come to live by that philosophy, the matter-of-fact explanation still felt cruel.

Jade rose from the couch. "I need to lie down." She announced her intention as if lying down hadn't been what she'd been up to for most of the afternoon. "I'm going to your room."

Before Jade made it more than two steps into the hallway, the buzzer sounded in the apartment. A visitor was downstairs, waiting to be let into the building. "You expecting anyone?" Abigay shouted.

Save for her mother, Jade still hadn't revealed the breakup to anyone. The only people who would expect her to be at Abigay's apartment were the police and Greg—and the police had been there earlier. "No, are you?"

Her mother's frown conveyed the answer. Jade strode over to the window and pulled back the curtain. From her position on the third floor, she could see the man loitering by the exterior buzzer. He appeared to have a gray buzz cut. "It's Greg."

"Oh dear Jesus. Should I call the police?" Abigay headed to the call box. "I'll send him away."

"Don't!" Jade surprised herself with the blurted command. Detective Ricci suspected that her fiancé had been trying to murder her. Yet, now that Greg was outside, Jade didn't want him to leave.

"He's not coming in here," Abigay said.

"I'll go down."

"Jade, have you lost your head?"

"I need to talk to him, Momma. I need to know the truth."

Abigay gestured toward the window like she wished to break it. "You think you'll get the truth from that man? He'll lie."

"Maybe. But I'll know. I'll see it in his eyes."

"You didn't see the two million dancing in his eyes before."

Abigay had a point, but Jade wouldn't concede it. Rational or not, she had to find out what Greg wanted and why he'd taken out that life insurance policy. She had to ask for herself whether their whole relationship had been a fraud.

She moved past her mother toward the door. Abigay stopped her before she could walk through it. She pushed it shut with her thick bicep, nearly taking off Jade's index finger. "Don't be foolish."

"If yuh bawn fi heng, yuh cyaan drown, Momma." Jade spoke the proverb in her mother's flat accent. *If you're born to hang, you can't drown.* The meaning of the saying was one that only Abigay subscribed to: A person's destiny could not be escaped. If Greg was meant to kill her, it would happen whether she spoke with him or not.

Abigay's jaw tightened. She didn't like having her belief in predestination used against her. Still, she couldn't battle the logic without embracing hypocrisy. And her mother prided herself on her uncompromising beliefs.

"Well, I'm coming too." Abigay's eyes burned like coal briquettes. Jade realized that anyone could kill with the right provocation, even a God-fearing woman. "Let him try me."

Abigay pulled back the door like she wanted to snatch it off its hinges. She led the way to the elevator bank. As they waited for the car to rise to the third floor, Jade realized she didn't want her mother's domineering presence dictating the conversation. There were some questions she needed to pose without Greg answering for Abigay's benefit.

"I'm going to take the stairs."

Before Abigay could stop her, Jade was through the stairwell door and sprinting down the steps. Her mother, formidable as she was, couldn't descend with the same speed. Years of hoisting patients onto operating tables had ruined her knees.

Jade burst from the stairwell into the bright sunshine. The

day was warm, the kind of late May weather that belonged in mid-June. The oversized sweatshirt Jade had borrowed from her mother was too heavy for the temperature. But she didn't dare remove it, despite wearing a tank from her teenage years that she'd unearthed in her old closet. The added layer was for protection as much as it was for warmth. It hid her body, providing a barrier against Greg's reach.

He seemed not to recognize her in her mother's clothing. Though he'd turned toward the sound of the door opening, he hadn't yet approached where she stood. Instead, he blinked in her direction, as if unsure whether she was the same woman to whom he'd proposed a few months earlier—the same woman he'd ejected from their home at gunpoint.

"Jade?" He finally stepped toward her. Without the Harvard cap hiding his buzzed head, he looked gray and gaunt. Old. Too old for her, Jade told herself. And yet he had the same ice-blue eyes that had made her melt.

"What do you want?"

"I talked to that detective." He held out his hand. Her cell lay in his palm. "And I heard the video. You were telling the truth."

She plucked the phone from his grasp, careful not to let her fingers graze his own, to feel the warmth of his touch. "That's not news to me."

"I'm sorry." Greg's body rounded, as if the apology itself was a blow. "I am so sorry."

The building's front doors banged open. Abigay approached like a bull, head down, eyes ablaze. "What do you want with my daughter, Gregory?"

Typically, her mother's accent was muted around non–West

Indians. But she was too upset to maintain the British accent of her schooling.

"I'm sorry, Abigay. I was confused. I'm sorry."

"You sorry? Fi wha? Kicking her out her home? Threatening her with a gun? Trying to kill her?"

Abigay's shouts alerted several women in the neighboring playground. They turned their attention from the elementary schoolers in their care to where the three of them stood in the courtyard, arranged like an acute triangle. Her mother stood at the sharpest angle to the strange man in their midst.

Greg raised his hands as though Abigay had a weapon other than her words. "It was never loaded." He rotated to Jade. "It was never loaded, I swear. I thought you and that man were working together. I believed you might attack if—"

"You thought she would attack you? When you were the one with two million to gain?"

Greg's face, already drawn, fell further. Jade saw recognition in the defeated expression. He knew *exactly* what her mom was talking about.

"The detectives called," Jade said. "I know you took out a life insurance policy on me."

Greg glanced over his shoulder at the wary people in the playground. In addition to the women, they'd gained the attention of a few young men on the basketball court, and they did not look pleased with Greg's presence. He took another step toward her. "It's not what they think, Jade." He lowered his voice, apparently wary of attracting more eyes. "I was getting things ready for the baby. I added you to my policy and then took out one for you. It's what you do when you're having a kid."

"Then why didn't you tell me?"

"I must have said something."

He glanced away. The broken eye contact lasted only a nanosecond, but it was long enough for Jade to realize he was lying. Greg knew that he'd never discussed any insurance policy with her.

"I think I'd remember a two-million-dollar price on my head!" she yelled, not caring about the onlookers. In fact, she wanted to court them. If Greg tried anything, it would be his word against that of multiple unrelated witnesses. Even his money and status wouldn't stand up against the statements of so many strangers.

"The policy accrues that amount in interest over time, and then we can borrow against it. Tax-free." Greg rubbed a hand over his mouth, perhaps trying to keep himself from revealing anything else. He let it drop with a heavy sigh. "It was just a way to set aside money that Leah couldn't claim in the divorce proceedings. If I didn't mention it . . ."

"You didn't mention it."

"It was because I didn't want to explain why I needed to put away our savings in such a strange way and end up in a complicated discussion of how much money my ex was after. I didn't want you thinking that I was stingy or that my finances were a problem—"

"But they are?"

"Not really. And definitely *not* after I secure that Brooklyn building. The bonus on that will have me back at the top of my game, and Leah's not entitled to any of it."

The emotion that had fueled Jade's furious descent down the stairs was fading. She wasn't certain whether she believed Greg or not. But she didn't burn with a desire to know the truth anymore. Sadness had replaced her anger. Sadness and shame. It wasn't only Violet who'd assumed she was a gold digger. Greg himself had believed she wouldn't love him if not for his wealth.

"I never cared about your money." Jade's voice broke as she said it. God, she was exhausted from all the fighting to be seen for who she was.

Abigay must have sensed her weakening. She strode over and draped a protective arm around her shoulder. "No, honey. *He* cared about the money."

"Please, Jade. You can't really believe I would have hurt you."

"No? She can't? You accused her of trying to have you killed." Abigay wasn't screaming anymore, but she didn't need to raise her voice to keep the crowd's focus. The whole group in the playground had moved toward the gates in order to better view their performance.

"I was confused. Hurt. Afraid. It was all too much for me to process. And then Violet was in my ear about a younger woman only wanting me for my money. I find out you're visiting a prison. That story about your dad..."

"I heard a story, too, Gregory." Abigay stepped in front of her daughter. "I heard that the car sending my child those hateful messages was registered to you. You've been trying to drive her crazy."

Greg's mouth opened in a "pained O" like Abigay had delivered a punch to his solar plexus. "The Audi?"

"Don't act as if you don't know it."

"I left that car with Leah."

The name was a slap, but not one intended to hurt, a cheek smack intended to wake someone up. It was so obvious, Jade realized. Violet hadn't delivered the messages or been involved with the attack. Greg's ex had been trying to send her running! Leah probably wanted another shot with her ex-husband. At the very least, she wanted to keep her children's stake in their father's assets from being diluted. All this time, Leah had possessed the strongest motivation to hurt anyone: protecting her children.

"She was writing those letters," Jade said.

"No. She's not like that." Greg shook his head for emphasis. "Leah wouldn't have had anything to do with this. She wouldn't hurt me."

The statement felt like a stab in Jade's back. Until that moment, she'd been considering forgiving Greg, in spite of everything he'd done. Yet, here he was, coming to his ex-wife's defense when he'd never come to her own. "Of course, *she* wouldn't. Not the perfect blond Brahmin after all your money. But me, on the other hand, obviously I'd be guilty, right?"

"Jade, please. I didn't mean it that way. It's just that Leah wouldn't have." He sighed. "I can fix this. I promise."

"You've done enough, Gregory." Abigay put emphasis on his name, making clear it would be the final word in their conversation.

Jade felt her mother tug her arm, pulling her to the safety of the brick building. She had a flash of herself as a child watching the courtyard through the window and her mother's strong hand yanking her back from the glass as voices began to rise, just before the pop of gunshots. Abigay had always known the right time to walk away.

"Jade." Her name sounded like a plea.

"Go home." Jade heard a twinge of her mother's accent in her own voice. "You don't belong here."

CHAPTER 31

From the window, Greg watched the black Audi pull up to the curb in front of the house. He saw Paul exit the driver's seat and tracked his advance to the front entrance. His son's gait recalled a horse's canter, a jumpy step followed by a loping stride, as though he struggled not to sprint. Greg didn't recall him having such a distinctive, jittery walk as a child or even as a teenager. College had changed him.

Greg withdrew from behind the partially drawn shade and walked to the exit. He opened it before Paul could hit the doorbell. The air that invaded the house possessed a sharp chill, a result of the threatening rain or perhaps Greg's own feelings about the coming confrontation. His awareness of Paul's actions had robbed him of the usual warmth he felt seeing his golden boy.

"Come on in."

Paul stepped back, perhaps detecting the suppressed anger in Greg's tone. "Hey, Dad." His smile flashed more bottom teeth than top, like an anxious dog. "What did you want to talk to me about so urgently that I had to come this weekend?"

One argument in front of a whole neighborhood was enough to last him a lifetime. Greg pulled back the door another inch. "Come inside, Paul. I'd like to talk where we can sit."

His son's strained smile grew even wider. "Okay. You're making me a bit nervous."

A bit of nerves was the least of what Paul deserved after apparently tormenting his fiancée while she'd been reeling from a violent attack. Greg ushered him inside and then led the way to his office. The master bedroom wasn't appropriate for a serious discussion with his kid, and every other nonbathroom had a camera. In the event Jade decided to press harassment charges, Greg couldn't have the conversation recorded.

The office's overhead lights were off, but the natural glow from the windows kept the room from being too dark. Greg gestured to the kitchen chair where he'd directed Jade to sit a couple of days earlier. The room was arranged exactly as it had been then. Only the gun had changed locations. Greg had returned the Glock to its combination-locked carrying case, which sat on his drafting table, waiting for Violet to return it to her friend.

Just as Jade had been unnerved by the solitary chair, Paul, too, was bothered by its rigid presence. "Wouldn't you rather talk in the living room?" he asked, frowning at the seat.

"No." Greg settled in his Eames and again pointed for Paul to take the other chair. His son lowered onto the seat like the rattan might have splinters. "I don't get the whole Guantanamo thing you have going on in here."

Greg jostled the mouse of his computer. The giant monitor flashed white and then took on a grayish green as it settled on the video image he'd cued on-screen. The black Audi was in front of his house. Paul's jacket-covered arm was stretched out of the passenger window.

"I almost missed this." Greg indicated the computer. "The video only saves for thirty days."

Paul squinted, as though he couldn't make out his car and his own arm in the still shot. However, his lips worked back and forth, betraying that he knew what he was about to watch. Greg hit the play button. The mailbox lid fell open, and Paul's gloved hand shoved something inside. He slammed the lid closed. A moment passed as Paul presumably slid over into the driver's seat. The car sped away.

"What am I looking at?" Paul's incredulity was obviously faked. His brow was furrowed to a comedic extent, and his head was shaking too hard. He'd never been a good liar.

"You were sending Jade threatening notes," Greg said.

"No. I was—"

"Don't, Paul. That's your car. The police matched the license plate."

Paul's jaw dropped. "The police are involved?"

"Of course! We'd been attacked. Jade thought the threats might be related and took them to the cops."

Paul sprang from the seat. His chest rose and fell like he was running a marathon, standing still. "I had nothing to do with that break-in. I was at school. I—"

Greg patted the air. "No one is accusing you of that."

At least, Greg wasn't. He was certain that there was a more innocent explanation for his son possessing the sonogram. Most likely, Paul had stumbled upon the picture while helping pack up the rental during Greg's hospitalization. He'd snatched it, perhaps in hopes of determining its authenticity.

Violet had certainly been in her brother's ear with her sham-pregnancy theory.

Paul stopped panting. He gripped the top of the chair and lowered his head, apparently steadying himself.

"But you did send the notes."

Paul kept his head down as he nodded. "They weren't explicit threats. I just wanted to let her know that Violet and I wouldn't disappear now that she was with you." He shrugged. "And that maybe it's messed up having kids barely older than your future grandkids."

The confession stoked Greg's anger. Though he felt certain of Paul's involvement, he'd hoped that his son would at least offer an explanation capable of lessening his culpability. He'd delivered the notes only at Violet's behest, for example, because his sister had been so certain of Jade's involvement in the attack and they'd been trying to protect him by driving Jade away. Such an excuse wouldn't have exonerated Paul. But it would have made clear that his hardworking and sensitive youngest was still the boy he'd imagined. That Paul had done something bad but for what he'd believed to be a good reason.

Instead, it seemed Paul had done something horrendous simply because he didn't approve of Greg starting another family at his age. "Even if you didn't threaten bodily harm, you knew how she'd interpret those letters. She'd been assaulted. Lost our baby. She was taking care of me with my head bashed in. And rather than support her—rather than show some damn sympathy—you tried to drive her away!"

"Because she doesn't belong here," Paul whispered.

"Who are you to decide? She's my fiancée. I love her."

"She didn't earn her place!" Paul looked up as he yelled. His pale blue eyes were bright and furious. Greg imagined they mirrored his own. "For years, you were sequestered in your office, climbing the corporate ladder to redraw the skyline, while we—Mom, Violet, and I—slaved to make you happy, to be perfect enough to gain some of your attention and affection. And then when I've earned it, you leave us. You start a new family with some woman less than a decade older than your own daughter. You start a new family to take your money, your time, everything we worked for. Everything I worked for."

Paul's hands went to his blond hair. He raked them through his bangs, pulling the strands far off his forehead, as though he were balding. "And we were supposed to just accept her? Accept that you were replacing us?"

The question doused Greg's rage, snuffing it out like ash on a fire. "The divorce wasn't about you kids. Leah and I didn't work anymore. We'd lost that passion. We didn't have things in common. I wasn't replacing you."

"Of course you were." Paul's eyes flared, but he spoke in a voice soft and bitter as smoke. "You were going to be with Jade and your new kid, maybe kids. And everything I did to earn your approval wouldn't matter. I'd done what you wanted, and you were done with me."

Greg's chest constricted. The feeling was different from the one that had preceded his panic attacks. His heart didn't feel as though it would break out of his chest. It only felt like it might shatter. "How can you think that? You're my son. I'd never be done with you."

"Dad, you were barely with me as a kid. I thought now that

I was an adult, and becoming an architect, we'd have more in common. We'd design the skyline together." Paul rubbed the heels of his hands beneath his eyes. Greg didn't see any tears, but the motion indicated their presence.

Greg's own eyes burned. "Maybe I wasn't the best father, Paul. I thought my job was to provide a nice house, to set an example of hard work and goals for you all to aspire to. I want a second chance to be better—for you and your sister."

Paul wiped beneath his nose with the back of his hand. Greg still didn't see tears, but it wouldn't be like his son to bawl. He'd taught him to keep his emotions caged, to *focus on winning, not whining*. It had been one of his choice dad phrases.

Greg stepped toward Paul and placed an arm around his shoulder, pulling him in. "We can all be a family." He patted his back. "But you need to apologize to Jade before she escalates this any more with the cops. She has to understand that you weren't ever a threat to her safety."

Greg felt Paul's nod beside his own head. "Give her a call, Dad."

CHAPTER 32

Time was relative to emotion. Jade felt the concept in her bones as she hovered by her mother's window as she had as a child, her body made brittle by sadness. The courtyard below was empty save for a few folks pushing strollers, returning from the playground due to the ominous clouds overhead. No man with a concealed weapon in baggy pants patrolled the area. No man with a head of graying hair called up to her from the courtyard. Yet, she could somehow see both of them below her, as if time had come full circle and she was seeing her past and future converge. Both timelines ended with her alone at the window, waiting for a man who wouldn't come back.

Water ran in the kitchen. Ostensibly, Abigay was cleaning the cookware. Really, she was making herself scarce so as to be sensitive to Jade's loss. Jade figured the act wasn't easy for her mother. Abigay considered Greg's departure a personal victory. She probably wanted to strut through the apartment with a revolutionary flag, hailing her daughter's independence from a man whom Abigay had never liked, much less understood. As far as her mother was concerned, Jade should be celebrating. She'd learned of Greg's true intentions before she'd committed to him before God. She was free to never see him again.

Jade couldn't feel relief, let alone joy. She'd loved Greg. Crazy as it would have sounded to her mother, she still loved him. In the past few months, he'd been beaten into a coma, discovered that they were no longer expecting, battled post-traumatic stress disorder, uncovered the truth about her father's criminal history, and thought he'd revealed an affair. Was it any wonder that he'd become unglued enough to accuse her of attacking him? She, herself, had become sufficiently disconcerted to believe, for a moment, that a man she *knew* loved her had tried to have her killed.

"Momma." Jade pulled herself away from the window and Greg's phantom presence. She headed into the kitchen where Abigay hovered over the sink. "I don't think he did it."

Her mother turned off the water. She didn't turn around.

"I know two million dollars is a lot of money," Jade continued. "But Greg stood to earn five times that amount on the Brooklyn building. A man with his wealth and earning potential wouldn't have risked his freedom for that amount. Plus, I know he loves me, Momma. I know it."

Her mother gripped the counter. "Jade, you don't need that man."

Abigay's careful response suggested that she also doubted Greg had plotted her murder. Perhaps she'd been giving his tearful apology more thought than Jade had realized. "He's not right for you."

"Why do you say that?"

"He's too old and set in his ways," Abigay said before finally turning to face her. "You'll end up doing whatever he wants because he's the more experienced one. If he says the house needs to be decorated one way, you'll do it. If he suggests that you need to give up your job to raise the kids, you'll do it. If he decides you shouldn't have kids at all because he's been a father and doesn't want them..." Abigay trailed off, allowing Jade to fill in the blank.

She wouldn't have given up on kids, though, Jade thought. She'd always told serious boyfriends that future babies were nonnegotiable for her. On their first date, Greg had mentioned having two adult children, and Jade clearly remembered responding that she wanted kids someday. *One girl and one boy*, she recalled saying, *that's just what I want*. He'd known a condition of their relationship was his willingness to have more kids—kids that Leah didn't want her to have; kids that, maybe, Greg didn't want to have either.

Jade's whole body shuddered. Though she couldn't imagine Greg trying to kill her, she could envision him trying to frighten her. He'd done that with the gun, hadn't he?

Greg had been so sure that Leah wasn't behind the letters. Was that because he had been? Maybe he'd never wanted their unplanned baby and saw its unexpected loss as a way out. He hadn't paid people to induce her miscarriage, of course. He'd have to be a sociopath to do that.

But he hadn't exactly been in his right mind after the attack. He'd been vulnerable and afraid, and hating every minute of feeling that way. Perhaps in his compromised mental state he'd decided to take advantage of her post break-in fear and scare her into not wanting kids? He'd known where she'd kept the sonogram photo.

The thought filled Jade with panic. If Greg was capable of sending her those notes and then claiming he knew nothing about them, what would he be capable of in the future? She'd rejected him. Surely, he wouldn't just accept it and move on.

Jade rushed from the window to the coffee table where she'd left her phone. She unlocked it and then scrolled to the security app. With luck, he'd forgotten to change the password. She needed to see what Greg was up to.

"Is everything okay?" Abigay asked.

"Yes." Jade heard a quaver in her own voice. "I need to check something."

Jade typed in the numbers 1, 2, 8, 0, 1—the earlier combination. The phone buzzed with an alert message: *Wrong Passcode.*

She brought the phone to her forehead as if it could somehow transmit the new digits to her brain via an invisible stream of ones and zeros. She had to think. Like most people, Greg couldn't remember too many different passwords so he chose important dates. The initial passcode had been Paul's birthday.

Jade tried Greg's birthday and got the same buzzing no. Out of desperation, she entered her own birth date, even though it seemed impossible that Greg would lock her out of the security system by changing the code to the numbers Jade would be most likely to remember. A note appeared on the screen warning that she would be permanently locked out of the system if she entered another wrong combination.

What was Violet's birthday? Jade racked her brain for a month and a day. She couldn't recall Greg ever telling her the date. But she could search for it.

Jade brought up a web browser and typed in Violet's full name along with the state where she lived, Connecticut. The page refreshed with a link to a Facebook profile featuring a pouty picture of Violet. She clicked on it. Since they were not friends, Violet's posts and profile information were invisible to her. Jade grumbled and returned to the main search page.

Ten links down, she got a better lead. A site claiming to search for public records said it had found "Violet Hamlin." Jade double-clicked and was taken to a page with Violet's full name, birth date, and town: Violet Anne Hamlin, 12/6/98, Greenwich, CT.

Jade reopened the security app and carefully entered 12698. The screen flashed. A grid of more than a dozen video feeds appeared on her screen.

She scrolled through the thumbnails, searching for the room containing her ex. He wasn't in the kitchen or his bedroom. The sitting and living rooms were empty. He didn't lounge on the back deck. Was he even at home?

She clicked on the image of the garage. Greg's Tesla was inside. Wherever he'd gone, he hadn't driven there. Jade switched over to the grid view a second time. He had to be somewhere in the house.

Suddenly, motion on one of the screens caught her eye. Greg emerged from the camera-free office into the neighboring room. A moment later, his skinny, younger doppelgänger entered the frame. Paul had come for a visit. With her gone, Greg's kids would be coming over all the time, Jade supposed.

She clicked on the video, enlarging it to fill the screen. The room's sound began transmitting over Jade's tinny iPhone speakers. "I'll apologize," Paul was saying.

"You'll do more than that," Greg replied. "This is going to take work to repair."

"What if she doesn't forgive me?"

Who were they talking about? Her? Hope throbbed in Jade's chest. She switched back to grid view and then clicked on the outdoor camera, silently praying that she would see what she wished. There, in front of the house, mere feet from the curbside mailbox, was an Audi. All this time, Paul had been threatening her.

Jade thought back to his kind overture at the hospital. If he hated her so much, then why had he gone out of his way to tell her that he didn't suspect her in his father's attack? Why had he outlined Violet's reasons for disliking her dad and taking it out on her?

Jade's gut clenched with the answer. She clicked back on the live video of father and son, hoping that she would see something to prove her wrong. Paul stood beside his dad, long and skinny with piercing blue eyes. Jade felt the fist that had driven into her stomach. Once. Twice. She recalled the ropey silhouette of the man who had delivered those blows.

Paul hadn't only delivered the notes. He'd attacked her. That was why he'd been comfortable confessing that he didn't suspect her of hiring those thugs. He was one of them. His nice act had been only to deflect suspicion from himself.

Jade's cell screen suddenly went black. For an instant, she thought Paul had somehow caught her staring and shut off the video feed. She frantically pressed the on button to return to the main screen. It didn't work though. Her phone had died, and her charger, like all of her things, was still at the house—just like Paul.

He'd killed their baby. Now he was in a locked home with the father he hated—and a gun.

CHAPTER 33

Jade wasn't answering his calls. Her phone went to voice mail before a single ring, indicating that she was hitting the ignore button as soon as his name flashed on her screen. She didn't want to talk to him, Greg thought. Perhaps she'd never speak to him again.

The realization transformed the handset in his palm into a brick. He set it down on Jade's beloved blue resin and marble coffee table, the one she'd said reminded her of the Caribbean Sea skimming over a reef. In his mind, he saw her smile as she'd shown him the piece. He loved that smile, the genuine one she had flashed so often before the attack, so big and broad that it crinkled her nose and pinched a dimple into her left cheek. Jade was beautiful, inside and out, Greg thought. They could have had a beautiful life. But he'd ruined it with ugliness, unfounded accusations, and threats. It was a miracle that she hadn't already changed her number.

He slumped onto the couch and dropped his head into his hands. His hair-dusted scalp felt soft and spiky, like a kiwi's skin. He rubbed a palm over his injury, noticing the fuzzy layer give way to the ridge of scar tissue where he'd been sewn back together. He'd never felt less whole. Over the past few months, he'd become someone else, a scared, suspicious shell of the man he'd once been.

"I'm so sorry." He whispered the apology to the memories of his fiancée and his former self. He'd betrayed them both.

"Any luck?"

Greg forced himself to pick up his head and look at his son. Paul's chin was tucked to his narrow chest, as if he didn't have the strength to lift his face, as if the weight of the shame was too much. It hurt Greg to see his boy that way, but he couldn't take that burden away—from either of them.

"She's not picking up." Greg felt pressure build behind his eyes. He couldn't cry in front of his kid.

"You didn't leave a message telling her, did you?"

Paul's pupils darted from Greg to the front door to the office, as if the answer might make him bolt in some yet-to-be-determined direction. He was afraid of the police using a recording against him, Greg knew. Harvard surely suspended any student charged with harassment.

"No. I think the news about you writing those notes, and your apology, has to be delivered in person."

Paul's head rose. "And if she doesn't want to see us?"

Greg sighed. "I don't know."

"Would you leave a message then?"

Greg supposed he could understand why Paul's primary concern would be the trouble he could get into, but he still hated the fact that his son was so self-centered. He should be sorrier, Greg thought. Paul should be asking what he might do to reach out to Jade and make amends.

Greg was about to say as much, but a buzzing on the coffee table stopped him. An alert dominated his cell screen: *Activity Detected!*

He picked up his phone and clicked the message. The security application opened with a full-screen view of the front door camera. A BMW had parked behind Paul's car. Greg watched as the driver slammed the door and rounded the vehicles. His heart swelled at the sight. It was Jade.

She was running toward the house like someone was chasing her.

Greg pocketed his cell, pushed himself from the couch, and sprinted to the front door. He flung it open without pausing to consider what could lie on the other side. Beeps emanated from the alarm system speakers as he ran down the walk, leaving the door wide open behind him. The only fear he felt was that Jade might change her mind and bolt back to her car before he'd had a chance to beg for forgiveness one more time.

"Greg!" There was a desperation in Jade's voice. Had she been imagining life without him? Was it possible the prospect devastated her in the same way? "Greg. Come here. Please. We—"

His arms were around her before she could finish the sentence. He held her like she was a life preserver and he'd been adrift. "You came back." His cheeks felt damp. "I'm so sorry, baby. I'm going to be better. If you give me a second chance, there won't be any more suspicion or assumptions. I love you. I love you."

He kept repeating the phrase as he felt Jade pull away. She no longer felt the same, he thought. Probably, she'd returned to get her things.

Jade stared over his shoulder at the open door. "I love you too. That's why we have to go. Paul was the one."

"Paul's been sending the letters. I spoke with him about it." Greg held her arms, trying to steady her trembling body. "He's sorry, Jade. He's so sorry, and he wants to tell you."

"But he—"

"It's my fault too. I wasn't the best father. I was focused on my work. All these years, he's been trying to get my attention by following in my footsteps. He thought that I would abandon him for my new family, and he freaked. He's not a bad kid."

Jade's head shook violently. "No. You have to listen to me. Paul was the one who robbed us."

The force of the accusation caused Greg to step backward, releasing Jade from his grip. She was mistaken. His son would never have hurt him. Sure, he'd sent some mean letters to his future stepmom in hopes of scaring her away, but that was different. Paul would never have raised a hand against him, or anyone. Growing up, his boy had always been studious and measured. Paul had never even gotten into a schoolyard scrap. Jade, in her fear and grief, was conflating the verbal attack against her with the physical one.

"No. He was responsible for the letters, and that was horrible. I'm sure he picked up the sonogram when he helped move boxes." Greg reached for Jade's hand. Her fingers dug into his palm. She pulled him toward the car.

Greg stood his ground. "But now he realizes how wrong that was. He wants to try to make it up to you. He knows how much I love you."

A thunderclap punctuated his statement. Jade jumped like she'd heard a gunshot. "Please, Greg."

The sky opened up. Rain tumbled down in a curtain. The water drenched his scalp and dribbled down his forehead into his eyes, blurring his vision. Jade's expression became unreadable. He could see only her torso shivering in a saturated shirt.

Greg gently tugged her in the direction of shelter. "I know he hurt you, baby. But he didn't attack us. He was in college at the time, a hundred eighty miles away in Boston. And he's my son. I know him. Please, just hear him out. He wants to apologize. He wants us all to be a family."

The tension in Jade's hand finally released. He led her toward the front door, slowly, despite the downpour. Each of her steps was tentative.

When they reached the landing, Greg saw that the front door was still ajar. He expected to hear the intruder alert blaring. But it wasn't. Greg figured that his son must have shut off the alarm with the key fob left by the base station.

They entered the vestibule, both standing on the black welcome mat. Greg shut the door behind him. He noticed Jade flinch at the sound of the lock engaging.

"Paul!" Greg shouted in the direction of the living room where they'd previously been sitting. "Paul!"

Greg stepped farther into the room, still calling his son's name. Jade remained on the mat, as if afraid to enter the house that Greg had ordered her from at gunpoint. He felt a stab of guilt. "Jade's here," Greg yelled. "She's willing to hear you out."

Paul entered the neighboring family room from the office. He slowly approached the vestibule, stopping himself in the area where the open spaces met, a nonthreatening distance from Jade. His son had always possessed a good grasp of what was appropriate, Greg thought. Paul knew that Jade wouldn't be ready for him to come within touching distance given his actions.

His son looked up at Jade's face and then down at his hands, no doubt too ashamed to meet her eyes. "I'm sorry. I thought that I could drive you away with those notes. I was wrong."

Jade eyed Paul with her back against the door. If she saw even a fraction of the boy that he did, Greg was certain she'd forgive him. She'd have to understand that Paul could never truly be violent. His son's lack of aggression was evident in the roundness of his shoulders and the way he dug his hands deep into his oversized jean pockets, seemingly afraid to let them out.

"You really *only* sent those notes?" Jade asked.

Paul's head snapped to attention. His eyes widened. "What are you implying? Huh? What are you trying to say, Jade?"

The voice that asked the questions didn't sound like his son, Greg thought. It was too high. The tenor was too hysterical. It was the voice of someone not in control of himself.

Greg considered Paul anew. He took in the sight of his son's jeans, belted tight around the waist and baggy at the knees in a way that wasn't fashionable in any circle. He noted the way Paul's button-down hung off his broad shoulders as though he were a hanger and not a human. He saw—really saw perhaps for the first time in a long while—his son's gaunt face and tortured expression. What had happened to his boy at Harvard?

Best place to become a speed freak. Violet's words rattled in

Greg's brain. He'd thought she'd been trying to diminish her brother's accomplishments because of her own insecurity at going to a less-renowned school. But when had Violet ever cared about renown? She'd taken years off to travel the world with a backpack.

"Are you abusing amphetamines?"

"What? No." Paul's Adam's apple bobbed, trying to swallow his blatant lie. "Why would you ask that?"

"You look too skinny, like a drug addict."

As he said the words, Greg had a flash of the thin assailant who'd run past him up the stairs, the one he'd tried to catch before the larger man had knocked him unconscious—the one who'd beaten Jade. *It can't be*, Greg told himself. Still, he stepped in front of his fiancée, shielding her from the sight of his son's barely contained fury.

"Well, I take Adderall sometimes. I mean, what do you expect me to do? Do you know how hard it is to compete there? To live up to your standards?" Paul's words stumbled over one another in their race to jump from his tongue. "How hard it is to measure up to Greg Hamlin, the famous architect? There's no sleep. There's no time. I need pills to stay awake. To focus. And then to deal with everything between you and Mom and her."

Paul growled the last word. Before Greg's eyes, his boy was changing, devolving from his sedulous son into a snarling animal. Greg had read an article on the meth epidemic once that said amphetamine abuse led to anxiety, depression, and uncontrolled outbursts of anger. Could Paul be suffering from such symptoms?

Behind him, Greg felt Jade's energy heighten, as if her body were a struck tuning fork vibrating the air around her. "You broke into the house." She nearly whispered the accusation. "You punched—"

"No!" Paul's hands flew from his pockets and landed upon his head where they transformed into claws, tearing at his hair. "No. No. All I wanted was to grab that ridiculous ring you put on her finger. It would have paid for everything I need."

Reflexively, Greg's own hands went to his ears. He couldn't believe what he was hearing. His son had turned into a drug addict. But how? Paul had always been a straight-A student. He'd been on the tennis team and gone to the state championship for doubles. His art had won national competitions. He'd been the model child.

Tears ran down Paul's cheeks and poured off his nose. Greg murmured his name, trying to make eye contact with him, to somehow make him retract what he'd just said. But he wouldn't look at him. Paul's pupils seemed extra wide and focused. They zeroed in on Jade.

"There wasn't more money for anything, thanks to you!" Paul was screaming and sobbing at the same time. "Dad gave Mom the house and some alimony, but then he cut her off. He cut us off. He paid tuition and room and board, but he left Mom with everything else. And how was she supposed to cover all those costs, huh? The taxes on the Greenwich house alone are over forty thousand a year. What's my mother supposed to do? Go back to work? After twenty years at home taking care of us and him, what would she be qualified for? Secretary? Grocery store cashier? While you gallivant all around Westchester in a fifty-thousand-dollar diamond, blogging about your new house and new baby?!"

"Paul." Greg spoke his name louder, hoping to pull his attention off Jade. "Paul!"

Paul's pupils narrowed on him, as if just noticing the light in the room. "I never meant for you to get hurt, Dad. My dealer was only supposed to keep you downstairs. But you punched him, and he reacted. I was already on the landing. I didn't realize he'd brought a crowbar. I didn't know! And by the time I realized, he'd already hit you."

Part of Greg had known what Paul had been building up to, but the confession still felt like a sucker punch. It coursed through Greg's body, inflaming his nerves, triggering a fight response. His hands curled into fists. "You stole from me," Greg roared. "You beat up my wife."

"I'm sorry, Dad. I'm sorry!"

"You're sick."

"Dad—"

The name felt like an accusation. This boy was not his son. The drugs had taken his boy away. "You need to be in an institution."

"You can pay for me to get help. I'll enroll in McLean Hospital. It's affiliated with Harvard. They have detox programs and sober-living homes—"

"I can't just pay for this to go away, Paul. You killed our baby."

A loud beep interrupted. It sounded from the security system's speakers, signaling that an exterior door had been opened. If the system had been armed, the beeps would have sped up. But his son had shut off the alarms.

Greg became aware of a buzzing in his pocket. He pulled out his phone and glanced at its face, still trying to maintain focus on his apparently psychotic boy. Alerts ran down the screen: *Motion Detected! Activity Detected! Person Detected!*

Someone was in the house. "Who did you call?" Greg shouted the question even though he'd already answered it for himself. Paul had deactivated the alarm to allow his dealer into the house. The gun was locked in the office. If he could just get to it, he could defend himself. He could make that man pay for what he'd done to them.

Before he could take a step toward the office, a figure emerged through the door into the living room. The shape was far smaller than the man Greg remembered, and he recognized the blond hair and fair skin.

"Leah?"

She strode toward them at a furious speed, her visage becoming clearer with every step. "Get away from my son, Greg."

Her arms rose. There was something in her hands. Greg couldn't make it out, or maybe he just couldn't believe what he was seeing.

"Gun," Jade whispered, as if any sound could startle Leah into pressing the trigger. "Greg, she's got a gun."

Leah came to a stop beside Paul. Close up, Greg could see the details of the weapon held in both his ex's hands. It was the same gun he'd pointed at Jade days earlier. "How did you get that? It was in a lockbox."

"Yes, Greg. *My* lockbox on *your* desk." Leah aimed the weapon above Greg's shoulder. "Where do you think Violet got it? It's *my* gun."

The way Leah handled the Glock confirmed her statement. Her right hand interlocked with her left on the grip. Her index finger extended to touch the trigger. "You will not make my son pay for anything, Greg. This is your fault. Whatever he did, you drove him to it."

In contrast to Paul's hysterical pleas and sobs, Leah sounded preternaturally calm. Greg had a flash of the arguments in their marriage. She'd never been one to yell or scream or cry. Leah would flatly express her disappointment and then carry on as if she hadn't lost the argument. Her tone was the same as then, Greg thought. But she was apparently done carrying on.

Greg couldn't let her win this one. "A rehab facility won't fix this. He has to face the consequences of his actions. We can't just—"

A deafening pop finished his sentence. The volume seemed to pierce Greg's eardrums. His head exploded with the sound. Out of the corner of his eye, he saw a shadow dive in front of him. And once again, everything went black.

EPILOGUE

Pain radiated through Jade's belly and into her back. She grabbed the edge of the kitchen counter and tried to inhale for more than a few seconds. One gulp of air and her lungs felt fit to burst. She exhaled and inhaled again, settling for the shallow breaths that were all she could manage since her stomach had shifted into the space formerly occupied by her left lung. Beneath her flowy shirt, she could see her swollen belly folding in on itself, like a bread loaf with a line cut down the center.

"You don't drink enough water." Abigay admonished her more gently than usual, perhaps acknowledging that her cramps were bad enough without being nagged.

"My bladder can't hold more than a cup of liquid," Jade groaned.

Abigay grinned like that was a good thing. She came around behind Jade and rubbed her back. The steady motion eased the pressure on her stomach. Jade released her death grip on the counter and gradually straightened her spine.

Abigay patted Jade's back, signaling the end of the mini-massage. "You're going to let me use the string and ring, right?"

"I already know the gender." Jade pointed to the cake stand on the counter and the concoction inside, encased in white buttercream. "I had to know for the filling."

"I only want to prove it works."

"There's no scientific basis for it."

"Let your mother have her fun!" Greg called out from the neighboring living room. He sat beside Violet and across from Michael, with whom he'd been chatting amiably for much of the past hour. A genuine smile lit his face.

The sight erased all of Jade's complaints from memory. Joy had been a fleeting emotion for her husband in these past eighteen months, seen only in flashes between distant looks. Jade knew he blamed himself for Paul's death, even though Leah had done the shooting. The guilt kept him from enjoying this pregnancy. But it also had hardened his resolve not to repeat the mistakes of the past. Greg was dedicated to becoming the best father and husband imaginable with the "second chance" he'd been given.

He'd been proving it with Violet. He regularly made the trip to Rhode Island to visit her and never failed to invite her to every major event in their lives—including today's gender reveal party. For her part, Violet appeared grateful for all the attention and forgiveness. Like Greg, she also suffered guilt over Paul's death. Had she been more vocal about her suspicions of his drug use and called an intervention with her parents, she believed that her brother might have gotten help. Instead, she'd tearfully confessed to Jade one evening, she'd become mired in jealousy over her dad's new wife, a choice that she'd *never be able to take back* and would *forever regret*—just like her mother.

Leah was serving ten years at the Danbury women's prison—a facility best known for housing celebrities with bad habits. The place was a country club compared to the maximum security prison where Paul's former drug dealer was incarcerated. Typically, it took only people accused of bloodless crimes, but an exception had been made given Leah's level of despair and extreme cooperation with police. There hadn't been a trial. She'd been so distraught over having accidentally shot her son that she'd pleaded guilty and willingly confessed to every action leading up to that horrible afternoon.

Apparently, she'd been watching them for weeks. Once Violet had told her about Greg's new security system, Leah had downloaded the app, typed in Greg's email address, and guessed that he'd continue using his kids' birthdays as passcodes. She'd insisted that her intentions weren't violent at the time she began watching them. She'd claimed to have only wanted to check out her ex-husband's new house and maybe use shots of his expensive new furnishings as fodder in her divorce battle. But then she'd started to see Greg's suspicions mounting against Jade, and she became glued to the video feeds, partially out of concern that Greg's new wife might have it in for him and partially out of plain lurid curiosity. According to Leah, the live feed had become like a reality show featuring an alternative version of her life. *Must-see TV.*

She'd been watching earlier that day when Greg forced Paul's confession about the notes. A mother knows her son, Leah had said, and she'd suspected that he'd done far worse.

Once she saw Jade return to the house, she knew that Greg wouldn't simply forgive their boy. He'd be forced to choose between his new wife and his son, Leah had said. And she'd known that "poor Paul would never win that contest."

Leah swore she hadn't driven over intending to kill Greg and Jade. According to her, she'd entered through the office simply because it was the closest door to the driveway, not because she'd known that the gun would be in there. She then saw her lockbox on Greg's desk and removed the weapon on impulse, thinking she could scare them into keeping quiet.

Jade doubted that to be the truth though. Leah was a smart woman. She'd have known that Greg wouldn't be intimidated by her. Jade was pretty sure that killing them had always been part of Leah's plan. Greg's ex had parked just beyond the base of the driveway where the cameras wouldn't register her car. She'd then run straight to the office, as if she knew that Greg had never removed her gun from the room. Jade figured that Leah had thought she could pass off their deaths as a murder-suicide, given all the mutual suspicion she'd witnessed. With Paul backing up her story and her reputation in the community, she'd likely thought that the police wouldn't ask too many questions.

Now Violet had a parent in prison. That fact had humbled Greg's daughter and brought her closer to Jade. *Friends* would have been too strong a word for their relationship, Jade thought. But over the past year and a half, she and Violet had developed a partnership of sorts, the purpose of which was to protect Greg from the worst of his sadness. For several months, they'd both feared that he would become consumed by the loss of his son, and they each did their part to draw him back out into the world, Violet by opening up to him about school and asking for help on projects and Jade by forcing trips to foreign places in which they could enjoy one another's company without staring down the past.

It had all helped. But the pregnancy had really resuscitated Greg, giving him a purpose that not even the Brooklyn building had provided. He'd spent days painstakingly designing the structure using recycled steel scaffolding and decommissioned shipping containers, but he hadn't seemed to derive much happiness from his effort. Jade hoped he'd feel differently when he saw the finished product. The critics were already calling it a "masterful marriage of Brooklyn's port history with its sustainable future." Greg said it would resemble a giant Jenga with some of the pieces missing. Violet had told her privately that the game was Paul's favorite as a boy.

Abigay picked up the cake tower. She led the way into the neighboring room as Jade waddled behind her, one hand on her back and one on her belly. Greg rose to take the dessert from Abigay and set it down on Jade's favorite table, the one that reminded her of the Caribbean Sea. The table fit better in the house since Jade had added several more island-inspired pieces. She was far from finished decorating, however. Lately, the homes of area interior design clients—and the nursery— had consumed most of her creative energies.

Abigay pointed to the chaise end of the sectional, close to where Michael sat. "Go on, sit down."

Jade complied, but with an eye roll to emphasize that she didn't believe the old wives' tale that a baby's gender could be pegged by the swing of a wedding ring over the belly. Her mother winked at Greg to show that she also didn't put much stock in the superstition and was merely bowing to tradition. They'd gotten along better in the past year. Abigay seemed to believe that Greg was God's way of letting her and Michael make amends for Mateo Bernal. She'd been unable to show kindness to Carlos Bernal as she would have wanted, but Abigay could help another man grieving the loss of a son.

Abigay put her hand out and opened and shut her fingers, a gimme gesture that Jade assumed she would someday see from a toddler. Jade twisted off the simple gold band that had been slipped on her finger by Greg in a small ceremony in Jamaica attended only by her parents, Violet, and a couple of close friends. She hadn't bothered with a wedding party. Choosing a best man in his son's absence would have hurt Greg too much.

She handed the ring to Abigay, who soon had it dangling off of a long white ribbon, apparently brought specifically for the purpose. Jade lay back onto her elbows and hiked up her blouse, revealing her domed stomach and the long dark line dividing it that her doctors swore was only temporary. Her mother hung the ring above its highest point.

"How does it work?" Violet stood beside Abigay, looking more interested than amused.

"Back and forth is a boy. A circular motion is a girl," Abigay said.

The ring barely seemed to move at all. If Jade had to pick a direction, she supposed she'd admit that the movement was more linear than circular. In spite of herself, she started to smile. Quickly, she pinched her lips together, hiding the revealing expression.

"A boy!" Abigay's eyes probed Jade's own, trying to wrest the truth from them early.

Jade sat up. "Okay. Now that that's done"—she adjusted her blouse—"time for cake."

Jade scooted over on the couch close to Greg. A large, flat knife lay at the base of the cake stand. Greg took it. She placed her palm atop his knuckles. "Ready?"

He smiled again. This expression didn't seem as genuine as before. The mention of a boy had, no doubt, reminded him of Paul.

They both pressed into the cake together, slicing a triangle into the center. Then Jade slipped the knife beneath the cut piece. "One...two..."

"Three." The room joined in on the last number as Jade pulled away the slice. Blue icing decorated the layer inside.

"I knew it," Abigay announced.

"It was a fifty-fifty chance," Michael quipped.

"Not from that. From the way she is carrying. All pointy."

A kiss landed on Jade's cheek. She turned to face her husband. Greg's blue eyes were red and watery.

A sob directed her attention to the chaise. Violet sat, forcing a smile despite the tears tumbling down her own cheeks. "A brother," she said.

Jade patted Greg's thigh, trying to show that she understood how bittersweet the news must be for both him and his daughter. As she did, she heard the doorbell.

Michael stood, likely expecting Greg to shuffle past him into the foyer. Instead, Jade grabbed her cell from its resting place near the cake. She clicked the security application and selected the doorbell camera. A man in a brown UPS uniform stood at the front door. In his arms was a cellophane-wrapped, two-foot-tall cupcake constructed from rolled-up onesies and diapers, a gift likely from one of Jade's New York City friends who hadn't been able to make the midday trip.

She held the phone to her mouth and pressed the intercom button. "Hi, you can leave it."

The speaker crackled with the delivery guy's "Okay." He stepped away from the house, snapped a picture of the package sitting in front of their door, and headed back to a marked brown truck.

Michael watched the whole exchange over her shoulder. "I didn't realize there was a camera there. When I came in, I didn't see one."

Jade handed her father the phone so he could watch the deliveryman drive away. "We only have the outdoor ones now."

Jade flashed a smile at Greg. She'd been so happy when he agreed to take down most of the devices. Privacy was important, even between loved ones—maybe especially between loved ones. Couples weren't meant to share every moment of every day with each other. They needed the space to do things they found embarrassing or unattractive, the freedom to vent about each other, the ability to have an internal life. Mystery was part of a marriage. It had to be, Jade thought.

"Well, we have the outdoor ones *and* the one in the baby's room." Greg gave Jade's hand a gentle squeeze as he corrected her. "We have to keep an eye on the kid."

ACKNOWLEDGMENTS

"Hindsight is twenty-twenty" goes the old adage. Looking back at everything that happened in 2020, it's a miracle that this novel wasn't delayed. I am very grateful to the team at Grand Central Publishing for guiding this book through one of the most challenging times in my life. I owe special thanks to Beth deGuzman, who believed in this story; and my wonderful editor, Alex Logan, who polished my words, improved my pacing, and kept this book on track while the ground shifted around us. I am also thankful for my agent, Paula Munier, who not only sells my work but also serves as a much-needed sounding board for me. Paula, your guidance is very much appreciated.

I am extremely thankful for the family and friends who support me, read drafts, listen to character quotes, and keep my spirits lifted. My husband, Brett Honneus, bears most of this burden. I love you very much, and I thank God nightly that you're my partner.

I owe a real debt to my daughters, Elleanor and Olivia.

Childhood and all the changes that happen during it are difficult enough without the world also turning upside down. You both have had to rethink the way you do nearly everything, and you've met the challenges with a good deal of bravery and optimism—often more than I have. I am inspired by both of you, and I appreciate your patience and forgiveness with having me as a somewhat addled homeschool teacher also trying to produce a book on time.

I must thank my parents, Angela and James Holahan. You two have shown me that love is strength. You guys got married—a Black Jamaican woman and an Irish American man—a little over a decade after it became legal in the US and years before it became accepted by many. You both dealt with stereotypes and suspicions, and you each taught me to never let someone else define my culture, my heritage, or my sense of self. If people take away any message from this story, I hope it is that stereotypes are damaging. Individuals should always be judged by their actions and their efforts.

ABOUT THE AUTHOR

Cate Holahan is the *USA Today* bestselling author of domestic suspense novels *The Widower's Wife, One Little Secret, Lies She Told*, and *Dark Turns*. In a former life, she was an award-winning journalist, writing for the *Record*, the *Boston Globe*, and *BusinessWeek*, among others. She was also the lead singer of Leaving Kinzley, an original rock band in New York City.

She lives in New Jersey with her husband, two daughters, and a food-obsessed dog, and spends a disturbing amount of time highly caffeinated, mining her own anxieties for material.

To find out more, visit:
CateHolahan.com
Twitter @CateHolahan
Facebook.com/CateHolahan